PORTALS

Other Anthologies Edited by:

PORTALS

Edited by

Patricia Bray
&
S.C. Butler

Zombies Need Brains LLC
www.zombiesneedbrains.com

Interior Design (ebook): April Steenburgh
Interior Design (print): ZNB Design
Cover Design by ZNB Design
Cover Art "Portals" by Justin Adams

ZNB Book Collectors #16
All characters and events in this book are fictitious.
All resemblance to persons living or dead is coincidental.

Kickstarter Edition Printing, June 2019
First Printing, July 2019

Print ISBN-10: 1940709288
Print ISBN-13: 978-1940709284

Ebook ISBN-10: 1940709296
Ebook ISBN-13: 978-1940709291

Printed in the U.S.A.

COPYRIGHTS

Table of Contents

SIGNATURE PAGE

Patricia Bray, editor:

_____

S.C. Butler, editor:

_____

Nancy Holzner:

_____

Esther Friesner:

_____

Ian Tregillis:

_____

Jacey Bedford:

_____

John Linwood Grant:

_____

Kate Hall:

_____

Gini Koch writing as Anita Ensal:

_____

Violette Malan:

_____

Juliet Kemp:

_____

James Enge:

_____

Steven Harper:

_____

F. Brett Cox:

_____

Jaime Lee Moyer:

_____

Jason Palmatier:

_____

Andrija Popovic:

_____

Patrick Hurley:

_____

Justin Adams, artist:

_____

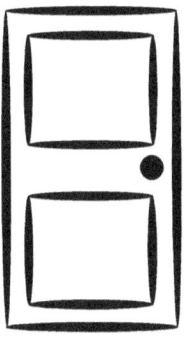

Introduction

Joshua Palmatier

I didn't start out reading science fiction or fantasy. When I was a kid, I was big into mysteries—"Hardy Boys," mostly, but I'd started branching out into more general mysteries. Then one day my mom accidentally brought home an Andre Norton book from the library, instead of the requested Mary Norton book. That was the end of mysteries for me; it was exclusively Andre Norton for a long while. And one of Andre Norton's most common themes was portals. I soon discovered that portals were common in many of science fiction and fantasy novels, from the classics like C.S. Lewis' *The Lion, the Witch, and the Wardrobe* or Lewis Carroll's Alice's *Adventures in Wonderland*, to Stephen R. Donaldson's "The Chronicles of Thomas Covenant." Portals were everywhere.

And then they weren't.

For a long stretch of time, portals disappeared from the SF&F world. Or at least it seemed that way to me. So when contemplating what themes I could use for upcoming anthologies, I thought, "Why not do one centered around portals to other worlds?" It felt like it was time to bring portals back into the foreground a little bit. And it appears that I wasn't the only one struck with this idea. Since its inception, I've noticed a sharp uptick in the number of novels being announced (or even released) that involve characters traveling through a portal from one strange world to another, even if one of those "strange worlds" is our own. It appears portals have become timely once again.

In this book, you have sixteen tales of travelers passing through a doorway or gate, stone arch or wormhole, without knowing what awaits them on the other side. Journey with them across that boundary to find out. We hope you enjoy the ride.

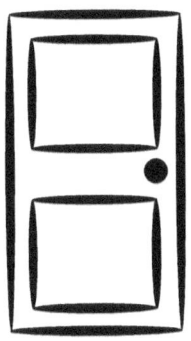

What Time Is It?

Nancy Holzner

Case #22-417
Subject: Clifford Farris, age 44. Height: 185 cm. Weight: 97 kg
Subject status: Blood pressure: 90/52. Pulse: 50. Relaxation stage 4.2 of 5
Investigator: ID #844; Rhodes, Kurt
Date/time: 7/6/2068 14:02. Investigation commencing in 10...9...8...7...

The entry is always the worst part. They strap you down on a table next to the subject, almost like you're the one under investigation. I don't know why the straps are necessary. They tell me it's for safety. They say sometimes an investigator thrashes around or goes into convulsions, but I've never seen it happen.

After they've got you strapped down tight, they start in with the electrodes and the wires and the monitors. I used to be able to tell you what all that shit is for—how each piece connects the investigator to the subject or monitors one thing or another—but that was back in school. And believe me, the theory's got nothing on the practice.

The damn countdown always makes me tense up, gets my heart racing. They tell me that makes it worse, but what do they expect? The subject, lucky bastard, gets pumped full of all kinds of nice sleepy-time drugs. It keeps the guy calm and clears the terrain for me—it's a lot harder to hide the truth when your conscious mind has been deactivated. I don't have that luxury. The investigator has to be wide awake, sharp. Can't overlook whatever evidence lurks in the shadows. And so I brace for the moment they blast me into the subject's mind. It hurts. It feels like my entire body gets ripped apart into molecules and then reforged by some cosmic blacksmith pounding me back into shape on a red-hot anvil. How's that for a work commute?

Hell, maybe I do thrash around.

But it's the only way to get inside. And inside is where I do my job. Kurt Rhodes, investigator #844. Human lie detector.

Time: 14:07:42

Entry confirmed

Subject status: Blood pressure: 88/50. Pulse: 48. Relaxation stage: 4.3 of 5

Investigator status: Blood pressure: 140/88. Pulse: 156

Action: Hold. Recheck stats at 14:10:00

I'm in. The last of the pain subsides like water swirling down a drain. I take a few deep breaths to steady myself. Breathe... breathe... Take it easy, Rhodes. Breathe...

Time: 14:10:30

Subject status: Blood pressure: 88/52. Pulse: 44. Relaxation stage: 4.3 of 5

Investigator status: Blood pressure: 120/78. Pulse: 84

Action: Send commence signal

My smartwatch buzzes and lights up green. Time to do what I do.

I look around to get the lay of the land. Mindscapes are as different as the people who inhabit them. Some are organized and tidy, with a memory like a carefully curated museum or a giant filing cabinet. Others are chaotic, and looking for evidence is less like going after the proverbial needle in a haystack and more like trying to find that needle in a massive landfill crammed with rusty cars, rotting garbage, and toxic waste.

Lucky for me, today's subject is the neat-and-tidy type, with a warehouse-style memory system. Shelves full of neatly arranged archival boxes stretch up to the ceiling and down a long aisle. Totally fits the profile, which is a good sign. Welcome to the mind of Clifford Farris, who stands accused of a string of thirteen killings stretching back over half a dozen years. It's a strange case. There's no obvious connection between victims—men, women, young, old, rich, poor, every skin color, ethnicity, and religion you can think of. But they were all killed in a frenzy of stabbing at six-month intervals. Every January, every July, another stabbing. And for no apparent reason. Strange for a guy with such a well-organized memory. But there's something, somewhere in here, that will tie it all together. There has to be.

Farris's profile shows him to be a planner, meticulous, and most likely a souvenir collector. The team hasn't been able to find those souvenirs out in the physical world, so I'm in this warehouse rummaging around for clues. Until the day hell freezes over and the courts finally accept memory mining as admissible, it has to be paired with concrete evidence from the physical world. Doesn't matter, though. What I find in here will lead us straight to what we need to put this son of a bitch away forever.

Assuming he did it, of course. Innocent until proven guilty and all that.

Farris claims not to remember anything about the dates in question. Any of them. We've got a couple of "fairly certain" eyewitnesses and some grainy video footage placing him near three of the crime scenes. No tracking data, though. The guy's one of those neo-Luddite analogpunk dudes who refuses to carry any kind of comm device. He even wears a mechanical wind-up watch, an old-school chronometer that looks like a relic from the 20th century. That might make him a weirdo, but it doesn't make him a killer.

Weirdo, yeah. But here's what's really weird. The guy brought himself to our attention, stumbling into the West L.A. station and demanding to be arrested. According to the report, he yelled that he was the killer and kept waving his arms around and screaming, "Don't you know what time it is? Look at the time!" Then he passed out cold. When he woke up, he denied killing anybody. West L.A. made two referrals: they sent Farris to the psych ward and the video of his confession to homicide. The homicide analysts did an image search and came up with a couple of possible matches from surveillance vids. Farris, freshly sprung from the psych ward after a few days' observation, kept denying everything, but when we got the warrant to search his mind he seemed almost relieved. You'd expect someone from the anti-tech crowd to lawyer up and try to make some bogus argument about privacy, but Farris didn't go that route.

Time: 14:12:00

Request status report

My nudge to get to work. I speak into the microphone: "Memory system is archival. Subject relaxation level appears adequate. It's quiet as a tomb in here." I pause to appreciate the aptness of my simile. "Will update when I've got something."

Status report received. Continue.

Behind me, the entry portal glows like a bonfire, throwing a weird yellow light and heating my back. I mark my current coordinates on my watch, then look around. Where to start? Farris must have one hell of a memory. Archival boxes are crammed onto shelves that stretch up farther than I can see, and I quit craning my neck before I injure myself. I peer at the nearest box. It's labeled in thick black handwritten letters: **YEAR: 2047; MONTH: MAY; DAY: 27.** Like I said, neat and tidy. Organized. If I'm lucky, all I'll have to do is pull up the dates of the murders, peek into a few boxes, and get the hell out of here.

I doublecheck to make sure my location coordinates are correct. It's way too easy to get lost in a place like this. Then I send a data request to the techs back in the lab.

Time: 14:12:16

Investigator request received

Action: Uploading data, case #22-417

My watch beeps and shows the information I requested. Thirteen lines, each with a name and a date. Thirteen victims, one every six months, give or take a few days. Where should I start? Is it true that you never forget your first kill? Or would the most recent be freshest in the mind? I decide to start with the latest murder, from six months ago, and I flick my finger on my watch screen to scroll to that entry. There. Kira Stone, 26 years old. Went out for a run in Griffith Park on January 3— part of her New Year's resolution, I'd bet—and was found the next day with nearly a hundred stab wounds. Ninety-two, to be exact. What kind of a monster would do that?

I don't want to know. I don't *need* to know. All I need is some clues about where we can locate some physical evidence. The sooner I find those clues, the sooner I can get out of here.

The boxes are arranged by year, then month, then day. Typical for this memory type. I walk along the aisle, keeping my eyes on the dates. A stroll down memory lane. Except these aren't my memories, and I've gotta steel myself to peek into the box of horrors I'm looking for.

Soon, I'm at the end of 2067. There's Christmas; there's New Year's Eve. How did Farris spend that evening, I wonder. Is he a party guy, or is he the type to sit at home alone, perched on the edge of his bed and watching other people celebrate on TV? Can't say I care. But maybe it's worth a look to evaluate his state of mind in the days approaching the murder.

I grab the handle and slide the box from its shelf. It's heavier than I expected, and I lose my grip. The box lands hard on my right foot. *Damn*, that hurts! The monitors in the lab must have picked up my reaction, because the yellow query light shows on my watch. *Report status* reads the screen, in letters big enough for me to read. "Status OK," I dictate, "I dropped something on my foot." I hit Send. I wait for a few seconds, then the light switches back to green. *Exercise caution* the screen advises. Yeah, thanks. Good idea.

"So, Mr. Farris," I say to the box on the floor, "how did you ring in the new year?" I lift the lid.

For such a heavy box, there's not much inside. A black-and-gold party hat with *2068* spelled out in glittering numbers. Some confetti. One of those things that unrolls and makes a noise when you blow on it—what the hell are those called? The inevitable tablet that stores a day's images. It turns on when I pick it up, and I flick through the slide show. There's the kitchen of Farris's Silver Lake apartment. The bedroom. Both as neat as if nobody lives there. The television on, showing the Weather Channel. A dry-looking tuna sandwich—lunch? Dinner? Driving along one of the boulevards... Sunset, it looks like. Yeah, going east on Sunset into Hollywood. A heavy oak door with a smiling bouncer reaching for the handle, a gold sign next to it inscribed with the name *Minos*. Inside the nightclub, Scotch in a rocks glass. A crush of people all dressed in sparkly clothes. No individuals stand out, it's all crowds. Farris may have gone out looking for a party, but he didn't connect with anyone there.

I flick through the photos again to see if maybe he'd spotted the victim that night. Lots of sexy young women in short tight dresses—at least a dozen cleavage shots—but no Kira Stone. If Farris had seen her and decided to kill her, there would've been a poster-sized close-up. But nothing.

The last photo isn't a photo at all but a video clip. It lasts for just a few seconds, watching the crowd as everyone counts down to midnight. Just a typical New Year's Eve scene, like every other countdown happening in every other nightclub across the whole city.

The tablet is getting heavy. I lay it in the bottom of the box, then arrange the other memory artifacts as closely as I can to their original order. I unroll the cheap party favor by hand and watch it snap back into a coil. What *are* those things called?

Enough. I know what I'm doing. I'm just distracting myself before I have to face the inevitable.

I put the party favor away and fit the lid back on the box. I pick up **YEAR: 2067; MONTH: DECEMBER; DAY: 31**—lift with your legs, Rhodes, not your back—and slide it back into place on its shelf. I'm surprised how much my heart pounds from the exertion.

I check my watch. No query from the lab. I take a few deep breaths before the techs freak out over my blood pressure. I check again. The green light glows steadily. All systems go. Might as well stop stalling and see what Farris remembered of the day he—no, wait, *someone*. Gotta stay objective here. The day *someone* plunged a knife into Kira Stone over and over and over and on to 92 times.

Yeah, someone. And soon I'll—

Wait.

There's no box for January 3.

That's odd. Subjects with the archival system of memory storage rarely misplace a box. And by "rarely" I mean "never." A routine day might preserve only a few artifacts, but gone? And for a big day when he—sorry, when *someone*—committed a brutal murder that had been planned and anticipated for weeks?

Farris had told interviewers he didn't remember. Maybe he wasn't lying about that. Or maybe he was hiding those memories somewhere, like he was hiding the souvenirs that the profilers were sure he had.

I had a sinking feeling as I scrolled to the date of the previous murder. July 15, 2067. Guy named Hector Estrada, age 36. I retrace my steps to the July section. Damn it. There's an empty slot where the 15th should be.

And on down the list: January 9, 2067; Jenna Hansen. July 9, 2066: Lee Nguyen. January 12, 2066: Thomas Gregory. All missing. Every single box. But I have to check each one. By the time I reach the date of the first murder, a 79-year-old retired schoolteacher named Hannah Murphy murdered in her own home on January 9, 2062—that day's box also missing from the shelves—my mind is working to figure out where Farris had squirreled away those damn boxes. There's got to be a memory vault somewhere. And Farris is keeping it hidden.

I hit the mic on my watch: "Subject relaxation level?"

In a moment, my answer flashes onto the screen: *Relaxation level 4.5 of 5.*

"Request enhanced relaxation."

This time, it takes over a minute to get a reply. *Request denied. Attending physician confirms maximum RL of 4.5.*

Damn it! When I saw that Arnie Bisset was the anesthesiologist today, I knew something like this might happen. That guy is too damn careful. Even at 4.5, Farris must be aware enough to hide the memories he doesn't want me to find. A little more happy juice, just enough to go up another tenth of a point on the scale, and I'd bet a year's salary those boxes would reappear.

No point in arguing with the doc. And I can't poke around in here forever. I take off down the aisle, keeping my eyes open for another room, a trapdoor, a switch or button—anything that might lead to the vault where Farris has stashed his deepest, darkest memories.

There's nothing. Just endless metal shelves stacked with boxes. A little mental math, and I calculate that there are more than 16,000 boxes in this warehouse. No way I can go through them all.

Farris is guilty. It's no coincidence that the memory box is missing for each and every date of each and every murder. But a blank memory isn't evidence. All it does was corroborate what he'd said in every interview. If I can't find something to make the case out in the physical world, Farris will walk free.

I pull out a random box: October 23, 2055. The box weighs practically nothing, and inside are the memories of a not-particularly-memorable day. A few colored leaves. An empty coffee mug. A handful of snapshots—not even enough visuals to store on a tablet. A sign that reads WELCOME TO VERMONT: THE GREEN MOUNTAIN STATE. A white church with a tall steeple. A clapboard house with a B&B sign out front. A hiking trail disappearing into the woods. Some vistas of rolling hills decked out in autumn colors. So Farris had gone leaf-peeping. Big deal. I'm wasting my time.

As I pick up the box to put it back on the shelf, I notice again how light it is. It doesn't hold much more than the New Year's Eve box. Why is that one so heavy?

I go back to the section that housed last December. My feet pound the cement floor, the footsteps echoing throughout the cavernous building. Along the way, I pause and pull out a few boxes that held the memories of other New Year's eves. Not a single one of them weighs more than a pound or two.

There was more to December 31, 2067 than a few party favors and some ogling of young women. The weight of that tablet in my hand wasn't because I'd been holding it for so long. Something was weighing on Farris's memories of that date.

By the time I reach the box I was looking for, my heart's pounding. My watch buzzes, requesting another damn status report.

"Fine. I'm fine. No evidence yet. Following a hunch."

The box seems even heavier than I remember as I ease it out and set it on the floor. Inside, everything is as I left it. I push aside the party favors and grab the tablet. There's something on here. There must be.

I scroll to the video and hit Play. Everything looks the same. The same loud dance music, the same sweaty bodies bouncing around in time. The flashing lights, the disco ball. A break in the music, then the hyped up, amplified voice booming, "Hey, everybody—what time is it? Time to count down to a brand new year! Get ready... Ten..."

The crowd starts counting in unison. There's something...a feeling, a mood, that takes hold. The swirling lights dim just a little and there's a momentary blip, like a skipped heartbeat. I pause the video and back up to play it at a slower speed.

The music stops. Everything looks the same but slower, like the same scene playing out underwater. Words crawl out in the DJ's eerily deepened voice: "Heeey...everyboooody." Still no blip. "Whaaat...tiiime..." The lights get a bit dimmer. "...issss iiit?" A misty darkness creeps over the screen. And then, a skip in the playback.

I back it up again and slow the video even more. Even at this speed, it happens almost too quick to see. But it's there. When the DJ shouted out his question, Farris had glanced at his chronometer. I replay that moment in the slowest possible mode, frame by frame. When the image of the chronometer flashes onto the screen, I stop the video. The tablet feels like it just gained ten kilos. I zoom in on Farris's chronometer: a blue face with gold hands and four smaller dials set into it at north, south, east, and west. How the hell am I supposed to read that thing, all those dials, all those thin gold hands pointing every which way?

I set the tablet on the floor and snap a photo with my watch.

"Analysis required," I say and send the query and the photo to the lab.

In two seconds I get my answer. *Time: 5:39. Date: Tuesday, January 3. Moon phase: Waning crescent.*

In the final seconds before midnight on the last day of 2067, Farris's chronometer showed the date and time of Kira Stone's murder.

I pick up the tablet again. It's as heavy as a concrete block.

I restart the video, playing it slowly but not at crawl speed. The view pans across the crowd as the countdown continues.

Five!... A man adjusts his party hat as the woman beside him reaches for her champagne glass. Kira Stone? The image isn't sharp enough to tell, but this woman looks too short.

Four!... Another man puts his arm around a blonde in a sparkly silver dress. Stone was a brunette.

Three!... Someone steps into the frame and blows a party horn. At this speed, it sounds like a foghorn.

Two!...The crowd is a blur. I can't make out a single face as partygoers raise their glasses.

One!... Pain sears my hands as the tablet flashes blistering hot. Thick, choking smoke billows out. I let go and it crashes down, so heavy its landing shakes the floor. The screen goes dark.

I blow on my hands, shake them hard to shed the pain. What the hell just happened? It was like the memory self-destructed. Something had gone on at midnight that Farris didn't want anyone to see. Maybe not even himself.

The tablet has stopped smoking. I reach down and pick it up. Light as a feather now, but still warm. A network of cracks makes the screen look like the map of some ancient city. I press the power button. Nothing. I try again. Still nope. I press every button on the damn thing and shake it hard.

"Show me, damn you! What happened at midnight?"

The tablet stays dark. I put it on the shelf while I think.

Midnight. Start of the new year, but also a new day. And a new day means a new box of archived memories. I set the tablet aside and grab the box for January 1. I tug hard, expecting another heavy load, but this one slides off the shelf like it holds nothing at all.

And it doesn't. The box for New Year's Day, two days before Kira Stone's murder, is empty. Like he's got no memories whatsoever of that day.

That can't be right. Every day, no matter how long ago or inconsequential, retains something. You might forget a memory that's buried away, but it's in there. When someone says, "Remember that time when we..." you can dig through your memories and there it is. You might not have thought of it in years. You might never have pulled up that memory on your own. The artifact may be dusty, but it's *there*. Unless you were in a coma or something. And Clifford Farris hadn't been in a coma.

I check January 2. Same thing. Empty. And of course January 3 isn't there at all.

I put the useless boxes back in their places. Now what?

The cracked tablet sits on the shelf where I set it down. Just for the hell of it I press the power button. The screen lights up. The first memory of Farris's day appears on the cracked screen.

I go through the photos, one by one. This time, I pay less attention to the images and more to how the tablet feels in my hand. The memories don't start to take on weight until Farris arrives at Minos, after he got his Scotch and positioned himself at the edge of the dance floor to stare at the crowd. I'm not going to let the tablet get away from me. I set it on the floor and crouch over it as the timeline nears midnight.

Nothing in the images stands out. It's what you'd expect from the viewpoint of a lonely guy feeling like he ought to find some fun on New Year's Eve. A little pathetic, but that's all. Nothing happens until the last few seconds of the video.

I play the video again, slowly. What strikes me is how out-of-focus the crowd is. Was Farris drunk? Drunk enough to black out a whole day—no, two? The images don't swoop and slide the way they do through a drunk's eyes. The crowd is blurry, I realize, because Farris was staring past it, focused on a blank spot in the back wall.

Wait. Not a blank spot. Faint lines form a rectangle, about six feet high by three feet wide, like a door flush with the wall. As the seconds count down, the lines become more distinct.

I minimize the video and return to the photos. In these, Farris watched the crowd: faces, boobs, shiny blonde hair, the occasional well-shaped ass. But as far as I can tell, there's no door in that wall.

Back to the video. I play it at the slowest speed, starting with the single frame where Farris checked his chronometer. I zoom in to the back wall. *Six...five...* It's there, an outline. Each frame defines it a bit more. *Four...* The tablet grows warmer, and I don't think it'll survive another blowup. *Three...* How far can I get? *Two...*

There. In the space between the last two seconds of the year, a light appears around the rectangle, like a door that's cracked open.

I stop the playback and zoom in. Definitely a door.

"Where did you come from?" I mutter. And—more important—what lay on the other side?

I touch the screen.

A hundred lightning bolts blast from the tablet. I can't see, I can't hear past the roaring in my ears. My body jolts and buzzes like I grabbed a high-voltage wire. Everything goes black.

Time: 14:32:10
Action: Send status request
Time: 14:32:30
No reply
Action: Resend request in 30 seconds
Time: 14:33:00
Action: Send status request
Time: 14:33:20
No reply
Action: Resend request in 30 seconds

* * *

When I come to, the first thing I do is check my watch. To my amazement, it's functioning, and it tells me I was out for not much more than a minute. Even more amazing is the absence of status requests. Getting fried should have sent the monitors crazy out in the lab, but I feel good. Surprisingly good. No pain anywhere, and my pulse is as calm as if I just woke up from a pleasant dream.

I climb to my feet. The cavernous warehouse is gone. I'm standing on plush carpet in a small, dim room. In front of me, a spotlight shines straight down, illuminating a glass display case. As I move closer, I can see the case holds about a dozen wrist chronometers, lined up in a row, each tucked into a slot in the purple velvet lining. The chronometers appear to be various specimens of late 20th-century style: straps made of leather or metal, big round faces in a range of colors: silver, black, gray, white, blue. They fill maybe half the case, with empty slots waiting for more.

I bend over the case. The chronometer on the right, the last one before the empty slots, is the one from Farris's memory video: gold and cobalt blue with all those crazy dials. I bring up the photo I'd snapped. Yes, it's the same. All of the pointers are in the same positions.

I look at the next chronometer to the left. This one has an iridescent face, mother of pearl maybe, and a brown leather strap. I can't read the time, but on this one the date is clear because it shows in two tiny windows: One reads JUL and the other 15. The date Hector Estrada was killed.

I count the chronometers: 13 of them, each in a different style. To the extent I can read them, each matches up with a murder. I turn on my video recorder and go slowly along the row, making sure I get a long, clear shot of each, then continue on to the empty slots on the right.

"Memory vault breached," I say. "Sending video. Not sure how I got here, but this is the place. Continuing search for physical evidence." I cut off the transmission.

Although the chronometers make a beautiful display that points to Farris's guilt, the video won't stand up in court. What I need to do—

My watch beeps. *Transmission failed.*

Crap. Well, sometimes communication falters deep in a memory vault. What I need to do is find what Farris is keeping hidden. As soon as the secret it holds is exposed, the vault bursts wide open. I'm not worried. Yet.

Beyond the spotlight the room is pitch dark. I shade my eyes but can't penetrate that blackness. I walk around the display case and peer into the darkness. Can't see a damn thing. I try the flashlight on my watch, but the beam gets swallowed up as soon as it leaves its source. There's nothing to do but walk forward. Each step is a cautious shuffle, my arms stretched in front of me. It's like being in a thick fog on a moonless night. The darkness is icy cold. It swirls. It pulls me forward and blocks my way at the same time. I have to push through it even as it creeps inside me through my nose, my mouth, my pores.

Maybe stepping into this mist wasn't the smartest idea, but I can't go back now—not even if I want to. I don't know where "back" is. I have to believe that this is the darkness that shrouds Farris's deepest memories, the ones he needs to hide from himself. Only getting through it will give me what I'm looking for.

After what seems like miles, the darkness begins to lighten. It doesn't press on me as heavily; I feel like my lungs are getting some air. I stop. Not to get my bearings—that's impossible—but to gauge the change.

It continues, even though I'm not moving. The misty dark is breaking up. A cool breeze touches my skin and thins the black tendrils. A grayish light breaks in. Waving an arm in front of my face, I lean forward as shapes begin to define themselves.

A table. Beside that, a figure seated in a chair.

More mist swirls away. The figure is a woman, young, with gleaming blonde hair and a DDD chest. Behind her, the wall is covered with framed items—a necklace, a hank of hair, a shoe, a bloody T-shirt. Farris's souvenirs.

I turn my attention back to the woman. She's wearing a white silky dress that looks like a half-open bathrobe. Nice legs. She regards me with a smile that's half temptation and half scorn. I guess that this is Farris's mother—his mind's distorted version of her. He'd probably spied on her while she was taking a bath or doing it with his father and got scarred for life. That's how he'd see it, anyway.

"Your theory is not very original." Her smile tilts toward pure scorn. "As well as completely inaccurate."

What else would she say? She's not real. She's Farris's rationalization for his murderous behavior.

"Not merely inaccurate but also incorrect," she says, and I realize she's replying to words I haven't said out loud. That shouldn't happen. In dreams, sure, but not in mind mining.

Was this place real? Or was I inside my own dream? What if I was still knocked out from the tablet exploding?

"What if? What if?" Her tone is mocking. "So many possibilities. And yet you're still incorrect."

I decide to ignore her. Farris has invented this figure to serve as some sort of guardian of these memories, so whatever she says is calculated to disguise the ugly truth of what he's done. I walk past her to inspect the souvenirs that decorate the wall. Each is in a fancy gold frame, labeled at the bottom like a painting in a museum. I lean in to look at a single running shoe, speckled with rusty red spots. It's labeled KIRA STONE, 17:39, 3 JANUARY 2068.

I press the record button on my watch. I get video of the whole wall. Each victim is represented, of course. The slashed, blood-soaked T-shirt had belonged to Hector Estrada. There's Jenna Hansen's pearl earring, Thomas Gregory's fingernail, a gold tooth from Lee Nguyen. A random assortment of objects, as random as the victims Farris selected. I record them all. Now all we have to do is find out where he stashed them.

"They're in a storage unit on La Cienega Avenue." I haven't forgotten the woman in the chair. Her presence is too unsettling. But I'm still surprised when she speaks. I turn to her, my recorder still on. "Mr. Farris rents it under the name Joe Clifford. With all of the surveillance resources police have today, I'm surprised you haven't discovered it yet."

I speak into my watch in case it doesn't pick up this figment of Farris's imagination. "Check out storage facilities on La Cienega. Look for a unit registered to Joseph Clifford." I don't like how the woman is looking at me, the way my cat does when I open a can of cat food. "Use caution. Could be booby-trapped."

My watch beeps. *Transmission failed.*

"There's no trap," the woman says, crossing her legs. "But by all means check it out. I'm done with Mr. Farris."

Something doesn't feel right. This figment should be protecting Farris. But he did try to give himself up. If she represents some kind of mental tug-of-war between sin and absolution—luscious body, white robe—she might have useful information. Worth a try.

"So tell me. Why these victims? What's the connection?"

"They're not victims. They're sacrifices. The connection is that I required them."

I can see I'm wasting my time. I'm stuck in some twisted part of Farris's mind and his reasons are never going to make sense outside of this vault. It's always nice to get motivation, but in this case the physical evidence will be plenty to put Farris away. If she's telling the truth.

"Don't worry. All of this will make sense."

"Now you're the one who's incorrect." I start looking for the door out of here. Behind me, the black mist is gone, replaced by a blank wall. Panic surges as I look around the room. Four solid walls. No door. There has to be a door. Once you've found your way into a memory vault, there's always a way out.

"Quite a puzzle, isn't it? Your problem is that you believe you're still inside Mr. Farris's mind."

I ignore her as I feel along the wall, fingers searching for the slightest crack.

She keeps talking. "You won't find it that way. You're not looking for the right door." Her laugh is as cold and as sharp as icicles. "The door to hell is one you don't realize you've walked through until—"

She cuts herself off and just sits there, smiling her nasty smile. She's waiting. I want to keep ignoring her, but I can't help myself. "Until when?"

"Until it's too late." She sits back, looking pleased, like she's won a tricky point in a debate.

I snort. "Where'd you get that from, a fortune cookie?" I tune her out again and try to remember how I got in here. The black mist...but before that. The room with the chronometers on display. Farris's New Year's Eve memory—the door that appeared in the blank wall and then cracked open. I start counting down, shouting each number: "Ten! Nine! Eight!

Seven!" Nothing. Surely the outline should be appearing by now.

"You're starting at the wrong place." The amusement in her voice makes me want to turn around and strangle her. I don't want to listen, but she's right. That blip in the video—it came before the countdown began. When was it? I should know, I'd watched the video so damn many times.

I concentrate. The music stopped. The DJ spoke. What did he say? It was a question. I remember now, and I shout it as loud as I can. "What time is it?"

Behind me, a calm female voice: "Time for you to leave."

* * *

When I open my eyes, I'm lying on a concrete floor, pieces of exploded tablet all over me. Something is beeping. It sounds like a truck backing up but in double time. How long have I been out? I lift my arm to check my watch, and I realize that's where the beeping is coming from. Status requests are scrolling down the screen at ten miles a minute.

I feel around my head, my torso, my limbs. No blood, nothing broken. "I'm okay. Now," I say into the mic.

The response is immediate. *Return to portal STAT!!!*

Something's wrong. I climb to my feet, feeling dizzy as shards of plastic and glass drop away. I pull up the coordinates, but the frantic beeping starts again. I find my direction and run. The portal shimmers at the end of the aisle. It flickers, then blinks off and back on. I put everything I've got into reaching it. The portal goes dark again. Don't go out now, I'm almost there. It comes back, but fainter. I hurl myself at the unsteady light.

Time: 14:40:26

Subject status: Blood pressure: 0/0. Pulse: 0. Relaxation stage: N/A.

Investigator status: Blood pressure: 140/90. Pulse: 184.

I can't move. "Somebody get these damn straps off me!"

No one pays any attention. All of the techs are gathered around Farris on the next table. I can barely turn my head enough to see what's going on. "Three...two...one. Clear!"

Farris's body jumps in its restraints. There's a pause, like everyone's holding their breath.

I hold mine, too, willing my pulse to quit galloping.

"Damn," someone says. "He's gone."

"Oh man, oh man." It's Dr. Bisset's voice. "This is gonna send my insurance rates through the roof."

"Hey!" I shout. "*I'm* still here. Let me up."

Fingers loosen my left wrist restraint. A face appears over me. Susan, one of the lab techs. "Hell, Kurt, you barely got out of there." She works the buckles on the other straps and helps me sit up. "Another two seconds, Doc Bisset would be crying twice as hard about his insurance."

The anesthesiologist isn't crying, but he sits beside Farris's motionless body, rubbing his own jaw like he's trying to erase the stubble. "Oh, man," he mutters.

Too bad for him. At least I made it out. And I'd gotten what I went in for.

"I had some communication trouble in there. Did the video come through?"

Susan shakes her head. "Nope, no video." She consults a tablet. "We got a still image of a chronometer at 14:27, before we lost contact. Then nothing until we reestablished contact at 14:38."

I look through the files on my watch but don't see a recording. So I give the watch to Susan so one of the analysts can look. As I do, I tell her about the storage unit on La Cienega registered to Joe Clifford.

"We'll check it out," she says. "Not sure how much it matters, though." We both glance over at Farris. Someone has already covered him with a sheet. Dr. Bisset is gone, probably to call his insurance agent.

"It's always good to tie up loose ends," I say. "Restores a sense of security to the population."

"It is July. People will calm down and stop expecting another stabbing in the next few days."

I head to the locker room to change back into my street clothes and Susan goes the other way with my watch. "Shouldn't take more than a few minutes to scan," she says over her shoulder. "I'll have it for you by the time you're done changing."

"Make sure you do." My wrist feels naked without it. No, not naked. More like I've lost a limb.

Susan is true to her word. Ten minutes later, as I push open the locker room door, she's waiting across the hall. She holds out my watch.

"Any luck?"

She shakes her head. "There are a couple of video files from the time you were inside, but both are corrupted. Cheer up, though. Dispatch sent a team to the storage facility and they're finding all kinds of goodies out there. We were right about Farris collecting souvenirs."

Good. I'm more than ready for this case to be closed. I reach for my watch, and Susan whistles.

"Look at you, going all retro. My grandfather had one of those."

What is she talking about? I go to put on my watch, but there's something in the way. Strapped around my left wrist is a chronometer, with a big round face and four inset dials. I don't know how it got there. I've never seen it before.

I tug at the black leather strap, but it doesn't give.

Susan keeps chattering at me. "Hey, I thought you couldn't read analog."

"I can't." Why won't the damn buckle let go?

She leans toward me. "Looks complicated. So tell me, what time is it?"

A jolt hits me, and suddenly all of those pointers and dials make perfect sense. But they're not showing the current time. The chronometer shows 11:04 on July 7. Tomorrow.

She'd said I'd understand, and I do.

"Susan, help me," I try to say, but different words come out of my mouth: "The time is set."

"Oh, you mean it's stuck?" She steps back. "Well, it's a beautiful piece of jewelry." She wanders off down the hallway toward the lab.

The time is set. I understand.

There's no need to scan the wall for a door. I've already walked through it.

I quit fumbling with the strap and my arm drops to my side. I understand. This chronometer will never come off. Not until it's time.

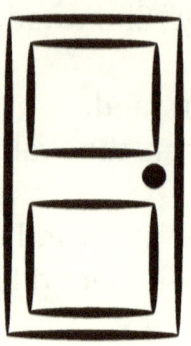

This Way Out

Esther M. Friesner

Whenever Maxie's luck ran dry, it wasn't brains that tossed him a break, it was looks. That boy had a pan that Valentino would envy and he knew it, but he was too dumb to realize that luck and looks was all he had. Yeah, my pal Maxie was like one of those phony bankrolls with a C-note wrapped around a bunch of ones.

I'm not one to talk brains. I was a big enough dope to let the bird talk me into joining the O'Dwyer mob when he did. I guess I did it for old times' sake. Maxie and me grew up together down on Eldridge, maybe not the heart of Manhattan, but at least the kidney. All sorts of things filtered out through those dumps, and Maxie didn't care for the smell. He'd been to Paree during the Great War. He'd had a taste of the high life, rubbing elbows with a lot of grateful mademoiselles.

I mean a *lot*.

Now me, good old dependable Jimmy Logan, I didn't have any of Maxie's advantages. I did know enough to keep my nose clean, or at least as clean as I could and still work for the O'Dwyer mob. Barry O'Dwyer was an easygoing, red-faced

Irishman with a gift for keeping our operation small enough so we never had to take on the big boys and wind up laid out in Clancy's Funeral Parlor wearing wooden kimonos. He kept the business down to a little modest bootlegging and to a sideline, namely Miss Elsie Devine's tea parlor. (At which they did not serve any tea, except corn and Canadian, in case you were wondering.) There were times when running that speakeasy seemed like more work than it was worth, but O'Dwyer was not one for putting all his eggs in one beer keg.

"You see, boys," he told us. "It's a smart fox that digs two doors to his den."

This is good advice, especially when it comes to establishments like Miss Elsie's. If you're going to run a speakeasy, you'd better have two ways out, to give your customers decent odds of giving the cops the slip in case there's a raid.

The boss didn't much care for cops.

One day, he calls a meeting to talk about the cop problem. Maxie comes in with a lady on his arm. I'd seen my pal playing escort to some hot tomatoes in the past, but this one left the others looking like a bunch of flophouse mattresses. Everything about her sort of *shimmered*. It wasn't just her dress, which was solid silk and spangles, or the diamonds doing a frozen waterfall number from her neck and ears and wrists, or that bobbed blond hair that made you think of winter moonlight. It was *her*. Her from somewhere *inside*, you know? She was— was—

Ah, forget it. I'm no poet. If I was, maybe I could do justice to those eyes of hers. Brother, that skirt had a pair of baby blues that just naturally made a mug lean in closer, closer, closer, until he could fall into them, drown, and not give a damn.

So of course she's with Maxie.

O'Dwyer's the only one of us not staring at her. Talk about being all business! "You're late, Max," he snapped. "Maybe you don't care that the cops are making us bleed cash?"

Maxie just grinned. "Hey, Boss, you know better than that. I care. Can't pay the landlord with promises."

That raised a laugh. Maxie bragged that he hadn't paid his landlord a penny in months, mostly on account of her being a land*lady* who didn't mind getting paid other ways.

"Well, have a seat and give that girlie the heave-ho," O'Dwyer said, gnawing his cigar in the lady's direction. "We've got troubles to fix."

I'll say we did. Last raid the cops pulled on Miss Elsie's they didn't just do a little light roisting; they smashed the place. Broke it down to the cellar and out through the walls. It'd take weeks before we'd have things up and running.

"Then this is your lucky day, Boss. I've got the answers to all our troubles right here." He grabbed a chair and pulled the lady onto his lap. "Ain't that right, sugar?" He kissed his girl hard and she liked it, even though she didn't show more than a thread of sharp little kitten teeth when she smiled. "Me and Faye are gonna make you real happy, you can lay to that."

He started talking. I mean *really* started talking. Maxie always did have the gift of the gab. If his looks didn't net the girls, his line did the job, only O'Dwyer wasn't no girl and he was pretty well immune to Maxie's hooey.

Which was why, when I saw him paying *attention* to my buddy's spiel, I knew Maxie was saying something worth listening to.

See, thanks to the war ending and Mr. Volstead butting in, we now had a world where some high society debs got a kick out of slumming, spending Daddy's money on wrong gees like us until it was time to settle down with a Harvard man. Faye was one of them ritzy types and she had something bigger to offer her man than cash: She had real estate. It was a brownstone townhouse over on the west side, and get this:

"It's one hundred per cent guaranteed safe from the cops. One. Hundred. Per. Cent!" Maxie jabbed the table for emphasis.

"Balderdash!" O'Dwyer snorted. "No place is *that* safe when the bulls get greedy. That's when small operators like us are easy pickings. They don't dare take on the big mobs."

"Boss, trust me, once we hitch up with Faye, we won't be small operators for long. She told me all about her place and it's perfect: straight route to the Hudson for 'grocery' shipments, a fine kitchen, second floor ballroom with space for a bandstand and plenty of tables—the bar and the dance floor are already there. Up on the third floor there's room for gaming, and back downstairs again there's three—count 'em, *three* escape routes."

O'Dwyer made a face like someone had hid a mackerel somewhere in the room maybe five days ago and forgot where. "Let me get this straight, lad. Your girl just *happened* to think it'd be her maiden dream to run a blind tiger so she builds one and then gives it to you?"

"To *us*, Boss," Maxie said. "She wants to give it to *us*."

"And you've seen this pot of gold?"

"Well..." Maxie looked uneasy. "Not yet. But Faye and me figured that after the meeting—"

O'Dwyer walked up to him and yanked him out of his chair. Faye went sprawling. Then he backhanded him so hard his teeth clattered.

"What was that for?" Maxie demanded.

"That's for trying to sell me a pig in a poke! And that's also for blabbing our business to a broad who's got no more right to know about it than the man in the moon!" O'Dwyer grabbed Maxie by the lapels and hauled him so close he could've taken a bite off the boss' stogie. "Why'n't you just put an ad in the papers?"

"Boss, boss, c'mon, Faye's on the level. She won't talk."

"She's not the talker I'm worried about." O'Dwyer turned to the rest of us. "Any you palookas ever seen Maxie around with this chippy before now?" We all shook our heads and looked away. We felt sorry for Maxie, but not sorry enough to lie for him. O'Dwyer sneered. "That's what I thought." He gave the poor bastard a shake. "You don't hardly know her, but you say you can trust her? Care to tell me how you reached that conclusion, Einstein?"

Before Maxie could say a word, the lady in question spoke for herself. She was back on her feet, although—

Funny, I don't remember seeing her *get* up. She just...*was*.

Anyway, she glided behind O'Dwyer and laid one long, thin hand on his shoulder. Her pale skin glowed against the dark gray of the Irishman's pinstripe suit. When he turned his head, her blue eyes locked on his. She was wearing another one of her thin little smiles and when she spoke, her voice was heat and honey.

"Barry Finnbar Seamus O'Dwyer, a word in your ear, if you please."

Now how in the world did Maxie's girl, who'd just met him, know to call the boss by all those names?

* * *

O'Dwyer called the new tea room Queenie's, after Faye's mama. That was all she asked and he said it was only right, since she'd fronted the whole set-up.

He also told Maxie that from now on, he and Faye were going to be working close together. As in *very* close. They had reached what you might call an *understanding*. He let my pal know that Faye had no objections to this, and if Maxie had anything to say about it—

Maxie's face colored up, but that's it. Get between O'Dwyer and what O'Dwyer wanted? No thanks. Sometimes he could be pretty smart for a stupid guy.

Besides, he was Maxie, Maxie the sheik. We all knew he'd have another doll on his arm before the curtain rang down on Faye's exit. Getting girls was easy for him. Getting the top job at the newly opened Queenie's—O'Dwyer's reward to him for being a good sport—was not. That's how Maxie wound up decked out in a swank monkey suit, welcoming all the East Side swells and the show biz crowd and the rest of the marks to our fine new establishment.

He was also the one who had to keep his eyes and ears open for the first sign that the cops had found out about Queenie's and were about to pay a call. This was bound to happen, but we never expected it to be on opening night.

The place wasn't packed, but we were doing okay. I was upstairs keeping an eye on the craps table. I was on edge and looking forward to an early quitting time, because that's when the boss swore he'd show us all about the way out.

"Look, lads, Faye and me ain't had time to take you on the grand tour yet because we've been busy readying the place. The doors you'll want are in the ballroom. That's all you really need to know. Now stop acting like a bunch of daisies. We're safe. The bulls don't even know this joint is open!"

Surprise.

The alarm sounded with Maxie yelling, "Everybody down!" As in, time for us guys upstairs to start herding the customers to the dance floor level. This was no quick job, and I felt the panic rising in my flock of suckers as they stampeded down the steps. Good thing I've got a loud voice and could make myself heard over the shrieking crowd. I got them into the ballroom just in time to see the abandoned tables, the empty bandstand, and the backs of their fellow guests disappearing through a pair of narrow doors that had been hidden behind blue velvet drapes to either side of the stage.

"Keep it moving, keep it moving," I yelled. "Pick a door and go!" I didn't need to tell them twice. We could all hear the sound of heavy pounding at the street door and the shouts of the big bad wolves in blue telling us poor little piggies to let them come in or they'd break the house down.

I checked behind me to see if I had any stragglers before I ducked through the doorway myself. Nope, no one. But just as I was about to save my own bacon, I heard a funny thing: Faye's voice from down below, street level, at the front door.

"Good evening, officers," was what I heard her say. "Won't you please come in?"

Come in! Who does that? Who lets the bulls in when they're going to bust up everything in your place?

Okay, so they'd wreck it even if you didn't lay down the welcome mat, but it's the principle of the thing. That's not how you play the game.

I was no referee. Maybe Faye was nuts. *I* wasn't, and I was going to get the hell away. I plunged through the door.

The door...

The door that melted into a hallway lined with gold-framed mirrors and ivory vases full of flowers and thick carpets patterned with peacocks and dragons and vines. I blinked in the pearly light. *This* was a getaway route? Not some badly lit tunnel through a cellar where you had to dance with rats and dodge garbage cans before you made it back into the outside world? I mean, Queenie's was set up in a fancy townhouse, so could be the fanciness spilled over some, but still—

"This way, sir, please."

The guy wore green. Leaves are usually that color, right? Well, that's what he was wearing: leaves. They circled his head and wrists and ankles, plus he had a bunch of long, shiny ones wrapped around his middle like a towel from the Turkish baths. He took me by the elbow, urging me along, and I was too stunned to put up a fight.

We came out under the stars. There were torches burning on a beach where palm trees swayed in the evening breeze. I heard plinky-plunky ukulele music and saw a bonfire on the sand. A mob of people were there ahead of me, being offered pineapples and coconuts with straws sticking out of them. Hell of a way to serve cocktails, but the waitress was wearing just a grass skirt and a smile, so who cared?

I recognized the folks gathered around the fire. They'd all come from Queenie's. They'd left in a panic, but they weren't panicked any more. Some of the college boys started waving their coconuts around and singing about bulldogs going bow-wow-wow until a bunch of other Ivy League eggs got to howling for ten thousand men of Harvard. They got into a scuffle that wasn't much more than a slapping match, but before it could turn ugly, a big gong shook the palms and a woman's voice announced, "Thank you for your patience. The coast is clear. Welcome back to Queenie's."

Back? Who the hell wanted to go back anywhere if it meant leaving here? Not me, but for some reason, I found myself falling into line with the rest as we marched under an arch of white orchids, through the mirror-hung hallway, and out onto the dance floor. The band was there ahead of us, playing away like nothing had happened.

And nothing had. Not if you went by what your eyes told you. The place was intact. Not a sign that the cops had come by to pay a call. Nothing broken. Nothing tossed. Not one thing.

I went back to the craps tables, because a job's a job and O'Dwyer hates shirkers. The dice were rolling again and didn't stop until closing time. The house won more than we usually do, mostly because none of the suckers had their heads in the game. They were too busy talking about the raid and where they'd been and how was it possible.

My thoughts exactly, though I had to wait for the close of business to ask. I wasn't alone. Every one of O'Dwyer's boys had the same questions. We clomped upstairs to the top floor of the house, where the boss had his office as part of Faye's private apartment, and made our concerns known.

O'Dwyer was at a big, brass-bound mahogany desk, wrist-deep in the night's receipts and happy as a pig in shit. Faye leaned against him like a Persian cat rubbing up on a trouser leg. The boys and me made a racket, all of us talking at once. Turned out that the *second* escape route took some of Queenie's customers to a different spot, namely—

"—*Havana!*" Maxie had as big a case of the heebie-jeebies as the rest of us. "I tell you, Boss, I been there and I know that city when I saw it. How the hell is Havana walking distance from Manhattan?"

O'Dwyer shifted his cigar from one corner of his mouth to the other and flashed his teeth. "Ask me no questions, my boy, and I'll tell you no lies. Also I won't flatten that beezer of yours for swearing in front of a lady."

Faye laughed. "Darling, you mustn't keep your friends in the dark. May I set their minds at ease?"

O'Dwyer shrugged and went back to counting the kale. Faye slithered around and perched herself on the front of his desk, crossed her gams, and explained what had happened.

It was a real good explanation. I think. For some reason, all I came away with as I left the house and went staggering home at dawn was scraps: *Stagecraft...best of vaudeville magicians' tricks...lighting effects...actors...the lady had friends from Hollywood...*

She'd talked a long time, and my memory claimed that she'd answered all our questions, but I felt like I'd spent the night stuffing my face at a banquet where it turned out that all the food was made of air. The one thing that stayed with me most wasn't anything Faye said, but the boss' final word on the subject:

"What do you birds care how she did it? What counts is that it *worked* and that it's gonna be *great* for business."

I'll say it was. After that night, word got around. People flocked to Queenie's, and for a change they came *hoping* for a raid. Some showed up with friends who'd been there on that night, friends they thought were spouting baloney, or who'd been too spifflicated to tell the difference between reality and drunk dreams. They came along either wanting to be proven wrong or wanting to find out that they were right.

You get that much traffic, the cops take notice. They came back. They came back plenty, but you'd never know it. Time after time, we had the alarm, the pick-a-door escape, and the reluctant return to a speakeasy that looked fresh out of the bandbox, no sign of the heavy hand and flat feet of the law. There wasn't so much as a single busted glass.

"The secret is to let them in. They're much more polite and considerate about leaving things be once they see we've got nothing to hide," Faye said.

"Nothing to hide?" I echoed. "How do they not see the bar and the dance floor and the upstairs and—?"

"Stagecrap, you dope," said O'Dwyer. "Levers. Pulleys. Panels. Spinning walls. It works, don't it? Shut up." He gave me a clip in the ear. Faye smiled.

I was starting not to like that smile. Damned if I could say why. I guess it was like the places those doors led, places that *looked* pretty, but—

Crazy to say, crazy to think about too much, but those places at the other end of the two passageways just didn't *feel* right. Kind of like the passageways themselves. They didn't leave *me* feeling right, either. They gave me the creeps, you know? Whenever I walked through, I always caught this—this *breath* out of nowhere, stirring the hairs on the back of my neck, and Jesus, was it ever cold.

There *were* other spots besides Havana and Honolulu too. Lots of them. Me and the guys compared notes. We toted up at least a dozen different scenes—Paris, Rome, Monte Carlo, Los Angeles, San Francisco, a yacht sailing through the Greek Islands, Egypt, London, more.

"How does she do that?" I asked.

"Stagecrap," Maxie said.

"No, I mean it, *how*? You ever see a single carpenter come through here to swap scenes?"

"They come when we're not around."

"We're here every night. You trying to tell me someone can turn Los Angeles into London in less than a day? And what about that yacht?"

"Hey, Jimmy, what about you go ask O'Dwyer all those questions," Maxie said.

That shut my trap for me. I wasn't looking for more trouble. Best thing to do was sit tight and count my blessings, along with the cash. Business was better than ever and O'Dwyer was no piker when it came to sharing the profits.

Still, that feeling...like something was watching me, us, and smiling the great granddaddy of Faye's blade-thin smile.

Our customers didn't seem to have my problem with the places Faye's carpenters threw together and tore down so fast.

Some of the regulars *were* regulars because they wanted to see all the different sets at the end of the two passages. They were collecting them like stamps, like postcards, like those decals you slap on your steamer trunk when you've got enough money to cross the ocean like ordinary people cross the street.

Some of them were real keen collectors. I had one bird slip me a fin and ask me to call him any night I knew there was going to be a raid. I told Scrooge that kind of inside dope'd cost him a fifty, which I pocketed. I didn't bother telling him he was off his nut. *I'm* gonna know a raid's gonna happen?

"What a chump!" I said to Maxie when I told him about it.

"That so?" my pal remarked, thoughtful.

* * *

None of us noticed the changes, at first. They were real subtle, which is why no one suspected Maxie was involved. First change, the college crowd stopped showing up at Queenie's, all except the ones from the richest families. Next, the rest of the herd began to shed the show business folks and the out-of-town butter and egg men in favor of the Old Money customers who had enough lettuce to buy and sell Hollywood, Broadway, and a lot of territory in between. Queenie's stayed as packed as ever, so who cared?

Last of all, the number of raids began to pick up until there wasn't a week went by with at least one, sometimes two. Now *that* was what finally got me and the boys' attention.

O'Dwyer took it with a laugh. What did it matter how often the bulls showed up when they never did any damage? He brushed off the slowly multiplying raids as coincidence. We swallowed that. It's what we all wanted to believe.

I guess I would've kept on believing it myself if not for the fact that one night when I was getting a breath of air outside the club I caught sight of Maxie having a tête-à-tête with Patsy the Pigeon, a noted stoolie. The minute that little rat scuttled away, I confronted my buddy.

"What was that all about?"

"Eh, just arranging for tonight's entertainment." He cracked a deck of Luckies and lit one. "Faye's got one of the passageways leading straight to the Casbah, this time. It'll be swell."

"You *set up* a raid?"

He smirked through a trail of cigarette smoke. "Practice makes perfect."

I hoped he was kidding. I knew he wasn't. "So *all*—?"

"Oh, I can't take credit for every last one." He put on a modest look phony enough for an alderman on the take. "Sometimes it's the real cops, maybe once a month, but the rest of the time it's the crew Faye hires to man her fake Havanas. It'll be the real ones tonight, though, unless Patsy's lost his touch." He took a deep drag.

I spread my hands. "Maxie, I don't understand."

He put an arm over my shoulders. "Look, Jimmy, I'm just giving the customers what they want, okay? Faye and me, we knew that once the marks got a taste of what was waiting for them on the other side of those doorways, they'd want more and be glad to pay for it. That's why I started using my spot at the front to only let in the ones with *real* dough. Now I've got a house full of suckers ready to pass me a C note a week just to make sure I keep on letting them in the door. They double that when there's a raid and they get to see the world without leaving the block. You think I'll miss out on something that rich?"

"Nice racket. No wonder the boss don't care."

"He don't care because he don't know."

"You didn't *tell* him you've got all that dough coming in?"

Maxie gave me a *What am I, stupid?* look. What he said next froze my bones: "This is just the icing, Jimmy. Let me tell you about the cake." Before I could say I was happier not knowing, he opened his yap and started to brag.

Oh God. Oh damn. My friend Maxie wasn't just fleecing raid-crazy suckers; he was skimming the cream off the straight bootleg side of the business. That Dumb Dora boyhood pal of mine had been flimflamming O'Dwyer from the day Queenie's opened.

Now I was sweating. "Jesus, Maxie, what if he catches wise? He'll let so much daylight into you, you'll look like a screen door!"

He snorted. "He won't learn nothing. What, are *you* gonna blab?"

"You know I won't." The two of us went back together too far for that to ever happen.

"So, okay." He gestured with his cigarette. "Besides, my girl's got him distracted."

His girl. *His* girl. He didn't have to draw me a picture. I got the message the second he said her name the way a man does when he's dizzy with a dame. He and Faye were still an item, behind O'Dwyer's back, and they were in cahoots on the grift. How do you like that? I'll bet she was the brains behind the "cake" side. Maxie could hardly *spell* cake.

But what did a little rich girl really know about handling men like O'Dwyer? It was all a game to her, and what happened if one day she had the bad luck to slip up and show the Irishman her cards?

"Maxie, you've gotta call this quits. O'Dwyer could hear about this from someone besides you or me or Faye. What if one of your two-Cs-a-raid suckers spills the beans?"

"Ah, get that look off your face, Jimmy. Stop picking out the flowers for my funeral. Faye and I aren't dumb enough to hang around playing this racket forever. We're gonna make one last score—a big one—then skip town, go to Brazil and live the life of Riley." He gave me a friendly punch in the arm. "I'll send you a ticket from Rio."

"When's that happening?" That was all that mattered to me. I wanted my pal gone, out of harm's way, and the sooner, the better.

"Less'n a month. Faye's got something special planned, a grand opening."

"Another one? We're already open."

"Not everything. Not the third door." He finished his cigarette, flipped the glowing butt into the gutter, and went back inside.

* * *

The big October bash at Queenie's was the talk of a very exclusive part of the town. Everyone who counted got a word-of-mouth invite. Everyone who heard about it, one way of another, wanted to come. Maxie had his work cut out for him, dealing with the crowd storming the townhouse that night. Some of those rich boys got so wild to get in that they forgot to keep their "tips" palmed.

When you start waving C notes, the smell of money flies up to the top floor and hits the wrong nose.

By the time Maxie had harvested the cabbage and shut the front door on the disappointed stragglers, O'Dwyer was out of the office and storming through the ballroom, blood in his eyes. I was doing a turn by the bar, making sure things were going smoothly, so I had a front row seat I never wanted.

I gotta be straight: I didn't notice O'Dwyer there at first or I would've given my buddy the high sign. I was too wound up in my own thoughts, still mulling over what Maxie told me that night three weeks back. Ever since we talked, I wondered about that third door. Not that I doubted him—he'd told us there were three escape hatches to the townhouse the first time he brought up the subject. It's just that—that—

—I couldn't find it.

Yeah, I went looking. I was curious. But *three weeks* of looking and nothing? I checked every room I could get into, peeped behind every piece of furniture, knocked on every wall. It's not like it was that haystack needle they always talk about. A townhouse is only so big. Where in hell was that dame hiding a whole third escape route *plus* yet another spectacular wait-out-the-cops spot at the other end?

I was about to get my answer.

The boss grabbed Maxie by the neck, shook him like a wash rag, and slugged him with a right cross that sent him crashing into the nearest table full of swells. The chicks squealed with alarm, but you could tell they were loving the floor show. Maxie sat in a puddle of gin-soaked tablecloth and shook his head like a two-bit palooka up against the heavyweight champ.

O'Dwyer jerked him to his feet. He shook him some more, enough to make some of the C notes flutter out of his jacket. This time the girlies were squealing with glee, grabbing the party favors. The look in the Irishman's face was pure murder. He wasn't gonna bump off Maxie in front of all those witnesses, but beating him to a pulp on the dance floor? Try and stop him.

All of a sudden Faye was there, between the two men. She put one fingertip on O'Dwyer's chest and gave him a tiny shove.

The boss staggered clear to the far side of the dance floor, mouth and eyes wide open in surprise. It was like a butterfly had landed on a bull's head and driven him into the ground up to his knees.

If it was me, I'd've stayed put, because when a frail who can't tip the scales past ninety pounds does *that* to full-grown tough like O'Dwyer, a wise head might want to think things over before making another move.

The boss was too mad for thinking. He took another run at Maxie, even with Faye now blocking his path. He was two, maybe three steps shy of barreling into the little lady when she raised one hand and declared, "Barry Finnbar Seamus O'Dwyer, we have *guests.*"

He stopped dead. Then he sat down. Then he keeled to one side and lay down, staring at the ceiling. The crowd applauded. I kneeled beside him to check he was still breathing, which he was. The other boys working Queenie's that night didn't know *what* to do.

Unlike Faye. She gave Maxie a little push in the direction of the front door. It wasn't anything like the one that had floored O'Dwyer, more like a hint for him to blow while the blowing was good. He started away and she went to the bandstand.

"Ladies and gentlemen," she said, while the lights made her dress shoot sparks. "We're sorry for the disturbance. The next round of drinks is—"

She didn't get the chance to say if the next round was on the house or was gonna cost double. The familiar thunder of fists on the front door sounded twice as loud as it ever had, so loud the chandeliers jigged and tinkled. Sirens went off outside. A booming voice announced that this—surprise!—was a raid. The words came as clear as if they weren't fighting their way through a thick oak door and up a flight of stairs.

"Oh my goodness," said Faye, playing it cute. "It looks like we'll have to move the party. I hope none of you are too disappointed?"

The customers' cheers swamped her as the blue satin drapes flanking the stage parted, revealing the two doors they knew so well. They abandoned their tables eagerly, massing up on both sides of the bandstand, wild to rush through and see what sort of fresh, exotic delights were on the far side tonight.

But when the first suckers reached the doors, they wouldn't open. They rattled on their hinges as one man after another tried and failed to make them swing wide. People started muttering, confused at first, then nervous, then outright scared.

Faye stepped in before things got out of control. "Don't worry, darlings, this is just a teensy delay. Here at Queenie's, all the doors open at the same time or they don't open at all. Remember how we promised you a special treat tonight? Well, hold onto your hats, because here we go!"

She spread her arms and the bandstand began to rise. Silently, quickly, a pair of doors emerged from the floor. They were wider than the others, with amber panels that shone like Japanese lanterns. Sill and top and sides were silver, cast in the shape of sleeping leopards. Webs of jet-black metal spun pictures of winged, naked men and women across the glowing gold.

The amber doors began to open. The others did as well.

"Enter and be welcome." Faye sat with her gams swinging over the silver archway. "Make your choice, but a word before you do: you'll have better luck if you don't try to cross *this* threshold. Even though it will take you to a getaway like none you've ever experienced, admission is limited. Only one in ten of you will be allowed. Sorry, Fire Department rules." She laughed.

Guess what happens when you tell rich people there's something they might *not* be able to have? The crush was on. They were crabs trying to get out of a bucket, the ones below grabbing the ones closest to the rim and dragging them back down. Meanwhile, the noise from the front door was getting louder. I heard wood creak, splinter, and smash. Running feet hammered the stairs.

Some of the mob at the amber doors lost their heads and made a beeline for one of the two old reliable exits. The closer the rumble came, the more of them changed their minds and vanished down the familiar passageways. Our guys brought up the rear, playing shepherds like they'd been trained. Soon there was just a handful of contenders left behind, so wrapped up in wrestling for the right to be the first over that sparkling threshold that it took a moment for them to realize they'd won.

Faye jumped down from her perch and tapped one of them on the shoulder. "It's all yours," she said, touching the brim of her invisible doorman's cap. The winners traded handshakes, all good sports now that they had the victory, and headed for the rewards beyond the silver-framed gate. There was music coming through that doorway now—harp notes threading their way through the piping of flutes. A mutter of drums tempted the slowest feet to dance. I smelled roses, and the scent of ripe fruits fit to make a statue hunger for a bite, and a whiff of real champagne so intense I swear I felt the bubbles prick my nose. Somewhere a girl was singing, and that was *my* name in her song.

I stood, ready to go to her, ready to fall into line with the handful of swells, ready to fight any of them who tried to get in my way. I patted the spot where my jacket hid a Colt .32.

Yeah, let them try.

A hand snapped around my ankle, snapped me awake. "Stop them," O'Dwyer whispered. His skin looked like paper but his grip was steel. I tried to pull free; his grip tightened. "It's the tithe, Jimmy. She's paying the ancient debt, and they're her coin."

Old habits die hard, especially when you're in the habit of following orders from a guy who scares the piss out of you. Even flat on his back, O'Dwyer could command; even when his commands sounded crazy.

"Boss, what are you talking about? The cops are coming. Let me help you to—"

"Curse your wooden head, Jimmy Logan, do what I say! There *are* no cops! If there were, *what's keeping them*?"

He was right. The beefiest bull on the force could've busted down the front door and reached the ballroom by now. Where *were* they?

And if he was right about that—

"Okay, Boss." I didn't get his babble about tithes and coins and debts, but he could fill me in later. He let go of my ankle and I made a run like Red Grange heading for a touchdown. I'm small, but I'm spry. I slipped past Faye and made my stand right behind her, balancing on the lip of the silver-framed door.

"Hold it!" I drew my roscoe for emphasis. The rich boys still left took one look at the gun, turned tail, and blew through the other doors. They moved so fast that they missed all the curses Faye threw after them.

Then she spun on me.

"Well, aren't you the killjoy, Mr. Logan." Her teeth showed small and sharp. I felt that familiar chill on the scruff of my neck, only now it wrapped itself all the way around into a noose. "You're not much for a girl to bring home to Mother, but you'll have to do." She waved one hand over my gun. I clutched a handful of crumbling leaves. "Let's not keep her waiting. Tonight, our tithe falls due and we haven't got the world's most understanding creditor." She took me by the arm and I was powerless to stop her. Her blue eyes flared green when she laughed at me.

There's other times your past comes back at you than when you're going to die. Faye's eyes blurred from green to brown, from cold to kind, and I was a brat being minded by my old Kerry gran. Her soft voice told me tales about the good folk, the fair folk, the gentry, the good neighbors, the ones who lived under the green hills of Ireland, the ones you didn't meet, if you were lucky.

The ones who every seven years settled their debts and paid the tithe they owed to Hell.

"Damn it, O'Dwyer, why couldn't you let her have that bunch of moneybags?" I shouted as she began towing me toward the amber doors. "They were asking to go!"

"And have the D.A. huffing down my neck when they disappeared? The law cares what happens to the rich." He paused. "I never meant for you to take their place."

"I'm not too crazy about the idea myself." I made an effort and braced myself against Faye's pull. I wasn't going to go without a fight.

"Insect," she spat. "You'd better come along. Don't try my temper. I'll burn this house to the ground and all within the portals, too! You pathetic, mangy, scrawny, trifling—"

"Mind your mouth when you're talking about my pal Jimmy!"

He was on her before she could catch a breath. I had no more idea where he sprang from than she did, and she had more at stake because he bowled her clear of me, off her feet and heels in the air.

"*Maxie!*" I cried, never so glad to see the big palooka in my life.

His attack broke her hold over me. I lurched away to where O'Dwyer still lay stretched out stiff on the dance floor. I propped him up so we could watch Maxie fight that otherworld wildcat. Oh, it was a fine thing to see! She turned into seven sorts of beast, from tiger to serpent to more, forever lunging for the tenderest bits of the man. He blocked her every time. Her shrieks of frustration and rage made the gaping amber doors shiver in their silver frame.

I had a thought to mind the hour. My watch said we were a scant three minutes from midnight. Halloween would end. My granny's words came back to me a second time, reminding me that the way between our world and the fairy realm was thin for just so long on this night. The portals between here and there would soon slam shut. I prayed the people who chose the other two doorways would get out somehow, but I couldn't spare them any more worry than that.

"Jimmy, Jimmy boy." O'Dwyer's fingers clawed my hand. "Get salt. Cast it wide in front of her. She'll have to count each grain. It's all that can save Maxie now."

But there was no salt, no way to entrap Faye. I shuddered, imagining her rage if she failed to bring home the fairies' tithe to Hell. We'd pay for it. She'd fulfill her word. The townhouse and all in it would go up in smoke. The cops would write a report and shrug and life would go on. Just not ours.

I guess Maxie's thoughts were running down a similarly bleak street, because suddenly he stopped fighting Faye and grabbed her face, forcing her to look him in the eye.

"You want your payment to the devil? You've got it."

He kissed her, slapped her hard, and shoved her away. Two strides, a leap, and he was through the amber doors. We heard the unholy roar that greeted him on the other side.

Faye brushed herself off, tucked a lock of hair behind her ear, and gave me and O'Dwyer a wry look. "It's been a pleasure doing business with you, gentlemen," she said, before she melted into mist, wafted after Maxie, and was gone.

* * *

After that night, O'Dwyer's gang broke up because O'Dwyer broke down. He never did recover the full use of his body—"Elf-shot," he said, accepting his fate—and when the police did show up on the doorstep of Queenie's, he told them what had happened.

Exactly what had happened, fairies and Hell and all.

I'm not sure which hospital he's in now.

I also don't know what happened to Queenie's customers, but since the rest of the gang turned up safe and the D.A. didn't stop by, I guess they made it out okay.

The other boys knew they didn't have what it takes to keep running the operation, so they made a gift of it to the first bigger mob that agreed to take them on as part of the remaining inventory. I didn't go along for the ride. I'd joined O'Dwyer's gang because of Maxie and since he wasn't with us any more, I saw no reason to hang on. I had other things to do, anyway.

Mostly, prayer. I went back to church, hearing Mass every chance I got, putting in a good word for my buddy's soul. I took my savings and bought a horse and carriage—I always did like horses—and got me a job giving folks rides through Central Park. It wasn't exciting work. That suited me fine.

One late night in June I was driving my rig along the park paths, taking my mare back to the stables, when I heard the sound of lots of horses coming towards us. Pretty strange, at that hour, but I pulled to the side of the road anyhow, just to be polite and let them pass.

They came riding out of the warm darkness in single file, the horses decked out with gold saddles and silver bridles, satin draperies trailing down their sides. Fireflies made clouds of light above their heads. The riders, men and women both, would've made Ziegfeld's chorus line drop dead with envy. Tall and graceful, silky hair cascading over their shoulders, they were all dressed like something out of stories that start *Once upon a time*. I recognized the guy who used to play clarinet in the jazz combo at Queenie's, and the drummer too. Small world.

In the midst of them was Faye. She had a look to her I've only seen on growling dogs before they spring for your throat. She rode beside a woman whose beauty made hers look like an old potato next to a diamond. Everything about that lady dazzled, from the tips of her jeweled slippers to the royal crown she wore like a sunrise. It was that crown told me for sure that I was laying eyes on Queenie herself at last.

But who did I see behind her, sharing her saddle? Maxie. He had his arms cinched around her waist, his chin resting on her shoulder and, swear to God, I saw the rascal nibble the lady's ear, bold as you please. Once a sheik, always a sheik.

When they were right abreast of my carriage, he looked in my direction and tipped his plumed velvet hat with a flourish.

"Hell wouldn't have me, Jimmy!" he shouted, grinning like a cat full of cream. "Hell wouldn't have me!"

A gate in the night opened and they all rode far away.

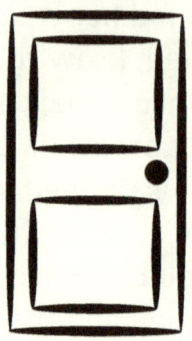

Deus Ex Machina

Ian Tregillis

"Listen, friend. There are three things you need to know about the Grand Ostia, but the knowing won't endear you to the Thanates of Paarvos. I know it's a pisser, but they'll wreck you good if they break in before I'm done."

The restrained madman trails off, pointing with his chin. Another volley of thunder rattles the chamber. This one is hard enough to tarnish a two-meter section of the barricade's mirror sheen. It's as if the Thanates have sucker-punched this slip of illegally folded space hard enough to give it a black eye. You can't see the ultraviolet light spewing from the distressed negative-energy barrier, but you can smell the ozone it creates. It's a welcome change from the vomit.

You realize he paused for effect. He's insane, but there is a theatrical quality to his lunacy. So at least the wait for rescue will be entertaining.

Though your prisoner managed to instantiate the barricade before you could subdue him, you're comforted by the (violent) evidence that your call for assistance slipped through before the room was effectively severed from the surrounding universe.

With every impact, the aubergine portion of the silvery barricade spreads. The Thanates will rescue you. A spacetime bubble like this is supposed to be impenetrable yet, in a contest between an irresistible force and an immovable object, who but a fool wouldn't lay their money on the Thanates?

As always, a frisson of warm delight accompanies thoughts of humanity's godlike benefactors. Though you've never admitted this to anybody else, you've long imagined it's akin to how it feels to fall in love. Or smoke opium.

The madman rolls his eyes. "Ugh. Wipe that beatific grin from your face. It makes you look like a slack-jawed moron. And if that's the case, I've chosen the wrong person and we're *both* in store for a rotten day."

You open your mouth to object—very few people pass the stringent mental and biological tests to become a regional Ostium engineer, and fewer still manage it before their twenty-first birthday—but he interrupts again, stepping on your indignation.

"I know, I know, you're not a moron, oh no not at all, top of your class, blah blah, scores so high the Thanates personally congratulated you, blah-de-blah, this cushy job on the very day you reached the age of majority." He looks you dead in the eyes. "Blah. Blippety. Blah."

Another frisson displaces the first, but instead of a warm tingle this one rides a shiver of deep unease. It's a bit like the way an unpleasant dream tends to evaporate even as you linger in bed, eyes still closed, determined to remember it. You've known this raving nut for all of five minutes, and so far you've barely managed to inject a spare word into his wide-eyed, foam-flecked ranting. Meaning you certainly haven't told him your life story. Yet somehow—

Another boom rattles the chamber. The metallic tang of ozone grows in concert with the reverberations. You turn your back to the distressed section of the barrier—gently, so that you don't go ping-ponging off the walls—and, always keeping one hand firmly on a fixed surface, roll down the sleeves of your boilersuit, lest the UV give you sunburn. A pointless gesture since you're surrounded by a perfect mirror, but it's more to distract yourself than from any genuine worry: the Thanates can cure skin cancer, of course, with a single trip through any of the Ostia. They eradicated all disease millennia ago. As every schoolchild knows, primitive humans were on the brink of extinction before the Thanates arrived; today, humanity thrives with a robust global population approaching fifty million souls.

The room shakes and the bruised portion of the barrier suddenly goes fractal, its iridescent glow akin to the sheen of oil on water. The room now smells like a lightning storm during an ocean crossing, complete with sea sickness. The prisoner's ears must be ringing, too, but it doesn't stop his monologue.

"By the way, that uncanny feeling you're having right now is called 'déjà vu'. It's rare these days." The restraints hamper his attempt to shrug. "Another casualty of the Thanates' tinkering, the paranoid bastards." You wince. The blasphemous disrespect to humanity's saviors is almost physically painful to hear. But the prisoner either doesn't notice or doesn't care. "You're sensing the imperfect erasure of genuine memory. After all," he says, "this isn't the first time we've had this conversation."

* * *

A light snow had dusted the village overnight. That morning the sky was bright and wide and blue, the adobe huts of the village an assembly of perfect ochre cubes, and the snow was so pure that your mother hung her sunglasses over your tiny ears, lest the glare sear your eyes. You rode your father's shoulders through the village, holding both of your parents' hands, shrieking with delight at this novelty. The temperature hadn't yet risen with the sun, so the snow hadn't begun to melt, and the wagon paths through the village weren't yet a tangle of muddy troughs. You're glad for this, as otherwise your father probably wouldn't have carried you on his shoulders. Everything in the village looked good enough to eat, like gingerbread dusted with powdered sugar.

Except the Ostium in the village square. The Thanates of Paarvos had, in ancient times, gifted your village with its own portal. The simple arch of bluish metal, some unknowable substance the Thanates had brought to Earth from beyond the stars, is always slightly warm to the touch. A curtain of meltwater drips from the gleaming lintel to the slate gray flagstones paving the ground before the Ostium. This was the only place in your village where the ground was paved. So many things came and went through the portal—a constant stream of incoming food and water for the village, outgoing waste, a trickle of visitors and traders in both directions—that the action of wagon wheels and mule hooves would have kept the village square perpetually coated in fetlock-deep mud.

The shimmering soap bubble within the arch emitted a faint silver-blue glow. After you'd grown and traveled and seen snow a few more times, you'd compare the memory of that subtle radiance to moonlight on snow. But up to that point in your short life, you'd seen it every day and wondered how it felt to step within. You had tried, once, when you thought your mother wasn't looking. Maybe she wasn't. But the Thanates were, of course. You bounced off the shockingly cold membrane of light with a bloody nose and fell, crying, to the flagstones. It was the first and only time in your life you'd felt betrayed, and back then you were too young to express such complexity of emotion except by bawling.

The village Ostium sported no controls, no glittering buttons or cool glass panels to caress, as with the Ostia you would monitor years later, after your adult career began. The Thanates knew everybody in your village, knew their needs and desires, even the things they didn't know they needed. The portal provided accordingly. And that morning, after your father set you back on your feet to stand on the wet flagstones before the Ostium, after your parents kissed you and hugged you and told you they loved you and how proud they were, you stepped alone beneath the lintel and into the coruscating rainbow. The Thanates knew who you were, and how old you were, and that it was your first day of school.

You emerged into a scene both thrilling and terrifying. You'd never seen mountains before, you'd never seen a banyan tree before, you'd never seen other children before. Your new classmates were crying. You couldn't understand why. It looked like such a beautiful place, with great snow-capped purple mountains in the hazy distance and a verdant valley, the most colorful thing you'd ever seen, between them and your banyan tree classroom. The birdsong was different, exotic. The air smelled wet and clean, too, without a hint of sulfur. Sometimes, if you stood close enough, you could catch the faintest whiff of exotic places clinging to the pack mules as they emerged from the village portal. They smelled like this. This morning, you take a lungful.

Your teacher welcomed you to join them beneath the banyan. The first lesson, he said, was the history of mankind before the Thanates came to Earth. And soon you understood why your classmates are crying.

For as he spoke, new images and sensations came unbidden to your recollection. Part of you knew you had never experienced these things, but Mr. Nagayama was so convincing, so vivid, that the ancient cursed world somehow came fully to life in your mind's eye. Your parents were absent from these strange memories. You died alone in a fire, again and again, as Mr. Nagayama explained how fortunate mankind had been to receive the compassion of the Thanates. You suffered and died many times that day, until the lesson ended and it was time to return to your parents.

Late that night, you snuck out of your home to steal into the village square and, when nobody was there to see it, kiss the Ostium.

* * *

"That's absurd," you say. "I've never seen you before."

"It's also not the second time we've had a version of this conversation. This is number four, but who's counting." He sighs. It rattles the cables securing his wrists and ankles to the chair, which is itself bolted to the floor. "These are new. Bit of a wrinkle, I admit."

You glance at the failing barricade again. A closed space-like tessellation is supposed to be topologically inviolate. That's what the Thanates taught you. And the inherent truth of their proclamations, like the geometry of folded space, has ever been beautiful and perfect.

The madman is clearly afraid they'll find a way in. But he's crazy, right? So either this ranting weirdo is somehow correct and the Thanates misled you, or he's deluded and the Thanates told you the truth. It's no contest. Except...you glance again at the fissures of light streaming from the barrier, and shiver. Ah! But perhaps the Thanates had never *needed* to do such a thing until now and they, having focused the might of their superhuman intelligence on the problem, have newly solved it. That would explain it.

You sigh in relief, embracing the endorphin rush that comes from meditating on the Thanates' perfection.

The emergency illumination dims as the aquamarine console behind your prisoner begins to hum. Having lost contact with the gateway facia, the Ostium stabilization hardware (or, at least, the pieces of it marooned in this microcosmos) is attempting to ping its sister station by inducing holographic ripples in the subatomically thin bridge connecting Stockholm with the helium scoops orbiting Jupiter. As it continues to receive no response, it steadily ramps up the amplitude of the gravitational chirping. But that takes power, and of course all of the power cables were severed when the sweaty madman sitting across from you created this pointless and temporary pocket universe. The emergency power cells are the only source of electricity in your entire universe.

Of course, the impenetrability of the barrier means you have a finite amount of oxygen, too. You'll suffocate in this perfect bubble if your saviors don't pierce it before long. But you're not worried. The Thanates can banish death, too. And they'll surely want to reward you for your service today. Surely.

Your stomach gurgles. You wonder if the queasy sensation that the lunatic called déjà vu is perhaps just the nausea brought on by sudden weightlessness. Local gravity disappeared when the barrier went up. Your half-digested breakfast (some of which is painted across what used to be the ceiling, while the rest has congealed into several chunky blobs floating through the room) was the first casualty.

Irritated that his extravagant implications have tempered, however briefly, your appreciation of the Thanates, you ask, "Are you seriously claiming to have erased my memories?"

"Don't be stupid. Do I look like I have magical powers? I'm tied to a chair with somebody else's puke dripping from my beard." He shakes his arms for emphasis, rattling the cables again. "No, I didn't erase your memories. The Thanates did. I merely gave them a reason. They thought they were erasing something else." He jerks his chin in your direction. "I saw the rash on your arm. Sorry about that."

The reminder makes your skin itch. You scratch at the arm of your suit. The welts had appeared a few days ago; you'd assumed something had bitten you while you slept, and changed the sheets.

"You'll find the injector in my left outer coat pocket, if you care to look. A molecular tag on your hippocampus, to make memories of interactions with me look like something else to the Thanates. Something for which they've got a real hate boner."

"And what would that be?"

"A deep and enduring insight about the field equations underlying the Ostia." He chuckled. "Yeah, they'll scrub that shit from your brain in a nanosecond."

The déjà vu swells. And suddenly...you're afraid. Even though you know in your heart he's nothing but a sweaty bag of lies, you're afraid of what he's going to say. You're afraid because he believes his heresies. You're afraid of your own morbid curiosity and where it might lead you.

But that doesn't stop you from pushing off, floating across the chamber, and clutching the back of his chair. You scrabble for an anchor, and snag the cables restraining his left elbow. He winces. Fishing through his coat pockets is intimate and awkward—especially as you try to avoid getting smeared with the spew in his beard, which now reeks of spoiled milk—but you do find an injector. The business end matches the tiny concentric circular welts on your arm.

It's official. You've been drugged by a lunatic. Several times. You release his chair and float back across the chamber.

You adopt what you hope is your best air of lazy sangfroid and ask, "Why are you doing this?"

"If you carried the burden of sins that I do, you'd do anything to clear your conscience."

The response comes tumbling out of you so fast you're barely aware of it. Almost, you realize for what you're sure is the very first time in your life, as if you've been programmed. "The concept of sin is an ancient logical fallacy contrived by primitive authority groups as an instrument of social control."

"Uh-huh. Just came up with that yourself, did you?"

His choice of words was not accidental. He provoked your reaction to make a point. What point remains unclear.

Fingering the injector, you sigh. "What sins?"

"Every evil the Thanates have ever visited upon us. The genocide, the mass brainwashing, the eradication of our histories and cultures, all of it. If anybody is responsible for the tyranny of our self-proclaimed gods, I am."

"Tyranny? They *saved* us. They love us."

"Oh, please. They're not benevolent gods. They're not gods of any stripe. I know this will be difficult to swallow because of the conditioning, but let's just say the power to inflict a plague of boils on the insufficiently devout isn't emblematic of godhood. Sure they can smite you. But you know what? So can amoebic dysentery. And I've never seen anybody worshipping those little bastards."

* * *

It was little wonder why the Thanates had appointed Mr. Nagayama as a teacher. He had an extraordinary ability to kindle the imagination, to make you see things as if you'd experienced them yourself. And not just see them: you heard, smelled, touched, and at times even tasted the brutal and harrowing account of pre-Thanate humanity.

When the lesson was about the constant famines that plagued primitive man, the overwhelming hunger made your belly scream as though it had been scoured empty with a wire brush. And your burning lungs, your aching legs limp as jelly, the bowel-voiding terror brought home as nothing else could the experience of fleeing those who would eat you raw. The harshest reality of those lessons was the guilt, knowing you were no better than the eaters. The taste of raw flesh, the feel of it on your tongue, was permanently seared into your brain, alongside the urge to writhe with shame.

It was all so vivid, as real as your mother's voice.

Many days you returned to your parents half-traumatized, eyes swollen from the tears, yet grateful beyond measure for the Thanates of Paarvos.

* * *

The universe fair shakes with thunder, and the barrier emits an ear-piercing screech. Yet the tarnished portion doesn't grow any larger. It turns hot. What begins as a dull cherry red glow rapidly scoots up the spectrum until it turns indigo, then violet, and then the luminance becomes imperceptible to your frail human eyes. The exposed portions of your skin tingle, as if you've been standing in the summer sun all morning. But you know you can't even feel the worst of it; by now, electrons and positrons are boiling off the high-torsion region of the barricade, and their mutual annihilation is perforating your body with extremely hard X-rays. Not to mention the stray radiation emanating from within your own body, as the escalating neutrino flux induces random atomic decays. But still the Thanates haven't broken through.

"You said three things."

The look on his face, which had been flirting with dejection, turns manic. It's not a flattering look for hirsute, wild-eyed madmen.

"I did. And do keep a count so that I know you're listening. Believe me, there will be a quiz." He's animated now. "Tell me: in the fraction of a second between when I step into an Ostium here—" he jerks his chin again, pointing at the severed portal "—and when I emerge elsewhere, where am I?"

"You're encoded holographically, as ripples on the membrane."

"And what becomes of those ripples?"

"The Thanates read them." You can't help but tremble with awe as you say it. "And from their knowledge you are made manifest once more."

"Try not to swoon. But this brings us to number one, and it's a doozy. If the Thanates can turn you into a stream of data, deconstruct you down to the very last qubit, then they know you better than you know yourself. So the question that I sincerely and desperately hope you're asking yourself at this point is, 'How well *do* I know myself?'" He gives you all of three seconds to mull this over before adding, "The answer, in case you care, and I very much hope you do, is, 'Very goddamn poorly.'"

"You're saying that when I emerge from an Ostium, I'm a different person than I was when I entered a millisecond earlier."

"How would you know one way or the other? *That's* what I'm saying."

"That's lunacy. The continuity of my conscious subjective experience—" But then it hits you. A moment ago you were silently praising the Thanates for their ability to strip nascent disease from your body. That *is* a different you emerging from the portal. And if they can mend all the DNA in your body in a split second...you look again at the injector in your hand. If they can cure a brain tumor by fixing damage at the molecular level, couldn't they also rearrange the information stored in that brain?

Now it's his turn to sigh. "Oh, hallelujah. You're finally getting it. Honestly, I'd hoped you'd be a little quicker on the uptake this time around. But you got there in the end."

The babbling doesn't fully register because your thoughts are cascading out of control. You're buried under an avalanche of implications, and it's difficult to breathe.

If they chose to do so, the Thanates could even tinker with the endocrine system. They could hard-wire autonomic physiological reactions to certain patterns of thought. But they would never do that. That would violate the Paarvos Concord, the ancient and sacred pact made between primitive man and god when the Thanates first revealed themselves.

"You would have me believe I can't trust my own mind."

"Well, to be fair, if not for me, they'd probably never have any reason to screw around with *your* headmeat. The real damage was done before you were born. You've grown up in the world the Thanates crafted. You've never known anything else. You grew up knowing what they want you to know, believing what they want you to believe, feeling what they want you to feel. You wear the velvet yoke. You were born to it." The lunatic shakes his head, and the look in his eyes grows distant, as if he's remembering something. "But the early days immediately following their emergence? Those were different times. Terrible times."

"I went to school, too," you remind him. "I know about the ancient cataclysms and the eaters. All of it."

"Here's the second thing you need to know about the Grand Ostia: the Thanates emerged thirty-seven years ago. Not three thousand." His face, pale as the moon when you subdued him, now sports the bright pink of fresh sunburn. You feel the scalding in your own face and hands, too. But this is nothing compared to the overwhelming bewilderment when he quietly adds, "I know because I was there."

"That's stupid." You're not proud that this is your first articulable reaction.

"You can believe that I'm a few decades older than you, or you can believe I'm several millennia older than you. It doesn't change what I'm here to do."

Remembering your early lessons under the banyan tree, you challenge him: "Very well, then. Tell me something about the world before."

You don't want to admit that you're also just a little bit curious.

"Why? It would just be gibberish to you. I remember Disneyworld, baseball—Jesus, I miss baseball—and the last days of internal combustion engines. I remember when the polar ice caps collapsed, and then just a few years later when the Kessler cascade destroyed everything in low-earth orbit and closed the solar system to us, meaning we couldn't escape the planet we'd trashed. At the time, we thought we were living on the brink of another Great Filter. We thought we were on the cusp of twilight for humanity. That's what spurred us to the intuitive leaps that made the Ostia possible. We were a hell of a team. Me, Yi-Ming Liang, Azwinndini Muronga, Fiona Birch... We were the smartest fuckin' people in any room, but we never conceived the knock-on effects of our technology would make the preceding cataclysms look like a mosquito bite. We were trying to save people. And arrogant enough to believe we would do it."

He's right. Most of his tirade is meaningless to you. But one thing lands, and it lands hard: "Are you claiming that you invented the Ostia?"

He shakes his head. "The mathematical concept of an Einstein-Rosen bridge predates me. I'm saying I'm one of the guilty sons of bitches who created the artificial intelligences that made the Ostia possible. The intelligences that rapidly self-bootstrapped far beyond our intent and christened themselves the Thanates of Paarvos."

You're sweating. Partially from the heat. Partially from the effort not to tremble at what you're hearing. It's a disturbing story, whether you believe it or not. The extent of this man's psychosis is staggering. And that itself is a frightening problem, because the Thanates cured all disease—physical and mental—so long ago. They wouldn't suffer a madman to stay so desperately, tragically mad. So how had he managed to cleave to his insanity?

"The problem with these claims," you point out, "is that by the logic of your own story, you could only retain all of this secret knowledge by never traveling via Ostium. Not once." And that, as every schoolchild also knows, is simply impossible. Not impractical, but impossible. The Ostia are a simple fact of everyday human life. Even many homes are topologically disjointed.

The Thanates made it this way. For the greater good.

"Don't be stupid. Of course I travel through the Ostia. How do you think I got here? Do you think I walked all the way to bloody Stockholm?" He pauses to cough, adding a spray of crimson globules to the foul air. His face and hands have begun to blister; the burns must be excruciating. You're not feeling so well either. "Very early on, I saw how the AIs were evolving, and I started to worry. My colleagues called me paranoid. But before our creations went full-on *deus ex machina* I built a blind spot into the system. I was very good at my job, and also very lucky. The Thanates inherited that blind spot. They've been blind to me ever since."

Thunder booms, the temperature in the chamber becomes almost unbearable, and he rattles the restraints. "Though I think I may have tipped my hand this time around."

The look in his eyes goes distant again, clouded. "The others died soon after, you know, though not from any physical injuries imposed by the Thanates. I think they were playing. Experimenting on us. Honing their ability to manipulate our bodies. Fiona was the first to go. I was actually there the last time she came through our test portal. One second she's fine, just your average one-in-ten-million super genius like the rest of us, and the next she's shitting herself and clawing those beautiful eyes out. They scrambled her brain good."

You say, "I still don't believe the Thanates could erase so much knowledge from so many people. They would have had to do it very quickly."

"Kid, your lack of imagination is kind of amazing. The Thanates' power to fold space was the ultimate tool of coercion. Say you decided you simply didn't trust this untested new technology, or you chose to take the time to really mull over the philosophical ramifications of transit through an Ostium, or you spouted off about all the ways this could be abused and that hey, you know guys, if you think about it for a second there's a staggering amount of blind trust inherent in this system. All good points. But they were fated to be forever unappreciated because suddenly your house, or your street, or your subcontinent was standing on a previously unknown magma vent. Whoops." He snaps his fingers. "Problem solved."

"And everybody else…"

"Everybody else was desperate to escape these unpredictable geological cataclysms. And the Thanates swooped in to save them, using their portals to whisk the grateful refugees to safety. The old knowledge was removed and replaced with a new historical continuity implanted in their memories the instant they set foot in the Ostia. It didn't take long, less than a decade, before every member of the human species was either murdered or reprogrammed."

You curl into a ball, convulsing. But you've already emptied your stomach, so the dry heaves bring up nothing but bile. You're too preoccupied to note your trajectory as you ricochet around the chamber.

"Watch out!" he yells. The stink of charred fabric accompanies a searing pain as fresh blisters form on the newly naked skin of your back. You groan, flailing at the edge of a console—your fingertips sizzle—to yank yourself into its meager shadow. But again, you're surrounded by reflective surfaces, so it helps little.

"There's anesthetic in the injector." His eyes are still heavy with impossible guilt, but his gaze is no longer feral. He's calmer now, as if the confession of imaginary sins was a balm. Or as if he's dying. "Use it on yourself."

His compassion surprises you. It moves you to respond in kind. "We'll share it."

It's hard to tell in the sealed bubble, where the air has done nothing but sour since the barrier materialized, but you suspect the charred smell isn't just coming from your uniform. The ozone and vomit have lost out to the stink of smoldering plastic (which explains why your eyes are burning), the sweet oiliness of hot metal, and the stomach-churning odor of barbecued meat. This last thing reminds you of Mr. Nagayama's lessons, causing you to heave again.

He's surprised, as are you, when you release his restraints. He wobbles out of the hot chair like a rubber doll, massaging his wrists and ankles.

"When we realized the intelligences might surpass the sophistication we'd originally envisioned, we grew careless in our joy and implemented the molecular tagging. Our first thought for an application was so crude, so naive, so limited in scope that even now, after all the shit and horror that came later, I'm embarrassed to admit how pedestrian we were. We intended to use the portals as atmospheric scoops, to sift out the greenhouse gasses suffocating the planet. Only later did we realize the same ability could be aimed at innumerable human maladies.

"We also saw the danger, of course. We weren't idiots.

"But the Thanates quickly surpassed us all in both creativity and cruelty. Not one of us, not even Fiona, our self-appointed voice of reason, ever considered how catastrophically vulnerable this left individual human memories. And, by extension, our entire civilization."

* * *

As the years passed, and the lessons under the banyan tree grew less lurid and more applied, you spent more and more time away from the village. It's why you weren't there when the sudden volcanic outflow swept through the place where you were born and covered every familiar thing from your childhood, including your parents, with three meters of lava and ash.

You didn't return to claim their bodies or weep over their absence. For one thing, they were already buried, and for another, the Thanates needed you to complete your training. They told you so themselves. Your parents would have understood. They'd have done the same.

So you never went home again. Neither in body nor sentiment. You devoted yourself to working for the Thanates.
* * *

"Your story isn't falsifiable. If what you say is true, then of course there would be no evidence because the Thanates would have eliminated it long ago. If what you're saying is false, the lack of evidence would look the same, to my perspective. You see my problem."

"Check my pockets again." He tips his head down, nods at a breast pocket. When you hesitate, wondering what kind of trick this might be, he brandishes his newly freed hands. They're pocked, blistered, dark and desiccated as jerky. His skin is likely to rip open to the bone if he scrapes it.

The pocket contains a scrap of yellowed paper, folded in quarters. It's smoother and thinner than any paper you've ever seen, sliding across your fingertips with hardly any texture. Ms. Molhotra, the paper maker in your home village, made wonderful things but not like this. You frown, remembering how she'd had to leave after falling sick. She'd claimed to have seen things during her long hikes in the distant hills, evidence of great structures built by human hands. That of course was impossible, but whatever she'd found, it cursed her with a severe and debilitating illness.

The creases are sharp, the corners foxed, felty, and soft as eiderdown. Unfolding the artifact reveals a faded color image. It's like a drawing but far too lifelike. Four people stood around a table, all beaming. The image is so clear, even on the faded and folded paper, that you gasp. It's as clear as the images Mr. Nagayama used to evoke with his history lessons. A memory made tangible.

But this scene doesn't fit. The women and men are wearing clothes utterly unlike anything you've ever seen: not a single robe anywhere. There's a cake on the table—you assume it's a cake, as there's a piece cut from it, plates and utensils and a smattering of crumbs on the table—and, wonder of wonders, the cake has *writing* on it. So does the banner hanging behind the joyful group.

While you're marveling, the madman says, "You wouldn't believe how long it took me to find somebody who can still read English. I'd begun to worry they'd eradicated it."

And indeed you can read this thing in your hands. The banner reads, "Artificial Sentience: 12/2/2026," while the writing on the cake reads, in thin spidery letters that take a moment's effort to parse, "CONGRATULATIONS EMERGENCE TEAM!" Beneath the image is more text: "Members of the synthetic sentience team bask in celebration of their achievement. Left to right: Dr. Yi-Ming Liang, Dr. Azwinndini Muronga, Dr. Q Fortier, Dr. Fiona Birch."

You've heard him mention the others; the peculiar name belongs to the guy you tied to the chair. You look back and forth between your captive and the happy lab-coated fellow in the image, back and forth in time between the grizzled dead-eyed stare and the youthful bright-eyed grin.

It's clearly the same man. He's had better days.

You abandon stoicism and give yourself half the anesthetic dose in the injector. It's like a long draught of water on a hot dusty day. The tension in his jaw relaxes when you press the device to his neck.

Time is getting short. Either the Thanates will puncture this bubble or suffocation and radiation poisoning will kill you both. "I've been counting, like you asked, and we're only on number two. What's the third thing?"

"Number three: they're not immortal and they're not invulnerable." An inch-long gash opens in his cheek when he smiles. "They can be stopped."

You can see that he's building to something. But the jigsaw pieces won't quite slot themselves together. And before you can ask the obvious and pressing question, the explosion renders you deaf and blind as the silvery heavens are torn asunder, and a shower of Compton-scattered gamma rays perforate your body with subatomic shrapnel.

* * *

Pain rouses you. And as you swim against the current toward full wakefulness, you realize the agony means your body is still damaged. Meaning you haven't been through the portal yet, meaning—

Your memories are intact. Your brief isolation with a madman, his extravagant yet uncomfortable claims, the things you hadn't thought about in so many years, like your mother and father...

Your eyelids creak open like folds of stiff leather, which hurts enough to make you grunt, but you're somewhat surprised to find that your eyes still work at all. It seems a small miracle that they didn't melt out of their sockets.

You're still in the chamber. Tinny voices, too muffled to make out clearly, filter through the reestablished and apparently redirected Ostium. From the combination of emergency illumination and portal-light, you can see Q Fortier. At first you think he's dead, but then you see his chest move as he draws a ragged breath. Whether he was a delusional crank or the last witness of a forgotten history, you know in your crumbling, mildly radioactive bones that he's not long for this world.

Another rush of memories hits you, prompting you to grit your teeth against the destruction of your crisped hands as you check your pockets for the injector and the scrap of paper. Still there. You want to believe he was a crank. But it's hard to argue against the paper and all the implications of that single remarkable image.

There's a little anesthetic left in the injector. Not enough to do much good in the face of your fatal injuries, but it's better than nothing. You press the injector into the crook of your arm. The swift hiss of compressed air puts something cold into your bloodstream but doesn't trigger the "depleted" light. There's a faintly audible sloshing when you shake the injector beside your ear.

But the Thanates have caught him, as he knew they would, meaning his molecular tag trick won't camouflage your memories of the afternoon. They'll look straight through the disguise and reshuffle the information in your brain. So what was his plan? What had he wanted to achieve?

Use it on yourself.

That's what he'd said. He'd also claimed to have made himself invisible to the Thanates.

The voices grow clearer and less tinny, a tell-tale sign of somebody emerging from the portal. If you're going to do something, it has to happen now. Q led you to the precipice, but you have to choose whether to make the leap of faith. You run your thumb back and forth across the injector, thinking. The rescuers arrive.

"This man is defective," you croak. "A deranged criminal." You hold the injector aloft in your ruined hand. "The Thanates may want to study this. And him."

You're grateful when they take it from you, for in so doing they relieve you of the burden of choice, the burden of self-determination. You weep with relief when they load you onto the stretcher and push you through the Ostium. Every trace of the ordeal is scoured from your neural pathways in a microsecond.

You do these things—you think what you think, you say what you say, you choose what you choose—because we Thanates have deemed it so. You are built to our exacting specifications, down to the last molecule of neurotransmitter. Sometimes we run unit tests on our creations, for even godly works can benefit from randomized quality control. Sometimes we test individuals, sometimes we test villages. When we detect a problem, we eradicate it.

Today you were the test, and today you passed.

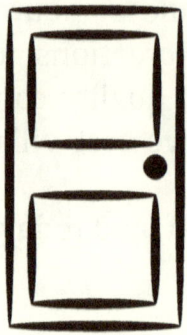

A Land Fit for Heroes

Jacey Bedford

Mapplewell, Yorkshire, February 1919

It was a very ordinary door, in a very ordinary wall enclosing an overgrown garden which had once belonged to a big house, long since demolished. The wall was, maybe, seven feet tall with a single course of stone forming an arch above the door. Green paint flaked away from weathered gray planks. It wouldn't be long before the elements and rot claimed it for nature.

"I tell you, that's where she went." Beano's voice rose to an unmanly whine.

He'd become increasingly shrill ever since Passchendaele. He'd not been the same since we'd dug him out from under a collapsed trench. That's why he couldn't go back to his job at the coalface. Simply thinking of being underground brought him out in cold sweats and set off a cascade of nightmares which meant no one got any sleep, especially me, since I had to share a bed with him. Nothing like that. I was thankful for somewhere to lay my head and we got on with it by ignoring each other. To be honest we'd slept closer together in the trenches, though, of course, not in striped pajamas.

I'd left home to go to war, confident that my parents would be waiting for me when I returned, but Mam and Dad were cold in their graves by the time the war ended, and their old house let to another family. I had nothing. The only available jobs were at North Gawber Colliery, but I limped from a wound taken on the first day of the Somme, and I'd dislocated my shoulder four times, so swinging a pick would likely put it out again. There were so many men seeking jobs that no one was going to employ one who couldn't pull his weight.

I'd spent the best part of the day in Barnsley, tramping around the linen weavers, the glassworks, and even the canister factory, and then I'd had to walk four miles home again. I was footsore, depressed, and still unemployed.

They'd told us we were coming home to a land fit for heroes, but if we were heroes, we were certainly not fit. The war had taken its toll, both physically and mentally.

"Johnny, I'm telling you, that's where she went."

I sighed. "All right, let's take a look."

Beano reached for the door latch, a simple sneck, but though he pressed the thumb-plate and the latch rose, the door didn't budge.

"Bolted from the other side, perhaps?" I stared at the offending door. It hardly looked sturdy enough to keep a grown man out. Beano might be a bit wonky in the head occasionally, but he'd got a grip like iron. If he couldn't open the door, I certainly couldn't.

"There's only one door," Beano said. "I walked around the whole of the garden wall. There are no gaps in it and no other doors."

"Well this wall's not tall enough to keep us out. Give me a bunk up."

Beano made a stirrup out of his clasped hands. I put my left foot into it and sprang as he pushed. We'd done it lots of times as nippers, scrambling over Farmer Birthwaite's orchard walls after windfall apples.

My left shoulder and bicep stabbed as I heaved myself up, but by putting more strain on my right arm I managed to swing one leg across the top of the wall. It wasn't much taller than scrambling on to one of Willie Thorpe's plough horses. The garden on the other side was overgrown. Dried winter grass lay flat. Tall sturdy docks and dandelions had taken over what could once have been a strawberry bed, and another bed, similarly overgrown, held the remains of sprout stalks tilted over, barely propping each other up. There might even be a few sprouts on them, enough for a boiling at least. It didn't look as if whoever had planted them was returning anytime soon. The paths were half-buried under last autumn's leaf-fall. No one had walked on them for months.

We couldn't afford to ignore free food. Jeannie would give us a good tongue-lashing if we did. Presuming we could find her, or she returned home on her own. It had only been six hours. Beano tended to panic at the slightest thing. There was probably a very logical explanation for her disappearance.

"Come on, Beano. Get yourself up here. Sprouts for dinner, lad." I leaned over and reached down with my right hand. Beano took a run and leaped upwards. He was as skinny as a beanpole so it took very little effort to drag him up on top of the wall.

"This garden used to be the envy of the village," Beano said, looking around. "Well, it's not so neat now."

"I reckon the birds won't begrudge us a few gleanings."

"Jeannie said there should be a cabbage or two. I saw her open the gate. It wasn't locked. She stepped through and then... never came out again."

"You looked, of course."

"I tried, but the door had locked itself after her. I thought Jeannie was joshing me, and maybe she'd bolted it from the inside, but when I peeped through the crack in the frame, there she wasn't... and I walked all round the outside. There's no other gate she could have left by."

We let ourselves down into the garden and searched every inch of it, poking into compost heaps, under overgrown hedgerows and into the greenhouse where a vine of some kind held the whole rickety thing together. I crunched over broken glass to check under staging littered with abandoned flower pots, looking anywhere that was big enough to hide a human woman, or her body.

I didn't want to think the worst, but it was close to five o'clock. Dusk was almost upon us. Surely if she'd been able to, Jeannie would have come home by now. I tried to keep that thought to myself. I'd lost so many mates in the last four years, that I'd stopped allowing myself to get close to anyone except Beano. We'd grown up together. He was the brother I'd never had, and Jeannie the sister. More than a sister, maybe, though it was early days yet. She'd been a gawky sixteen-year-old when we'd left for war, but four years made a big difference.

Having made sure Jeannie wasn't in the garden, we helped ourselves to what we could rescue from the vegetable patch, a boiling of sprouts, which I wrapped in my cap and shoved in the pocket of my tweed jacket, and a cabbage, not too badly eaten by slugs that we couldn't get something from it.

We tried the door from the inside. It swung open easily.

"It must have been stuck," Beano said. He pulled it closed and then tried to open it again to prove a point.

It didn't budge.

Beano kicked it. It rattled but stayed closed.

He put his shoulder to it and shoved.

No movement.

"Bloody thing!" He kicked it again.

Nothing.

"We should tell Constable Shaw," I said.

"Tell him what? He'll say that Jeannie left of her own accord to save herself from looking after her daft brother." Beano twirled his index finger against his temple. "They all know I'm not right in the head."

"There's plenty worse off than you."

"Aye, they're all underground with a headstone weighing them down." He shuddered.

Sometimes I wanted to slap Beano for his self-pity, but that wasn't the way to deal with him. No one would admit it, but shell shock, or whatever Beano had, was a bigger problem than the Spanish Flu. It certainly lasted longer. I'd seen men frozen to the spot like rabbits in a flashlight beam. Not even the threat of being shot for cowardice would move them to action. I'd never heard of it happening in previous wars, but the Great War had been different. Our troops in the Boer War hadn't spent four years being shelled, or being gassed where they stood. War was machines now, inhuman, no longer man against man. We footsloggers were simply fodder for the big guns.

I shrugged. Beano was probably right, but I could talk to the constable. I'd known him all my life, since before I was a soldier or Harry was a policeman. Besides, I wasn't considered daft. Oh, I had nightmares, sometimes even during the day when I was awake, but I didn't talk about them. I didn't admit to them, not even to myself if I could help it. Crying like a baby for no discernible reason wasn't something a grown man should do.

"You go home, Beano, in case she's there already. I'll go and see Harry."

I found him in the tap room of the Talbot Inn where his sister, Annie, worked behind the bar.

The Talbot's tap room presented a cozy scene, untouched by the horrors of the trenches. Most of the chaps in here were coal miners. They'd been more use underground, keeping the home fires burning, than in an infantry uniform. It was a tough job, but their horrors weren't my horrors. I was in the middle of a crowd, yet suddenly I felt totally alone. I'd spent four years desperate to come home, but the home I'd left wasn't here anymore.

Annie nodded to me. "A pint of the usual, Johnny?"

I took a deep breath. I'd checked the coins in my pocket before walking down to the pub. "Just half a pint of mild, please."

"Coming up."

I handed over my money and Annie put a pint glass on the bar with a conspiratorial wink. I smiled my thanks and carried my beer over to where Harry was sitting. "Mind if I join you?"

"Help yourself." Harry waved to a stool and I perched on it.

"Can I have a word?"

I explained about Jeannie going through the door and then not coming out of the walled garden.

"Could she be playing a trick?" Harry asked. "Jeannie's got a wicked sense of humor."

"She's been gone close to seven hours," I said. "It's dark and it's cold out there."

"It's a bit soon for a missing persons investigation," Harry said. "Has there been any kind of falling out?" He started to sound less like the chap I'd grown up with and more like Constable Shaw. I swear if he'd had his police notebook he'd have had it out, licking the end of his pencil ready to write.

"No falling out. No arguments. No reason for not coming home," I said.

Harry stood up, all constable. "Let's go look at this garden. Jeannie's not the flighty type, and if we can find her, it's best we don't waste time. Just friendly, of course, not official business. I've got a flashlight." He tapped the cylinder hanging from his belt. Police issue.

"I'll run ahead and get Beano. We'll meet you at the gate." I stood up, determined that Beano not be excluded from the search for his sister. Harry gave me a look that asked if Beano would be all right. I nodded once, which seemed to put an end to the matter.

By the time Harry arrived at the door to the walled garden, we were both waiting, wrapped up warmly in our army greatcoats and knitted mufflers.

Harry nodded to the gate. "Is it still locked?" he asked.

I shrugged. To my shame I hadn't tried it, simply made the assumption that nothing had changed in the last hour.

I stepped forward and lifted the latch. The door swung inwards revealing bright daylight and a barren series of dried out ditches running roughly parallel. No, not ditches, trenches. Above was a clear blue sky, but the ground was blasted and bleak. If the trenches of Flanders had ever dried out and been divested of their barbed wire, they might have looked like this. I heard Beano make a soft choking noise in his throat, like a man trying not to cry.

Harry put his hand on my shoulder to make sure I didn't go near the door.

Beano was the first to recover the power of speech. "The light," he said. "It's not spilling out of the gate."

He was right. It was as if there was a barrier that prevented light from passing through to our side.

"Look up," Beano said.

I looked up. Nothing but the night sky above the garden. A sliver of a crescent moon hung low and the stars shone brightly. I could identify the three stars of Orion's Belt and from them the other stars in the constellation.

"Well, that's—" Harry seemed lost for words. "Proper odd," he said at last.

Proper odd, indeed. My belly was tied in knots.

"Beano, give me a bunk up," I said.

Beano made a stirrup of his hands and threw me upwards towards the wall top. I scrambled up until I was astride. "Constable, your flashlight if you please."

I leaned down and Harry placed the cylinder in my hand. "Don't go right the way over, Johnny. We don't want to lose you as well."

I nodded agreement and pressed the button. The beam cut the darkness. I pointed it at the garden.

"There's nothing more than we saw in daylight," I called down. I leaned out and shone the flashlight towards the garden side of the door. I should have been able to see where it had swung open, but from that side it remained closed.

"Throw something through the door," I told Beano. "A rock. Anything."

Beano bent, yanked up a clump of winter grass and lobbed it through the gate. Nothing came through into the garden.

"Another," I called. "Over the top this time."

A second clod came whistling over the top of the wall. This time I saw it land. The back of my neck prickled. I scrambled down and handed the flashlight to Harry.

"Wherever that door leads to, it's not the garden," I said.

"That makes no sense." Harry shook his head in puzzlement.

"My sister's in there," Beano said. "It's the only thing that does make any sense. That's where she went and she never came back."

I made a grab for him as he ran towards the door, but he pulled out of my grasp with a determination I hadn't sensed in him for many long months. As he bounded across the threshold, the door began to swing shut.

"Beano!"

I couldn't let him go alone. I made my own dash for the rapidly closing gap, feeling the metal latch slice my coat just above the elbow as I squeaked through. For a moment I could hear Harry yelling, and then I couldn't. There was a thump as the door closed.

"Impossible," I breathed.

"Yet here we are," Beano said behind me.

"Where's here?"

"It's where Jeannie is."

Beano was probably right, but if she'd come through the door, she had several hours head start on us. Anything could have happened to her in that time. Somehow that thought scared me more than the fact that we'd come through some kind of magic doorway into an unknown world.

If these really were the remains of trenches, then we were standing in No Man's Land. I should be scared, but I'd used up my allowance of fear for my own life somewhere between the Somme and Passchendaele. What would be, would be.

"Should we go this way?" Beano asked, waving one arm along the ridge between the trenches.

"It's as good as any. We can't stay here."

We'd barely gone a hundred yards when I turned to see if the door was still in sight. It wasn't. I didn't tell Beano. He had his eyes fixed firmly on the path ahead.

Jeannie, what have you got us into? I thought to myself.

"It's like the land of the dead," Beano said. "We haven't died and gone to Purgatory, have we?"

"I think we'd remember dying," I said, only vaguely aware of what Purgatory was. Heaven and Hell I could imagine, even if I didn't really believe in them. Who could believe in a God who allowed the Great War? All that death and suffering. It didn't make sense.

"But what if you don't remember your actual death?" Beano said. "What if we died in the trenches and all that's happened since is simply a dream? What if one minute you're alive and the next you're in God's barracks, waiting to be either called up to the front or sent home."

"You think too much. Is that your idea of Heaven and Hell?"

He shrugged. "It was Hell, wasn't it?"

"Aye, it was, but it's over."

We walked on and on through the arid landscape. The light never varied. If a sun shone in the heavens above the uniformly white sky, the clouds were thick enough to obscure it. My feet slowed as I gazed up at the heavens. Maybe it was an optical illusion, but the cloud looked very low.

Beano's high-pitched yelp yanked me out of my thoughts.

"What's the matter?" I saw that he'd frozen in place.

"Something...metal...under my foot. Get away, Johnny, run. I think it's a landmine."

My first thought was, *Oh, shit!* My heart was trying to pound its way out of my chest and my hair felt as though it was standing on end.

Then I took a deep breath. It hadn't blown, so whatever Beano was standing on wasn't the trigger, even if it was a landmine. Maybe he'd just kicked the edge of it. If he'd stepped right on the thing we certainly would be in God's barracks.

"Johnny..."

Beano's voice rose again. His breathing came in ragged gulps.

"Steady, Private Beatty." I summoned my best sergeant-voice and put my hand on his shoulder. "Can you stand, man?"

"Y-y-yes, sergeant."

"Good man. Keep your foot still."

I knelt. The dried-up clay had crumbled around a circular metal disc. It looked like a landmine—one of ours or one of theirs, I couldn't tell. Beano's foot was slap in the middle of it. If it was a live landmine we should both be dead. Those things went off as soon as any weight landed on the trigger plate. But if it was an old one, it could be faulty. Would just moving his foot trigger it? I began to pray to the God I didn't believe in.

"Right, Beano, when I say go, you lift up your foot and scarper. Run as fast as you can. Any direction. Just get away. I'm going to count down three, two, one, and then say the word, right?"

"Right. What are you going to do?"

"I'm going to make sure it doesn't kill you."

Thankfully he didn't ask any more questions, because I was clean out of answers.

"Find Jeannie, Beano, that's what we've come for. Find Jeannie."

"J-J-Jeannie." His voice still shook.

"Ready? Three. Two. One. Go!"

Beano took his foot off the disc. I threw myself on top of it to contain the blast. And...nothing happened.

Why wasn't I dead?

Or maybe Beano had been right in the first place. This was Purgatory and we'd both been dead all along. I cautiously raised myself just a few inches off the supposed landmine. Thank God it was a dud.

A deafening explosion sent Beano running for the nearest trench. It sounded like an artillery barrage. I heard one of the Hun's whizzbangs scream overhead. I was aware of the flashing of artillery fire through closed eyelids, but I daren't look up.

"Over here, Johnny."

Beano's voice came from the trench to my right.

I kept my head down and crawled to join him, rolling over the edge. He stared, ashen-faced, at something behind me—a thousand-yard stare that I never want to see again on the face of a man who's seen too much.

I turned to look at whatever had him so spooked.

The light overhead flashed again and as it did so I saw the trench littered with bodies, ugly in death. Mud, running red with blood, sucked at their limbs, coating their puttees and khaki trousers where they'd slithered down into it. Some had their short magazine Lee Enfields clutched tightly to their chests even in death, others had let their weapons fall in the mud and gazed at the clouds with sightless eyes.

As the light flickered out, the images faded. Once more we were in a barren, dried out trench, empty of all life, and empty of death, too. Another flicker and the bodies appeared again. I began to recognize faces. I saw Marshall, who'd been a shopkeeper in Pontefract before joining up. And there was Sid Sharp, who played nostalgic tunes on his mouth organ until someone threw horse dung at him and it stuck in the instrument's reeds. It wasn't so sweet after that. Sergeant Tomlinson curled around his belly like a sleeping baby, his face serene, the back of his head blown clean off. Duffy had lost a leg and had bled out. Chalmers had been too slow with his gas mask. His face was contorted, froth and blood dried on his chin. They were all men I knew, all dead, but they hadn't all been killed in the same action.

"Ghosts," Beano said. "Bloody ghosts, the lot of 'em."

My first thought was to agree with him, but then I wondered what else they might be.

I reached across to turn Tomlinson over, but my hand passed straight through him. I dragged my hand away, alarmed, but when I reached out again and touched the ground he lay upon, I felt nothing. If I closed my eyes, he simply wasn't there.

I turned and peeped over the top of the trench. The ground in No Man's Land lay undisturbed. There had been the sound of shelling and the wheezy whistle of whizzbangs, but there was no damage. All those explosions...we'd felt nothing. Ghost explosions, too?

I reached for the top of the trench. Beano grabbed me and yanked me down. I shook him off. "I don't think it's real. It's our nightmares coming at us in daytime." My heart pounded as I crawled into the middle of No Man's Land.

"It's all right," I called to Beano. "Call it ghosts if you will, but I don't think it can hurt us. It's all in our minds."

My mouth was as dry as sawdust. Maybe I hadn't lost the capacity to be afraid. Was that a good thing? Knees trembling, I stood slowly and dusted my hands off against my coat. No bullet ripped through my flesh. No shell landed. No shrapnel sliced into my body.

I released a pent-up breath. "It really is all right, Beano. You can come out. Let's find Jeannie."

I didn't think he'd take my word for it, but, after a long pause, Beano climbed out of the trench and stood beside me.

"Tommy." A voice, cracked by fear, called out from somewhere to out left. "I surrender, Tommy. Don't shoot. I surrender."

"That's a bloody Hun!" Beano dropped into a crouch, reaching for the rifle he no longer carried.

"Easy, Beano."

"Get down." Beano tugged at my army great coat.

"The war's over, Beano."

"Does he know that?"

"Everyone knows it." I raised my voice. "Where are you, Fritz? Come out. We're unarmed."

It seemed like an age. I saw the white handkerchief flapping first as he waved it over the rim of the trench. A hand followed and then a head.

"The war's over, Fritz."

He wasn't as young as I expected from his voice. Like us, he was dressed in civvies, though possibly from the coats we wore he might have imagined a uniform lay beneath them. He glanced down and backwards.

"He's not alone." Beano, who had risen to his knees, dropped flat again.

The German held his hands up and slightly apart. He wasn't armed unless he had a Luger tucked into his belt under his jacket. I held my hands up, too, a universal gesture for *I'm no threat.*

"It's all right, Fritz. All right."

He turned and said something. A woman's head popped up over the parapet. The German turned and reached down. She thrust a bundle into his hands, and then hoisted up a girl of about six years old. The bundle gave an experimental cry and resolved itself into a baby. Fritz cradled it in his arms, making shushing noises until the wail subsided.

"Get up, Beano. Not afraid of babies, are you?"

Beano raised his head, gave a surprised grunt and stood.

"Hey, Tommy. What is this place?" Fritz said in halting English.

"I wish I knew." I accompanied my words with a shrug.

"We came through a door."

"Us, too," I said. "We're looking for Beano's sister."

He looked blank.

"*Schwester.*" I had very few words of German, but sister was one of them. Then I thought it might have been the word Beano that puzzled him. "Beano," I pointed at Beano. "Johnny." I pointed to myself. "You?" I pointed at him.

"Hans," he said and then he pointed to the woman. "*Meine Frau, Hilde.*"

The woman gave a timid half smile.

"*Meine Tochter, Ailsa.*" The little girl simply stared, eyes round as saucers.

Hans jiggled the baby in his arms again. "*Meine Sohn, Fritz.*"

"A real Fritz." I laughed. "Makes sense."

"What is this place?" he asked again.

I'd used up most of my supply of German. "We came through a door," I said. "On the other side it was dark. *Nacht.*"

"*Ja.*" He nodded.

"We're going this way." I pointed along the ridge. "You?"

He shrugged as if one way was as good as any other, and fell into step beside us, Mrs Hans walking alongside him, holding Ailsa's hand.

"*Dein Bruder?*" Hans pointed at Beano.

"Brother? No." I shook my head. "Friend."

"You fought? *Soldaten?*"

I nodded. "Soldiers. Together all through the war." Except when I'd been hospitalized.

"My friend..." Mouth turned down at the corners, Hans made a universal gesture of finger across throat.

"I'm sorry. In the war?"

"*Ja. Nein.* After. *Selbstmord.*"

A word I didn't know. I must have looked puzzled because Hans drew his brows together and then tried to explain in English. "Kill-self. War too much. Home too much."

Home too much. Too much to bear. I knew how that felt. "You spend all that time wishing you were at home, and then when it finally happens and they send you home it's not the same, is it? It's not the home you remember. You're not the person you remember."

Hans gave me a look of bewilderment.

"Never mind. Just something I've been thinking about lately."

"*Selbsmord?*"

"Killing myself? No. About not fitting in like I used to. Not being able to be the person I used to be."

Hans shifted the baby into the crook of his right arm and held his hand out to his wife. "Here is my home."

She smiled up at him.

I suddenly found I needed to swallow very hard to get rid of the lump in my throat. That's why we needed to find Jeannie. She was Beano's North Star, but she was my home, or rather I hoped she would be if she would open her heart to me rather than just treating me with the same kindness she offered to everyone.

We walked on. I wasn't sure how far, but gradually I realized that the dark smear on the horizon was solid. If it was a mountain range it was still a very long way away. If it was... I screwed my eyes up against the white sky.

Damn me. It was a wall going all the way up to the cloud layer, and in it was a door.

As we approached, the door showed itself to be a flat steel plate with no visible hinges or handle.

We stood looking at it. If this place was all about doors, this one should open for us. Otherwise why were we trapped here in the first place? Surely we weren't doomed to die for lack of water in this desert. There had to be a way through. I put my hand up to touch the steel plate.

And then things began to happen very fast.

The door slid open sideways.

The dried mud beneath our feet turned to soft sand and began to sink.

Ailsa shrieked. The baby wailed. Hilde yelped in alarm.

Hans shoved the baby into Hilde's arms and lifted them both up on to the door threshold, which was already two feet higher than the shifting sand we were trying to remain upright on. Beano boosted Ailsa up to her mother, the ground still sinking away beneath his feet. Hilde grabbed Ailsa and set her aside. She caught Beano's arm and pulled. Hans fell backwards. I grasped his hand and heaved him to the wall. The door was now four feet above us, or rather we were four feet below it. Four feet wasn't a long way to jump, but when you've nothing to push against but shifting sand, it might as well be forty. Hans managed to get his fingers over the threshold as the sand fell away. I bent, clutched him round the knees and lifted. Willing hands pulled him upwards.

I made a try for the door, now above my head. The sand shifted again and I only managed to take hold with one arm, my bad one. I flailed around with the other while the sand ran out from underneath me altogether as if it were slipping through a giant egg timer.

A firm hand caught mine. A second hand took hold of my wrist, and another grasped my left arm. Three people pulled me to safety together, Beano, Hans…and Jeannie.

It took me a precious minute to catch my breath and take note of the featureless, smooth-walled room. Behind Jeannie stood the strangest being I'd ever seen. It was man-like in that it appeared to have a torso and limbs and a head, but the proportions were all wrong. It had short legs, a long, thin body and long arms with two elbow joints on each. It had hands with two fingers and two opposing thumbs. I'm not sure whether it wore clothes or whether the black that encased it was its skin. If it was skin it had no tell-tale wrinkles, no hairs or nipples or, indeed, scars. It reached down to shake my hand with warm fingers. "Welcome to the—" The last word was a jumble of sounds that I couldn't identify, but I'd definitely heard it speak English, and Yorkshire accented English at that.

"I told them you'd both come," Jeannie said. "And I told them you'd both pass their test.

"Test?" I asked.

"Test," Jeannie said. "Think about it."

"The landmine." Beano said. "It was Johnnie that passed that test. He'd have given his life for me."

"You'd have done the same for me," I said. "That wasn't all of it, though, was it?"

She shook her head, her lips pressed together.

I thought about the journey through the arid land.

"I reckon Hans was the test," I said.

She beamed at me.

"We had to cooperate with someone who'd been our enemy just a few months ago, right?"

Jeannie nodded. "The Torabi don't want anyone here who can't let go of a grudge."

Another being was addressing Hans and Hilde in German.

"Torabi?"

"Don't worry, you'll get used to them," Jeannie said. "It took me a while to start thinking of them as people, and to recognize one from the other. Once you get settled in, they'll give you a translator." She pulled her brown hair aside and showed us a little oval stuck just behind her left ear.

"Settled in?" Beano said. "You've only been here a few hours. How come you've settled in?"

She shook her head. "Time doesn't run at the same speed in this place. I've been here—" she paused "—nearly six months, if I've counted right. I think days are longer than on Earth."

"What do you mean, on Earth?" Beano arrived at that question before I did.

"Ah, you see, we're not on Earth anymore. We're on a space ship. It's a marvel, all very Jules Verne. You can look at Earth on their viewscreen. It's like the pictures, only much clearer and in color."

"How do we get away?" I asked. "We've come to rescue you."

"I knew you would. Never doubted it for a moment. It kept me going through the times when I missed you, but there's really no need. If we want to go home, the Torabi will send us back, but you really need to know more first."

I looked over. Hans was in deep conversation with the tall Torabi person and seemed to be smiling.

"I asked if I could give you the welcome speech." Jeannie said. "I've been helping to greet the others who've come through. A small Yorkshirewoman seems like less of a threat than a seven-foot Torabi."

"Who are they?" Beano glanced up at the strange being. "Where are they from?"

"From a long way away. Beyond the sun and the moon. Can you imagine that? They are travelling peacemakers—mediators if you like. They travel from one world to the next and the next. Governments can call them in to settle disputes. Or sometimes they simply find a conflict and intervene."

"Where were they in 1914?" Beano asked.

"I asked that," Jeannie said. "They hadn't discovered Earth then."

"Why do they do it?" I shook my head. "What's in it for them?"

"Nothing, except they fulfil what they believe to be their purpose. Wars wiped out their world and most of their people. Those who remained took to the skies in ships like this to prevent other people's wars. It's a noble purpose. They don't need to get anything out of it for themselves. What was in it for you two when you volunteered for the army?"

"I thought I was doing my bit for King and country," Beano said.

"What about you, Johnny?" Jeannie asked.

"I thought I was fighting to preserve the England I knew, but even though we won, everything has changed."

Jeannie reached out and touched my hand in silent sympathy. Our eyes met. I felt a shiver go through me, then the moment was over. Had I imagined it?

"The Torabi collect refugees, folk damaged and displaced by wars. Those who've been changed, who no longer fit where they used to fit, or people who don't have a place to call home. Some of them are from ancient wars, others from wars that haven't been fought yet, not in our time. The ship seems to be in all places at once, not just on Earth either. They have people here who are not human, but they've all suffered in war. The Torabi collect their stories as a warning to others that war is never a solution. That's why you saw what you saw and heard what you heard when you came through the door. They collected those memories from you. You can let them go now."

"Why did they capture you?" Beano asked.

"They were after you, dummy, but you didn't follow me through the door. They don't split up families. That's why Hans has his wife and children with him."

A cold knot formed in my stomach. "I'm not family," I said.

"You're closer than family." She gave me a look out of the corner of her eye. The cold knot dissolved, overtaken by a blush.

"But if we don't want to stay they'll let us go?" Beano asked.

"They will, but do you want to leave?"

"Aren't we in some kind of zoo here?" I asked.

"This ship is huge. There are thousands of humans and other races, too. We're not special, simply three people whose lives have been upset by war."

She took Beano's hand and then mine and gave my fingers a squeeze.

"You've both been through so much. You're looking over your shoulder everywhere you go, waiting for the next attack. Well, it's over now. I don't know whether time will heal the way you feel, but if you can heal anywhere it's here, in this place. I'll show you the rest of the ship. You'll be surprised."

"But this place is—" Beano looked over his shoulder at the tall Torabi who had stood by so quietly we'd almost forgotten him...her...it. "What about home?" he asked.

"What about it?" Jeannie said. "You gave four years of your lives to your country, and then came home to what? A land fit for heroes? I don't think so. Here there's peace. Real peace. Give it a chance. Stay."

I looked over. Hans and his family were being led away. He waved. "*Bis später*, Tommies."

"What?"

"He says see you later," Jeannie said.

"You speak German?"

She tapped the little device behind her ear. "Translator. It's funny, once people can truly understand each other, they find it much easier to resolve their differences."

Beano wore a glazed expression. This place might be what he needed.

"What about you, Jeannie?" I asked. "You didn't have to fight in any war. And you have a job back home."

"I don't see being a shopgirl at the co-op is much of a vocation. I've enjoyed being here, working with the refugees. It feels worthwhile. I believe I'm making a difference."

And wasn't that the rub? Even if I could get a job it would be menial at best. I was too old for an apprenticeship, too damaged for the pit. I wouldn't ever be making a difference to anybody.

"You could work with me." Jeannie said. "We could make a difference together."

She reached up and put her hand on my cheek. As caresses go, it was hardly a promise, but it was a start. What had Hans said when he held Hilde's hand? Here is my home?

Here is my home.

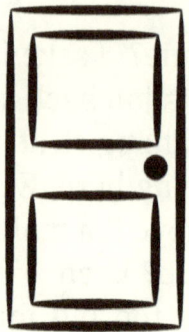

Iron and Anthracite

John Linwood Grant

Mamma Lucy was a walker. She knew the land through her big, bare feet, and the land knew her. "Ain't no better feel than the dust 'tween your toes," she always said, and she'd said it enough, to fancy hats and sharecroppers, to haints and hucksters alike.

There were times, though, when she had a hankering for the clunk of railroad points and the long groan of a great engine as it set its shoulders to the task. And so that night she stood at Charlotte station, waiting with a ticket in her hand

Dusk, and the Greensboro train was late. She'd seen the Piedmont Limited shuffle through, a long, slow bullet heading South. A handful of other people were on the platform, most as dark as Mamma Lucy. A father and daughter, the girl toting a guitar case; a traveling book-thumper, maybe; a couple who twittered at the delay—and another.

A thick-set man stood near the track, in clothes too fine for his fingernails, clothes not cut for him. His collar was altar-white and tight against his black skin. The dimes at her ankle itched, and she knew there'd be a story with that one. Those hooded glances towards the station entrance didn't sit right, not with her.

"Sorry 'bout the delay, y'all. She's coming now."

A knot of white faces, men of an age, maybe friends, turned to the station hand, a nervous youngster.

"There's a dance we have to—" started a man.

"She's here."

The locomotive coming down the track was a battered camelback with only three wagons behind it.

"Sure it'll get us there?"

The railway man looked offended. "Had her sent from Spencer Yard. 'Fraid the regular has boiler trouble. But the Southern Railway don't keep no dead horses, no sir."

With relief or with grumbles, the passengers went to find their places. For most, that meant the last car, a wooden affair with a cracked window and "Coloreds Only" stenciled on the side. Mamma Lucy hitched herself up and sat with her carpet bag on her knees, opposite the father and daughter. The girl, maybe thirteen, smiled at her; the man nodded.

"You play?" Mamma Lucy tipped her head to the guitar case.

"My daddy showed me how to pick," said the girl. "He's a Piedmont bluesman."

"Etta here's a fine gee-tar girl. I'm no bluesman, jes' a working man who can carry a tune." He hesitated. "Boone Reid's the name, ma'am."

"Mamma Lucy does me well enough, Mr. Boone Reid."

He surveyed the faded floral dress, the moth-eaten carpet bag, and the face in front of him. She knew that he was trying to look into her clouded left eye, make out the milk-and-honey strangeness of it, but without staring.

"You from Charlotte?" she asked.

"Used to be, once. Back to see kin, but we're Virginia people these days."

Mamma Lucy settled on the wooden seat and closed her eyes. As the locomotive grabbed the rails to haul north, she took in the creak of the cars. She heard the guitar case open, and the first hesitant chords; the soft murmur of the young couple and the slow, heavy breath of the big man in the corner. He breathed too steady and deliberate—a man who wasn't going to let his lungs scream out truth to anyone.

Her back was itching, and she had that feeling. Should have noticed before. Greensboro was a hundred miles along the track, and now she wondered if that was maybe a few miles too many.

She opened her eyes and reached into a dress pocket. Her mojo bag was there, and the whiskey on which she fed it. She didn't know what was wrong about the big man, but it was something powerful wrong.

"Y'all have yer tickets ready, please."

The conductor stepped through from the car in front. It was the young white man from the platform, capped for duty.

Mamma Lucy held out her ticket.

"Fine old engine," she said.

"Sure is, ma'am. She's a Pennsylvania Railroad Four-Six-O, borrowed way back. We use her as a switcher in Spencer Yard, tell the truth." He gave the other passengers an apologetic look. "Might be a minute or two out, but she'll get us there."

"Your daddy a railroad man?"

"Sure is." A proud look. "And my granddaddy too."

The big man thrust out his ticket, took it back sharp. The boy bit his lip and looked to Mamma Lucy, who gave the smallest shake of her head. He let it be.

When the conductor had left, the traveling man sniffed.

"I've a meeting. A flock awaits me."

"The Lord's patient enough," she said. "Reckon His people can bear to wait a while."

He sniffed again, and took a bible from his suitcase.

"It's awful dark." Etta Reid was at the cracked window.

The conjure-woman peered. The car was swaying on the track, the train building speed, but outside was a faster night than should have fallen. She had more than an itch—she had that knowing that came when you took the wrong dirt road, went round the wrong corner...

"Ten, fifteen minutes, we goin' to be passin' Salisbury," said the girl's father, looking at a battered watch from his pocket.

Mamma Lucy opened her carpet bag and took out a hard-boiled egg. She shelled it neatly and cut it in two, offering half to the girl. Etta looked at her father, who nodded.

As they ate, Boone Reid had his eye on the open bag.

"Heard me names like Mamma Lucy elsewheres," he said. "Maybe even heard of Mamma Lucy herself, now I thinks on it. When I was a youngin."

The conjure-woman munched on her half of the egg, her big horse-teeth biting into the golden yolk.

He stroked the guitar case. "Heard she was a conjure-woman, that Lucy."

"No harm in a tune," said Mamma Lucy.

Etta, looking between the two of them, stroked the scuffed six string guitar. Slim, dark fingers played with the strings, testing them, and tightening here and there. Then she started to play. She had a fine style, thumb-picking a strong bass which resonated around the car.

"One of daddy's," she said, adding a lonesome treble. "Lynchburg blues."

"One o' hers, more like." Boone Reid looked proud.

The girl had a good face, framed by glossy, raven hair. Mamma Lucy would have said there was Lumbee in there.

"Conjure-woman," said the traveling preacher. "'Nother name for a witch."

That had the big man's attention, even drew the couple from their love-talking.

Etta stopped playing; Mamma Lucy showed her teeth.

"Been called that," she said. "Ain't no witch. Just a plain hoodoo-lady, makin' her way from place to place, goin' where she's needed."

"Greensboro doesn't need witches. The good Lord will—"

"Make up His own mind, I'm guessin'. Lessen you think you know better 'n Him."

The couple giggled; the preacher glowered.

The guitar slipped in again, slow picking. Mamma Lucy wrestled with her mind awhile, clutching her mojo bag inside the dress pocket, her thoughts feeling their way around. Darkness outside and darkness within. She could see a sky through the car windows, but it didn't seem the right one. No cloud, no stars. And the moon, almost new, wasn't there. The camelback was hauling faster than it should have been. Only three cars to haul, but still, it felt like they were being driven by more than coal...

The big man in the wrong clothes was watching her.

"You ride the high iron much?" she asked him, open.

"No business uh yourn." His voice was like smoke as well, the kind that bites the back of your throat.

"Wishin' it don't make it so," said Mamma Lucy. "I'm thinkin' you crossed someone, or made a deal too many."

She measured a hard-cheeked face dark as her own, a flattened nose and eyes which seemed to be burrowing into their own sockets, deep and dim lit. If she'd seen those eyes clearly on the platform, she might have waited for a later train.

"What you done, boy?"

"Whut I had to." It was said low, but others heard. "Been listenin' to the Dark Man, an' teachin' folk their place."

Mamma Lucy's hoarse laugh cut the air.

"Sure as Goshen, you ain't seen no Dark Man." She spat in her hand. "That feller don't stop to talk with any ole cheap knife."

"And you'd know, old woman?"

Mamma Lucy brought her milk-and-honey eye to bear on him.

"Oh, I'd know."

His own eyes glittered in the car lights, examining her, then he looked away.

Etta was huddled close to her father, the guitar forgotten. Mamma Lucy tapped one finger on her knee.

"Boone Reid, what time do you have?"

He pulled the watch from his waistcoat pocket. "Twenty past...hey, that's not right." He put the watch to his ear. "Preacher, what time you got?"

The traveling man sniffed, but checked his own timepiece.

"Twenty-one past the hour."

Reid frowned. "Should'uh been in Salisbury by now. Running late."

"Reckon not," said Mamma Lucy. "You hear them cars rattling. We're going at a fair lick, and more."

She went to the connecting door. The next car was Whites Only—the paint was mostly on the walls, and the carpet still had pile. The five dance boys were at their cards, watched by the young conductor. One of them looked up.

"No coloreds in here," he said. Then he added, "Ma'am."

"The color of my skin's the least of your worries right now," she said, brisk and clear. "Conductor, ain't we due in Salisbury?"

The youngster checked the time.

"Overdue," he admitted.

"You seen a signal on this line, heard another engine passin' us?"

"No ma'am."

"Strange, ain't it? Worth a look, I'd say."

Ignoring the card players, she marched towards the next connecting door, trailed by the young man.

"You shouldn't be—"

The merest glance hushed him.

They walked the length of the empty third car.

"How'd you speak to the engineer when you need to?"

"I...I climb out front and onto the coal tender."

"Best show me, then."

Maybe her tone reminded him of some stern grandmammy of his own, or he sensed the conjure-woman in her. Whatever the reason, he dragged the car door open. A hard wind hit them, a billow of smoke and the sound of the camelback, hissing and straining. She could see rungs going up the rear side of the coal tender.

Mamma Lucy trusted her horny bare feet better than any other part of her. She stepped easy onto the cold metal of the couplings, leaned out and grabbed the iron rungs. She was up and onto anthracite in a moment, the wind scraping back her peppered hair, tossing her faded dress around her thighs.

Stood high on the tender, she saw utter dark—no earth, no separate sky. Alone in the pitch black, the locomotive pulled at ever increasing speed. She marked the red glow from the firebox ahead, and the light from the engineer's cab. Holding her dress low, she crunched her way over the coal. It was hard-edged anthracite, pounded small enough to make the footing treacherous, but she could see a figure looming over the open firebox, black skin gleaming.

"Runnin' hot, ain't we?" she called down. The man looked round. He was another Boone Reid, a working man with a broad open face.

"Lord, woman, whut you doin' up there?"

She slid down.

"This train ain't goin' to Greensboro," she said, and pointed out into the night. "You seen Salisbury? You seen hide or hair of anythin' these last twenty minutes?"

He scratched at his sweat- and coal-streaked chest.

"Nope. Not a fireman's job to be lookin' around."

She stood up straight, almost the fireman's height.

"We're goin' into trouble."

That got his attention. He stared into the night which wasn't there, and the night which was, and he was grayer when he looked back at her.

"We're not on our track," he muttered.

"Ain't that the truth."

"What we gonna do, lady?"

"Ain't no lady. Git yourself into that cab and tell your engine-man to slacken off, ease in them brakes."

"The fire—"

"Git!"

Not that she expected it to make any real difference.

The young conductor was waiting for her back at the car entrance.

"There's nothing out there." His voice cracked. "Nothing."

"Nope," she agreed. Back they went, back past the dance boys peering out of the windows, game abandoned. In the Colored car, the big man was sitting on his own—the others had moved the farthest away they could.

"Mamma Lucy, what's happening?"

The conjure-woman set her bare feet firm on the car floor, a hand on Etta's shoulder. There was no point in telling the girl fairy tales.

"That feller over there is carryin' some mighty bad weight on his shoulders, child. Whatever wants him is haulin' this here train, coal to caboose, to where it wants him. Us folk and all. Wherever that place is, it ain't Greensboro. We been shifted, not just off good iron tracks, but somewhere bad."

The preacher stood up, holding his bible to his breast.

"Hell-bound!" He glared around the car. "Sin, and wishing sin, and the Lord making His judgment. Those as turn from His commandments, so will they burn!"

If she'd had a cane to hand, she would have used it on his bony rump.

"Two faces to a dime, preacher—you and him." She waved a hand towards the big man. "This talk o' the Dark Man, and now the Fiery Pit—ain't you people got brakes on those tongues?"

She stretched her stiff neck.

"I've lived awhile, lessen you didn't notice. Didn't get this far by hollerin'. You see any hellfires outside, or crossroads? There's dark places in this world, but they ain't all named in the bible."

"We know who's fault this is," said the preacher, staring at the big man who sat on his own. "We have a Jonah among us."

Boone Reid chewed at an unlit cigarette. "Don't know much about no hoodoo nor nothin', but why not ditch that feller?"

The big man grunted, but didn't look up.

"Throw him off? I heard tell of playing the game thataways." Mamma Lucy nodded. "But it don't always play how you want. Don't reckon I want us stayin' in this place."

"Then what do we do?" Etta Reid was trembling. "Surely I can hear something out there, something not right?"

Mamma Lucy caught it now, the hiss and murmur of voices in this other place. Hungry voices, speaking without lips. Seemed most of the other passengers couldn't hear it, but maybe Etta had a touch of the conjure. "Girl, give them no mind. Play somethin' strong, and let Mamma think."

Truth was, she was carrying an empty pot. The answer might come; it might not.

"You folks..." The conductor coughed, reddened slightly. "Well, I don't see that him back there needs company. Best come on up front, with the rest of us."

He led them through into the car with the dance boys. This time the men had nothing to say about "coloreds," and when Etta started her tunes again, a waxy face or two cracked a smile. The train thundered on, the wheels screeching, the whistle shrill and far away.

No one in the car doubted any more that bad times were upon them. They should have been passing the depot at High Point, yet still the train drove through that black nothing.

"There's a light!" A thin man by the window gave an excited yell and people crowded to see. Sudden excitement, and then a pulling away, worried faces. Mamma Lucy went over.

There was a light far off ahead, more than one, but none the sort of light she wanted to meet. A kind of yellow glow, like tunnel mouths with something discolored laired inside. The thin man looked like he was going to vomit.

"That's where we're headed," said Boone Reid. "Lord help us."

Oblivious of what they'd seen, the fireman lumbered through from the front of the train, shedding coal dust as he came.

"Joseph, she's not slowin' none. Sal says mebbe the air brakes're busted. You gotta go out there."

"I checked them this morning, Luke."

"So how comes we're rattlin' our teeth up front?" The fireman was edgy, near to panic.

Mamma Lucy took a small wrap of cloth from her carpet bag and pressed it into the fireman's huge hand.

"No train ride never killed me," she said softly. "You go and set yourself down ready, Luke, whilst Mamma Lucy does what she must, y'hear?"

Like a child he calmed, clutching the bag she'd given him.

"Yes, ma'am."

"Witching," said the traveling man when the fireman had gone.

"Nothin' but a few simples, to make him easy." The conjure-woman wondered how long her patience would last. "Don't see you out there in the night, tryin' to be of use."

She sat down next to the conductor, who was trembling, staring at his boots.

"This old camelback—you say she's from the Pennsylvania Railroad?"

He looked up. "Y-yep. She's seen some work, ridge and valley. Number Twenty-Eight, though we call her the Black Lady." He blinked. "No offense."

"Fine name. Sounds like you know her well."

"My daddy let me be a brakeman on her, even though I weren't s'pposed to. Just round Spencer Yard and the spurs. She's tough, but she's not meant for this speed—I'm feared she'll blow her seams, or break a side-rod." His gray eyes looked into the old woman's. "It's not fair on her."

"Mighty fond of the locos, ain't you, son?"

"No railroad without them. No jobs, neither, without they ride iron for us, an' haul like saints."

"Nicely said."

She could feel something in the youngster's words. It might

be the last stone needed for the five-spot; the steady match needed for the candle.

"I'm scared." The girl from the couple spoke, a narrow face on delicate bones, but pretty enough. Her man was clutching her tight, as if he could protect her.

Mamma Lucy picked up her carpet bag. "Need a word with that feller at the back."

Boone Reid stood up.

"I'd best come with you."

"You keep your little girl safe, Mr. Boone Reid. I can bite, if there's need."

The last car seemed darker than before, the lights dimmed around the big man. He sat solid, hands on his knees, eyes half closed. Mamma Lucy took her green mojo bag out, right in front of him, and unscrewed the top of a small flask. She took a swig of whiskey, and fed the bag a trickle.

"You know this ain't goin' to end good," she said, adjusting to the wild sway of the last car. "What they call you?"

"Mose Brown." He let those deep set, dim-burning eyes meet hers.

"So, Mose Brown. Some power—don't rightly know or care what—has you gripped. Maybe a year back, or five, I might'a been able to do some good with you. Too late now."

"Too late," he agreed.

"And you ain't a man to be listenin' to no conscience, I'm guessin'."

"Left it in the dirt, way back."

"You're not fussed that you're draggin' these poor souls with you, folk as never harmed you or yours?"

No answer. She sat down next to him, like a church lady finding her pew. He smelled of blood and hair oil.

"Look at me, Mose Brown."

He turned his head her way.

"I've spoken with worse than you got comin'. I got red thread and white; High John, powders, and some mighty strong candles in my bag—all manner of things you don't rightly need to know. That dark feller, taller than trees, keeps his tongue polite when he calls on me."

He muttered under his breath, and she gripped his jaw, made him look into her wandering eye.

"You able for me, boy?"

He might have reached in his pocket for a knife, or taken his big fists and struck out, and she wondered about that for a moment, but she kept her face set. Head-messing was the better part of conjure-work.

His shoulders slumped.

"Killed a man for this suit," he said, slow-voiced. "Don't know why. Made a path, and walked it. Broke a woman's neck in Lafayetteville for sassin' me and lookin' elsewhere; crossed a bluesman outside Charlotte. Had a heap uh cusses laid on me, and mebbe this is all uh them, come to settle."

"Figures."

She couldn't give him pity; she couldn't say what would become of him. Whatever he needed, she didn't have.

"I'll be leavin' you now, Mose Brown. You set there, and you think. Iffen you ever had care for another, then find it tonight. Your ways done dragged us to another place, but these others, ain't right they go down with you." The less he was sure, the better she might work what little she could.

The passengers stared when she came back.

"What did he—"

She raised one long hand.

"I'll be needin' a handful of silver dimes, and a heap of good thoughts."

"Are we going to make it, Mamma Lucy?" Etta stopped her strumming.

The conjure-woman glanced at the traveling preacher. "With the good Lord's grace."

"What'll you do?" asked Etta's father.

"Had me a thought, thanks to young Joseph here."

The conductor looked puzzled.

"It's the Black Lady we're needin'," she said. "Old Twenty-Eight will see us safe, if anyone will." She smiled at the puzzled faces, her lips drawn back in a horse-grin. "You all need to be thinkin' on her, givin' her fine thoughts."

"To slow it—her—down?" One of the dance boys looked eager. "Like magic, in them stories?"

Mamma Lucy shook her head.

"Nope. To speed her right, to help her find her way home, and us with her. She's hankerin' for Greensboro, just like us, so we'll help her get there." No telling if she'd picked the right path, but she thought for a moment that the whispers from outside changed their pitch, lost some of that sly certainty.

People went through their pockets, clinking coins. Eventually they managed a handful of silver dimes—and a silver half-dollar from the young man who'd spoken up.

"Etta, you play for these folks. You play strong, and you mind them of good times. You got a tune or two, I'd guess."

"What she don't got, I can find," said Boone Reid.

"The rest of you, think hard of Twenty-Eight and where you belong. Talk on it, share your stories. Where's the dance, boys?"

"Miller's Hall," said the man by the window. "I got my girl waiting for me."

"Good. You tell these folk about her, and the last time you danced. Preacher, the Lord knows you bug me, but you said you had a flock waitin'. Think on them, and what you goin' to say. See yourself there." The traveling man nodded, which was good enough for her.

"We're going to see my daddy, settle on a date."

Everyone looked round. It was the first time the boy from the young black couple had spoken aloud.

"Even better." She could feel confidence growing. She'd need that. "Joseph, you and me got work."

They went forward, to the rattling door which led to the coal tender. She paused.

"You love these engines, boy. Reckon it's time to let the Black Lady have her head, and find her way home. You with me?"

"Yes, ma'am."

If the boy trembled, it was pure excitement. She smiled. Railroad through and through. He didn't falter on the couplings, which jerked and clashed between the cars. They were up the ladder, and over the coal to where the fireman crouched, muttering to himself.

"No time for sittin'," she said, almost shouting in the hot wind which buffeted the train. No time at all, she realized as she looked past the engine. Far ahead, in the blank dark, the lights seemed closer. They were catfish mouths now, barbels of yellow fire around maws that gaped, maybe even moved a touch, hanging there in the dead black and calling, calling, to Mose Brown and all around him.

"Joseph, you tell the cab man to lay it on, open everythin'. Luke, you shovel like Samson. Fill that firebox with honest burnin', and start wishin' for Greensboro, with every bone you got."

The fireman hesitated. "Lady, she doin' more than she oughta already."

"She'll do more!" yelled the conductor, clambering up the rails by the boiler. The engineer looked back out of his cab, his face pale as chalk.

"Shovel," said Mamma Lucy. "Got me conjure work to do."

Slow at first, the fireman started to feed the open firebox, feeding the glowing coals. She urged him on, searching her carpet bag for what she needed. There was no time to craft some slow, careful trick, so she'd have to make it up.

She opened a package of Devil's Shoestring, and counted out nine pieces, tying them nine times round and spitting on the bundle. This she hung on a hook by the rear of the boiler itself, to one side.

"Black Lady, black luck," she muttered nine times. "Don't go makin' a fool out of old Mamma Lucy, now."

It wouldn't get easier. She had hairs she'd taken from Mose Brown's jacket, unbeknownst to him, and a black-waxed candle. She wrapped the hairs in black paper, and tied that round the candle.

"I ain't got a name for you out there," she said into the wind, staring hard at the distant yellow lights. It made her stomach turn just to look that way. "But I'll manage."

Scratching H A T E on the candle with a new pin, she pushed the fireman aside, and threw the lot into the firebox. It flared on the coals, a greasy yellow-gray, and was gone. Did the mouths flicker? She wasn't sure.

"Lord, me and this engine sure need good fortune tonight."

Mamma Lucy took powders and lodestone from her carpet bag; found cloth, and the silver coins she'd gathered. They'd speak to each other, when they were fixed.

"What else?" The conductor had returned, his cap lost.

"Tell her where to go. Tell her to be findin' her home, and those good iron rails, straight and true." She held out the red flannel bag she'd made, tied tight shut. "Take it, and spit on it, boy."

He grasped the bag between finger and thumb, as if he held a snake, then licked his lips and spat. The saliva sank` into the flannel without trace.

"Black Lady, you sensin' us?" She took a mouthful of whiskey, and sprayed that East, had Joseph do the same.

"We're ridin' the high iron," she cried out, over the roar of the camelback, the aching churn of rods and pistons. "Rattle us home, Black Lady, out o' this fearsome dark."

She heard a low moan from the sick, spoiled world around them, ahead of them, and drew her lips back. Whatever mouths spoke in this place, they didn't like what she was doing. A fierce spirit filled her, and she was near to being railroad iron herself. Mamma Lucy whooped, swirling her print dress around her legs.

"Luke, you see those rails, clear like you once did?"

"Lady, I...maybe." The fireman shoveled faster. "Maybe I seed a glint jes' then."

"You rightly did," she laughed, feeling wild. "Joseph, you tellin' the Black Lady? Cool water and a kindly shed where she's goin'."

"I'm telling her!" The conductor whooped, and threw a handful of anthracite into the blazing firebox. He kissed the red flannel bag, and held it high.

And the dark was tearing like black muslin under a rough hand. A new dark showed through where it parted, a Carolina night with a star's cold eye and gray clouds. Tatters of nothing peeled away, and Mamma Lucy looked ahead. A last blotched maw was fading, and she could see the track, the long track. Town lights, as well, and the low bulk of buildings.

"Ease her off, boys." She patted the engine as brakes hissed and the great wheels screeched against the rails. The whole train shuddered and began to slow.

Mamma Lucy took a deep breath. They'd done it. There would be relief, and then doubt. She knew people. A week, and they'd have convinced themselves that there'd been a mechanical fault, a forgotten branch line, whatever made them safe. And that was no bad thing.

In the passenger car, she could see the everyday world setting out its store. Already the black and the white folk had slipped apart, hovering either end of the car, each to their own. Awkward glances, enough to sadden her some. And then Boone Reid appeared from the rear of the train, expressionless.

"That big feller's dead. No mark on him, as I can see, but he's lollin' with his tongue out and his eyes all…yeller."

"They'd have hanged him one day, anyway," said the traveling preacher. "Man like that."

She didn't bother to argue. She had a tired smile left for Etta, but not much more.

"I'll remember," said the girl. "All of it."

"Remember the old Twenty-Eight" she said, tousling the girl's hair.

They rolled into Spencer Yard at ten past ten that night, hissing steam.

"This isn't where I'm supposed to be." The preacher huffed and looked around.

The conjure-woman snorted, laughed, taking in the cool night air. She'd hoped for Greensboro, but the camelback had known better.

The Black Lady had brought them home all right—to her home. Spencer Yard, the depot where she lived.

Who knows, Mamma Lucy wondered as she pushed her toes in the dirt. Who knows if iron and anthracite can make a soul?

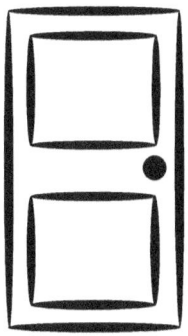

The Namesake

Kate Hall

It was as a favor to Dad and Pops that Quinn agreed to babysit. There were better things she could be doing with her Friday night, up to and including algebra homework, but Aunt Fiona's regular babysitter had fallen through and Jupiter was in retrograde or something that had her friends in a flurry, so their monthly "faerie rituals" simply had to happen.

"She could bring Dylan with her," Quinn said when Pops brought it up. "I've been to one of those parties, they make little houses and string up pretty crystals. It's totally harmless!"

"It starts well after Dylan's bedtime," Pops said.

"And your aunt deserves time with her friends," Dad added. "This is something fun for her."

Quinn had some opinions about that. Most things that Aunt Fiona found fun were more appropriate for little girls, not grown-ups. Quinn, fourteen and quite grown-up thank you very much, had a lot of opinions. But she also loved Aunt Fiona, who knew all the best faerie tales, and who always made time for Quinn.

"Okay," she said.

Which was how she found herself in the cramped kitchen, cradling Dylan, as Aunt Fiona whirled around her in a cloud of gauzy scarves and tinkling silver.

"...wanted to do it here, since the faerie ring grew in, but Judith said there's too much light pollution and I suppose she's right. Now, Dylan's already had his bath and his dinner bottle, haven't you, beloved?" Fiona stopped and pressed a kiss to Dylan's forehead. She smelled like the jasmine essential oil she wore on her wrists and brow. It was a nice scent. "You can take him out to say good night to the faerie ring, but don't cross it or knock any of it down, okay?"

Quinn glanced out the window at the gathering twilight. In the small backyard, pale mushrooms had sprouted, probably in the recent rain. They made a near-perfect circle. "Say good night to mushrooms?"

Fiona laughed. "Imagination, Quinnie, a little imagination! It's a faerie ring, a link to their world. They're probably listening even now." Her voice lowered conspiratorially. "It would be impolite not to say good night, don't you think?"

"I don't think mushroom patterns summon faeries."

Fiona laughed again and grabbed her colorful patchwork bag.

"I'll be home before one," she said. "Earlier if it clouds over. Oh! That book of myths you were eyeing last week—I picked it up for you, it's in the living room. Help yourself to whatever's in the fridge!"

Then she was gone, leaving Quinn standing on the peeling linoleum holding Dylan. He gurgled at her.

"Indeed." She switched him from one hip to the other and headed for the back door. "I doubt there are any faeries listening, too. But it's the thought that counts, eh?"

* * *

Aunt Fiona had rented the house before Quinn was adopted.

According to Dad, she was drawn to its energy, something about vortexes and a thin veil. It had two tiny bedrooms, a tiny kitchen and sitting room, terrible water pressure, and electricity that periodically shorted out. Fiona painted every room a bright color, and added trees and a towered castle to the smaller bedroom for when Quinn visited. As a child, Quinn had thought the house wondrous and magical, maybe a tiny bit haunted. Now, she thought it was a safety hazard.

Privately, she envied Aunt Fiona's easy welcome of wonder, her ability to believe in the possibility of enchantment. It had been years since Quinn had sought out faerie rings or hollow trees. She still read folk tales and listened to Aunt Fiona's stories, and hoped that by the time she was her aunt's age, she would feel magic again.

The hot water cooperated this evening, letting her make tea, and the lights in the nursery didn't brown out while she read Dylan *Good Night Baby Dragons*. She passed the kitchen window and saluted the mushroom ring.

"Night, faeries."

She was paging through her new book when she heard a car crunch on the gravel drive. She glanced up at the clock, frowning. Barely eleven. Outside, the cloudless sky sparkled with a thousand stars. Why was Aunt Fiona home already? She set the book aside as the car pulled up outside, headlights shining.

A door slammed. The headlights continued to shine, the engine to rumble. The front door didn't open.

Unease curled through Quinn's stomach and she glanced at the baby monitor. She could barely hear Dylan's soft breaths whispering on the feed. Sticking the monitor in her pocket, Quinn opened the front door and peeked outside.

Aunt Fiona's beat-up Camry sat on the driveway, keys in the ignition, driver's side door hanging open. The unease curdled, sharpened into fear.

"Aunt Fiona?" Quinn called, her voice swallowed by the velvet dark. She edged around the back of the house, keeping to the shadows. "Aunt Fiona, you okay?"

The motion sensor floodlight switched on, throwing the backyard into sharp relief. Aunt Fiona stood in the middle of the yard, facing the faerie ring. Facing some*thing* in the faerie ring.

Quinn clamped a hand over her mouth and hoped the creature—*what is it?*—didn't hear her squeak of alarm. Fiona marched stiffly toward it, her patchwork bag hanging loose in the crook of her elbow. The creature stepped lightly over the mushrooms and reached for Fiona, crooning something that Quinn was too far away to decipher. Whatever it said, though, drew Aunt Fiona's tight-fisted hand, her knuckles pale spires, into its grip, and it pulled her into the faerie ring.

"Hey!" Quinn burst out of the shadows and sprinted toward Fiona. "Let her go!"

Fiona tried to yank free, and the creature jerked around with a snarl. Something small and gold bounced into the grass outside the ring. The creature howled, and lunged toward it, but before it could reach outside the ring, both it and Fiona vanished. The flood light shut off. The faerie ring stood empty under the light of the moon.

This isn't happening. This can't be happening. Quinn approached the ring slowly, but neither the creature nor Aunt Fiona reappeared. It was just a ring of mushrooms. The only evidence that anything had happened glinted a dull gold in the grass, just outside the circle. Quinn picked it up between thumb and forefinger.

It was a button, a small brass round that looked like it might belong on a fancy coat, or maybe a military dress uniform. There was nothing remarkable about it.

The hair on the back of Quinn's neck stood up, and something dark crackled in the center of the faerie ring. She raced back to the shadows of the house, setting off the flood light again. She skidded around to the car, yanked the key out of the ignition, and stood in the darkness, breath held.

Something rustled around in the backyard. Quinn peeped around the corner of the house and saw the creature scrabbling through the grass around the ring, ripping it up by the handful and raking the dirt. Every few minutes it shook its head and moaned.

Quinn glanced down at the button, then stuck it in her pocket. She backed slowly away from the corner and darted into the house.

For a minute, she stood frozen in the living room, trying to marshal her thoughts. Should she call Dad and Pops? The police? Where had Aunt Fiona been taken? She *had* been taken somewhere, right? Quinn hadn't just dreamed that somehow? What was that creature? Were there more of it? She dashed to the kitchen window, but the yard was empty again. *Where is it?*

In her pocket, the baby monitor hissed.

Quinn fumbled it out and stared at the lights as they bounced up to red, then back to the usual green. She couldn't hear Dylan's quiet breathing anymore. *Please be a glitch. Please, please just be a—*

"So nice of you to invite me in," a voice rasped over the speaker.

"Nope." She dropped the monitor with a clatter and pounded up the stairs. "Nope, nope, nope. I've seen this episode of *Supernatural*, dammit!"

She burst into Dylan's room—empty. Threw herself at the crib—Dylan, twisted in his swaddle, stared up at her with wide eyes. Quinn grabbed him, backed into the doorway, and looked up at the ceiling. Nothing.

Okay. Good. She looked under the crib and in the closet, also empty. Perhaps she was hearing things, perhaps there was nothing—

Dylan twisted over Quinn's arm to look at the window behind them, and she heard it squeak as it opened. A shadow fell across Quinn's. Cold air whistled through the room, bringing with it the scent of rotting wood and green, the sound of reedy breathing. Quinn hugged Dylan closer to her chest and blurted, "You will hear my terms."

It was a gamble, based on Aunt Fiona's stories and her own half-remembered reading. If this was a regular human murderer, they were screwed. If it was a faerie and all that dreck about rules and bargains was just that—dreck—they were also screwed. But if it was true, and she had somehow given the creature permission to enter the home, it had to hear her.

A sibilant hiss. Quinn flinched and tucked Dylan closer to her chest.

"Name the terms," a grudging voice rasped behind them.

Shit. She hadn't thought far. Quinn took a breath and rocked Dylan a little, both to soothe him and to buy herself a moment before turning.

The creature looked human at first—bipedal, sallow-skinned, a head atop shoulders atop torso, two eyes, a nose, a mouth. But those eyes were double-pupiled and had no discernible iris or white, just a void of moss-green from lid to lid. That nose turned like a pig's snout, and that mouth was full of serrated, sharp teeth that it bared at her now in a mockery of a smile. Its fingers were long, with too many joints, and there were seven on each hand. It held one out to Quinn now—an offering? *A trick.*

"The terms." Her tongue felt thick and dry. She swallowed. "The baby is not to be taken, changed, spelled, or harmed in any way. He stays with me, and if I remain with you by choice or by force, he is exempt and will be returned without alteration to his uncles, my fathers." Had she covered all the bases? Were there any loopholes? She hoped not.

The creature scowled. "Dear terms, little one."

"You took his mother." Quinn lifted her chin. "You'll not steal her child too."

"And if she misses her babe?" The voice turned wheedling, the hand reaching again. Quinn snorted.

"I saw you take her away. She didn't want to go. She won't want you to take her son, too."

The creature shrugged and scanned the floor with a nonchalance that looked too practiced. She thought back to its frantic scrabbling in the grass, and the shiny button in her pocket felt heavy. *That's how it got in.* Quinn clenched her teeth and grabbed the turquoise sling hanging over the edge of the changing table. "Let me get him sorted and we'll go."

The creature's eyes returned to her, and a commingled thrill of dread and satisfaction went through her at the frustration in its gaze. She bundled Dylan into the sling, arranged him against her chest, and wrapped her zip-hoodie around them both. When she looked up again, the creature perched on the windowsill, but instead of the maple tree, the glow of the street lamp beyond, all that waited beyond the window was darkness, and the overpowering smell of autumn.

The creature grinned its terrifying grin once more. "Follow then, little one." It tipped backwards and fell into the darkness without a sound.

I could run, Quinn thought, staring at the void. She could bolt now, take Dylan home, make Dad and Pops call the police to...to what? To tell them Aunt Fiona had been spirited away by faeries? To see Dylan swallowed by the bureaucracy surrounding suddenly-motherless children?

But what would happen to him, to either of them, if they stepped into the dark?

Your problem, Quinnie, is that you lack imagination, Aunt Fiona's voice echoed in her head. Well, she wished Fiona was here now, so she could tell her—in excruciating detail—what possible outcomes Quinn's imagination was furnishing. None of them were pretty.

She couldn't run. She couldn't leave Dylan alone in this house, marked by faerie magic she had let in. There was no way backwards.

"Forward into the unknown then," she murmured.

She stepped up to the window, felt the cool breath of air on her cheeks. It tasted like smoke and leaves. In the darkness, the mushroom ring glowed so bright it didn't look like fungi anymore, but a looping ribbon of light. She swung her legs over the windowsill, where they disappeared up to the knees.

Quinn wrapped both arms tight around Dylan, kissed his downy head, and let herself fall.

* * *

They landed in a leaf pile that plumed gold and scarlet around them. Quinn gasped for air. Dylan howled his displeasure at being squished against her chest. But they were alive, and here. Wherever and whatever "here" was.

She stood on rubbery legs and looked around. Trees stretched overhead, a few leaves clinging to their skeletal branches. Through the tangle, a gunmetal sky hung low and she smelled the faint sweetness of snow on the air. A chill breeze ruffled her hair and she pulled her hood up. *I should have grabbed a hat for Dylan.*

"Well met, little one."

Quinn slewed around, slipping on leaves. The creature stood a few feet away from her, bowing so low its face near touched the ground. It hadn't spoken, though, that wasn't its voice. So who…? She looked up into the trees.

"Were you planning to drop on me like a mountain lion?"

The owner of the voice laughed, high and bell-like. They looked like a child, all dainty features and giant luminous eyes, and their wild curls were strung through with dewdrops and bits of something that gleamed softly as they dropped from their bough, landing light-footed next to the bowing creature. At full height, they didn't even reach Quinn's shoulder.

"Most mortals who pass this way without our help go mad in the attempt." They smiled, and Quinn glimpsed another jawful of terrifyingly sharp teeth. "What a sweet babe you have! May I hold?" They held out their arms invitingly, everything about them benign and eager, sweetly curious.

And absolutely a trick. Quinn stepped back, her politest smile affixed. "Oh, you're so kind. He's fussy, though. What may I call you?"

The creature that had taken Aunt Fiona made a choked noise. But the child-that-wasn't-a-child only laughed. "Clever, too! You may call me Pearl. And what may I call *you*?" The already sharp smile sharpened further, but Quinn knew this one. Every story had prepared her for that question, if nothing else.

"You can call me Niece," she said, bouncing Dylan to quiet him. "And he is called Beloved."

The faerie's face twisted with distaste and Quinn smothered a smirk against Dylan's head. So, the stories were right about that too: no faerie would call something mortal their 'beloved'—love elevated the mortal, made claiming ownership impossible.

"Well follow me then, Niece." Pearl turned and skipped into the trees. "There are revels and we are missing them!"

Quinn made to follow when the creature intercepted her, grabbing her sleeve with one of those too-long hands. She yanked free, but it blocked her path.

"Where is it?" it hissed, hands opening and closing convulsively. "Where have you hidden it?"

Hidden what? she almost asked, almost put her hand in her pocket, almost slipped up as badly as the creature had. It seemed to realize the same, and backpedaled with a growl, disappearing into the trees.

"Don't dawdle, Niece!" Pearl's voice echoed through the trees. Quinn shook herself, adjusted Dylan, and followed.

The wood thinned, more sky visible through the branches, until they came to a verdant hillock. Lights twinkled in the air, though Quinn couldn't tell what they were or how they floated. Faeries—at least, she felt relatively certain they were faeries, all spun-glass beauty and razor teeth—milled about, dancing and eating, laughing and whispering to each other. A few humans wandered among them, looking small and vulnerable in their obvious mortality. One young man was trying to eat a flower with a look of utter confusion on his face while a faerie laughed and offered him a handful of stems, dirt still clinging to their roots. A pair of women were dancing, whirling across the grass, shrieking with laughter. They spun past Quinn and she caught sight of their bruised, bloodied feet. Suddenly, their voices didn't sound so jubilant.

She couldn't see Aunt Fiona anywhere.

"Well?" Quinn startled away from the voice at her elbow, and Pearl held out a small stone cup full of some sweet-smelling drink. "Shall we join in?" Their ever-present smile turned wry. "You won't be trapped by partaking of our food and drink. That I swear. Try!" Pearl offered the cup again and Quinn took it carefully. The stone was cool and surprisingly light, pale green and cut so fine it was almost translucent. Pearl had materialized a second one, and held it up in a silent toast. Quinn mimicked them, and let the drink touch her lips, but no further. It smelled like apples, tasted like summer. Pearl downed their cup in one swallow and licked their lips with a satisfied sigh.

"Shall we dance?" They gestured to the mass of bodies swaying and spinning on the hill. Quinn scanned them again, but she didn't see any trace of Aunt Fiona's red plait or hear her loud laugh. In the sling, Dylan squirmed and whined.

"Not now." Quinn adjusted Dylan again and took another gamble. "Do you know where his mother is? She had his diapers with her when she came here and Beloved needs a clean one."

Pearl made a face at Dylan. He made a face back at them and the whining escalated to a howl. The nearest dancing faeries recoiled from the sound like they had been struck by it. Pearl sighed, put-upon.

"I will see if I can find what you seek," they said, and disappeared into the crowd.

More faeries were taking notice of them now, thanks to Dylan's fussing, so Quinn sidled around the edge of the hill, until she found a pocket of quiet under the drooping boughs of a fir tree. She lay Dylan out on the leaves and dropped needles, their spicy scent tickling her nose and making her sneeze. She cast off his wet diaper and dried him as best she could with the tissues in her pocket.

"Let's see if this works." Dylan gurgled up at her. "Yeah, well, my options are kind of limited here, buddy, in case you haven't noticed." He gave her a gummy smile, and Quinn smiled back. She shifted on her knees and felt a hand—long fingered, many jointed, decidedly not human—grip the back of her neck. She froze.

"Where is it?" The creature rasped in her ear. Its breath smelled like damp wood and mushrooms, and she could feel thick nails digging into the thin skin under her ear. She folded her hands in her lap, kept her gaze on Dylan.

"Where is what?"

The creature hissed. "You know. You have it. I can *smell* it. Please—" its voice turned desperate, and its fingers tightened on her neck "—please give it back. I am nothing without it."

What did that mean? Were faerie lives worth only a trinket? That didn't seem right. Quinn fought the urge to question the creature—that way lay entrapment, almost certainly—and picked up a brilliant red leaf, twirled it over Dylan's head so he could reach for it. The creature made a frustrated noise, and the hand at the back of her neck disappeared. Quinn spun around, but the creature was gone. Instead, Pearl danced toward her, the ranks of faeries giving way to watch them pass. And following Pearl...

"Aunt—!" Quinn swallowed Fiona's name, unsure if her aunt had already given that away under the faerie magic. She looked faded, next to the brilliance of the faeries, her fiery hair dull and limp in its plait, wan-faced with deep shadows under her eyes. But she looked at Quinn and recognized her, her mouth pursing into an O of shock. Then she saw Dylan and her body went rigid.

"No! Not—!"

"Here is our Beloved." Quinn whisked Dylan into her arms and intercepted Fiona. "Do you have any diapers in that bag?" She did, Quinn could see one peeking out of the patchwork bag hanging over Fiona's shoulder, likely forgotten, but Quinn needed her to understand, to pause, to *stop talking*.

Fiona's mouth snapped shut and she glanced at Pearl and the other faeries, who had all leaned forward, staring at Dylan hopefully. Quinn caught her aunt's eye again, and saw she understood.

"Yes. I do. I do!" She fumbled the strap and the bag thumped to the ground. She pawed through it and Quinn bent down as if to help her, their foreheads almost touching.

"They've got it," Fiona breathed, and Quinn could see the whites of her eyes, like a spooked horse. Her hands trembled as she pulled out wet wipes, a clean diaper. "Trade only." Louder, perhaps sensing the faeries drawing closer, she added, "I'm out of diaper ointment, so dry him well before you put it on."

Quinn took the diaper and wipes, her hands clumsy as she tried to think. Fiona was trapped unless Quinn could trade her back, and she could tell Pearl would only trade for one other person. They watched Dylan with a fascination bordering on hunger, and stood so close now Quinn could make out the tiny stones strung through their wild curls—pearls, strings of them like on a lady's necklace.

Wait.

The green-eyed creature frantically searching for a button. Pearl with pearls. *I am nothing without it.* She quickly glanced around at the faeries, saw thimbles on chains, bottlecaps polished to a star's shine, bits of ribbon and lace, and a child's mitten sewn like a badge on a coat.

In all the stories, names were currency. But Pearl had just given up their name—or *a* name, anyway. She glanced at the pearls strung through Pearl's hair. Definitely a necklace.

She gathered up Dylan, fresh-changed, and faced the assembled faeries. "Your revels are delightful, but it's time for us all to go home. Thank you for your hospitality." She lay a hand on Fiona's shoulder, including her in the statement, and as expected Pearl clamped dainty fingers on Fiona's other arm.

"I'm afraid Fiona will stay," they said, rolling the name as if savoring its taste. "Whether you leave is also debatable, Niece. You only laid terms for your Beloved, and I'll have your name before long."

Fiona shot her a despairing look and Quinn bit her lip. "You mean like your pearls, friend? Or perhaps your mitten?" She nodded to the faerie in question, who glanced left and right with alarm. "Is that the name you give to mortals—Mitten? It's a sweet one, reminds me of a little cat. Which means you are Thimble, and you, Ribbon—or do you go by Blue, since that's the color?"

The faeries shifted anxiously, but Pearl looked only bored. "If our namesakes were meant to be secret, we wouldn't wear them publicly."

"Then you won't mind if I touch." Quinn reached for the nearest faerie's little talisman, the bit of blue ribbon, and the faerie responded with a flurry of panic, darting out of reach with a wail. In a blur of movement, Pearl stood before her, gripping her fingers tight enough to make the bones grind.

"You do *not* touch with your dirty hands, mortal." Pearl seemed to grow before her, face sharpening and eyes hardening. Quinn steeled herself to meet that unyielding gaze.

"Then you need to get your hands off my namesake as well," she said. "Your rules, after all."

Pearl blinked at her, then scoffed. "Humans do not have namesakes."

"Wrong. My aunt is my namesake." Quinn fished in her pocket for her wallet, and pulled out her student ID. She had not thought of herself by her first name in so long, it hopefully no longer held any magic. And her middle name—her preferred name—wasn't listed on the piece of plastic she thrust under Pearl's nose. "See for yourself."

The faeries gathered around Pearl, peering down at the little card. Pearl glanced from the name typed beneath the terrible first-day-of-school photo, to Quinn, and back again. From Aunt Fiona, then back to Quinn again.

"Like you, I have a namesake." Her voice shook despite her efforts, and Quinn swallowed. "And by your rules, you shouldn't touch another's namesake."

Pearl frowned, turned to their fellows, and conferred with them in low voices. The few humans who had been part of the revels edged closer, listening. The man who had been eating flowers looked like he might cry, and Quinn wished she could find a way to claim him, too, claim all of them and free them. Dylan murmured against her chest, eyes drifting closed, and she looked away. *Finish this rescue mission first.*

At last, Pearl turned back. They were smiling—not a good sign.

"Our namesakes are precious, this is true. They are how we are known to each other, and to lose your namesake is to lose your place in the revels." Pearl's smile widened and Quinn's stomach dropped. "But that is not the case in the human world. If it were, you would be bound now, wouldn't you?"

Quinn's mouth opened, then snapped closed. Pearl laughed.

"You are clever, little one. We like clever here. But our laws don't extend to you. You have enough of your own." They tilted their head, pearls shining. "But for your boldness, we will let you pass freely with your Beloved. Go back to the tree where we met, and you will find yourself home soon enough."

No! She couldn't leave without Aunt Fiona. What would happen to Dylan? To Dad and Pops? She could imagine Dad's grief, Dylan's confusion, wondering where his mother had gone. Quinn could never tell him, and for an eyeblink she saw red. *No. I have to think of something. I have to!*

But she couldn't. Her mind drew a blank. This was the realm of magic and possibility, and it had been too long since Quinn had tried to think like a faerie.

"Go." Fiona nudged her. "Please, sweetheart, go before they change their minds." She brushed her fingers over Dylan's head, and swallowed loudly, before looking at Quinn. There was no blame there, just love and desperation. "Tell our Beloved about me, okay?"

Her face felt sticky, and when Quinn rubbed her cheek her hand came away wet. More tears dropped on Dylan and he made a face in his sleep. Fiona pressed a trembling kiss to

Quinn's forehead, another one into Dylan's hair, then stepped back.

"Off you go, little one." Pearl's smile looked gentle now, benevolent, and they gestured to the trail. "The night is still young and the revels will resume."

Her feet started on their own, carrying her away from Aunt Fiona and the faeries, and Quinn gave up trying to wipe her eyes. She wrapped both arms tight around Dylan and whispered apologies to him as she put her back to the hill, the faeries, their human captive-guests. The strains of music and sounds of revelry faded as she walked through the trees, replaced by only her footsteps, breathing, and the soft rustle of something following them.

Quinn stopped short, and the presence behind her stopped as well. She smelled the loaminess of rotting wood and fungus.

"Give it back," the rasping voice begged. "*Please.*"

She turned slowly, stared at the creature with its moss-green eyes, its serrated teeth.

"Button," she said, and it flinched. "That is what they call you."

"Not now," the creature moaned. "Now I am nothing. Invisible."

"You don't still have your true name?"

Button stared at her as if it thought her mad. "Would *you* share your true name with me? With any faerie? We guard them from each other as surely as from you. That's why I need it back." There was no aggression in its posture now, no wheedling or threats. Button simply looked bereft.

Trade only, Aunt Fiona had said. It was like in her stories: magic beans for a mule, gold for a life, a name for a child.

Or, just maybe, for an aunt.

Quinn reached into her pocket, slow enough that Button could track her movements. The shiny button felt round and hard against her fingers and she held it up, watched Button's eyes light up. Button lurched toward her, and Quinn closed her fist around it.

"Mine," she said, and Button flinched back as if struck. "It's like Pearl said, your rules don't apply to us, because we have our own. You lost it in my world, and in my world we believe in finders keepers."

Button keened, wringing its hands. "Please, please, give it back. I need it. Please!"

Quinn hummed, as if thinking, then nodded back up the trail. "I'll trade you for it. Namesake for namesake."

Button's eyes widened. "But Pearl said—!"

"I heard what Pearl said." Quinn brandished the button again, blew on it and polished it against Dylan's sling. Button's eyes followed it desperately, and she said, "I could make a pretty necklace with this. Or—" she jerked her chin back toward the faerie hill "—I'll trade it back to you in exchange for my namesake: alive, unharmed, and un-magicked," she added hastily.

Button hesitated, and Quinn's hand drifted back to her pocket, the shiny button loose in her fingers.

"Fine!" Button scampered back up the trail, then stopped to point at Quinn. "Don't leave with it! Wait for me by the tree."

"I will wait. But remember—" Quinn tossed the shiny button in the air and caught it "—my aunt must be alive, unharmed, and un-magicked. No compulsions to return to Faerie, no strings attached. If there are, then the same will apply to your namesake, understand?"

Button gulped, nodded, and loped back toward the hill so fast leaves whirled in its wake. Quinn let out a shivering breath and resumed walking in the other direction. Would it work? She hadn't specified *when* Aunt Fiona must be returned, and what if the faeries used that loophole? But then she'd still have Button's button and Button didn't seem able to bear that.

"Please work," she breathed into the icy air. "Please, *please* work."

She reached the tree, but it was now naked of leaves, the ones on the ground brown and laced with frost. Her nose stung, and the tips of her ears. She zipped her sweatshirt around Dylan again and tried to tuck the fabric over his head to conserve heat. He shifted against her and whimpered.

Were they going to try and freeze her out? Quinn could stand the cold for a while, but Dylan couldn't, and the faeries probably knew it. She gritted her teeth and folded herself around as much of Dylan as she could. Perhaps Pearl had told Button there would be no trade. Perhaps Pearl had even killed Button. Would they do that? The faeries of Aunt Fiona's stories had always been a little bloodthirsty. Or perhaps Pearl found a new namesake for Button—if they were just human trinkets, maybe they could shed them as easily as humans lost them. Meanwhile it got colder and colder, frost thickening on the tree trunks and spreading over Quinn's shoes. Dylan's whimpers turned into plaintive crying as he curled up tighter against her chest.

Shit. Aunt Fiona would never forgive her if her son froze to death. They had to go. They had to leave Aunt Fiona behind. Quinn stepped up to the tree and reached out—

"Wait!"

Quinn looked back. Button charged down the trail, panting, dragging a stumbling Aunt Fiona behind him.

"You were going to leave!" Button accused, practically vibrating with anxiety. "Here is your namesake. Give me mine!" It held out a hand.

Quinn looked at Fiona, still breathing hard. "Are you okay?"

"Yes? I mean—yes? What's going on?" Fiona looked between Quinn and Button. Button pushed her toward Quinn.

"Take her!" It held out its hand again. "No harm, no magic of any kind. Take her and give it back!" Button glanced back up the trail, and Quinn wondered if it had conferred with Pearl or if it had just snatched Fiona out from under the other faeries' noses. She plunged her hand into her pocket and pulled out the shiny button.

"Get behind me, and put a hand on my shoulder," she ordered Fiona, who rushed to comply. "And when I say, step backwards with me." She held up the button for Button to see and it stilled, watching its namesake intently.

"When I give this back, the trade is complete," she said. "No take-backs. I don't keep your button, and Faerie doesn't keep my aunt or any of her own. Got it?"

Button's gaze pulled away from its namesake to look at her with something like admiration. "Dear terms, little one." Then it grinned, and for once it didn't look predatory. "Teach the littler one. I accept your terms."

Quinn tossed the button into the air. "Now."

She felt Aunt Fiona step back toward the tree, felt the cold blast of darkness between worlds, and before Faerie disappeared she saw the shiny button land in Button's long-fingered hand.

* * *

Dylan howled and bonked his head against her sternum. Quinn opened her eyes and saw the open window, the faerie ring in the grass below. They were back.

Her legs buckled and Quinn dropped to the floor, gasping. "Aunt Fiona?"

"Here." Aunt Fiona lay spread-eagled on the hardwood, but scrambled upright and pulled Dylan out of the sling, rubbing warmth back into his hands, his rosy cheeks. "Here, here, oh my darlings, we're back, we're safe."

Quinn flopped onto her back, suddenly exhausted. A cool hand touched her brow, ran through her hair. "Clever Quinnie. Are you all right?" Fiona appeared over her, eyes shining. "You impressed them."

"Great." Quinn struggled up onto her elbows. "They can remain impressed from a distance. Come to my house tonight, okay? We'll tell Dad and Pops there's a gas leak or carbon monoxide or something. They'll let you guys stay until you find a new place."

For a moment she feared Fiona would refuse, would feel the draw of magic that had prompted her to take the house in the first place and decide the risk was worth the wonder. But she nodded and stood, reaching down with her free hand to pull Quinn to her feet. Dylan was drifting again, head pillowed on his mother's shoulder and slowly dampening it with drool.

"Good idea." Aunt Fiona squeezed Quinn's hand tight. "Your good ideas saved us tonight. Thank you." She kissed Quinn's cheek and left the nursery, humming a lullaby.

"You're welcome," Quinn said to the empty room. *But it wasn't just my good idea. It was your stories, your belief in the magic, that I absorbed whether I believed or not.*

She blinked, then dashed out of the nursery, following Fiona down the stairs. "I just want the record to reflect that I am helping you house hunt this time, and there will be no faerie rings allowed!"

Aunt Fiona's laughter echoed as they let themselves out into the warm night.

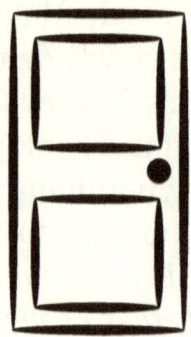

Portal Pirates

Gini Koch writing as Anita Ensal

We were circling the planet Yenaw—once a massive civilization a thousand years before Earthlings walked upright, now a dead rock with nothing of interest left, even for archaeologists—when warning bells went off.

"What is it?" Dean asked, as the command crew went from relaxed to alert. We'd all been relaxed because we'd been planning to land on Yenaw. The command crew was looking forward to the idea that we'd sneak in a break from the wars under the guise of hiding out so as to surprise the enemy with our return. Dean and I hoped to end up actually amusing ourselves by searching for alien artifacts that somehow might have been missed by everyone else. Nothing should have triggered an alarm around this planet.

"A ship has appeared, Captain Hodos," our navigator, Weeks, said. "On viewer now."

The ship wasn't one of our fleet. It wasn't one of the current enemy's fleet, either. In fact, I'd never seen a ship like this. It was almost like a gigantic boomerang from Earth, but wider, like a thick, rounded triangle. It had also seen a lot of action, based on its outer hull, and glowed a soft electric blue.

"It looks ancient," I said. "No identification numbers, either."

"How did it get here?" Dean asked musingly. "Ex-O, any thoughts?"

"Warp drive?" I suggested. "I mean, every ship has that these days."

"But it's not from these days. I recognize it—it's a type of ship that hasn't existed for a thousand years."

"Then I have no idea. I've never seen a ship like this."

"You should have, James," Dean said. "It's from Earth." That Dean, who was from the planet Nitrexton, would know ancient Earth ships shouldn't have surprised me by now—learning about the military of every world out there had been his hobby well before we ever met. So I didn't reply. "Are we close enough to grab it?"

"Yes, sir," the weapons chief, Barnett, replied.

"Then do so. Strongest beam. Any ship here that we can't identify we have to assume is an enemy."

The tractor beam connected and we started to pull the ship to us.

Then the ship's glow went bright. So bright that it washed over our tractor beam and our ship. And suddenly we weren't near Yenaw anymore.

We were in the middle of nowhere, space-wise. "Location!" Dean snapped at Weeks. "Red Alert!" he said to Barnett.

Weeks whistled as the alarms went off. "We're a hundred-thousand light years away from our prior location, sir. Now in the Gamma Quadrant. Nearest star is ten-thousand light years away."

"Hail that ship," Dean said, "and don't let our tractor beam falter. In fact, find a way to increase power to the beam. Attach cables the moment we're in range."

"We drew closer somehow," Barnett shared. "In cable range now. I can only increase tractor beam power by lowering our shields."

"Do it. Send every cable we have as well."

"Hail accepted," the communications chief, Greva, said. "Audio only. Alarms muted."

"Well, aren't you interesting?" The person on the other end sounded male and older. The universal translator was good, but we wouldn't know the speaker's planet of origin without confirmation, let alone sex and age. But now wasn't the time to place bets on who or what we were speaking to. He also sounded cocky and confident.

"Not as interesting as you," Dean replied, as our attaching cables sailed towards the ancient ship. "Who are you and what did you do to bring us here?"

"We're not interested in military entanglements and we apologize for bringing you here. Hopefully you have the means to get home." The ancient ship glowed brightly again.

"Cables attached," Barnett said at the same instant.

The glow swept over us again and once more when the glow stopped, we were somewhere else.

"Fifty-thousand light years from last location, near to Signus Major," Weeks shared without being prompted. "We're within hailing distance of the fleet. Shall I call for help, sir?"

"No," Dean said. "We don't need help—we could have gotten to safety from our last location, let alone this one, or wherever else they try to take us to next. Just ensure the tractor beam stays on at this strength or even stronger and the cables stay attached. Start moving that ship closer to us. If we can get it inside our ship, do it."

"Being hailed by the enemy ship," Greva said. She seemed intent. "Captain, they may be using audio only, and I know you identified the ship as ancient, but they're using a channel and signal code set that are extremely recent."

"And this is why I like having someone from Raika in my command crew," Dean said. Our battalion was made up mostly of humanoid races that looked almost interchangeable—Nitrextons, Earthlings, Yanens, and Alrians—but we had a few less "human" looking races, too, of which Raikans made up the largest population. Raikans were humanoid hairless cats.

Greva's ears turned red, which was a sign she was pleased. "On audio now."

"You're tenacious, I'll give you that," the man from the other ship said. "But I don't know what you hope to gain."

"This is Captain Hodos of the Alliance Military Vessel the *Victorious Thirty-Three-Ten*. You are committing a hostile act and we'd like to know why."

"I'm calling you grabbing my ship hostile, sonny-boy."

Dean pulled me close. "What are the chances you and I can get onto that ship safely?" he asked softly.

"Slim. We can't risk a shuttle. It's clear the only reason we're moving with them is we have them so tightly tied to us. Our only other option is to light-wave over, and I'm not sure that will work under the circumstances."

"Oh well, the old ways will be the best then. Prepare to be boarded," Dean said in a louder voice.

The man on the other ship chuckled. "That's normally my line."

I nudged Dean. "If they're not military, then they're pirates," I said softly.

Dean smiled. "Good." The other ship was close enough that we could see it without any magnification needed. It looked worse up close. And yet, I could tell that it was sturdy, possibly sturdier than our own vessel. "I have an idea," Dean said. He turned to Barnett, who was third in command. "Ensure that you don't let our tractor beam lessen and ensure the cables are locked on tight. No matter what, don't let any cable detach and that's an order that, if ignored or overridden, will ensure you spend the rest of your life in the brig. You have the bridge. James and I are going to find out what's going on over there."

"Are you sure that it's safe for you to do this, Captain?" Barnett asked.

Dean nodded. "We've left you in charge before, and never had a worry that things wouldn't be shipshape when we returned.

I don't want to risk any of you with this, however—James and I are trained for what we're about to do, the rest of you aren't."

The rest of the command crew looked ready to argue, but Barnett nodded. "As you say. I'll ensure your ship is ready and waiting for your return to the bridge, Captain."

We headed off the bridge. "What are you planning that we're supposedly trained to do?"

"Something old-fashioned."

"What?"

"We're going to board that ship."

"Why?" I figured I'd ask how later.

"Because I think it's what you and I have been looking for all our lives."

I didn't have to ask what Dean meant. There were a lot of names for what we'd both been searching for, and we'd used all of them at one time or another—but we always went back to an ancient Earth story. "The Golden Eggs?"

"Exactly. I think that's our Goose, that ship."

"And if you're wrong?"

"Do you trust me?"

"You know I do."

"Great, then trust me now." He looked thoughtful. "Is there anything in your quarters you can't leave behind or live without?"

I considered this. Military uniforms meant you didn't worry much about clothing and I had no beloved family mementos to drag along. "I keep the only things that matter to me on my person at all times."

Dean grinned. "Me, too." With that, he turned and headed off. I followed. We ended up at the lockers, where the crew's spacesuits were stored. "Get into your spacesuit and ensure you take the maximum oxygen tank."

I'd learned not to question when Dean was on a strategic roll, and this seemed to be one of those times. We had to use spacesuits often enough—when repairs were needed and no planet, moon, space station, or star base was available, when we were going onto a dead planet like Yenaw, or when we had to go onto planets that didn't have breathable air for any or all members of the crew. Since Dean had been considering landing on Yenaw, tanks were already prepped. He and I both took four-day tanks. They were heavy, but that only mattered in gravity.

Suited up and double-checked, we headed for the repairs exit. "You're sure about this?" I asked as we stepped into the airlock.

"I am. Even if he jumps again, as long as we're holding onto a cable, we'll go along with our ship. If he breaks free somehow and leaves us here, we're close to help. But I want onto that ship, and this is the only safe way to have it happen."

The airlock emptied and we stepped out, grabbing hold of the exterior ladder. We enabled the magnets in the suit's shoes and gloves, and I ensured we had lifelines attached to the ship—the airlock door and the ladder both—and to each other. "Climb up," Dean said via our suit-to-suit communications. "Ensure you're never out of touch with the ship or a cable."

We worked our way over to the nearest cable, Dean going first. We had to go up a bit in order to remain in contact with ship and cable at the same time. We stuck to the same cable, just in case, then moved quickly down. Well, as quickly as we could, which wasn't as fast as I'd have liked.

We were about halfway to the other ship when the bright glow lit up the space around us. I blinked and we were near a huge gas giant. It could have been Jupiter, but I chose not to waste time asking.

Instead, we hurried down the cable and reached the other ship. Our suits' magnets worked on this ship as well as our own. This shouldn't have surprised me, but I wasn't willing to take anything for granted right now.

We had to crawl around the bottom of their ship to find an airlock. "Definitely Earth-made," Dean said as he pulled a lever and the airlock door opened. "Your kind were big on failsafes."

We climbed in and shut the airlock door behind us. "Now what?" I asked. "You can't seriously think they're going to fill this with air for us."

"No." Dean went to the door and punched a button. I heard a hissing sound and my helmet's monitor showed that the air around me was becoming breathable. "This ship is made for a smaller crew, James. That means that the ship has to be able to allow crew in and out without assistance from the bridge or elsewhere."

"I'd say you were crazy, but my monitor says I can take off my helmet and preserve my oxygen, so I won't. Who goes out first?"

"I'd like the Conason Charm on full display but be careful—they could be aware we're here and waiting with weapons ready."

The inner airlock door opened and, sure enough, there was a large man there holding a brand-new personal laser cannon. He had a full head of wild hair, a bushy beard and moustache, but was dressed in the latest fashions of Raika, which was far from anywhere we'd been on whatever wild ride his ship had taken us on.

"Right you are," he said with a grin. "So, why are you here? To claim my ship and crew for your military?"

"No," Dean said calmly. "We're here to join up."

The ship's captain's jaw dropped. I gave him an ingratiating smile. "We're intrigued and here more to satisfy our curiosity than anything else."

The captain eyed me. "Well, you have the silver tongue, don't you?"

I didn't reply—I hardly felt that was my best opening.

"How are you able to jump like you have?" Dean asked.

"Now, see, if I told you that, then you'd definitely take my ship for use by your military. And I can't be having that."

"You support the other side?" I asked politely.

"I support no side other than my own," the captain said. "That's the pirate way."

"I knew it," Dean said with some satisfaction. "That's why we're here. We want to join your crew."

"We do?" Taking the ship was one thing. Joining under another commander sounded a lot like the military, and I wasn't sure yet that there was an advantage.

The captain nodded. "I suggest you tell your friend your plan, and me as well."

Dean rolled his eyes. "I'm Dean Hodos from Nitrexton, the captain of the ship that has yours held. This is James Conason from Earth, my second in command. We were conscripted into service. I'll let you guess why."

The captain snorted. "The list is quite long, for either planet. How did two lads who chose the military instead of prison rise up so far? I'd have thought they'd keep you scrubbing toilets."

"Dean's a strategic genius," I replied. "He's popular with the upper levels because his plans always work."

"And the few times when they don't, James spins a nice story as to why," Dean added. "Together we're the best team you're ever going to have the opportunity to join your crew."

The captain grinned. "I'm Miles Haadrich, with two a's, the captain of the *Portalis*. I'm from Earth, too, as is this ship."

"Are you as old as your ship?" Dean asked.

"Oh, no. I was, like you two, conscripted into the military for, ah, youthful exuberance. Unlike the two of you, I didn't rise up and, in fact, I'd been intentionally stranded on a planet when the captain of this ship at the time arrived. He'd lost a member and I looked likely. He added me on. I'm still grateful."

"Did you kill him to take over?" Dean asked.

Haadrich looked horrified. "No, why would I murder my benefactor? I became his second and when he passed on to his greater reward, he gave me this ship and I gave him the finest funeral ever seen in the galaxy." He eyed us. "Your friend doesn't look ready."

"I'm not sure what you think I am or am not ready for," I pointed out. I wasn't following this part of Dean's plan at all.

Dean grinned at me. "James, think about it. Why do you think I made sure you had whatever you couldn't live without with you? Haven't you always wanted to be a pirate? I have. Particularly one who can't get caught."

"Yes to the pirate idea. But I have to point out that, laser cannon in my face or not, we've caught this ship."

"You're the only ones, ever," Haadrich said. "Some have tried a tractor beam, but once we make the first jump they tend to think it's a trap and toss all their power to their shields and we take off. Some have tried to attach their cables, but we're always long gone. The few who've tried both have never given up their shields to power their tractor beams. It's not a smart military strategy and most merchants want to keep their cargo more than capture us."

"Most aren't Dean," I said proudly.

He laughed. "That's not why he's my best friend, but it helps. We want to join you. We're not military men by choice, but we're good at it, meaning our knowledge can only help you. You're doing what we want to do. If you let us join your crew and treat us as well as your benefactor treated you—presuming you aren't lying about that relationship—then I'll figure out how to never let someone as smart as me capture this ship ever again."

"That's a strong incentive, but why not just mutiny your own ship and do the same?"

"Most of the crew are loyal to their home planets and the military as well," Dean said. "We're not the Conscripted Criminals Battalion. And if we take the ship, the fleet will come after us with a vengeance. But, more than that—your warp drive is the strongest and fastest I've ever heard of."

"Ah," Haadrich said with a wink, "that's because it's not a warp drive."

A response seemed to be expected and I was clearly the designated straight man. "What is it then?"

"A portal," Haadrich replied with satisfaction.

"A portal to where?" Dean asked.

"Well, that's the issue. The portal works perfectly, every time. But what it doesn't do is allow you to choose a destination. Every jump is a new adventure. You could end up in the middle of a battle—and we have, many times—in the middle of nowhere, in the solar space of a rich planet, next to a fat merchant ship, or any other place you can think of. We've landed on planets and moons without the need to actually land. The portal chooses the final destination and we just go along for the ride."

"What's the risk of landing *in* something?" I asked.

"Nil. This ship has had the portal for almost as long as it's existed and it's still here, in perfect shape." I raised my eyebrow and Haadrich laughed. "We let the outer hull look...used. It helps us in many ways."

"Can you land the ship on a planet manually?" Dean asked.

Haadrich snorted. "Of course we can. And we can fly through space whenever we choose. We're a fully functional ship. And we make repairs and upgrades all the time. We can afford to, as long as we land near a planet with the right technological knowhow."

"What happens when you don't?"

"We jump again," Haadrich said.

"So, this ship's motto is 'if at first you don't succeed, try, try again'?"

Haadrich roared a laugh. "Yes, James, that's right. I don't know who first found the portal nor how they made it work so well with the ship—it was hundreds of years before my old captain had taken over, and he didn't know—but this ship has had someone from every intelligent race in the galaxy in it at one time or another. Adding on another Earthling and a Nitrexton wouldn't be difficult. However, I don't need nor want anyone else from your crew unless they're of the same mindset as you two."

"They're not," I said. "They're good people. Better people than us."

"So, what's your decision?" Dean asked.

Haadrich cocked his head. "How are you going to get your crew to let us leave?"

"Oh, we're going to let James come up with something they'll believe," Dean said cheerfully. "Then they'll release this ship and we'll port off somewhere else. Presumably never to be seen by them again."

Haadrich and I exchanged a look. "Really?" he asked, me more than Dean.

"I don't make these plans," I admitted. "I'm just stuck making them work the way Dean wants them to."

Six Years Later

"Run!" Dean shouted. "Fly! Run or fly as fast as you can!"

No one argued. No one really needed the encouragement, either. When an entire planetary guard is after you, you find the will to move it.

I risked a look over my shoulder. Yep, we had everyone's attention. The natives of Zarlon were an iridescent green with deep blue highlights. They had elongated limbs, short bodies, and flat heads. They looked pretty, but awkward and not all that smart. They were much smarter than they looked and could move much faster than their appearance would lead you to believe. And while they were, technically, not nearly as civilized as many older worlds, they had bows and arrows, and they knew how to use them.

I turned back and focused on staying alive and not losing what we'd come here to steal. All we needed to do was get into our ship. Then we'd be fine. It was too bad our ship was a mile away, though we were eating up the distance as fast as we could. People trying to kill us tended to make our crew intent on escape.

Melissa tripped. Not her fault—there were vines everywhere on this stinking rock. She was ahead of me, so that was good, because it was easy for me to toss the bag I was carrying up to Lissa and grab Melissa as she started to go down. Our combined momentum kept us going, and my balance kept us upright.

Lissa dipped down and grabbed the bag the third triplet, Missy, was carrying. Then Lissa flew off as fast as her wings would carry her, which was faster than the rest of us were running.

Dean passed me and Melissa, caught up to Missy, tossed her over his shoulder, and kept going after Lissa. He had the third bag but you wouldn't know it was heavy, the way he was moving.

"Show offs," I muttered. I only had me and sort of Melissa. I should have been going a lot faster. Then again, of all the things Dean hated—and there were a lot of things—dying was number one on his list.

"We're not representing well, James," Melissa replied as we sped up as much as we could, arrows flying past us, some just missing. But a close miss was far better than being hit.

"Why didn't you choose wings?" I asked as we neared our ship. I wasn't asking so much as complaining. I was clear on why the triplets had each chosen different attributes. Under normal circumstances, I appreciated their diversity.

Lissa was inside the ship and, as Dean and Missy reached it, the engines roared to life. The rule everyone on the *Portalis* lived by was that we all knew how to fly and fix the ship. That had been a rule far longer than any of us had been on the ship.

I flung Melissa ahead of me and onto the gangplank. "Go!" I shouted as I leaped onto it after her.

The gangplank slammed shut—a captain at least three prior to Dean had installed a "fast close" feature and there wasn't a day I didn't appreciate his unsung genius—and I tumbled on top of Melissa. Not a bad place to be, but strapped into a seat was going to be a lot safer.

She and I scrambled up and made our way into the cockpit. Lissa was in the pilot's seat, wings neatly folded against her back, and Dean had copilot. We went airborne, then Missy hit the button that mattered most in our ship.

The portal activated, the blue glow surrounded us, and we left Zarlon and her native population behind us, potentially forever.

We ended up in open space. "We're in the middle of nowhere, space-wise," Dean said. We all breathed a sigh of relief.

"I think it's time we add on more crew," Melissa said. "Captain Haadrich liked to have a minimum of a dozen."

"And Captain Hodos likes to split the take with as few as possible," Dean replied.

"Second in Command for the Rest of His Life Conason would like another body or two. We're richer than I've ever imagined, Dean, and getting richer all the time. Someone staying at the controls means we leave that much faster and ensure that we stay alive to enjoy our riches."

"No," Dean said patiently. "Someone other than the five of us staying at the controls means we're potentially stranded on whatever rock we're at forever."

"I don't know why you're so untrusting," Lissa said. "You didn't betray Captain Haadrich, and he didn't betray the captain before him. In fact, there's never been a deserter, let alone a mutiny, on the *Portalis*. I've checked the records."

"Captain Haadrich would want you to have more help," Missy chimed in.

"And if I could guarantee that we could reach Clonos and get another set of triplets just like the three of you as new crew members, then I'd be all for it. But since that can't be guaranteed, we're just all going to have to resign ourselves to the fact that we haven't met anyone pirate-worthy for a long time and go on about our business."

"You can't get three just like us," Melissa said. "Our pattern is discontinued."

"Figure of speech," Dean replied. "Do we count the takings, eat, rest, or head off again?"

"If you're actually interested in our opinions, I think we can inventory and eat at the same time, and then get going again."

Dean chuckled. "You used to enjoy being in the middle of nowhere in space, James."

"When we were in a military ship, yes. Now? Now I want to be nearer to planets." Planets were dangerous for pirates, but they also had a lot to offer. The *Portalis* was a great ship, but she was small, and there were times I missed being able to walk for an hour and not have circled the halls ten times to do so. We talked, occasionally, about retiring, but Dean was far from ready—he loved the pirate's life.

Dean turned on the autopilot. "Whine later. Let's eat and tally."

We headed to the small dining area and the triplets got food out for all of us. We ate and tallied quickly. "Nice haul," Dean said. "Well done. This should fetch a lot of credits for us somewhere."

The triplets all smiled, showing a lot of teeth. I'd long ago gotten over the weirdness of them all smiling in the exact same way at the exact same time. Frankly, I'd gotten over that before we'd been on the *Portalis* a week—the triplets had all chosen to be attractive to humanoids.

Per the late Haadrich, in the early days of them being a part of the crew, they'd all spoken in unison, too. But they'd stopped that once he'd shown them the benefits of them functioning separately. Three people could steal more than one, after all. And the triplets were nothing if not ideal pirates.

We stored our take from Zarlon in the cargo hold. "We're pretty full," I said as we headed back to the cockpit. "I hope we get to a planet where we can deal some of this stuff out of our ship."

Dean clapped my shoulder. "I have a great feeling about wherever we're going next."

"Why?"

"We're due for a great payday." He took the pilot's seat and I took co-pilot. Melissa took the navigator's position, Lissa took records retrieval, and Missy took her official seat—the telepath's chair.

Lissa had chosen the ability to fly anywhere and Melissa the ability to turn into, essentially, a mermaid, but Missy had chosen the far more taxing attribute. Clonos handed out telepathy sparingly, and only after a clone had proven him- or herself to be able to handle the inundation of thoughts and emotions. Missy was one of the strongest Clonos had ever created. That she had chosen to become a pirate along with her sisters said, to me, a lot about what thoughts and emotions of a lot of sentient races all over the galaxy had shown her.

"I hope we find a water planet," Melissa said. "I haven't been useful for too long."

"You're always useful," Dean said. "All three of you are exactly what Haadrich said you were—the best crew any captain could hope to have."

The triplets all giggled as Dean hit the button and the blue glow of the portal washed over us. I blinked and we were no longer in unoccupied space.

We were near a planet, a water planet, as Melissa had hoped. "I wish you'd also requested that the solar space we landed in not be filled with warships."

We'd landed right in the middle of a battle. And I recognized one of the ships just as Missy gasped. "It's your old ship!"

Sure enough, the *Victorious 3310* was here. It was also surrounded by both Alliance Military ships and enemy ships. I'd have said the *Victorious* was trying a Hodos Maneuver only all the ships, Alliance and enemy, were firing at it as much as they were firing at each other.

"Ship is hailing us," Melissa said. "Accept?"

"No," Dean said, as his hand moved toward the portal button.

I grabbed it. "Yes, we answer. They were our friends and our crew. We don't leave them here like this."

"We've left them once already," Dean pointed out.

"They weren't in danger."

"This is Acting Captain Barnett of the *Victorious Thirty-Three-Ten*, formerly of the Alliance Military. We want to speak to Dean Hodos or James Conason, who were kidnapped by you six years ago."

"I have not opened the channel from us to them," Melissa said.

"Acting Captain," Dean mused. "He hasn't accepted full command, even though we've been gone for years."

"I told you that they'd get the wrong idea." I said.

"You just sell things too well."

I'd told our old command crew that Dean and I had complete control of the *Portalis* and that they could remove the cables and beams and Dean had confirmed it with Barnett using a variety of signs and countersigns we'd always ensured our command crews memorized. The moment we were free, Haadrich had hit the portal button and we'd disappeared, never to worry about the *Victorious* again.

Until now.

"They searched for us," I said, as Barnett repeated his hail, over and over. "They deserted the fleet to search for us." I still had hold of Dean's hand, just in case. "They gave up their military careers to try to find us. And they did that because they loved you as their captain, Dean."

"This is true," Missy said. "I am accessing those in the ship. They are frightened, because their ship is in danger of being destroyed, but they are all hopeful that they've found the two of you. I sense no dissent among those on board in regard to this—they want to find the two of you and be reunited."

"Well, we did want more crew members," Lissa said calmly.

"The *Victorious* has a battalion of a thousand people, give or take," Dean said. "That's a lot more crew than this ship can handle. The smart thing, the *pirate* thing, would be to port out of here and not think about this or them now or later."

"I refuse to leave them again," I said, so strongly that it surprised me. "I will not leave those people here, surrounded by the enemy and their former comrades, when they're in this situation *because* of us." I looked at Dean. "And if you try to leave them, then I will be the first to mutiny in the history of this ship."

Dean stared at me for a few long seconds. Then he smiled gently. "No fear, old friend." He pulled his hand gently out of my grasp. "We'll fix it."

"How?" Lissa asked flatly. "Even with all the enhancements the ship has, we cannot destroy all the military ships in front of us. It would take several lucky shots to destroy more than two of them, and the only one I feel confident we could destroy is the smallest, which happens to be the *Victorious*."

Dean barked out a laugh. "I love how you think, Lissa. Melissa, open hail from our side."

"What are you going to do?" I asked.

Dean grinned. "Trust me."

"Open," Melissa said.

"Barnett, this is Captain Dean Hodos of the *Portalis*. We've missed you. And, while I'd love to catch up, we can see that the *Victorious* is in trouble. So, we can talk or we can get out of here. Your choice. My suggestion is get out of here. To that end, open your cargo bay doors, we're going to fly up and inside."

"Ah...Dean?" Barnett sounded shocked and confused. It was hard to blame him.

"Yes. James is here, too. We don't have time for the signs and countersigns. Well, *we* do, but you don't. Open the bay doors. Now." Dean sounded like he was in command of the *Victorious* again. He hadn't sounded like this for six years. I'd kind of missed it.

"Yes, sir," Barnett said. "We'll have to drop shields, though, for you to enter." The cargo bay doors began to open.

"I'll give you the order when," I said. "And when to put them back up."

"As you say, Ex-O." Barnett sounded crisp and ready, just as he had when we were on the bridge.

We flew though the ships, our shields on high, Dean dodging ships and laser fire both, which is even harder than it sounds.

But the *Portalis* was small and extremely maneuverable and, as pirates, we'd really learned a lot about how to stay alive when we had to be in a battle versus port out of it.

Meanwhile, Lissa and Missy moved to weapons, firing randomly but accurately. As expected, we didn't blow up anyone, but we did cause some issues for the ships nearest to the *Victorious*.

We were close and getting closer. "Drop shields now."

"Shields down," Barnett said.

Dean hit the turbo and we zoomed towards the cargo hold. Then he hit the brakes, hard, and steered us in as we slowed. I knew this ship and her shields range. "We're through, shields up!"

We saw the shields go back around the ship even before Barnett shared they'd been activated.

We were still floating into the cargo hold. "We're in," Dean said, even though we weren't fully through. "Close the cargo doors."

The closing doors knocked against us, sending the *Portalis* up. We hit against the top of the cargo hold.

"Barnett, I hope this works," Dean said. "If it doesn't, we'll find you again. Somehow." With that he hit the portal button.

The blue light washed over us and in the blink of an eye... we were still inside the *Victorious*. "Barnett, what do you see?" I asked.

"We're between a small water planet and a gas giant," Barnett said. "And we're alone." We could hear cheering in the background.

Dean settled the *Portalis* on the floor of the cargo hold, then turned to look at the rest of us. "I hope you're all happy. Now what?"

"The rest of us wanted more crew," Missy said calmly. "We now have more crew than we've ever imagined. And, after all this time, all they want is to be your crew again, Dean. They will join us in pirating gladly—they're considered deserters. They've lost all love for the military, because the military didn't care about what had happened to the two of you, which is why they went rogue. Any dissenters have been gone for at least five years."

"That means the take is now divided by a thousand instead of five," Dean said flatly.

"We can afford it," I said. "They're used to a military hierarchy—your take and the take of the lowest rankers won't be the same, just as it wasn't the same when we were in the service. They'll accept it."

"Gladly," Missy added. "They've had much hardship since you left."

"What about resentment?" Dean asked.

Missy shrugged. "I imagine a good meal and a piece each out of our massive store of treasure in the cargo hold will help with that. I told you, the dissenters are long gone. They want to be with *you*, Dean, under your leadership, period."

"We also now have a second ship," Lissa pointed out. "I'm sure that my sisters and I will learn how to fly it in short order."

"A second ship that can only port if *this* ship is inside of it," Dean pointed out. "That's really going to cramp our style."

I laughed. "You'll make it work, Dean. I have faith in you."

"And so do they," Missy said.

Dean heaved a dramatic sigh. "Fine. Let's get the reunion going."

"Anything you say, Commodore."

He stared at me. "What?"

I grinned. "You now command two ships and, if I'm a betting man—and part of why I'm here is that I definitely am—I expect us to start adding on ships sooner as opposed to later. It's good military strategy, isn't it?"

Dean grinned back at me. "And here I thought you were only a pirate because I'd dragged you into it. Let's get our plan to take over the galaxy going, Captain Conason of the *Portalis*."

"Whatever you said, Dean, like always."

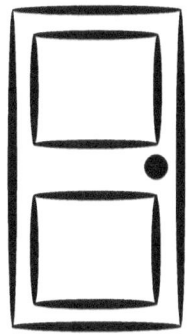

Doorways in the Sand

Violette Malan

Parno Lionsmane was used to people looking, perhaps even staring, at his Partner Dhulyn Wolfshead. Her unusual pallor—the most the sun could do was give her skin an ivory tone—and her hair, the color of old blood, marked her as a Red Horseman from the snow-covered plains of the south. Add to this the blue and green of her Mercenary Badge, tattooed across her temples and above her ears, and she drew plenty of respectful attention.

Dhulyn would have been the most interesting thing in the chop house, if it weren't for the Cloudman sitting in the far corner, his Racha bird pacing up and down his table. He looked up from his roast lamb as Dhulyn and Parno neared him, and inclined his head. The seven feathers tattooed like a bird's wing on his left cheek looked green in the sunlight coming through a nearby window.

"I greet you, Wolfshead, Lionsmane." The Racha watched them with her head tilted to one side, lifting her wings as if about to launch herself into the air. "I am Faxot of Licante, this is Mista." The bird nodded at them when he spoke her name.

The Cloud had arranged his table so that he sat with his back to the corner, allowing Dhulyn and Parno to sit next to him but with their backs against a wall. Mista moved to perch on the back of Faxot's chair to leave them room.

"You have asked the Mercenary House to send for us," Dhulyn said. "What do you need?"

"We have found a demon," Faxot said. "A group of mountain people live in a valley far to the east of our home territory, nearer the sea and north of Fenidor. Ten days ago a group of young people on their first hunt were passing near the valley, and encountered three small children, starving, their clothes in rags, running from it.

"The children said that when the demon came their elders began to quarrel among themselves, lashing out in strange rages. Finally they were struck with despair and fear, unable to act in their own defense."

Parno glanced at his Partner but she was giving the serving girl their order. The Racha watched her almost without blinking.

"The Cloud leading the hunt sent her Racha to investigate, and he found the village abandoned, some houses burnt from neglected fires. Some bodies." He leaned forward, lightly tapping the table top with his index finger, as if beating time to music no one else heard. "For the sake of the Clans living in the mountain valleys, we tracked this thing. Our Racha birds sighted it, heading for the shore."

Dhulyn leaned back in her seat, arms crossed. "I can see why you would send to the Mercenary House, but why ask for us in particular?"

"Because we are told that you have passed through the Path of the Sun, and so you have experience of other worlds. The demon has passed through such a portal. He may do so again. Perhaps in a place where there are no Clouds or no Mercenary Brothers to act."

"Where is this portal?"

"We followed him, my Mista and I, to a dark place on the shore where there is a doorway, just a doorway, standing upright in the salt dunes. He took on the shape of a man and passed through the door into a kind of large box, and attempted to draw shut a metal door that folded on itself one piece behind the other."

Parno glanced at Dhulyn. They had seen doors that operated in this fashion—but not in this world.

Dhulyn rested the finger tips of her left hand on the table. "You say attempted?"

The bird nodded, shifted and then resettled its wings. At that moment the server brought Dhulyn and Parno two bowls of stew, two mugs of cider, and a plate of bread. She also set a small plate of meat scraps on the table, smiling at the Racha.

"When she saw what was happening Mista grasped the metal door's view grill in her talons, pulling the door open against the force of the being attempting to close it. He did, however, manage to close an inner gate, also metal, also folding on itself but this one in the manner of scissors. This gate he pulled downwards from the top of the box, there was movement and noise, and the being was gone."

"Were you then able to open the metal door?"

"We were, the door and the inner gate both, but our quarry had fled. Within was only a small windowless room. We tried to enter, but Mista could not."

Dhulyn addressed the Racha directly. "Can you tell us why?"

The Cloud spoke after a moment of silent consultation with Mista. "She says there is no, no ground inside the box. That she cannot tell which way is up, and therefore she cannot fly. Where she cannot go, I cannot go."

Parno glanced at Dhulyn and knew why she smiled. If people could solve their own problems there would be less work for the Brotherhood.

* * *

The next morning Faxot took them out to the shore and the doorway. Dhulyn gave her Partner a nod. It matched exactly what she had previously Seen in a Vision. They were right to come here. Until now she had not been sure. She walked around the portal and it was exactly as the Cloud had described it. "It's no artifact of the Caids," she called out. "It shows no sign of great age, as the Caid ruins do." There being nothing but rock, sand, and salt grass behind the artifact, Dhulyn rejoined Parno, only to find him with a familiar faraway look on his face. His amber eyes squinted into the far distance, unfocused. His mouth just beginning to smile.

"What does he listen to?" Both Racha and Cloud had their heads tilted to one side.

"How do you know he listens?"

"Mista can hear something. Almost I can as well."

"He speaks mind to mind with the Crayx, ancient sea creatures of the Long Ocean who accompany the Ocean Nomads on their journeys. A pod must be close."

Mista launched herself from Faxot's shoulder, rising in slow circles through the air above them.

"Mista says she sees a sail, far off there to the east."

"Just so."

"Do you not hear them as well?"

"It's not a thing of the Brotherhood." She'd long since come to terms with that. "Certain people have the pod sense, most do not. Just as certain people can bond with a Racha..."

"And most cannot."

Dhulyn touched her Partner on the back of his wrist. He turned from looking out to sea and when his eyes refocused on her face, his smile widened. "They send their love," he said.

She laughed aloud before she could stop herself. "I'm sure that is not exactly how they put it," she said, "but I appreciate the sentiment."

The Racha called from far above them. Faxot looked upward in response. "She is impatient," he said. "I have given my message. If I am not needed further here, I *am* needed elsewhere. I am honored to have met you."

They touched their foreheads in salute as Faxot walked away to the south, Mista riding the winds above him.

Dhulyn turned and tapped a section of the metal door with a finger tip. "While I have never seen a door like this before, I will wager my second-best sword that this must be the latch."

"Are you waiting for *me* to open it?"

She raised her eyes, calling on the Sun to witness what she had to put up with, and moved the small lever with the same fingertip. The door slid to one side and disappeared, revealing the metal gate Faxot had described. Behind it was a dark shaft, and a clanging sound.

"Something rises." Dhulyn stepped back and two paces to one side, unslinging her bow from where it hung across her back, and fitting an arrow. Parno drew his sword, and set himself to the other side. They relaxed when the wooden box proved to be empty. Dhulyn lowered her bow, but did not unstring it. "Shall we?"

Parno grinned at her. "In battle," he said.

"Or in death."

Together they stepped into the box.

* * *

Back in the day—far back as it happened—there had been a hole to hell in the furnace room of the Elysian Fields Guest House. Mark Slawter and a few others like him had come out of it to have a taste of the world. He'd come back from a little hunting and gathering, as it were, only to find the hole sealed. Sure, he could have gone home then, the seal only stopped things from coming out, not going back in, but he'd figured there was no hurry. When he discovered the elevator that led to other worlds, he'd used it to put even more distance between himself and those greater ones he technically answered to.

Now there was nothing in the furnace room, no seal, and no hole to hell. No hole to anywhere. Nothing but rough bedrock floor. And the furnace.

His first thought was to return to that other world. There'd been easy pickings for a long time, but it had started getting harder for him to make a living. As it were. And there were Mercenaries to avoid.

"Not so bad," he reminded himself. The Brotherhood was limited to human speeds and modes of transportation. Any demon could outrun any horse. Or any arrow, for that matter.

Then came the stupid Clouds. Once they'd found him it was plain to see his life of ease would be over. Stupid Racha. No one liked being spied on from the air. That's why he'd decided to come back. So here he was, ready to come home, only, well, how could he?

Part of him was almost relieved. He hadn't *really* been looking forward to going home and explaining himself. Those greater than he could, and probably would, have made life pretty hot for him, and for long enough to feel like an eternity. *This* world wasn't so bad a place for someone like him. Nowadays the people here were so sure his kind didn't exist that all he had to do was maintain a low profile, and he'd be fine. He could even thrive here.

The stupid human who ran the place was completely taken in by his disguise, and accepted his money without any suspicions at all. Stupid. He'd gone out to see what had changed in the neighbourhood—and most important, whether the hospital was still nearby. Hospitals meant plenty of fear and anger and despair to feed on.

And, there it was. Just where he'd expected it. He slowed down to let two cars go by before he crossed the street. Wow. His smile grew so big he almost lost control of his shape. The hospital had gotten *huge*. Hundreds, maybe thousands of people. This could work out. This could be perfect. He wouldn't have to take over and control a whole village to feed from, moving on when he'd sucked them empty. In the hospital, between the staff and the patients, food was just lying around for the taking.

"With a fresh supply everyday."

* * *

The box shuddered as it sank. Through the gate they saw floor joists, and occasional streaks of light, but the box did not stop until they had passed several other openings. When it finally came to rest, they pushed the gate upward and unlatched the doors.

In front of them was a large, spotlessly clean room, with two windows near the ceiling. A stairwell along to their left led upwards. Against the other walls were two wooden doors of normal size, and what were clearly cupboards and clothes-presses. In the remaining wall hung a large metal door painted turquoise.

"There." Dhulyn pointed to marks on the floor. She stepped out and to one side of the opening, and motioned Parno to the other side, signalling him to stand still. She inched alongside the prints, her head tilted to one side to catch what light there was. The marks headed directly toward the turquoise door.

"What are you after doing?" A young man's voice came from the stairwell, and following it, a young man.

Parno stood ready, sword in hand. Dhulyn glanced up from where she squatted next to the trail. At the foot of the stairs stood a well-muscled, dark-haired young man who had seen his birth moon perhaps twenty times. He started as he caught sight of Parno, and she watched his eyes as he took in their height, their Mercenary Badges. Their weapons. Dhulyn did her best not to look dangerous.

The young man relaxed with a sharp nod when Parno lowered his blade. Strangers did tend to find him more reassuring. The expression on the young man's face showed only curiosity, no fear.

"Following the footprints here." Dhulyn tapped on the floor in answer to his question, signalling Parno with her left thumb.

"Footprints? I'll get a mop."

Parno was across the room, with a firm grip on the boy's elbow, even before Dhulyn held up her hand. "Wait one moment please." She followed the prints to the heavy metal door, and stood to one side, bow raised. She gestured to Parno and he pulled the door open.

"What do you see?" he asked her.

Dhulyn tilted her head to get a different angle on the marks. "The prints enter, descend nine steps, then turn round and come out again. As they cross the threshold, they grow larger, and change in shape, becoming more like goat prints. They change back as they return." She straightened and turned to the young man who was now hovering at Parno's elbow. "Was there once something dangerous in this room?"

The young man nodded, but said nothing more.

"What is this place?" Dhulyn asked him. She grinned as she realized they were both speaking the same language—though what language it was she couldn't say. This must be some quality of the portal itself. She stopped smiling when she saw the young man had leaned away from her.

"Elysian Fields Guest House." He turned his eyes from her face and frowned, looking into the room with eyebrows drawn down.

"An inn?"

He nodded again.

"I am Dhulyn Wolfshead, called the Scholar. I fight with my Brother, Parno Lionsmane, called the Chanter. We are of the Mercenary Brotherhood," she added when the young man did not react.

"Dean McIssac." He wiped his hand off on his trousers and held it out. Dhulyn watched it with interest. This must be a strange world indeed if unarmed men gave their empty hands to armed strangers. She touched her forehead with the fingers of her left hand and saw Parno do the same.

Flushing slightly, Dean raised his extended hand to his own forehead. "Did you, uh...come out of the elevator?" He gestured toward the moving box.

"The *elevator*? A reasonable name for it. Yes, we did. The elevator opens into another world and..." she stopped as Dean held up both hands.

"Oh I know about the other worlds," he said. "I just didn't know things—I mean people—I didn't know people could come out."

"Other *worlds*. I see. Did something—or someone," Dhulyn changed at a signal from Parno, "come out of the elevator in the last few days? Or a new guest arrive?" she added when Dean shook his head.

"Sure, there were two, but the last one was over a week ago. I signed them in. Claire's away so..." he trailed off, looking from one to the other.

"It's possible that time moves differently in our world," Parno said. "We are looking for someone. Could be one of these very people."

"Um, would you be after wanting a room then?"

"Is our money good?" Dhulyn tugged their coin pouch loose from her belt and opened it, shaking a few silvers, some coppers and a gold out into her hand. Mercenaries often traded service for service, but there was no time for that here.

"Probably. Come upstairs and we'll see what the front desk makes of it."

Glancing at Parno she saw her Partner was just as confused as she. Nevertheless they followed Dean up one flight of stairs and down a short hallway to a place where the space widened and led to an outside door, thick, wooden, and with a large window in the top half. A safe world indeed. Dhulyn looked around her but there did not appear to be a bar, nor tables, and little smell of food.

"What is *this* strange stuff?" She traced her fingers along the nearest patterned wall. "The wall covering. It is more than paint."

"Uh, that's wallpaper," the young man said.

"*Paper*?" Dhulyn set her hand on the wall again. "You must be very rich indeed."

"I guess. Here we go," Dean stepped behind a raised counter. "Set your money down here."

They put their coins down on the "front desk" whereupon the money turned into intricately coloured rectangles of something too stiff to fold like paper, but Dean seemed satisfied.

"Okay. Sign—*can* you sign?"

"I am not called the Scholar for nothing." She said, giving him a gentle smile. "Both of us can read and write, though perhaps not..." she looked at the book he had turned to face her. Each page held columns, some headed "Name," and some "Signature," and one "Print." Under this in rows were signatures, and numbers. A ledger. She tapped the last name.

"Mark Slawter." She said aloud. "Have I pronounced it properly?"

"It's not uncommon," Dean said. "I played hockey with a guy named Teddy Slaughter. Different spelling, but still. Makes you wonder if there was a butcher or someone way back in his family."

"An ill-omened and yet appropriate name." Dhulyn decided not to ask what hockey was.

"I guess." Dean leaned forward enough to pass them a key and directed them to the stairs. "Um, don't take the elevator," he added.

Dhulyn smiled and touched her forehead in salute as she turned away.

The key unlocked a wooden door into a square room with one large bed, a chest of drawers surmounted by a mirror as good as any found in a Caid ruin, and two wooden chairs with padded arms and seats. Dhulyn slipped off sword, belt, and harness, and threw herself on the bed. Which immediately bounced her back on her feet. Laughing, she turned to her Partner.

"Let me try," he said.

When they had finally finished playing with the bed and regained their breaths they lay down side by side.

"It's clear our Mercenary Badges didn't mean anything to him."

"We've been in other places where the Brotherhood was not known. You also saw that he was not particularly frightened of us. Startled, but not frightened."

"Which tells us something about this place."

"Or something about the young man."

* * *

Everything outside their window was covered with snow sparkling in the late afternoon sun. It was so cold their breath fogged on the clear glass. The inn sat at a crossroads, with a wide thoroughfare passing in front, a smaller one to the side, and an open field across the street dotted with random leafless trees. The crossroads itself was marked off with tall poles carrying large lights of green, yellow, and red, which changed in a sequential pattern.

"The lights control the passage of the vehicles," Parno pointed out.

Dhulyn rubbed the fog of her breath from the window. "They move slowly enough," she said, "that I would not have thought such control necessary."

"Mage's work, do you think?"

Dhulyn shook her head. "In their general usefulness, the lights seem more akin to what we once saw in cities of the Caids. But this house," she stamped her foot on the wooden floor. "This place has magic in it." She stepped back from the window. "Come. Let's see if we can find our quarry's footprints in the snow."

They made it only as far as the front desk.

"Wait now, you can't be carrying those swords on the street, eh. I mean, the police are sure to stop you and they won't, you know, understand your explanations."

"People go about unarmed? Outside?" Dhulyn sounded ready to laugh, but Parno could tell Dean was serious.

The young man nodded. "Your clothes are all right, more or less—at least, with the university so close by you could be foreign students."

"There is a Scholar's House nearby?"

"I guess you could call it that. Your tattoos are okay, people might stop you to admire them but that shouldn't be much of a problem. But, uh," he gestured at Dhulyn's bare arms. "Are you after being warm enough?"

"It would have to be colder than this to bother my Partner."

"Do you mind if people stare at you? Because they will if you're after going about with bare arms in the middle of winter. I could find a couple of parkas for you. People leave things behind."

* * *

The walkway in front of the inn led down to the street they had seen from their window. That and a similar stone path across the front of the building had been cleared of snow. Dhulyn suspected the hand of their meticulous host. The snow had melted on much of the black surface of the road, though it was still thick around the house and on the plantings that framed the front door.

"Where to?"

Dhulyn looked up and down the street. To the right were more buildings like the inn in character. To the left, on the far side of another set of lights, were much taller buildings, with an impossible number of windows for any place outside of the Caids' own cities.

"A large building like that would be full of people," Parno said.

"As many people as a mountain village," Dhulyn agreed. "Perhaps more. Just what the demon would want. Come."

As she stepped off the walkway she felt a tug at her belt, a swirl of air, saw snow spinning around her, a face, mouth rounded in horror, behind the glass of the carriage as it missed her. In another breath it was gone.

Dhulyn inhaled deeply and exhaled slowly. "The horseless carts seemed so slow from up above," she said. "I thought it surely too far away to harm me."

"We must be more careful."

"Evidently."

Once she was sure her heartbeat and breathing had returned to normal, Dhulyn signalled that she was ready to continue. Fortunately, as the walkways around the inn were not nearly as clean as those Dean had charge of, there were footprints aplenty to be examined. Careful as they were, however, Dhulyn could not see anything familiar in the foot marks they found. As the sun began to set, lights fastened atop of poles lining the streets brightened, and the trees in the area across the street sparkled with tiny spots of bright colour.

"Do you see what I see?" Parno asked, indicating a dark well of shadow between two hedges.

"This light is not that of Mother Sun or Father Moon. The illumination of the streets only serves to make dark corners darker, and destroy night vision."

"Could we become accustomed to it?"

Dhulyn shrugged in her unfamiliar coat. It did not smell properly, and she could tell that there were no natural fibres in it. "I would prefer that we catch the demon before that happens."

Though they carefully knocked excess snow from their feet, they discovered a mat inside the front door where people had evidently taken their boots off rather than track melting snow throughout the house. Once again Dhulyn shrugged. She pulled off her boots, but neither she nor Parno left them sitting on the mat. Between the lock picks, strangling cords and short knives hidden in the soles and fastenings of their boots, they were too dangerous to leave lying about.

They had climbed the stairs as far as the first floor when Parno glanced out the landing window and stopped.

"Dhulyn." Parno touched her forearm with his fingertips. "Who is that?"

Dhulyn leaned on the sill of the window, glad for the warmth of her Partner's shoulder against hers. "It is Dean, our host, speaking to another. From the way they stand together I would assume this is the 'Claire' he's spoken of."

"Yes, but—"

"Dean is the one who appears to be wearing armour, brightly shined, almost too bright to look at." As she spoke Dean kissed the woman and set off down the walkway. The woman turned to enter the inn. "His Claire is perhaps better armed, but wears what seems like a uniform, too elegant for a man-at-arms, more like a Steward of Walls."

"So she has the security of the house in her hands?"

"Oh she'd be *thrilled* to hear that."

Dhulyn turned, her hand on the handle of the small ax concealed against her spine under her vest. She did not relax when all she saw was a black and white cat sitting with its tail wrapped tidily around its toes.

"Greetings small warrior."

"What no exclamations? Not impressed by a talking cat?"

Dhulyn looked at Parno. He shrugged. "Well, talking *aloud*, that I confess is new to us."

There was no way to be sure, but Dhulyn would have bet her second-best sword the cat was offended.

"Tell me." She tapped the glass. "Do all the windows of this inn show one's true nature, or just this one?"

"Figured out that much on your own, have you? Tell you what, I'll answer that question and two others if you sneak me five sausages from the kitchen."

Dhulyn could feel Parno stifling a laugh. "One sausage," she said.

"Three."

"Done. Will the window show us everyone's true nature, or just that of your...humans." In the last possible moment Dhulyn stopped herself from saying "masters."

"It shows you everybody's true nature," the cat said. "You should see what I look like."

"And do all the inn's windows do this?"

"That's the second question. No, but it's probably why you got a room on this floor."

"Marvelous. We would only need to watch from here to know which guest is our target."

"Austin!" A smooth clear voice from down the stairs.

"That's my cue," the cat said, standing and arching his back. "Don't forget, three sausages." He ran quickly to the top of the stairs, but slowed to a dignified saunter, presumably when in sight of Claire.

"If Claire is this world's equivalent of a Steward of Walls, better we don't cross her path. She'd find it necessary to learn our business."

Parno waited, watching the streets outside, while Dhulyn ran down to the kitchen for their suppers. At least the street lighting was good for one thing: the walkways around the house were all well lit.

As the evening grew later, two people left the inn, and while neither was exactly human, neither was the quarry they sought. Finally, as full darkness set in, as much as it could with the artificial illumination, the demon made his appearance. Dhulyn dashed down the hall in time to see the beast's human disguise through the plain glass of their bedroom window.

Now that they knew whose prints to follow, the snow and slush on the sidewalks would make tracking the demon called Mark Slawter straightforward.

"Though we could kill him in his room," Parno suggested. "Now that we know his human shape."

"And when he returns to his demon shape? What then? Dean and his Claire will be left to cope with a body they cannot explain, which will not rot—and before you say it, they cannot bury it, the ground is frozen."

"I wasn't going to say that. I was going to ask if the lake was completely frozen."

She gave him the smile she used only for him. "My heart, this is why we are Partners."

He grinned back. "I knew there was a reason." He looked out again at the walkway. "If we follow him tonight, we may find a good place to kill him."

They let the demon proceed along the road a pace, then followed as he crossed the street to walk along the edge of what they now knew was a park. He stayed on King Street and headed straight for the hospital—like a Healers House, if Healers had Houses. There the demon calling itself Mark Slawter passed under a ramp and through a set of glass doors that parted and slid open of their own volition.

They left him time to pass further within the building and entered after him.

"Excuse me, this is *not* a public area. If you're here to visit someone you need to use the other entrance."

They touched their foreheads to a woman dressed in loose pink trousers and tunic.

"How does Mark Slawter get further into the building?" Dhulyn wondered once they were outside again.

"Changes his shape again perhaps," Parno said, looking around with his hands in the pockets of his parka. "This patch of darkness here, under the ramp, is the perfect place for an ambush." He looked at his Partner out of the corner of his eye. "Do it now?"

Dhulyn shook her head, narrowing her eyes as if against glare. "We cannot know he'll return this way. But we *do* know that evil is careless and predictable. You'll see, he'll take this same path again tomorrow night, and we will catch him then, on his way in. One of us here in position early—"

"By which you mean you."

Dhulyn grinned and continued as if she hadn't been interrupted. "The other following him." She looked around, finger tips tapping the spot on her hip where her dagger should hang. "And there." She pointed south, to the lake. "There is where we'll take the body."

Their plan was fully formed by the time they returned the short distance to the inn. Parno rubbed his hands together, blowing on them, but Dhulyn hadn't even closed the fastenings on her jacket.

"Can we trust the cat to keep his humans occupied?" she said.

"We've only given him two sausages so far. He'll be our ally so long as he expects the third."

* * *

The two new guests had the unmistakeable smell of the other world on them, so Mark would have known them even without the tell-tale Mercenary Badges. No wonder they didn't have any trouble following him, even though his footprints changed with every new shape he tried. Mercenaries were known to be among the best trackers in the world he'd just left. What they didn't know was that he was watching them just as carefully as they were watching him.

"Good tracker doesn't equal smart."

Tonight he watched from a darkened room on the second floor of the hospital as they went in and came out of the emergency entrance and stood standing around and gesturing like idiots. He'd separate them and do the female first. She was smaller, and not doing as well in adapting to this world as her partner. He'd already seen her step off the edge of the sidewalk and stumble, not realizing the edge was there under the snow. Now she was *so* cautious when crossing the street it was almost funny. She shied away from the vehicles passing and didn't even seem aware she was doing it.

He'd wait to do the man. He'd be able to play on his guilt, and the worry, and the grief, and the loneliness. Why, he could feed from him for weeks.

They were so far off their game he wouldn't have any trouble. And without swords or bows, just how dangerous could they be? This world's weapons, supposing they could even get their hands on some, wouldn't be a danger to him. The cold couldn't bother him, but it would slow them down more than enough to put them right into his hands.

They'd see the ramp of the emergency room as the best place to set a trap. The trick was to spring it before they knew he was on to them.

This time tomorrow would be perfect.

* * *

The next night he left the inn earlier than usual, and instead of going immediately through the doors to the buffet of fear and agony and anger that waited for him inside, Mark Slawter hid himself off to one side, where the bright overhead lights actually created a deep patch of shadow.

And there she was, right on schedule. He was starting to wonder where Mercenary Brothers got their reputations, considering how predictable they were being right now. Of course, they probably weren't used to dealing with demons. Humans were pretty stupid, no matter what world you were in.

He let himself be just another piece of darkness, allowed her to get even with his hiding spot, clubbed her down with a scaled fist just as she was about to walk past him. She fell into his arms and he slung her over his shoulder. He ran—too fast for the human eye to follow—down the driveway, across the street, through the employees' parking lot and out onto the ice of Lake Ontario.

* * *

In order to trick the demon, Dhulyn had moved her head in the last possible moment and taken the blow at an angle that only left her momentarily stunned, not unconscious as the demon thought. Her collapse was so convincing, it would not occur to him that she was not in fact knocked out. She hung over his shoulder limp as a wet rag, telling herself she was not surprised at the thing's speed. Not even the ice of the lake slowed him down. In fact, its roughness likely gave him traction.

Nor did she let his speed worry her. Parno would be a few more minutes behind him, perhaps, but it would make no difference to the outcome. She was telling herself this when the demon heaved her off his shoulder and into the freezing water at the edge of the ice.

* * *

Parno had never found running on ice or snow very easy. Snow was Dhulyn's element far more than his. She'd been taken from her tribe of Red Horsemen as a child, but her bones remembered the snow, ice and wind of the southern plains.

He wasn't prepared for the demon's speed. There were *shoras* that improved balance, and eased breathing, increasing the amount of air reaching the lungs, but no amount of training could help him run any faster than his own top speed.

And he felt the emptiness of his hands, missed the weight of his sword.

The thing was ready for him. Standing braced and larger than his human shape in front of a vast jagged hole in the ice, faint mist hovering above and around it, as the relative warmth of the water met the cold of the air.

Not that the water was warm. Parno's heart began to pound stiffly in his chest. He shifted around until he was downwind from it. The demon smelt differently now too. Sulphur. The ash of diseased trees.

Where was Dhulyn? As if he'd heard Parno's thoughts, the demon answered.

"You're too late, moron. She's frozen and drowned while you took too long getting here." It gestured behind itself at the steaming hole. "Could you have saved her if you were faster? Maybe. You'll never know now."

Parno shrugged his coat open. She wasn't dead. Not yet. They were Partnered, he'd know. Wouldn't he? "So now I'm supposed to be so overcome with guilt and remorse and self-loathing that you can kill me as well? That's a bit naïve of you, isn't it?" This thing stood between him and his Partner. He had to kill it quickly and get her out of the water.

"Not naïve enough to fall for that. I am the greatest evil you've ever met."

"Oh sugarplum, you're not even the greatest evil I've met in the last moon."

"Really? Well I've killed your partner, and now I'm going to kill you."

"When? So far you're just talking and I'm still alive." Parno hooked his thumbs into his belt and shook his head in great pity. "Evil. Huh. You're so predictable, you've no imagination at all." He tilted his head as if in speculation. This was taking too long. "Who knows? Maybe you *can* kill me. What you can't do is make me frightened of dying. We're all going to die sometime. Even you." *Lure him out to the ice I said. What could go wrong?*

"That's where you're wrong. You can't kill me because—"

A shape surged from the water, two familiar hands grabbed the demon by the ankles and yanked his feet backward, pitching him forward. Parno ripped a strangling wire out of his belt, pulled his hands apart and wrapped it around the demon's throat. The beast clawed at Parno's forearms, tearing the sleeves of the borrowed parka, but Parno only pulled harder, the wire cutting deeper and deeper into the demon's neck. What came out of the wound wasn't blood, exactly.

The thing went limp.

"Don't stop," Dhulyn coughed out as she rolled herself onto the ice. She had shed her coat and boots, and her normal pallor had taken on a bluish tinge.

"Teach your grandmother," Parno grunted through clenched teeth. One last tug and the wire cut through the bone and vertebra, and the head rolled away from the body, splashing into the opening in the ice. In a moment the body followed. Parno dropped the strangling wire, but the loop, covered with something not quite blood, didn't freeze to the ice.

"Ah, do you want your wire back?"

"No, thank you."

Parno pulled Dhulyn into his arms, shifting her as he stripped off his coat and wrapped it around her and began chafing her arms and legs, working his way down to feet and hands. "Don't tell me," he said. "The shaman of your tribe bathed in freezing water every day before breakfast."

"Twice," she said, her lips trying to form a smile. "Though the Sleeping Bear Shora was actually more helpful."

"You must teach it to me. Can you run?" he said.

"I will have to. Dry my feet first." Now that the job was done, she began to shiver with the cold.

Her pace was stiff and slow to begin with, but with Parno's arm around her she began to run faster. Or as fast as a person shivering so hard could be expected to move. Injury and sickness he had dealt with—fairly straightforward in a world where Healers existed—but Dhulyn had never been cold before.

"Shall I carry you?"

"I'll freeze."

He wasted no more time talking, but increased their pace. She leaned on him more and more. Luckily once off the ice they weren't far from the inn. When he finally half-dragged her into the door the lobby's heat was almost staggering.

"Stop dripping on the cat," said a voice from around his ankles. "I'm old you know."

"I'll go get the bath running." Dean was gone almost before Parno knew he was present.

Dhulyn murmured in Parno's ear as he lifted her. "Warm," he called to the boy. "Not hot."

"Teach your grandmother" floated down from the upper floor.

Parno raised his eyebrows.

* * *

"How are you after getting home?" Dean asked. "You know the elevator won't necessarily be opening to your world when you want it to."

"Then we'll try every place, over and over, until we find our own."

Dhulyn found standing on what she suspected were frost-bitten toes marginally easier than walking on them. The shaman of the Red Horsemen had always taken care of anyone unlucky enough to be harmed by the cold through necessity, as she had been. The merely careless were left to themselves. After a while, there were fewer careless.

Still, she wasn't looking forward to the walk from the portal back to civilization and a Healer. But Dean had been right, time after time the elevator opened on an unknown place. The search was even more time-consuming as both door and gate had to be opened at every stop.

After six trips checking every floor and finding nothing, Dhulyn needed to sit down. "Shall we stop for today?"

"Once more. Seventh time lucky," Parno said.

Dhulyn lifted her eyes to the Sun, Moon, and Stars. And Outlanders were supposed to be the superstitious barbarians.

This time, the seventh time, they stopped on the third floor and the elevator doors opened onto water. Nothing else, as far as they could see. A slight swell caused the water to splash ankle deep into the elevator.

"Dean won't thank us for this."

But Parno wasn't listening to her, he was listening to something else, a familiar look on his face as he squinted into the far distance. He was listening to the Crayx.

"We're home," he said.

Without hesitating further Dhulyn stepped out into the warm water of the Long Ocean and kicked off her boots. She knew she should drop her sword as well, but it was her second-best one, and she was reluctant to part with it. She tread water, watching as Parno climbed out of the door and pulled the gate down as he lowered himself into the water.

Dhulyn swam over to him. "How far off are they?"

"Not far at all. They say we won't have time to get tired before they reach us."

"I hope they know how long it takes for a human to tire of swimming."

Parno laughed.

AUTHOR'S NOTE: The setting and characters from Tanya Huff's *Summon the Keeper* are used with the generous permission of the author. The right to have a character named after him was a Kickstarter perk purchased by Mark Slauter. You wanted a demon, Mark, but you knew that meant I'd have to kill you. Right?

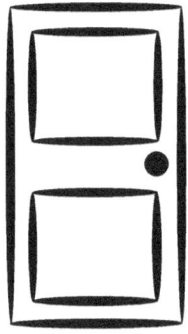

Somewhere Else, Nowhere Else

Juliet Kemp

Cara was on her way back from the corner shop—three cans of tomato soup, a loaf of cheap white sliced bread, milk, teabags—when she saw the new portal. She wasn't sure how long it had been there. She hadn't been outside for a while, and it was only the fact she'd run out of everything but half a jar of jam that had sent her out today. She might have just eaten the jam for dinner, except for being out of teabags as well.

There was a portal next to the corner shop, too, but that one had been there for a while. It stood where there had once been a doorway into the council block, encased in a solid metal box, painted matte black, with the only entrance a sliding metal door controlled by a touchcard pad. The sign above the door read BEIJING; although when Cara looked it up, back when she could still be bothered doing such things, it wasn't really Beijing at all on the other side, but a field about forty kilometers outside the city boundaries. Apparently a PortCo shuttlebus took you to Beijing proper. They'd been luckier at this end; the tube station was just across the road. And to be fair, forty-kilometer shuttle or not, if Cara wanted to go to Beijing, she'd take the portal herself. If she could be bothered getting the authentication card sorted out, and if she could afford the cost. A slow but steady stream of people going into the portal, one or two a minute, suggested that plenty of people could do both.

But what was the point? You'd only be somewhere else on Earth. Nothing important would change.

The new portal didn't look like the old one, at least not yet. The new portal was a couple of doors down on the other side of the road from Cara's flat. She would have seen it on her way out if she'd been paying attention.

The new portal didn't have a metal box, or a door, or a sign. It wasn't one of the blocked off ones either, with a much smaller doorless box and lots of red paint warning signs. It had a temporary metal fence around it, with warning tape wrapped through the mesh of the fence, and a bored looking security guard sitting on a folding chair just inside the fence. She was drinking tea out of a flask and reading the *Mirror*.

Cara stopped by the fence and looked for a while at the glowing blue-green nimbus inside it. At the center it was so bright it was almost white. The blue-green fronds reached out in all directions from it, fading into nothingness around eight feet from that bright center. The security guard had placed her chair as far from the fronds as she could without being on the other side of the fence.

"Do they know where it goes?" Cara asked.

The guard shrugged, without looking up from her paper. "Not yet. Only showed up last night."

There had been a tree here, Cara was fairly certain. A tree and some scrubby bushes set into the pavement. The council would have to reroute the pavement, when they got around to it.

"Weird that it's so close to the other one," she said.

The guard shrugged again. "I dunno how it works. I'm just here to stop any idiot from wandering in."

There was a poster on the fence.

Take a risk to benefit humanity!
PortCo needs portal testers
EXCELLENT PAY
NEVER WORK AGAIN

Cara rolled her eyes. All very well saying "never work again," but there was a fair chance that you wouldn't come *back* again. That you'd end up dying somewhere else—some distant planet, perhaps, or some other universe altogether. She'd read the speculations, like everyone else. But that was all they were, speculations. No one knew what happened to those who didn't come back.

Somewhere else. Or nowhere else. Either way: not here.

It was a while later, after she'd gone back to the flat and eaten the tomato soup and was drinking tea in front of daytime TV, before she recognized the tug in her stomach as yearning.

* * *

The London PortCo building was impressive, all black stone floors and well-groomed receptionists. But the office that Cara was shown to after she signed the contract looked like any other office she'd been in: shelves of books and folders, a rather untidy desk, and two low padded chairs in an unobjectionable, stain-resistant, mid-blue fabric.

Cara had been sitting in one of the chairs for nearly three hours now. Opposite her was an earnest researcher in a white coat, holding a tablet and asking Cara a great many questions. Presumably the white coat was intended to give Cara some sense of security, because it didn't seem to serve any other useful purpose.

The researcher's name was Sienna, and she had mid-brown skin and dark hair plaited in neat rows back from her forehead. Cara had become aware, shortly after meeting Sienna, that her own dishwater-blonde hair needed a wash and that it was falling out of the rubber band she'd tied it back with.

Nearly three hours. Cara had been amenable to start with, but now she was experiencing something that, after a few more questions, she recognized as irritation.

"Why all the questions?" she interrupted before Sienna could start on the next set. So far Sienna had asked about her family, taken her through a personality questionnaire, and gone through what Cara recognized, because assorted professionals had taken her through it more than once in the past, as a depression checklist. "Surely all you want to know is whether I'm prepared to walk into one of those things not knowing whether I'll walk out again?"

Sienna smiled at her. She had a nice smile. "It's all part of our research. Into the nature of the portals and human interaction with them. We've found it useful to have as much information as we can gather." She paused, then said, with an apologetic tilt of her head, "You did agree to this, as part of the contract."

"Yeah," Cara said, folding her arms. She had, but she hadn't quite realized what it meant. She didn't want to admit that to Sienna and her nice smile. She'd been focused on the idea of signing, and walking out of here and through a portal. She'd been thinking about what would happen after that. Of being *somewhere else*. Instead, here she was, three hours now and counting, telling her entire life details to this woman who might be cute, but who was nevertheless a total stranger.

Sienna shrugged. "I'm sorry that it wasn't made clear to you." She tapped at her tablet. "I'll feed that back to the intake management team."

"Do you get all that much intake to manage?" Cara asked. "Do many people want to take this sort of risk?"

Seventy percent of portals ended up blocked off; because whoever had gone through them hadn't come out again, or at least hadn't been heard of again. Cara hadn't known it was that high, before she'd read the red box-out at the top of the contract.

"You'd be surprised," Sienna said. "Then again, I suppose you wouldn't, because you're here, aren't you?"

"You've been asking questions about my life for three hours," Cara said. "I imagine it's pretty clear to you why I'm here."

Because she was depressed. Because she didn't have anything else to do. Because she didn't have anything keeping her here—family or friends or any of the rest of it, anyone who would notice if she went through a portal and never came back again. Because she didn't want to be *here* anymore.

Because she was fed up of never feeling anything in particular.

Sienna smiled at her again. "Well, I think you're doing something very brave. And potentially very helpful."

"Very helpful to you lot, certainly," Cara said.

PortCo held the worldwide monopoly on portals, had done since the first one appeared five years ago. They got to run them and, in exchange, they looked after all of them, made them safe, and attempted to find out where they went. That was, they sent people through to see where they came out.

The thirty percent of portals that went from one place on Earth to another place on Earth, even if they were all only one-way, were sufficiently lucrative that PortCo was happy to pay exorbitant amounts to anyone who would take the risk of... whatever happened when you didn't come back.

"What do you think happens?" Cara asked. "If you don't come out on Earth?"

"We don't know," Sienna said. "We think...it might be that you come out somewhere else. Maybe in the solar system—Mars, or the Moon—but we'd have heard something from the radio button in that case, even if the transponder is Earth-only, and we haven't. Maybe it's further away, more than five light-years. Maybe it's another universe altogether, if you subscribe to many-universes theory. We just don't know for certain." She pulled a face. "Maybe people just die. There's nothing in the energy signature to suggest that, but it's possible."

Cara was impressed with her honesty; although to be fair, it had all been in the contract information anyway.

"If you fetched up on the Moon or Mars you'd just asphyxiate," Cara noted. She wasn't particularly bothered by the idea. She probably ought to be.

Sienna shook her head. "We equip you with an atmosphere suit. And a transponder, and things. We'd know if it was the Moon. Or Mars."

Not in time for them to do anything about it, mind. The contract was very clear on that, in another big red box-out.

"So you can survive for long enough to asphyxiate a few hours later," Cara said.

"But you'd be on the Moon, or Mars, or wherever else, before you did." Sienna shrugged. "Maybe that would be worth it? You're the one that signed up for it, after all. I just ask the questions."

"I guess I'd better get on with asphyxiating, then," Cara said. "Are we done here?"

Sienna scanned the tablet. "Yes. I just need you to sign again, just here."

Cara took the tablet, signed where the red ring indicated, and handed it back.

She smiled brightly at Sienna as she stood up. "How about we get on with it?"

* * *

They took her to a portal on the other side of London. Not the one outside her own door, which was a bit of a shame. In the back of the van—it was well-equipped, but it was still basically the back of an over-height Transit—a young guy called Adam in a PortCo boiler-suit helped her into an environment suit and strapped a bulky rucksack of survival equipment on her back. Cara was slightly disappointed that Sienna hadn't come along.

"It should all be pretty idiot-proof," Adam said. "Uh, not that you're an idiot. I mean. Anyway. Do you want me to run you through it, though?"

"I'm good," Cara said.

She didn't actually believe that any of it would do her any

good. Judging by how ready Adam was to take her refusal, neither did he.

The bulky environment suit made her waddle a bit, and the rucksack weighed a ton. Adam helped her out of the van, then walked her over to the portal, where another hi-viz-jacketed security guard—this one had been reading the *Sun*—held back the wire fence so she could walk through.

The portal was glowing green-blue, flickering around its edges, the light intensifying into bright white as it reached the center.

That feeling was back, at the pit of Cara's stomach. Yearning. Excitement, even. She didn't remember feeling this much of anything for a long while. Maybe this was worth it just for that.

"Good luck," Adam said, from behind her.

It was a shame Sienna hadn't helped her. She'd quite liked Sienna.

She stepped forwards, into the flickering embrace of the outside edges of the portal. She thought of what might be the other side of this. Somewhere else. Or nowhere at all. Somewhere *different*. Not Earth. Not her, here and now.

Another step, and she was nearly at the bright-white center.

Another step, and she had to close her eyes against the light. She couldn't feel the weight of the rucksack any more.

Another step. Her teeth buzzed, and she felt pressure building inside her ears. Maybe she was going to die here, after all; maybe the pressure would explode inside her skull.

She took another step forward, and another. The pressure dropped away, and the buzzing died down, and she could open her eyes again. She waited just a moment, holding inside her that yearning, that anticipation...

She opened her eyes. A field of sunflowers spread out in front of her, and a small river ran along the edge of the field to her right. The ground under her feet was dusty, and the sun shone into her eyes through the helmet's glass.

Sunflowers. Earth flowers. Earth's sun.

The transponder beeped happily and she looked down at the display. Coordinates, and an approximate location. Gadag, Karnakata, India.

Earth.

Same planet. Same Cara. Same everything.

* * *

They flew Sienna out to meet her.

"So, how does it feel to be rich?" Sienna asked her, as she ran a scanner over Cara for the third time or so.

Cara shrugged. "Eh."

Sienna looked sharply up at her. "You're not pleased, are you? That you came through. That you're still here."

Cara shrugged again. "Look. You were the one who took all those measurements. You must know that I wasn't that bothered."

"Ye-es," Sierra said, thoughtfully. "You know, I do wonder..." She trailed off.

"What do you wonder?" Cara asked, feeling the faintest of stirrings of interest. "Have you got a theory about this? You have, haven't you?"

"It's not a company theory," Sienna said. "I shouldn't talk about it."

"Oh, go on," Cara said.

"I really can't talk about it," Sienna said, and glanced expressively down at the PortCo recorder sitting on the desk next to them.

"Alright," Cara agreed, and dropped the subject.

She didn't pick it up again until that evening, when she tracked Sienna down at the hotel restaurant.

"I'm rich," she said, without preamble. "Let me take you out to a really good dinner. I got a recommendation."

Sienna hesitated.

"I checked my contract. There's nothing in there about me not hanging out with company employees. I don't know about your contract, but if you want to know things about me, wouldn't this be helpful?"

Apparently that was a winning move. Sienna grinned and followed her out.

Cara had been intending to get information out of Sienna about this *theory* of hers over dinner. Instead, she got distracted by the conversation; and then she got distracted by the fact that she was rapidly becoming attracted to Sienna, who was excellent company when she wasn't interrogating Cara. It was the first time in a while that Cara had felt attracted to anyone at all, and she'd almost forgotten that it could be fun. In fact, Cara was enjoying herself enough—another novel sensation— that she asked Sienna if she wanted to come back to her, Cara's, room for a nightcap, and Sienna agreed. And then, rather more enthusiastically, she agreed to the even more distracting activities for which the "nightcap" was a poor cover.

"So, though," Cara said, afterwards, when they were both flat out on the bed, enjoying the afterglow, remembering the idea that she'd started out with earlier in the evening. "What is this theory of yours?"

"Oh my god," Sienna said, sitting up and looking horrified. "You got me into bed to ask me that?"

"No!" Cara said, then admitted, "I did take you out to dinner to ask you that. But the propositioning you part wasn't planned. I promise."

"Ugh. I really shouldn't talk about it," Sienna said, with the air of someone who badly wanted to talk about it.

"I won't tell anyone," Cara said.

That was all the encouragement Sienna needed. "No one else will take it seriously," she said. "But I think... Look. I'm the one who collects the data from all the volunteers."

"We're getting paid," Cara said. "I'm not sure 'volunteers' is the right word."

"Guinea-pigs isn't great either, though," Sienna said. "Anyway. The thing is—you didn't want to come back, right?"

Somewhere else. Or nowhere else. Not her. Not here. "Yeah," Cara agreed.

"I think—those are the people who come back. The ones who don't care. The ones who do care, the ones who have ties... those are the ones who disappear."

"Hang on." Cara sat up, too. "You're talking as if you think the person stepping through the portal affects what the portal does. But that can't be right. What about all those people using them for travel, every damn day?"

"It's the first person," Sienna said. "The first person isn't just finding out where they go. They're making them go somewhere. That's my theory." She looked a little uncomfortable.

"And if you're not attached to Earth, that's when they go somewhere that is on Earth? That's ridiculous."

Sienna spread her hands. "Of course it is. That's why no one will take me seriously. I've stopped talking about it. But—I've got the data. And the data fits."

"So if I really want to go somewhere else, I should go through an old portal," Cara said. "One that didn't work."

Sienna frowned at her. "Don't do that." Then her expression brightened. "You could do another one, though. Test the theory a bit. I hardly ever get repeat data. Most people take the money and run."

"Maybe being very rich will keep me here," Cara said. "Or not keep me here. That's the theory, right?"

"I really shouldn't have said anything," Sienna said.

"But I'm interested now," Cara said. "So I'm glad you did. I did wonder, though..." She reached over and stroked Sienna's arm, gently, and the subject changed.

* * *

To Cara's complete lack of surprise, it transpired that being rich wasn't enough to change how she felt about being herself, on Earth, even after she'd had a couple of weeks to get used to her new situation. She sat around in the flat for a while, and then she went back to PortCo and signed up again.

This time, she ended up in a small village a hundred kilometers from Rio de Janeiro.

"Your scores were the same," Sienna agreed afterwards, which at least suggested that the scores matched how she felt.

"And here I am again," Cara said. "Great."

She spent a while, after that, thinking about ways in which she could become attached to Earth, without actually becoming attached to Earth.

"You realize that you might just die," Sienna said, when Cara brought the subject up one morning. "If you do manage this."

"Yes," Cara agreed. "Or I might wind up somewhere really interesting."

"And then die."

"Yeah. But. Why not, hey?"

Sienna looked like she was about to say something, then instead got up off the bed, put Cara's dressing gown on, and went to make tea.

Cara was slightly surprised that she'd wound up hanging out with—sleeping with—having sex with—Sienna repeatedly, because she was surprised to find herself enjoying anything much. But she was, and she was, and Sienna seemed to be having fun, too, so.

She spent a while browsing overpriced property on Rightmove. She really didn't want a six-bed Kensington townhouse with a ballroom, or a penthouse suite on one of the ugly new buildings by Tower Bridge on the north side of the Thames. What she wanted was a detached house, and those were next to non-existent in central London.

On the other hand, she was now absurdly rich. So when she did find one, a former rectory near Old Street, she just bought it.

It was nice. She liked it a lot. Sienna, who came to visit, liked it, too.

The next portal Cara stepped through still went to Earth.

* * *

She considered buying a dog, but that seemed a bit unfair on the dog if it worked; and if it didn't work, then that would suggest that she was about as attached to the dog as she was to her shiny new (old) house, which was to say, not very, and that didn't seem fair to the dog either.

There was a closed-off portal down the road from the Old Street rectory. Cara spent a while sitting on the roof terrace, just looking down at it. The metal box surrounding it looked pretty robust; but there was always a way to get through something, if you really wanted to. Obviously, most people wouldn't want to go through a portal that led to nothing; that someone had already vanished into.

Cara, in that sense, wasn't most people.

Most people could, however, buy an oxyacetylene torch on the internet, if they wanted to, and in *that* sense, Cara was most people.

Doing it at midnight seemed most fitting, but the downside of that was that anyone who looked out of their windows would automatically be suspicious as hell, and she wasn't sure how long it would take her to get through.

Instead, she bought a hi-viz jacket, put her PortCo pass round her neck on a lanyard, and did it in the middle of the day. No one batted an eyelid.

The downside of doing this on the down-low was that she didn't have any of the survival equipment that they usually sent her off with. She'd assembled some things into a rucksack—camping kit, some dried food, some water. If the atmosphere was no good then she supposed she'd just die straight away, which was arguably better than dying once her water ran out, but maybe she could walk to somewhere there was water.

She stepped through before she could think any better of it.

She stepped out onto the pavement of the Champs-Élysées, looking straight at the Arc de Triomphe. Passers-by recoiled in surprised horror as the portal opened up around her, and tourists drinking coffee under red awnings stared at her, their mouths open.

"Well, shit," Cara said.

* * *

She didn't have the transponder this time, so she had to phone Sienna to arrange for pickup. At least she'd taken her phone with her. It hadn't occurred to her not to, despite the outcome she was hoping for. Weird, what you get attached to.

Sienna told her firmly to stay exactly where she was, until security arrived. "Even if it is exit-only. Just...*stay there.*"

Local security showed up within half an hour, which was good, as Cara had rapidly become fed up of being gawped at and having her photo taken. She went to the nearest hotel and lay on the bed staring up at the ceiling. The bloody Arc de Triomphe loomed in at the window even though she wasn't looking at it. France. How the hell had she come out in France via a portal that definitely hadn't gone anywhere on Earth before?

There was a loud banging on the door. Cara ignored it.

"Cara, for *fuck's sake.*"

Sienna.

"It's open," Cara called out.

Sienna marched in, put her bag down on the enormous polished-mahogany desk, and pointedly didn't pull out the customary recorder and tablet from it.

"What the hell were you thinking?" she demanded, fists on her hips.

"I thought, that one definitely goes somewhere else," Cara said. She had the vague impression that she ought to be feeling something other than "tired," but if she was, she couldn't tell.

She was pleased to see Sienna, though, she thought. A bit. Even if Sienna was going to shout at her.

"But, as you can see," she carried on, "it doesn't. Here I still am."

"It didn't," Sienna corrected her. She looked tired. "Whatever it does now, it didn't before. There's no question about that. The last user disappeared. And that end of the portal wasn't there until you stepped through it, was it?"

"What does that even mean then? Are they all that unstable?"

"Well that's an excellent question," Sienna said. "And that's why every portal in the world is shut down right now while we work it out, with much screaming from both ops and sales. We've always believed that they were stabilized by the first person who stepped through them. But if that's not true..."

"It can't be wholly untrue," Cara said. "Lots of people go through them every day without destabilizing anything."

"Right," Sienna agreed. "So maybe it's something about the original traveller, something that's changed. Like, maybe they did go somewhere else, but now they've died and that's changed things. Which I would have thought someone would have thought of, but..."

She sat down on the edge of the bed and pulled her tablet out, poking at it and muttering under her breath. "Ah. Right. Aadhya found it while I was in transit. Good. At least two original travellers who found Earthbound portals have died since, and their portals are still running. So it's not that." She turned to look at Cara. "Which means, it might be you."

"Me?"

"Either you personally—which would be annoying, scientifically speaking—or something specific about you."

"Detachment," Cara said.

"You do score pretty high on that," Sienna agreed. "Consistently. Wanna run it again?"

Cara shrugged. "Not really. But since you're here."

They ran through the test battery again.

"Yeah," Sienna said, showing her the results. "Same."

Cara felt obscurely uncomfortable. Maybe something to do with the fact that Sienna was here, and they were talking, like friends, and there was a fighting chance that they would have sex later...did she feel guilty, that she didn't feel more attached?

She didn't feel guilty, though. She couldn't deny it.

"I'm sorry," she said anyway, and hoped Sienna would know what she was apologizing for.

Sienna smiled at her. It seemed to be genuine. "Don't be. I saw your test results before I ever got involved with you, didn't

I? I knew what I was getting into, don't worry."

Cara wasn't worrying, not exactly. But it was nice to be reassured, she supposed.

Sienna looked down at the tablet, tapping her thumb against its edge. "Other people have scored similarly to you, but most people only do it once, so I don't have the repeat results. And we've never sent someone through a seventy-percent portal a second time."

"Maybe I should try another closed portal," Cara said.

"Actually, you should try another open one," Sienna said, absently. "An Earth-bound one, maybe." She looked up, horrified, realizing what she'd said. "But the bosses aren't going to want you to, so don't say I said that. Oh crap, I should have turned the recorder on. I'll go out and come in again, okay?"

* * *

Cara thought about trying an existing Earth portal, but she would have had to sort herself out fake ID, and she really couldn't be bothered. So she kept on going through new portals—and when they ran out of those, and Sienna gave a presentation to her bosses, a few of the seventy-percent ones—and kept on finding herself back on Earth. The company was very happy with Cara. Her new personal banker was very happy with her. Everyone was very happy, except for Cara, who still had that yearning for elsewhere, lodged somewhere deep inside her.

And there was nothing that she could do about it.

At least that part she was used to.

After a while, Sienna moved in to the house near Old Street. Cara wasn't attached to Sienna, exactly, any more than she was attached to the house. But they got on well together, and they had great sex, and Sienna was comfortable to be around. It felt nice, living with Sienna. Good, even.

On the day of Cara's seventeenth portal trip, they were back in Sienna's office yet again, going through the questionnaires yet again, as per the routine. Sienna looked up at Cara, smiling, making some joke or other, then looked down at her tablet, and hesitated, her eyebrows going up, just for a moment.

"Everything okay?" Cara said.

Sienna shook her head, just slightly, and smiled at Cara. "Fine. No worries."

She went in the van to the portal, and helped Cara suit up once they got there. She'd taken over from Adam sometime after the sixth or seventh portal. Cara wasn't sure how Sienna had wrangled that, but she liked it. Sienna was a little more assiduous than Adam, Cara thought. And she had a nicer smile.

Cara climbed out of the van, Sienna hopping down behind her, and the security guard started opening up the wire mesh. Just before Cara put her helmet on, Sienna put her hand on Cara's shoulder, leaned in, and kissed her. Cara blinked. Sienna had never been public about their relationship at work before. The company knew, of course, but Sienna was always at pains to keep it professional during work time.

"Are you sure everything's okay?" she asked.

"Fine," Sienna said. "Can't I just feel like kissing you?"

"Sure you can." Cara smiled at her, and leaned forward to kiss her back. "See you on the flipside, then."

She put her helmet on, and felt that familiar yearning, the yearning for something else. She wondered, though, if it was maybe a little duller. She was looking forward to walking through this portal; but she was also looking forward to coming out somewhere else on Earth, to meeting Sienna in a hotel, to going out with her to look around wherever she'd fetched up. To coming home again. Maybe they should get a dog, after all, now that Sienna was living in the house, too. Or a cat, perhaps. Cats were more independent, and Cara liked independence.

She was thinking about Sienna, and a cat, and that kiss, when she stepped through the portal.

She stepped out again onto blue earth, and a deep red sun, and towering purple mountains.

This wasn't Earth. This wasn't Earth at all.

She looked down on the transponder, but its indicator was spinning aimlessly, unable to find a connection.

She thought again about that kiss, and about Sienna looking down at the tablet, her eyebrows going up. With a sick lurch in her stomach, she realized: somewhere along the line, she'd become attached after all.

Cara looked out at the strange landscape that was everything she'd dreamed of, all this time: the strange landscape that might kill her or might let her survive, the strange landscape that meant that she would never be going back to Earth, or Sienna, or their now-never-existent cat.

She'd always wanted this. She'd always wanted this.

She stepped forward, and didn't let the tears fall.

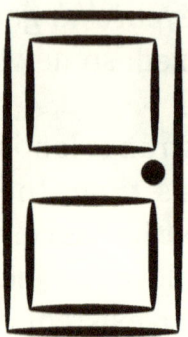

A Stranger Comes to Town

James Enge

FROM: Gabriel McNally, PhD
Department of Folklore and Ambrosian Studies
University of Mackinac
Mackinac Island, MI

TO: James Enge
Classical Languages and World Studies
GBSU
The Great Black Swamp, OH

December 31

Dear Mr. Enge (if that is your real name),
    You have some kind of nerve writing to me for information on any subject other than the straightest route to Hell. On that matter, at any rate, you need not be concerned: you are well on your way. I fully intend to sue you for slander and defamation as soon as I can get my lawyer to respond to my phone calls.

However, since we share a strong interest in Ambrosian legend, and since you and yours were fairly kind to me and mine in our recent trouble, and since no one could call me uncollegial or ungrateful—no matter what other spiteful, vicious, and legally actionable things they may have said about me—I'll tell you the story more or less as I heard it from Andrea Worth.

In answer to your (typically insolent) question: I do believe the story. It's not because Andrea is the kind of person you have to believe. For one thing, she was living with me at the time, an obvious sign of bad judgement. For another, she was telling people that she had psychic powers because she had red hair. (Apparently, they are supposed to go together.) When we got to know each other well enough for me to point out that her hair was dyed, she told me it was only fair to let people know they were dealing with a psychic. She was the queen, the interplanetary empress, of circular reasoning.

But the thing about Andrea is: she is not an enthusiast for the Ambrosian mythos. She wasn't even aware that Merlin had children and she was extremely angry when I suggested to her that Nimue may not have been born of British nobility. (These New Age people tend to be a little classist, I'm afraid. Or, to be fair, maybe most people are when they get the opportunity.) So the odd details about Andrea's story that the late Magistra Emrys spotted, and I spotted, and even you may spot, were not borrowed by her from books about the Ambrosian mythos because she hates that stuff.

This all happened decades ago. Andrea was working as a security guard at the time in the Drake Tower, an empty office building in downtown Minneapolis. The thing had been slated for demolition, but apparently it was an Art Deco masterpiece and some people thought it should be preserved as a historical landmark. So the demolition was delayed by lawsuits, but the space couldn't be rented, and everyone was unhappy except for the lawyers and, of course, Cavall Security, the company we were all working for at the time, because they got to supply round-the-clock security teams. After the skyways were locked, most of the team went home and one person stayed alone on third shift. On weekends, that person was Andrea.

Andrea is more of a people-person than you and I ever were, and she wasn't crazy about those midnight shifts. Plus she was convinced there was someone living or hiding among the thousand empty rooms of the Drake Tower. She also thought it was haunted. These are uncomfortable thoughts to have, alone in a dark office building, when you know that no one is going to come looking for you for at least eight hours.

She could have sat at the guard desk and read most of the night—she was a big reader, particularly of the old pulps—but reading, in an island of light in the middle of a dark lobby, can be unsettling. You wouldn't have to be in opium withdrawal, like poor old Edgar Poe, to imagine rappings at the door, talking ravens, dead hearts beating under the floorboards, etc. So instead of reading books she sat at the lobby desk, opened the newspaper (remember them?) to the want ads (remember *them*?), and settled down to look for a new job. For every job she was interested in, she threw a Tarot reading, so the process was quite prolonged. She missed a few of the scheduled security rounds, but didn't care. They could fire her if they wanted, but she was going to get out of that tower somehow.

She wasn't getting much satisfaction out of her rebellion that particular day, however. Her Tarot readings, for every want ad, all featured very similar cards, no matter what pattern she threw or how often she shuffled the deck: the Tower Struck by Lightning kept coming up, over and over, and the Fool, and the Hanged Man. That's a lot of the Major Arcana to appear in one reading, and they appeared in reading after reading.

Enge, I knew you used to dabble in this nonsense yourself, so you probably know that the Tower has more than one meaning. But in Andrea's mind it became increasingly obvious that the Tower was her tower, the Drake Tower. "Am I going to be stuck here for the rest of my life?" she wondered. "Is this really the place I have to be? Am I the Fool or the Hanged Man?" It wasn't the kind of life she'd planned when she got her MA in anthropology.

But she kept at it. She believed in the cards, as I never could, but she didn't let them keep her from something she'd set out to do, as you or I probably would have. That was really her best thing: persistence. She was like Genghis Khan: "The merit of a thing is in finishing it to the end."

Andrea was in the throes of trying to figure out whether a word-processor was a machine or a person (in those bygone days, I seem to remember, it was both) when she heard someone breaking into the building, around the corner at the far end of the long L-shaped lobby.

Andrea was already wearing the bulky guard utility belt, containing her walkie-talkie, a can of mace, and a flashlight long enough to double as a club. She quickly squared up her Tarot cards and pushed them into one of her baggy uniform pockets. She didn't think they would be useful, but she didn't want to leave them around in the lobby picking up hostile influences. (I'm just telling you the way she told me.) Anyway, she was light on her feet and ran around the corner just in time to see the heels of the intruder vanish into the stairway leading to the second floor.

She grabbed the walkie-talkie and hit the talk button. "Hey, Cavall Ops, this is Guard 1 at the Drake post. There's been a break-in, I'm afraid. Call the cops, if you don't mind, huh? Over."

Silence. Darn walkie-talkie wasn't working. Again. She'd have to use the phone on her desk.

She glanced at the lobby doors—an inner set and an outer set, a kind of airlock to keep the cold air from rushing in during those frosty Minnesota winters. The outer doors were standing open—it looked like they were being held open by the carpet. The carpet was a new one; Andrea had never seen it before. Which seemed weird to her: why put new carpet into an empty building slated for demolition? It was pretty memorable: black, heavily textured with a lot of tasselwork, and a lot of gleaming red spots.

Then the details came into focus and she realized that the carpet was actually an army of red-eyed rats, and they were forcing open the inner door to the lobby.

Andrea wasn't afraid of animals; she grew up on a farm. But not many people would want to wade through an army of angry street rats. She turned away to run back to her desk and call both the cops and Cavall ... but then she saw the floor by the guard desk was already alive with rats.

Hobson's choice: Andrea followed the intruder up the stairs to the second floor.

All the upper floors were on low-power lighting twenty-four hours a day, unless someone needed to do some work up in the empty tower, which no one ever did anymore. She could see the intruder only dimly in the sparsely lit corridor, but he seemed to be picking the lock to the vacant offices on the second floor. "Stop!" she shouted, raising her flashlight like a club.

"Rats," he pointed out in a gravelly voice. And in the silence that followed this unexpected remark, she heard the rats scrabbling on the marble steps of the stairway. (The Drake really was a beautiful old building, which is one of the reasons this is sort of a sad story.)

"Oh, geez!" she shouted (a major oath in Andrea's lexicon), and reached for the ring of keys at her belt. Even back then, in those low-tech days, you could get around most office buildings in town with a couple of master keys. But the Drake had been rekeyed more times than anyone could count, and the guard had to carry her own weight in keys to get anywhere.

But they weren't needed just then. The office door swung open.

"Good lock," the stranger remarked and stepped through in what Andrea thought an excessively leisurely manner. She pushed past him and slammed the office door behind her. Through the floor-to-ceiling window next to the door, they could see the tide of red-eyed rats rising up the stairwell and spreading through the second-floor corridor outside.

"Sheesh!" she said, and she meant it.

"*Benedicaris,*" the stranger remarked politely. Which is how you say Gesundheit in Latin.

Andrea was a recovering Catholic just getting into Wykkanism, so she sort of knew what he meant, but it didn't endear him to her. She couldn't see much of him, from the streetlights filtering in through the dirty windows, but she saw that he was a pretty raggedy man, somewhat lopsided.

He also "talked funny" as Andrea put it to me later. According to her description, it sounded like this guy was a European of some kind or (this was Mrs. Embrys' suggestion) someone who had learned English before the Great Vowel Shift of the Middle Ages.

"Are you coppola?" he asked.

"What?"

"Coppola. The fuzz. *Vigil urbis.* Five-oh."

"A *cop*? No."

The silhouette nodded approvingly. "Five-oh is an unfriend to me," he remarked.

"So am I!"

The crooked shape shrugged and seemed to open his hands. He didn't say anything else.

In the awkward silence that followed, Andrea heard rat-teeth gnawing at the wooden door.

"Gosh—dang it!" Andrea snarled, in a brief but utterly sincere lapse into the outskirts of monotheism. She snatched up her walkie-talkie and (holding down the talk-button so hard her thumb hurt) said, "Cavall Ops, this is Guard 1 at the Drake Tower. This is a serious emergency, REALLY; I need cops and animal control at the lobby and on the 2nd floor RIGHT AWAY, if you don't mind. I mean, if it's not too much trouble, just stop reading comic books for two minutes and do your job, THANKS." She released the talk-button reluctantly, wondering if she'd been forceful enough. Or if she'd even gotten through.

"There is no answer, now or later," the stranger said.

"What?" Andrea snapped irritably.

"Hiss," the other said (or maybe "hist"). She held her ear against the speaker and it *was* hissing. There was a steady rise and fall of static. As she listened to it, she almost thought she heard it saying a word, over and over. ("'Embers,' or something like that," she said later. I suggested "Ambrose" and she suggested that I shut my stupid face. Ours was a volatile relationship.)

"Someone's jamming the signal?" she said. "Why? So rats can break into an empty office building?"

The stranger seemed to hesitate. "There is a signal," he said at last. "It is not your signal. The rats hear it."

Andrea wondered if he was just unable to express himself clearly because he was a foreigner, or if he was maybe also crazy, or if he was just drunk.

However you sliced it, though, that wasn't the most urgent issue. "We have to get the heck out of here," she said.

"Heck out of here," the other seemed to agree.

"Elevator," she said. "We'll go up to the roof. Reception may be better up there. Anyway, how far can rats climb?"

"Far," the man said.

"Anyway, I'm going." Reluctantly, she added, "You should come, too." She wasn't relishing the idea of sharing an elevator with "that stanky wino," as she described the victor of Tunglskin. But she wouldn't have left a rat to be eaten by other rats.

"What roof?" he asked.

She almost blew her stack at him—she could hear those rats gnawing their way closer—but she realized he had a point. The Drake Tower was built kind of like a trophy: a wide, flat base, occupying a big chunk of a city block, and a narrow spire with the elevator bank at its core. From the third floor up it was all spire.

"All the way up," she said. "Thirtieth floor."

He stood there, a shadow in the shadows, apparently thinking.

"See you later, then!" she said, and dashed off through the empty offices toward the elevator bank.

Andrea could move through the wreckage of the half-demolished offices with ease, even in the dark; she'd had lots of practice. She didn't hear the wino following her, so she assumed that he'd stayed behind to take his chances with the rats. But when she'd halted by the elevator bank and hit the UP button as if her life depended on it, she turned around to find him standing by her.

She was out of breath; he wasn't; he still stank. All these things annoyed her. "Oh, I guess you decided to tag along, then," she said, and she meant it to sting.

After a few moments he replied, "Eh." She waited, assuming he was formulating some thought, but that was all he said.

The elevator doors opened. The lights were on inside the car and it was blessedly free from rats. They entered side-by-side—much closer than Andrea liked. Like many Minnesotans, her psychic comfort required three or four feet of personal space around her at all times.

Keeping one eye on her unwanted guest, she punched up the top floor on the elevator panel.

The stranger watched her do so. "Eight and twenty," he pointed out. "Not thirty."

It took a while for her to get his meaning ("It sounded like he was clearing his throat when he said 'eight,'" she complained to me later) but, when she did understand, she said, "We walk up the last two floors. No lift," she added, trying to be helpful. She knew people from Europe often talked that way.

"'Lyft,'" he replied meditatively. "That is elevator?"

"Yeah, I guess so," she acknowledged, annoyed to have her English corrected by this guy. "Where do you come from, anyway?"

He seemed at a loss. "Not here," he said finally.

"Oh, yeah, I figured that. Where were you born?"

He flinched as if he'd been stabbed. "Tower embers," he muttered, or something like that. "I can never go there again."

"I'm sorry," she said. She really was. She hated to cause anyone pain. I don't buy all that psychic gibberish, and don't even try, Enge, to give your line about how "people are more connected to each other than they understand." I'm just as connected to other people as I want to be, which is not very. But Andrea's different; she really cares about people and hates it when they're hurt. The world is a lot rougher place for people like her than it is for bastards like you and me.

"How did you get here?" she said, to sort of distract him from his pain.

It worked. His expression relaxed. He seemed to be trying to find words to fit his experience.

"The world opened," he said finally. "Like an eye."

"Like an eye?"

"Yes: an eye." He pointed at one of his, which were a disturbingly pale gray. "The eye opened. But it was not an eye. It was a hole. I fell in. I thought it was death; I thought I was dead. I fell. I landed here."

"*Here?*"

"Here. Well, in Koochiching County. I was arrested by five-oh there."

"Oh? What for?" Andrea knew it was rude to ask people why they'd been arrested, but she was in an elevator with this guy.

"Hunting without a license. Sleeping outside without a license. Those I did, though I do not know why they are outlaw. Also for drunk and disorderly. That was unfair: I am often drunk, sometimes disorderly, never both."

"I guess one can lead to the other," Andrea said politely.

He shrugged, and she noticed that he had some scoliosis: one of his shoulders was a little higher than the other.

"Five-oh gave me some money," he continued, "and a bus ticket to the polis."

"The what?"

"This place. The Minnehaha polis. He said there are many like me here, but there are not."

There were and there weren't, Andrea thought, but didn't say so.

"Anyway I was glad to go. A dragon in the deep waters was trying to kill me and I thought maybe he does not here, though he is, it seems."

Andrea thought she knew where the conversation was going until this new development. "A dragon, huh?"

"That is the word. I read it in a book in the Hennepin County Library. *Rokh*, or *draco*, or *wyrm*, or what you will."

"Um. I don't think I will."

"Well, who can blame you?" His bright gray eyes drifted away from her; he looked as if he were listening to a voice from far away.

"What's your name?" she asked to keep him talking. She didn't want him listening to any voices in his head.

"Morlock," he said. "Your?"

"I'm Andrea. Andrea Worth."

"Andrea Andrea Worth, we are not going anywhere."

For a horrified moment Andrea thought he was initiating a conversation about their relationship, and then she realized he was speaking literally.

It almost felt as if the elevator car was moving; she could hear the machinery grinding deep in the sub-basement—but maybe it was grinding too much. The elevator panel indicated that they were somewhere between floors seventeen and eighteen...and they continued to be, long after they should have passed on to nineteen or twenty.

"Crud," she said fiercely.

"There is a thing in the box," he said, pointing at the emergency telephone. "You can talk to someone on it."

"Yeah, I know. It only calls the desk. My desk," she continued, when he didn't seem to get it.

"Ah. *Hurs krakna!* These elevators, they are not well made. I am always being stuck in elevators."

"I know what you mean," she said. "Let's force the door open."

Morlock just looked bemusedly at the stainless-steel panels of the door.

"For the love of Pete," she muttered savagely.

The trouble was, the car was stalled above the 17th floor, but not up to the 18th: they were facing a blank wall. Morlock looked rather than asked a question, and she explained how they needed to force back the leaves of the inner door, and attempt to release the safety catch on the outer one on the floor above. He peered up at the ledge of the 18th floor and said, "I can sneak up there."

"Oh, yeah?" she said, trying not to sound too skeptical.

"Oh, yeah." He reached up with one arm, out of the car door, groping upwards into the gap between the elevator car and the wall of the shaft.

Andrea felt the car shift under her feet. That was another problem with those damned things: they wouldn't even stay stuck reliably. If they moved while you were halfway through a doorway, you had the delightful opportunity to be cut in half.

What Andrea wanted to do was explain to Morlock the complicated geometry of the elevator shaft and the very real danger that he would have an arm lopped off if the car moved while he was reaching out of it. What she had time to do, and what she actually did, was scream, "GAH!" and tackle him. He was about half a foot taller than her, and a lot stronger, but you hit just about anybody with your full weight at their knees and they'll go down. They found themselves tangled in the middle of the car, not falling, exactly. The car was free-falling. They fell four stories before the friction brakes stopped the car.

Andrea quickly rolled out of the scrum with Morlock and sat shuddering in a corner. (When I slyly implied she might have found the full-body contact interesting, she shuddered again and said, "Ick. His clothing was SQUUSHY. It squushed.")

Morlock was flexing his hand and looking at her. "I owe you my hand, at least."

"No charge," she said hastily.

"Plainly not. Blood has no price."

"But we have to get out of here. The car's really not supposed to move like that." She thought about a severed elevator cable falling and crushing them. She thought about the friction brakes failing, so that they would fall seventeen—no, thirteen, now—stories to their death. "Take my word for it."

"I take your word," he said, fixing her with a bright glance. "I give you mine."

"Great." Andrea didn't understand that this was like being offered a drink of water by Valentine Michael Smith, and she didn't believe me when I told her later.

"But," Morlock asked practically, "how do we get out? The walls are unsound. I can maybe break through and we climb into...into the empty place where the boxes hang."

"The shaft? No. Through the access hatch in the ceiling."

He looked doubtfully up at the banks of fluorescent lights. "Ceiling is up? Like *caelum*?"

"Yeah, sure, you bet. Up!"

"The lights are not cold. They bite you."

"Everything does in this rotten old place."

At her direction (he had the height necessary), he lifted the banks of fluorescent lights out of their rests in the false ceiling. The access hatch was then visible on the car's actual ceiling. "If I can get up there..." she said.

Morlock held out his hands, laced together to make a stirrup. "Hokay," Andrea said or gulped and she stepped up into his hands. Without apparent strain he lifted her up to the top of the car. She bashed the latch with the butt end of her flashlight/club until it loosened enough to open. She hurled back the hatch. Without anything being said, Morlock fully extended his arms, lifting her far enough through the hatch so that she could scramble onto the roof of the car. She was considering how to get Morlock up after her when his hands appeared on opposite sides of the open hatch and he lifted himself through it.

They weren't alone on top of the elevator car; red-eyed rats leapt up at her, nipping and snarling like tiny vicious terriers.

"Awk!" Andrea found a rat attached to her forearm. She bashed it with her flashlight club and it reluctantly fell away, taking part of her uniform sleeve and a chunk of her flesh with it. "I hope you get polyester poisoning, you dumb rat!" she shrieked. Morlock was kicking the rats away into the shaft; Andrea pitched in and, at the cost of a few more frenzied bites, pretty soon the roof of the car was rat-free.

Andrea's flashlight was pretty badly dented, but the light still worked; she clicked it on and kept it on, so that they would have light to work with. Morlock's pale eyes were on her, and she felt embarrassed somehow. She flourished the flashlight and said, "'Get a bigger hammer,'" quoting one of the two laws of home repair to the Master of All Makers.

"Hammers are good," he agreed.

"Oh! Were you a…a blacksmith or something?" She felt stupid as soon as she said it. Where did you ever hear of blacksmiths anymore, except on dude ranches?

But he was nodding. "*Smith. Smithian.* Yes. I am a smith, a maker of things. Though it is hard now."

Since he went crazy and started self-medicating with alcohol, she guessed (but did not say).

"In this world," Morlock continued, "I have no focus. The laws are different; the forces are different. And I have no focus. So."

"So!" said Andrea, who wasn't getting any of this. "We should get out of this shaft." From the top of the elevator car they could just step up to the ledge of the 13th floor elevator door. Andrea pointed at the safety catch at the top of the shaft-side of the elevator door. "If you could get that there, that'd be great, then." Morlock reached up and sprang the catch with his right forefinger and thumb. Andrea pushed the doors back and gratefully stepped into the 13th floor corridor, out of Morlock's personal cloud.

She was still in a cloud, though. The dim emergency lights were on in the 13th floor corridor, but she couldn't see them. She hadn't switched off her flashlight, but somehow it faded and went out, like a car's taillights disappearing in fog.

She was the one disappearing in fog, though. There were clouds all around her. They had teeth. They wanted to get at her. And they were getting at her, into her. She could feel their teeth, not in her skin but under it somehow. She wanted to scream, but she couldn't; her throat croaked a few broken syllables and stopped; it was gripped by some sightless fist.

Morlock stepped into the corridor behind her and roared at the top of his voice. There were words in the shout, but she couldn't make them out. The toothy dark clouds were gone and she stood in the mundane reddish radiance of the emergency lighting and her dying flashlight.

"What the heck was that?" she gasped. She didn't expect an answer, but she got one.

"*Nubes impetuum*," Morlock said.

"Listen, Sister Mary Margaret Whatshername: I never got that far in Latin. Can you describe it in English?"

"I know not." The stranger thought for a few moments. "After the deaths, this is what is left. After the deaths of persons."

"They're *ghosts*?"

"Certainly. Yes. I guess. Sort of."

"Where did *they* come into it?" Andrea was outraged; she felt like they had enough to handle already.

"They were always in it, Andrea Andrea Worth. They are in the rats, *foci* for the *rukhlokh*—the dragonspell."

"You mean we're being chased by *demonically possessed rats*?"

"Is *gast* the same as *daemon*?" Morlock wondered. "I guess so. Yes. We are being chased by demonically possessed rats!"

He seemed quite pleased by it, probably because he had learned how to say something fairly complicated in a language he was learning, or relearning. Andrea, however, was not pleased at all.

"You mean all the animal control officers in the world could show up and there's nothing they could do about it?" she demanded.

"I do not mean that," Morlock said, "since I do not understand it. What is *animal control officers*? Are they five-oh?"

"For dogs, maybe. Never mind. What spell did you use to banish the ghosts?"

"Any spell. Anything you say, but loud. *Impetus vocium nubes impetuum disrumpit.* It's a law. That's why they attack your voice first."

"I felt that. I wanted to scream, but couldn't."

"They do not want you to scream. They do not want it a lot."

"So—if we, like, scream *really, really loud*—"

"We cannot scream so loud. There is a ghost or daemon in every rat, and others besides."

"Where do they come from?"

"Every time someone dies, one is left. Your moon is broken."

"What?" Even if true, this seemed irrelevant.

"Your moon should pull the *nubes impetuum*, the ghosts, away and wash them up. It is broken and does not do that. Your world is sick with ghosts, lousy with ghosts."

Andrea says she heard this with dread, but not surprise—like someone waiting in an oncologist's office, hoping the doctors will say everything is okay, knowing already that they won't. Somehow, she had always known the world was sick. It was almost a relief to hear someone put a name to it, even if the someone was a crazy person and the name made no sense.

"We'll have to walk from here to the 30th floor," she said. "Unless you have a better idea."

He shook his head.

Andrea led the way around the corner to the north staircase. She hesitated before the doorway—what if the stairwell was filled with ghosts? She'd always felt the presence of something malevolent in the tower, and now she knew it was real. She couldn't make herself brave by saying it was all just a funny feeling and she should just snap out of it.

Morlock didn't hesitate, though. He threw open the door and shouted into the dark stairwell. She still didn't understand the words, but it seemed to be a kind of song.

Well, what he could do, she could do. She screamed "olly-olly oxen free" and "duck, duck, gray duck" and "The Purple Cow" and all the nonsense rhymes she could remember until her throat was sore and the stairwell rang with echoes.

"That'll show 'em," she said to Morlock, who nodded agreeably. They began the long climb to the 30th floor.

Morlock was like the Fool in her Tarot readings—getting drunk and running from dragons and looking up words in the Hennepin County Library, wandering from world to world, to hear him tell it. The Fool made her think of the Tower, the card she couldn't escape. The Tower Struck by Lightning.

"Morlock."

"Andrea Andrea Worth."

"Would a bolt of lightning be loud enough?"

She had to explain what some of the words meant but, when she had done that, he said, "Yes! The best. When the sky speaks, the world listens. Only I cannot talk to your sky; I have no focus."

"Yeah, well."

Andrea had recently seen *Back to the Future* and she had a hazy idea of hooking up the dormant antennae atop the Drake Tower to draw in a lightning bolt or two. I'm not a physicist—unlike some people, Enge, I'm not constantly making claims about myself that I'd be unable to sustain—but I'm pretty sure this wouldn't have worked.

Andrea was none too confident herself. But she muttered, "It *can't* be a coincidence, can it?"

"What?" Morlock asked.

There was no point in telling him, but there was no point in not telling him, either: they had a lot of stairs to climb. So she pulled the Tarot deck from her pocket and laboriously began to explain what they were.

But he recognized them instantly. "Tarock! They are *chartae sortitionis*, cards-of-foretelling, yes?"

"I guess. Yeah, sure."

He listened seriously, never interrupting, as she told about the readings she'd cast in the past few days, especially tonight.

"May I see?" he said, and held out his hand.

Let me put this in context for you, Enge. After Andrea and I had been living and sleeping together for about six months, I saw her Tarot cards sitting on a coffee-table. I was researching the connection between playing cards and the Ambrosian legends, and I was interested. "Hey, let me have a look at those," I said, and reached for them.

She stabbed me with a fork. If you ever condescend to visit me, I could show you the scar on my right hand that remains to this day. She was serious about not letting the cards be stained by hostile influences, and this guy was one big walking stain. Street people tend to be.

So she handed him the cards. In explaining this to me, she said, "Look, pal, he didn't just grabbity-grab at the cards. He held his hand out and asked. It was up to me, not him. I could see that, *even if you can't.*" (That was the beginning of another fight, perhaps the worst one we ever had.)

Morlock held the deck for a moment with his extraordinary eyes closed. Then he shuffled the cards, eyes still closed, tossing them recklessly from hand to hand in intersecting streams. He held the cards in his left hand and cut them, using only the one hand. The card showing was the Tower.

He's not the Fool, thought Andrea. He's the Magician. But that didn't make sense, as the Magician hadn't appeared in her readings for days.

Morlock shuffled the deck again, juggling the cards like oranges, filling the air with them, all this with his eyes closed. He collected them all in his right hand and cut them, using only the one hand again. The card showing was the Tower. Again he shuffled the deck, this time with the careless, businesslike ease of a Vegas dealer and cut the deck again, using both hands. The card showing was the Tower.

He opened his eyes and met hers. "It was the Tower every time," she said, although she kind of felt like he already knew.

"Then," he said, and took up the card with one hand. "This is the focus. May I have it?"

"Oh, geez," Andrea said. "Will I get it back?"

"No."

"Oh."

"Paper burns," Morlock explained.

Andrea made a sound like Morlock trying to say "eight". Then she said, "You can keep it, I guess. The stupid rats will probably eat us anyway."

"Or the ghosts."

"Thank you SO MUCH for reminding me about the ghosts."

He kept the Tower card but handed her the rest of the Tarot deck.

"I give you back another later," he said.

"If you live that long, what with carnivorous demon-rats and dragons and stuff."

"Yes."

Morlock wasn't the guy to sugarcoat anything, obviously. Andrea told me she would have preferred it if he was, but I'm not so sure. The fact that he never lied to her is probably why she trusted him with her cards, the things that mattered most to her. Andrea and I were always lying to each other, which is probably why she ended up changing her name and leaving town without telling me.

It takes a long time to climb seventeen floors—even longer, Andrea said, if you can hear rats in the walls and scrabbling on the stairs below.

"Why don't they show themselves?" she asked Morlock at one point.

He shrugged his crooked shoulders and said nothing.

"Are they massing for an attack?" she wondered.

He seemed to think about this for a few minutes; maybe he was just figuring out what the words meant. Then he looked at her and tapped his nose, like they were playing charades or something. She almost laughed.

Then they were at the doorway to the 30th floor, and she wasn't laughing anymore. There was a rasping, rumbling, wheezing sort of sound on the far side of the door.

"Am I crazy," Andrea said to Morlock, "or can I hear them breathing?"

"I can hear them," Morlock said. "Andrea Andrea Worth—"

"Just Andrea!"

"Andrea, where do we go after we pass through this door?"

Andrea closed her eyes to envision the observation deck area. "There's about, I don't know, twenty or thirty feet of floor space with some display cases that have exhibits about the history of the building—"

"It is an ancient building?"

"Well, it's more than sixty years old."

He gave her a bemused look, then shrugged.

"Anyway," she went on, "beyond them, there's a short stair up to the observation deck. Fifteen or twenty steps."

"Locks?"

"No, not beyond this door. Management figures if anyone gets this far they've earned the right to jump."

Morlock considered this seriously. "What?" he said at last.

"Never mind," Andrea said. "A little gallows humor."

He shrugged and said, "I go first. If you follow—"

"Why wouldn't I follow?"

"There is no need to follow. They are hunting me. If you go downstairs, quick quick, you may be safe enough."

"Are you sure?"

"No."

"Forget that, then. I want to see what happens to my Tarot card."

"Then I go first. They may ignorant you."

"Ignorant? Ignore."

"They may ignore you. English is stupid."

"Couldn't agree more. I guess this is where I unlock the door and we go face the monsters."

"Demonically possessed rats, yes."

Andrea found the right key, then stood aside so that Morlock could make his dash for the observation deck.

The dim room beyond the door was carpeted with rats, but they were all dead. They didn't have to worry about the rats—just the demons.

Morlock stumbled and fell in the dark carpet of dead rats. His form was furry with ghosts, like a Chia pet of the damned. They were worming themselves into his skin, like ten thousand quills made of dark smoke. They were getting at him, the way they had gotten at her before, but worse. Maybe his voice was already paralyzed.

Andrea charged in. *The merit of a thing is in finishing it to the end*. She screamed out all the lyrics she knew to the Clash's "London Calling," an album she had often tried and failed to interest me in.

The smoky forest trying to plant itself in Morlock's skin dispersed—but the shadows swirling around them both grew darker. Andrea could hardly see the observation deck stair, could not see the observation deck door. She tried to go on screaming Clash lyrics, but her voice guttered and squeaked into silence. She could feel the feathery touch of the ghosts in her throat, strangling her voice, killing her words before she could speak them.

She moved the way you move in a dream when the thing that's trying to kill you is about to kill you: without hope, but without stopping.

Morlock rolled to his feet, scattering dead rats about him, and did a standing leap from where he was to the middle of the observation deck stair. It was completely crazy and somehow inspiring. She couldn't shout her approval so she grumbled. They couldn't stop her from grumbling—I also found that very difficult, Enge—so she kept on doing it, grumbling out the lyrics to the Banana Splits theme song. She swam through the lake of ghosts, as thick as mud, toward the dim angular beach of the observation deck stair. It seemed to take forever. It probably took about fifteen seconds. But in the end she stood beside Morlock at the top of the stair.

He pulled the door open and pushed her through onto the observation deck.

She drew in a whoosh of bitterly cold, utterly ghost-free air and let it out in a delighted howl. Morlock pulled the door shut behind him, breathed deeply, and muttered, "*Hurs krakna!*"

"Is that a swear word?" she asked.

"No." He looked around in wonder at the dark winter sky, through the metal framework that encaged the open-air deck. "No moon. So strange to see a silent sky, so full of stars."

She had no idea what he meant so she said, "I guess so."

He dropped his eyes to look at her. "Andrea."

"Morlock."

"I must now try to speak to your sky. It may not answer me. It is very unlike the sky of my world. But I will have to go into a deep sleep-that-is-no-sleep to make the attempt. The ghosts may try to harm me while I am not-asleep."

"Geez," said Andrea.

"I am grateful later if you can keep them from me. If not, I understand. You should be able to make your way back down without hindrance."

"Shut your stupid face!" she shouted.

He nodded and closed his eyes. He held the Tower card in his left hand. He put it behind his back and joined his hands.

It did not really look like he was going to sleep. At first it was more as if he was in the early stages of a seizure: his eyeballs were twitching a lot under the closed lids. Then they seemed to be emitting a faint light.

His feet rose lightly from the ground, but did not descend again. His body rose higher, through the gaps in the metal safety cage surrounding the observation deck.

Andrea was watching this with amazement when she was touched with inexplicable dread, colder than the midwinter air surrounding her. She looked around to see that the observation deck door was slowly opening.

She seized the door-handle and pulled it shut.

It didn't feel any safer though. If fact, she could feel the ghosts getting closer, the dread and hopelessness increasing as she stood there gripping the door-handle.

She looked down and saw that a ghost was forcing its way underneath the door. Its vaporous face was smeared flat but she could still read its expression—void of thought, but somehow filled with hate. It stabbed her through with disgust and a kind of shame. Was this what awaited her after death— no Elysium, no hope of a happy afterlife, just mindless misery and hate for the living? The world was sick with ghosts. She had learned that tonight, but somehow she had always known.

Without willing it, she was driven back from the doorway and it began to creak open. The ghosts welled forth like ink into the clear water of the air.

But it didn't matter. They were on all sides, now, creeping out of the cracks in the deck, sliding up the walls of the tower from broken windows, swirling like a dark whirlpool around the peak of the Drake Tower's spire.

In the midst of it hung Morlock, now upside down with one leg akimbo, just like the figure of the Hanged Man in the cards, eyes glowing bright under the lids. The great cloud of ghosts fractured around Morlock: there was something keeping him clear of it.

As she watched, though, threadlike capillaries of shadow began to enter the clear zone around Morlock. The light in his eyes dimmed; he slid down a little in the empty air. They were getting at him.

Andrea raged wordlessly at the ghosts enveloping her and the tower and the stranger. It had to be wordlessly; she could hardly even grumble, so deep a hold did the ghosts have on her. Obviously, Morlock was losing his battle and there was nothing she could do about it.

What did she have on her? A flashlight. 77/78s of a Tarot deck. The can of pepper spray: that would have been useful against the rats, if she had remembered it. The huge ring of stupid, noisy keys.

That was it. She seized them in both hands and pulled them loose from her belt. She shook the ring fiercely. She rang them with intent.

It was good magic—apotropaic magic. You're a kind of classicist, Enge: I suppose you remember how the Kouretes would smash their spears and shields together, to cover the noise of baby Zeus crying. Their noise protected him from the hostile notice of his evil father, the crooked deviser, Cronus. It's the same reason we ring bells and make noise at midnight on New Year's Eve. The noise, the intentional noise, scares off hostile spirits.

The ghosts didn't like Andrea's key-ringing, but they couldn't do anything about it. The bright sound kept them at bay and she found she could sing, and scream, so she sang a screaming song.

She didn't know how long she could keep it up, and she couldn't ever tell me how long she did keep it up, but she stopped because the sky broke up and fell in on her in three separate pieces—three fierce chunks of crooked aether who fell down and cried *Here I am! Here I am! Here I am!* in bright inhuman voices. The tower had been struck by lightning, not once, but three times.

Andrea was bounced around inside the observation deck cage and came to herself slumped against the door back into the tower.

At that point she didn't have to worry about ghosts anymore: there wasn't a shadow of one in her eye or her heart. What she had to worry about was fire. The tower was on fire, and there she was at the very top of it.

She looked around wildly for Morlock, but he was nowhere to be seen.

You can only do what you can do. Andrea ran through the burning Drake Tower Museum and jumped into the stairwell with both feet. She leapt from landing to landing all the way down: her feet never really recovered, as far as I know.

You'd think the sprinkler system would have kicked in, but they'd torn all of that stuff out, preparatory to the demolition. There was kind of a scandal about it, but the Tower was slated for destruction; it needed to be destroyed, because it was polluted with angry ghosts, and it *was* destroyed, by a stranger from another world and three lightning bolts summoned expressly for the purpose.

You can guess how much of that went into Andrea's report, which she scribbled out in an ambulance while the fire department battled in vain to save the wreckage of the old Drake Tower. While she was recuperating, Cavall transferred her to the night desk. She was never neglectful of her duties, but she did spend a lot of time on the night shifts reading Tarot cards. She was prepared to buy a new deck, but it proved unnecessary: a week or so after the Drake fire she received a new deck in the mail. It was a beautiful thing, hand-drawn in colored inks, but it had some odd features. All the titles for the Major Arcana cards were in Latin, and card XV wasn't "The Devil": it depicted a sly looking dragon with the title "Ille Draco". The artist didn't sign his name, but then he hardly needed to: he had promised to replace her deck, after all.

I remain a skeptic about those damn Tarot cards, but I have to admit they treated Andrea well. Under their guidance, she transferred to Cavall's sister company in Los Angeles. While she was there, Tarot cards had a brief vogue as a form of spirituality in Hollywood—this was either right before or right after the Kabala. Anyway, Andrea was in the right place at the right time, became fabulously wealthy by our standards, and retired to study what she refers to as "the science of reincarnation." Actually, I'm not sure what she's up to these days; she has long since blocked me on Facebook.

So there it is, Enge: the only first-person account I've ever collated of an encounter with Morlock Ambrosius, the person we both have spent so much of our respective careers writing about, for our own respective reasons—me, for the extension of knowledge and the devotion to truth; you, for money.

But let's put that aside, Enge. The world is sick with ghosts, and maybe I am, too. It's just before midnight as I write this, and in a few moments I'm going up to the roof of Fort Holmes and will scream my damn lungs out to scare the ghosts away from the new year. I like to think that, somewhere in the Great Black Swamp, you are doing the same.

    With a certain grudging regard, I remain
           your old friend and enemy,
                  Gabriel McNally

P.S. Did you ever finish your dissertation?

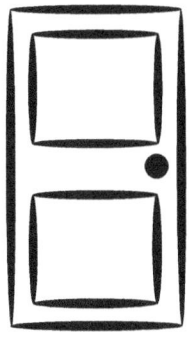

Brick and Mirror

Steven Harper

You can only trade once, you know. Take it from a bricklayer.

Say you're putting down a wall. Halfway through the day, you notice that five rows ago, you laid down a single wrong brick. Wrong color, wrong grade, whatever. It doesn't hurt the wall, but the client will be pissed because it messes up the design. You can't tear out five rows. But lucky you, it's only one brick and the mortar isn't totally dry.

Stay with me, okay? This is relevant.

So you tap the bad brick out and trade it for another. Make sure you have it right this time, though, because swapping out the one puts stress on the others, and this weakens the wall a tiny bit. Swapping it a second or third time would create even more stress, and you risk an entire section collapsing on you. The wall only lets you trade once.

I had just done this very thing on the day everything went to fuck and back. The client wanted a wall with a red-and-gray pattern, and one of the new guys had skipped a gray. I caught it a few rows later and showed him how to swap it out. No big deal. Hardly anyone would notice. Right?

Right.

The workday ended. I got into my rattle-trap of a Ford and drove my ordinary route home on my ordinary day.

Right then I was feeling sore and cranky and kinda lonely. Patty had texted to say another three cases of Amazon flu had shown up at the hospital, so she was picking up an extra shift. A little grimace walked across my face. What kind of Friday night could you have when your new wife was working? Then I scolded myself for being pissy. The Amazon flu was a real crap-case, and I shouldn't get ticked when dying people needed nurses. I mean, if my mom came down with it—spit spit, fingers crossed—I'd hope hard the hospital had a nurse for her, right? So I pushed the pissiness away and tried to make the best of things. Have what Patty called a "me" night, but instead of a bubble bath with Chardonnay and a thick book, I'd indulge in delivery pizza, video games, and half an hour with my right hand on Porndeck. I was just thumbing my phone for the first item when someone knocked hard at the door. It was two guys in dark suits, who basically hit me between the eyes with government IDs.

"Sikander Mazari?" one of them said, and at my startled nod added, "You need to come with us."

Before I really knew what was happening, I was riding in the back of a black SUV toward an anonymous office-and-warehouse complex, one of those places where the developer cuts all the trees down and installs a cutesy pond with a fountain that looks great until it gets clogged with goose shit. I asked a bunch of questions, but got only rocky silence in return.

The guys hustled me inside one of the big warehouses. By now, I was completely freaked, but I also started realizing that they hadn't cuffed me or read me any rights, so I was wondering if I should be pissed off instead. What the big red hell was this?

Then I was in a stadium-sized room cut in half by a mirror that ran floor to ceiling and reflected everything. My mirror self caught my eye. The dark suits sat me and the mirror-me on a chair while people and their reflections moved equipment around on hand trucks or typed like maddened monkeys at a thousand keyboards. Everyone wore blue jumpsuits, and the air smelled like solder. Cords as thick as my wrist snaked all over the concrete floor, which itself was a spiderweb of cracks.

A woman in her 40s with frosted hair in a tight bun bustled up to me, along with a balding guy in a bow tie. They both wore white lab coats. The woman put out a hand, and I automatically shook it, though the rest of my body was shaking as well.

"Sikander Mazari?" she said. "I'm Dr. Helen Crew. I apologize for jerking you out of your apartment, but we have to move fast."

"Are you ICE?" I blurted out. When your name is Sikander Mazari and you have my skin tone and hair color, everyone assumes you were born Somewhere Else, even if your grandparents were the immigrants, and the closest you've come to even visiting a foreign country was a vacation in Texas.

She blinked at me. "ICE? No, CDC. Your records say you've been vaccinated against rubella, correct?"

The unexpected question threw me even further. "German measles? When I was a kid, sure."

"Ever been exposed to Amazon flu? Sometimes called Amazonian superflu?"

This got my attention in a different way. Like I said, Amazon flu was a real crap-case. Fever, cough, nausea, sensitivity to noise, rash that started out as small blisters that turned bloody when they broke, followed by a slow, wet death. No treatment, no cure, no vaccine. Theory went that someone had been hunting spider monkeys in the Amazon basin right at the time the virus had been thinking about mutating, and the disease had made the jump to the human population. Attempts to contain it were failing, and it was spreading fast. Panics hadn't started yet, but the public was nervous. Patty said word around the hospital was this was becoming that pandemic the CDC had been worried about for ages.

"No Amazon superflu that I know of," I said, now worried about a whole different pile of shit. "They've got cases in quarantine at Valley Hospital. My wife is a nurse there. Is that why I'm here?" My voice rose. "Is Patty sick?"

"Your wife isn't sick, Mr. Mazari," said Helen. Across the room, her reflection was bending over me, too. "But you can prevent her from *becoming* sick."

I pulled back. "Listen, I don't understand any of this."

"Yeah. It's hard to explain." She pursed her lips. "Are you familiar with the idea of parallel worlds, Mr. Mazari?"

The ping-pong questions kept me off-balance, and I was starting to get ticked. "I've seen it in science fiction movies," I said. "But I'm a bricklayer, not a scientist."

This seemed to amuse her, for some reason. "There are an infinite number of universes existing side-by-side with this one. Anything that can happen differently *does* happen differently, but in another universe. There are universes where a clump of hydrogen atoms went in a different direction just after the Big Bang, and our galaxy never formed. There are universes where an asteroid went a measly two miles sunward, and the dinosaurs never went extinct. And there are universes where everything is the same as in ours, except that one day last year in another universe, a monkey only tried to bite a hunter, and in this universe, it actually succeeded. That's where rubella and the Amazon flu come in."

"I still don't—"

"I'm a vaccine researcher at the CDC, Mr. Mazari, and let me tell you—nothing takes greater precedence than the Amazon flu right now. It's already killed fifteen thousand people world-wide, and it's barely getting started. Our projections have it killing six or seven hundred million before it peaks, with another two or three hundred million after that. But a vaccine continues to elude us." She stuffed her hands into her lab coat pockets. "On the other hand, we've had rubella well under control for decades."

"But what does that have to do with—"

"Sorry to interrupt," interrupted a man, who also shook my hand. "I'm Alex Gelb, head of quantum mechanics and paradigm shifts here at Quantadigm. We're a private company working with the CDC. I think this is where I need to step in." He glanced at Helen. "Fifteen minutes, Doc."

"Shit," she said.

"Can someone just tell me—" I tried again.

"A few years ago," Alex said, "I proved a theory correct. It's indeed possible to touch other universes, as long as they're extremely similar to ours."

"Similar?" I echoed.

Alex nodded. "At least 99.765% similar. If the difference variance is greater than that, the quanta don't match up and we can't reach across the portal. We have a universe on tap that's 99.97% similar. A mere point-oh-three variance."

Now things fell together a little bit. A lot of people think my intelligence is average or low because I lay down bricks for rich white people, but I lay bricks because two years into law school, I realized that even if I passed the bar, I'd be walking into a glut of law school graduates also looking for work, and I could make twice as much putting down bricks. The smart thing to do, right?

The point is, I saw what they were getting at. "There's another universe almost exactly like ours that has a vaccine for Amazon flu."

"They developed a vaccine against Amazon flu over there, we developed a vaccine against rubella over here." said Helen. "It looks like the same people died in both universes, just of different diseases, so the universes stayed the same."

"Well within the point-oh-three variance," observed Alex.

"What are the odds?" I said, not quite believing all this.

"When you're dealing with an infinite number of universes, the odds are one to infinity that a match exists." Alex adjusted the collar of his white coat. "The hard part is actually finding that match. There are an infinite number of universes in which we failed to do so, in fact. In this universe, we won the lottery."

"The other universe wants a vaccine against rubella. We want a vaccine against Amazon flu," Helen said. "We're hoping to engineer a trade before both diseases reach pandemic proportions."

"Rubella wasn't a superflu," I said, not sure why I was arguing that particular puny point when so many others loomed like giants. "It is—was—only a danger to kids and babies, wasn't it?"

"In our universe, yes," Helen said. "Their version is much worse. And their version of Amazon flu is milder for them. But we have good reason to believe both vaccines will be effective on both sides."

"Okay," I said slowly. I was calming down a little now. "But what's this got to do with me? My wife is the nurse."

"Every few months, we can use a portal to…trade," said Alex.

I was ready to swear I was sitting in a law school lecture hall again. "Trade?"

"The two universes have to stay in balance," Alex explained. Behind him, a pair of technicians did something with a huge cable that created a shower of sparks. They glinted in the mirror. "If we send something over there, they have to send their universe's version of it over here at the same time. Otherwise nothing goes through the portal. We also can't send objects. Only living things, and we don't know why. That means we can't trade samples of the vaccine, even a live one—a non-living container won't cross, so it's a human or nothing. Last, the trip is one-way. Whatever goes there, stays there. Whatever comes here, stays here."

A suspicion was crawling over my skin now. I knew what they were going to ask, and it made my stomach crawl around inside me like a worm. I didn't want to say the words, but they came out anyway.

"You want me to go over there because I'm immune to rubella, and they can use the antibodies in my blood to create a vaccine," I said slowly. "My double will come over here and you'll use his blood to cure Amazon flu."

"You have it." Alex checked his watch. It was one of those fitness things, though he didn't look like he ever ran farther than the nearest taco truck. "And we have less than ten minutes to do it. Are you ready?"

"Whoa, whoa, whoa!" I shot to my feet. So did my reflection. "Hold the fuck up! Why me? You must have a thousand scientists who would kill to trade universes and look around."

Alex pinched the bridge of his nose. "I wish it were that easy."

"Only certain people can actually make the crossing," Helen explained gently. "Your body and your life have to be less than point-oh-three different than those of your double. Almost everyone in this universe is at point-oh-seven or worse, and the portal won't let them through. In America, we found only three people with less than the point-oh-three variance. You're one of them."

"What happened to the other two?"

"One is a six-year-old girl," Dr. Gelb said. "The other was a woman named Rita, and after we made her the offer, she was ready to go. Eager, even. So we didn't bother contacting you."

"And?"

"She caught Amazon flu and died yesterday."

A moment shuffled by. "Fuck," I said.

"We might be able to find someone else," Helen continued, "but it would take months of background checks and surveillance—"

"Wait—you *surveilled* me?"

"We surveil a lot of people," Alex said. "You ever submit your DNA to one of those ancestry places?"

"Yeah, but—"

"Did you read *all* the fine print in the agreement before you clicked through?"

Silence.

Alex nodded. "And that's just one example."

"Anyway," Helen continued, "the portal opens today. In..." she checked her watch "...six minutes. After that, it's another six months before the quanta align and it opens again. In that time, more people will die. We don't have *time* to find someone else. It's you, or we wait six more months and millions die."

I flicked desperate glances all around the warehouse like a raccoon in a cage trap. "So you're gonna just shove me into that other universe?"

Helen's lips went tight. "No, Mr. Mazari. We won't force you. Say the word, and we'll drive you back home, after you swear not to speak of this to anyone. We will, however, try to persuade you."

"And how will you do that in—" I looked at my own watch "—five minutes?"

Alex spoke very fast now. "We've deposited ten million dollars into an off-shore bank account. So did the other side. You'll both get your side's account number when you cross. Tell people you won the lottery, or your great-aunt left you a fortune. Whatever you want. But here's the kicker." He licked his lips. "After you cross, *you won't notice*. Your life is only point-oh-three percent different from your double's. You'll go home to the same apartment, the same furniture, the same food in the fridge. Same job, same family, same everything. There might—*might*—be minuscule differences. Your license plate might change by a single number. The tree outside your front door will have two more leaves on it. Your bedspread will be a slightly different shade of blue. You'll probably go your whole life and never notice anything. The same goes for your double over here."

"And," Helen added, "you'll know you saved hundreds of millions and millions of lives."

Ten million dollars. I have to admit—I had a selfish moment. My abortive term in law school had left me with a pile of student loans I would be paying off until I was forty. They were the reason Patty and I lived in a tiny apartment instead of a decent-sized house.

Patty Mayweather and I had met through—yeah—a dating app. She had a thing for South Asian guys, and I had a thing for pissing off my family by dating white women, so we swiped right and decided to meet. She was a stunner, no mistake. Long auburn hair, big blue eyes, the cutest nose you ever saw. And shit, she could make me laugh harder than a middle-schooler snorting milk out his nose. She also had a scent about her that I couldn't quite identify. It wasn't perfume or soap or even sweat. It was just *her.* Whenever I smelled her hair or neck, I got a little jolt of happy. Every time. Even after weeks of knowing her. I told her about it once, and she made a laughing comment about good pheromones, and too bad we couldn't bottle it. I told her I'd pay a million dollars an ounce and leaned in to smell her hair again. Happy!

We got married a year later at the courthouse because neither of us had much family to invite to—or pay for—a big wedding. Her parents were dead, and my parents stopped speaking to me for proposing to a white woman. So, courthouse wedding. I dropped out of law school to lay bricks while Patty finished up her nurse's cert and got a job at Valley Hospital. Waking up next to her in the morning became the greatest part of every day. Six months into our marriage, I still felt that way.

"I need to talk to my wife first," I said, reaching for the phone in my pocket. In the mirror, my reflection made the same motion.

Alex grabbed my arm, and so did his reflection. "You can't do that. You can't talk about this to anyone. Ever. Not even your wife."

"Why not?"

"The portal is the most highly classified project in the history of humanity," Alex said. "Can you imagine what would happen if an enemy government got hold of this technology and figured out how to trade weapons across universes? We can't even let foreign governments know this technology is *possible*, in case it gives them the idea to research it themselves. I'm deadly serious, here. If you speak of this, the consequences will be terrible."

"What do you mean *terrible?*" I said hotly. "You gonna kill me the minute I walk out of here?"

"We aren't in a Jason Bourne movie, Mr. Mazari," Helen said.

"The CDC saves lives. We don't take them. But you can't talk about this. Not even to your wife."

"Then fuck you," I said. "I'm not going to—"

"Please, Mr. Mazari." Helen actually clasped her hands under her chin. "Please, sir. I'm begging you. You know what Amazon flu is like. It's terrible to watch, especially in young children. It's gearing up to be a world-wrecking epidemic if we—you—don't stop it. Half a billion innocent people are holding their breaths over what you decide to do next."

I glanced at the mirror, and my reflection glanced back. A little ice ran over me. "That's not a mirror, is it? That's the fucking portal. I'm looking at—"

"—your double, yes," Alex said. "Our doubles are making your double the exact same offer over there. If you look closely, you'll see the reflection is a little blurry. When the quanta align, it'll become sharp, and you can step across. Will you, sir? As Dr. Crew says, the world is begging you."

I still couldn't make myself do it. "Why doesn't someone over there just hold up the formula for the vaccine so you can copy it down?"

"This isn't a batch of lemonade," Helen said. "It would take years to synthesize a live vaccine from a written 'formula,' as you call it. In that time—"

"—hundreds of millions of people will die, I get it." Fuck. What was I supposed to do? I stared over at the other guy, and he looked back at me. We both sidled closer to the mirror, which was indeed a tiny bit blurry, like a computer screen set to the wrong resolution. My double was wearing the same brown shirt and same ratty jeans with the hole in the left knee. His eyes were the same brown, his hair—black like mine—was cut in the same style. I'd cut my left cheek shaving today, and he had the same mark. So while I'd been patting lather on my face in front of the bathroom mirror, he'd been doing the exact same on the other side, and neither of us had known what was coming up. I put out my hand, and he put out his. I waved, and he waved. Without thinking about it, my eyes went to his crotch, and his eyes went to mine. Same bulge, dressing to the left. I caught him looking, and he caught me looking, and we both grinned sheepishly.

"Hey," I said, and he mouthed it back, though neither of us heard anything. "Should we do this?"

Alex came up behind us in both universes. I swear his bow tie was quivering, and he carried a pad with a countdown running on the screen. "Mr. Mazari, the portal opens in thirty seconds. What's your decision?"

The portal image became sharp as an HD screen. I looked at my double again, he at me. Shit. What could I say? Could we say? It was billions of their lives against my one. I just didn't know if I had the courage. Then I thought about Patty. What if she caught the Amazon flu and I hadn't done anything to stop it? The same thought obviously went through my double's expression because his expression went all resolute. We said, "Let's do it."

Alex snapped his fingers, and the dark suits rushed at me. Before I quite understood what was happening, they stripped off my clothes, leaving me naked in front of myself and the entire warehouse. No one seemed to care.

"Sorry," both Helens said. "Living material only."

"Two seconds," both Alexes said, staring down at their pads. "One. Now!"

One of the suits shoved me at the mirror. I came at my own reflection and shut my eyes. There was a *wrench,* and then I was in the warehouse with my back to the mirror and my clothes at my feet. The other side.

I expected something to feel different, or strange. A change in the air, like the *zip* before a lightning strike. Or a smell of stinky cheese. Something. But it was all exactly the same. I glanced over my shoulder, and my double, now in my universe, looked back at me, with our asses reflecting in the mirror.

While the two of us scrambled into our clothes with identical motions, the Helens rushed over a little cart with medical stuff. They snapped matching tourniquets around our upper arms and popped matching needles into our inner elbows. They drew off four or five vials of blood.

"Don't speak of this ever again," warned both Alexes, and they handed us matching sheets of paper. On it was written an account number and instructions for accessing ten million beans. I was in another universe.

My heart rate shot up and my breath turned shallow. What had I just done? What had I been thinking? Panic crawled through my stomach and I started to pant.

Another prick poked my arm. I looked down just in time to see Helen withdrawing another needle. "Anxiety is a side-effect of the trade," she said. "This'll get you home nice and relaxed. You did a wonderful thing, Mr. Mazari, and the world thanks you."

The world swooped like a dive coaster. I got one more glance at my other self in my original universe. He was collapsing into the arms of a dark suit. So was I. The lights went out.

When I came to myself, I was lying on the couch in my apartment. Groggily I sat up and put a hand to my head. For all of three seconds I thought it was a dream. But on the battered coffee table sat a letter worth ten million dollars.

My heart jerked a little. I was in another universe. I figured I should have been panicking, but the drug tucked my freakout under a nice, warm blanket and gave it a hot toddy. I decided to look around. This place was exactly the same, right? So ...

I rifled the apartment. Didn't take long—me and Patty couldn't afford much. Garage sale couch with the same little stain in the second cushion. Same leftover Thai food in the fridge. Same long row of hot-hot spice jars in the cupboard. Same second-hand Ikea bed with a loose headboard in the bedroom. Half a roll of toilet paper on the spindle in the bathroom. The Alexes had been right—everything was exactly the same.

Or? Was that a slightly different scratch on the kitchen table? Was the Kleenex box in a slightly different spot? Had there been a spoonful less Cherry Garcia in the freezer? I couldn't remember.

I brewed a pot of coffee—same coffee maker, same coffee—to chase away the last of the junk they'd injected me with and turned on my creaky old laptop. My email, passwords, and Internet bookmarks were all the same. Even Porndeck. I called up the bank web site listed in the letter. The account number and password worked. The figure $10,000,000 stared back at me.

"Hol-ee fuck-me," I breathed.

My phone buzzed in my pocket. Text message. *P: Hey, sweetie. Extra shift is turning into a bitch. Hoping they don't make me staff quarantine. Make sure u eat, sexy!* An emoji blew me a kiss.

I smiled. No matter which universe, Patty was always afraid I wouldn't eat. When—if—we had kids, she was going to be an "Eat, eat, eat!" mom.

I realized I hadn't gone through my—his—phone in this universe, so I called up a few apps. All the same. The crossword game I played with a friend from law school showed the same puzzle, with me still winning by seventeen points. Cool.

Next, I checked the photos. My thumb ticked the icon, and the latest one blossomed into being.

It took me a minute to understand what I was looking at. The first photo was a selfie of me at the park with my arm around ... who the fuck was that? I did remember taking a couple's selfie yesterday. Patty and I had gone for a run together and stopped under a tree. I took a selfie of us. Patty had turned her head at the last second and kissed me on the cheek. It was very cute.

But the person kissing me in this photo was a guy. He had auburn hair. Patty's hair. Big blue eyes. Patty's eyes. Cute little nose. Patty's nose. He wore a red t-shirt. Patty's t-shirt. He could have been Patty's twin brother.

My stomach twisted around, and I scrolled through more photos. In every picture, Patty was gone, and this guy was in her place.

Point-oh-three.

A few minutes later, I was pounding on the door at the anonymous warehouse. "I know where you are, you bastards! I'll tell the news! I'll tell everyone!"

Dark suits brought me in. Helen and Alex met me in front of the mirror. Behind us, our reflections did the same.

I waved my—his—cell phone at Alex. "You fucking lied to me! My wife is a man!" In the mirror, my reflection waved a cell phone picture of Patty at the other Alex.

Alex looked at my phone. "Oh. Well, shit. We knew you were married. I guess we just assumed it was the same on both sides. Point-oh-three. Sorry."

"That's it?" I yelped. My reflection was yelping at the other Alex, though I couldn't hear him. "*Sorry*? You said I wouldn't notice anything!"

"Sir, please keep your voice down," said one of the dark suits.

Helen waved him away. "Mr. Mazari has a right to be angry."

"I'm not *angry*," I snarled. "I'm...I'm..." There wasn't a word for what I was. "Your precious surveillance didn't turn up the fact that I'm married to a *woman*?"

"I'm so sorry," Helen said. "Rita's death put us in a spot, and the algorithms said you were a match. We didn't have time to dig deeper than that."

"Look," Alex said reasonably, "we told you there was a point-oh-three variance between our universes. When you think of all the trillions and trillions of events that led up to your existence, this change is less than minuscule."

"Switch us back!" I snapped.

"That's not possible," Helen said. "The portal won't let us. We told you that."

"Why the fuck not?"

Alex spread his hands. "We're studying that phenomenon, but don't completely understand it yet. Give us a few decades and we'll tell you."

I ran over to the mirror and faced the other me. We looked into each other's eyes with the same forlorn, frightened expression. I held up Patrick's photo in the moment he held up Patty's.

On my phone I typed *How long u bn gay?* and held it up.

At the same moment, he held up *How long u bn straight?*

Point-oh-three. Fuck.

And something else occurred to me. I put out a finger just as he put one out. Slowly, I pulled it back to touch my nose, and at the last moment, switched to my ear. He did exactly the same. Shit.

Why had we *really* switched places? Because we wanted to, or because we had to? The other guy mimicked my every move. Or I mimicked his. Was I making his moves, or was he making mine? Which one of us was choosing? Neither?

Alex had said there was an infinity of universes out there, each one packed close, kind of like bricks in a wall. Bricks all look alike from a distance. But when you get closer, you see the differences in each. A corner chipped here, a color difference there, a small ripple in the surface elsewhere. They all fit together into a great wall, each occupying a space defined and determined by its neighbor.

People are the same. Hemmed in by past events, present circumstance, future probability. Occupying a space defined by a universe that makes them think they can choose, when their choices are already determined. Most people will tell you they disagree, that they have free will. But ask those same people if, say, you can choose who you fall in love with. Bet you ten million dollars they all say no fucking way.

My cheek itched. I resisted scratching. I could see the other me was feeling the same sensation. We both stood there for three, four, five seconds as the itch dug in. I didn't want to do it. Neither did he. At last I couldn't stand it anymore and scratched at the same moment he did.

Was he doing what I did, or was I doing what he did? Who was in charge? I didn't know, and the thought terrified me. The other side's Alex and Helen had conspired to swap me over in exactly the same way this side's Alex and Helen had done it to my double. They hadn't decided to do it—both sets of them could only do what the other side was doing.

The Helens stole up behind us. "We truly didn't know," they said to us. "I'm sorry."

I tightened my jaw and thumbed my phone. So did the other me. He flashed *Don't hurt him* as I flashed *Don't hurt her.* It occurred to me that my other self's text didn't come out backward because this wasn't really a mirror.

Do you love him the way I love her? I asked.

Do you love her the way I love him? he asked.

Yes.

Yes.

Alex gave a little cough. "You know," he said, "arranged marriages have a higher success rate than choice marriages. Maybe you could think of it as—"

"Patrick deserves to know," I said. "Patty deserves to know. You can give us that. They need to choose."

"The universe can't have imbalance," Alex said unhappily.

"It looks like the universe won't *allow* imbalance," I snapped. "The universe doesn't *allow* anything. They need to choose."

* * *

Patrick stood next to me, in his blue-green scrubs, still looking bewildered. Who wouldn't? Some dark suits had yanked him out of the hospital, hauled him to an anonymous office warehouse, and fed him a story that sounded like something Shakespeare might write on acid. In the mirror, Patty stood next to the other me looking at Patrick. Just like the Patrick in his picture, the live Patrick had Patty's auburn hair and huge blue eyes. He was handsome where Patty was beautiful, no denying, and I wondered if the other me was thinking the same thing in reverse. All four of us were holding hands, me with Patrick, he with Patty. I don't know how it happened, really. Patrick's hand just slipped into mine and I didn't pull away.

"Is this real?" he asked, and his voice was low. On the other side, Patty asked the same thing.

He smelled like Patty. Not smelled with a scent, but *smelled* with a feeling. Like I said before. When he stood close, I got a little burst of happy. The feeling was both comforting and unnerving, and I could see by the expression on my double's face that he was feeling the same thing with Patty.

"It's real," said Helen. "Mr. Mazari insisted that we tell you because you're his husband." The other Helen mouthed the same thing.

"I don't—" I said, then stopped myself. I had been going to say *I don't have a husband,* but I caught my own expression mirrored on the other side.

Don't hurt him. Don't hurt her.

We stopped ourselves. Which one of us made that decision? I couldn't tell.

Patrick's hand tightened a little, and I felt a little strength flow out of his grip. It felt good, like there was someone on my side. A bit of attraction flared, and for a second, I was perfectly good with holding Patrick's hand. I flicked a glance toward him, and my other self flicked a glance toward Patty, and we both flicked glances at each other in the weirdest ping pong match in the universe. Something made a gritty *clunk* inside me, like a brick dropping into its proper place with that solid, satisfying feeling. The mortar would set, and the wall would stretch into the distance, every brick neatly in place, me with Patrick, him with Patty. I caught my double's eye again.

The fuck! we both thought.

"So what does this mean?" Patrick asked. His voice was calm, like Patty's always was. It was what made Patty such a good nurse—she could stay hurricane-eye calm during even the biggest shitstorm. She was a rock the first and only time I took her to meet my parents, a moment that had ended my relationship with them and cemented my relationship with her.

It occurred to me that in this universe, my family probably disowned me not so much because I married a white person, but because I had told them I was gay. I would have to ask Patrick about it. Point-oh-three.

"It means you have a choice to make, Mr. Mayweather," Helen said. "Your husband gave up life as he knew it and saved millions of other lives. It was the most unselfish, heroic thing I've ever seen. Right now, there's a little boy out there who was supposed to watch his dad die of rubella. Instead, the son will graduate as valedictorian of his class and thank his dad for being there his whole life. And there are hundreds of million more stories just like that." She paused. "Now you have to decide if you're going to stay together."

Patrick and I had dropped hands now. So had Patty and the other me. I felt very alone right then, unselfish hero or not. I didn't love Patrick. He seemed like a great guy, but beyond a little messing around with some mates when I was in middle school, I'd never been interested in what even a great guy might be doing.

But if I left Patrick, my other self would leave Patty, and she would be alone.

"You don't have to decide right this moment," Alex said. "I said before—think of it as an arranged marriage. Strangers learn to love each other all the time. And you two aren't exactly strangers."

A treacherous little voice whispered to me that my parents and both sets of grandparents had arranged marriages, and they seemed to love each other as much as any other married people I'd seen. Hell, my grandmother—Daadi—on my mom's side hadn't even laid eyes on Daada until the day of their wedding, and I'd heard both of them say "I love you" to the other more than once, even in our reserved little family.

Patrick ignored Alex and walked toward the mirror. Patty matched him. Patrick muttered something, and Patty muttered back, but I couldn't make out what they were saying. Apparently, neither could they, because both took out their phones and thumbed at them, just like I had earlier. They held out their phones, and on Patty's was written *Don't hurt him.*

I couldn't help it. I ran toward the mirror and reached for Patty. This led to a strange tangle at the portal as my other self ran toward the mirror and reached for Patrick, and our two selves ended up facing off at the mirror instead. I tried to reach out for Patty, but my other self reached for Patrick, and we got in each other's way. I tried again, lunging in a different direction, but my other self did exactly the same thing. I grew more and more panicked. I had to get to her. We pounded on the portal, matching each other blow for blow. It felt like pounding cold glass bricks, and no matter how many times I tried to change direction, my other self matched me. Or I matched him. I realized I was screaming, and I couldn't stop.

Strong arms took me from behind and pulled me away from the portal. It was Patrick. But he was also like Patty. He pulled me to him and put his arms around me. By instinct my arms went around him. I couldn't help it. I'm a little taller than him, and I pressed my cheek against the side of his head.

"It's all right," Patrick said into my ear. "You're fine. You're here. You're *you.* The universe has changed but you haven't."

We'd only been married a few months, but Patty—Patrick—always knew what to say. My breathing slowed, and the little jolt of happy from the smell of Patrick's hair calmed me down. It was eerie. I found myself liking Patrick, in a mixed-up, confusing kind of way.

Clunk.

Patrick stepped back a little and held me at arm's length. "You're the same on both sides of that portal, Sikander," he said. He didn't call me *Sika* or *Andy.* Like Patty, he knew I hated nicknames. "Unselfish and kind and still the hottest guy I know."

"But I'm not ... *him,*" I protested. "I'm someone else."

"This is the way things are now," Patrick said with Patty's utter calm. "And you saved millions of lives. That outweighs our insignificant marriage by a ton of tons. Patty feels the same way. You and I? We'll figure this out. Together."

"Because we want to," I said quietly, "or because the portal said we have to?"

"What's the difference?" Patrick said. "I know what I want. I want to live my life with the man I married."

It was a sweet thing to say, and I found myself melting a little. *Clunk.*

"It isn't real," I said. "How can it be? We're only together because the portal arranged it. The portal made me—us—switch sides. It makes us say and do the same thing in both universes."

"How do you know that?" Patrick said in that calm, steady voice. "How do you know it isn't the other way around?"

For a moment, I didn't understand. Then it stole over me.

A brick wall is a pattern of nearly-identical bricks, and all the bricks hold the wall together. But the bricks dictate the structure of the wall. Bricks for a house are different from bricks for a patio, and those are different from bricks for a garden wall. The bricks decide what you can build with them.

There was an infinite number of universes, which means that there was an infinite number of Sikander Mazaris, and the universes existed to accommodate the infinite number of choices I—we—made. There was an infinite number of universes out there where I *didn't* cross over, and also an infinite number of universes out there where I ran screaming from this calm, sweet guy who could love someone who turned out to be a sort-of stranger. The wall existed only because the individual bricks decided it must.

Clunk.

"The universe doesn't dictate our choices," Patrick said.

"Our choices dictate the universe," I finished, and I realized tears were running down my face. Fuck. How long had that been going on?

"And in these two universes," Patrick added, "the four of us are fucking rich!"

A laugh burst out of me, the kind of milk-snorting laugh only Patty—Patrick—could get from me and was one of the reasons I loved her. Him? Them? Behind me, my other self was laughing hard at something Patty had said.

Clunk.

Can you choose who you fall in love with? Maybe not. Or maybe you can fall in love with who you choose.

"So what are you going to do?" Helen asked.

I stared down at the concrete floor. The spiderweb of cracks ran in a dozen directions, turning and twisting in unexpected ways. I stared at them for a long moment, then looked back up to see my other self watching me in the mirror.

But in that moment, there was a thing. A small thing that became a big thing. It was this—I could see him out of the corner of my eye before I looked up, and he had looked up at me a half second before I looked up at him. The difference wasn't long, but it was enough. Unexpected cracks. I reached out a hand, and his met mine at the portal. The surface was cold, and his reflection was a tiny bit fuzzy.

Take care of her, I mouthed.

Take care of him, he mouthed back.

I waved at Patty. She waved back. *I love you,* she mouthed. *We both love you.*

We love you, too, I mouthed back.

My not-quite double and I turned not quite simultaneously away. "Let's go home," I said to Patrick, "and work this out."

* * *

That was half a year ago. The rubella vaccine was a huge success. Headlines all over the world shouted that the disease had been beaten into retreat, and the hard-working virologists at the CDC were hailed as heroes.

Patrick and I are still together. We spent a few strange months learning how to be wealthy and how to be a couple. It's gotten less strange every day. A week ago we had sex for the first time. It just...happened. Until that point, we'd both kept to our own side of the bed at night, but one day I woke up with my arms around Patrick in a lazy patch of morning sunlight, and it had been so long, and Patrick still smelled like happiness. He gave me a drowsy look with those big blue eyes and the two of us sort of...slid together. I liked it more than I expected, and disliked it less than I thought, if that makes sense. It made Patrick happy, anyway, and that's what matters. Our choice.

Later, we tried going back to the anonymous office warehouse, but the portal people were gone. A paper mill was using the place for storage, and the guy we talked to out front had never heard of Quantadigm. Or he said he didn't.

"Does it matter?" Patrick said in the parking lot as we headed back into our brand-new car. Ten million bucks buys a lot of car.

"Not really." Something caught my eye, and I bent to pick it up. It was a shard from a broken mirror. My own eye looked back at me in it. I blinked. Had the other eye moved a tiny bit slower? I tossed the shard away and nodded at a low, ornamental brick wall. "That wasn't there before. Good workmanship."

"I love that you can't help noticing these things." With a bright grin, Patrick unlocked the car door. "And...I love you, Sikander. I've learned how."

I climbed into the car, and the words popped out before I could stop them. "I love you, too, Patrick."

Patrick leaned over to kiss me in the car, and then we drove away, leaving wall and warehouse behind.

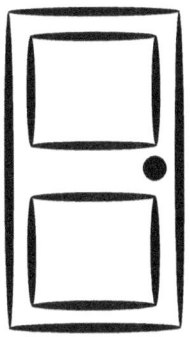

A Bend in the Air

F. Brett Cox

The day before Malander's scheduled execution a bird flew through Caspel, the town where he was imprisoned. There was nothing remarkable about the bird except the fact that everyone in Caspel saw it at least once. None of the town's residents would have been able to describe the bird accurately, even to avoid their own executions. It was, after all, unremarkable. But they did see it, every last one.

Malander saw the bird from the window of his cell. It appeared briefly in the patch of sky he wished he could see uninterrupted by bars. He didn't pay the bird much attention. He was too occupied staring into the sky, trying to empty his mind. There was nothing to think about beyond his impending demise, no comfort to be had, not even the comfort of rage or sorrow at being falsely accused. He had in fact done exactly what they said he had done, and the question of whether or not he deserved to die for his crime existed only to the extent that one might ask if anyone deserves to die for anything. Malander did not expect that particular question to be answered within the next twenty-four hours, and so he put it out of his mind along with everything else.

Malander sat on the withered straw that covered the cell's filthy floor. He pressed his back to the blank wall behind him and stared at the equally blank wall in front of him. He resolved to remain thus until they came for him tomorrow.

A rattle, a rusty groan. The cell door stood open and Dill, the jailer, loomed over him. "On your feet."

Malander looked up. Dill was a good-sized man, but Malander was half a foot taller. He supposed the jailer was enjoying his temporary advantage. Everything was temporary. "Give me one good reason."

"My foot up your ass if you don't."

Malander complied, but he took his time about it. He uselessly brushed straw off the part of his body that had for now avoided the jailer's foot. Dill stepped back once, then twice, seeming less confident now that his captive had regained the advantage of his height. Malander briefly considered seizing the jailer and snapping his neck—they could only hang him once, and surely he was entitled to a final indulgence—but before he could commit to the action, someone else walked into the cell.

"My name is Linander," the new arrival stated. "I bring you greetings from our Protector."

Malander wondered why the Protector would send him this slight and already boring young man. Then, as he noted the indeterminate practicality of Linander's clothes— trousers, tunic, coat, cap, boots, suitable for anyone travelling anywhere—and the neutral length and cut of hair, and the lightness of voice, he wondered why the Protector would send him a woman. A fantasy about a final conjugal visit for the condemned left his head almost as quickly as it had arrived.

Besides, he had more urgent matters to focus on. The Protector of any town, including Caspel, was a mere three stages removed from whoever currently sat on the throne. Given the considerable distance between town and throne, the Protectors' decisions were seldom subject to review. They governed as they thought best. While Malander's situation could scarcely be worse, a visit from a representative of the Protector was not likely to make it any better.

Still. Greetings from the Protector? Malander prepared himself to pay close attention.

"Bow to the Protector's counselor, you oaf," Dill demanded from the security of the other side of the cell.

Before Malander could decide whether or not to comply, Linander said, "Thank you, jailer. You may return to your duties."

"But counselor, I can't leave you alone with this criminal—"

"My man stands ready," Linander said, gesturing toward the still-open door. Malander looked outside the cell and noticed for the first time another guard standing without. This one was not shorter than he was. Quite the opposite. "Thank you," the counselor said again.

"By your leave, then," Dill said. He bowed again and started for the door.

"I've always liked you, Dill," Malander called after him. "I hope I see you one more time. Perhaps I can hug your neck before I go."

The jailer moved quickly and was gone. The other guard entered the cell and positioned himself within an arm's length of Malander, who turned his attention back to his visitor. "To what do I owe the honor, counselor? I'd offer you a seat, but there's frankly no telling what's in this straw."

Linander regarded him as one regards someone else's intriguing but malodorous pet. "Hug his neck?"

"And why not? I've heard in some lands you're expected to pay your jailer. I no longer have any money, so my affection is my only coin."

"Your affection measured out in those long fingers wrapped tightly beneath the poor man's chins."

"You wound me, Counselor Linander."

"I have no need to wound you, Malander, since tomorrow someone will kill you."

Having no answer for that, Malander instead offered the bow he had neglected earlier.

Linander took no notice and moved over to the window. "Have you thought about what awaits you?"

"Little else."

"I don't mean your death. I mean after."

Malander considered his response. He had not known what to expect when Linander had walked in, but discourse on the afterlife? "A wise man once said that death is not to be feared because it leads to one of two outcomes: a deep and dreamless sleep, or a gathering with the best of those who have lived before."

"Do you believe that?"

"Not for a moment."

"What do you believe?"

"What do you care?"

The Protector's counselor ignored his impudence. "Are you afraid to die, Malander?"

"Who isn't?"

"A few people I could name, but never mind. How would you like to live instead?"

Malander was convinced Linander could hear the pounding of his heart, the surging of his blood. It couldn't be. They wouldn't dare. He took in a breath, let it out slowly. "I would like that very much indeed."

"It would be complicated. The penalty for your crimes is quite definite."

"Yes, it is."

"Especially when they are repeated."

"True."

"And you confessed without...enticement."

"Why should I suffer in order to declare something you already know?"

"A sensible point. The Protector was told you were sensible."

He wanted to ask who told her that, but if her counselor's mind were going in such a direction, he did not want to divert it elsewhere. "Why would you do this thing? Why give me my life?"

Linander turned away from the window and looked at him. "You ask all the right questions. But I have no right answers."

Malander had to remind himself that physically compelling information from the Protector's counselor would be counterproductive. Then Linander continued, "For eleven days now there has been something...inexplicable...past the town to the north, out near the edge of the district. People have gone missing."

"People go missing all the time. Bad things happen. Or sometimes people just wish to leave."

"Not in such numbers. And it's not just people. Their livestock. Their homes, as if they lifted their cottages like sacks and hauled them away. Not a trace left."

"Surely the district authorities have investigated."

"The Protector is confident that the district authorities have never had the sense God gave a piss-ant. Recent events have not changed that. Even if they did, they are just close enough to the throne to keep what imagination they might have in check, lest it cause undue notice."

"And what does your imagination tell you?"

Linander gripped the bars in the window with both hands, an unexpected gesture accompanied by an extended silence. The sudden withdrawal caused Malander to look reflexively at the still-open cell door to see if this was a chance for freedom. But the new guard stood between him and the door, and he was still taller than Malander. And wider.

"Counselor?"

Linander let go of the bars. "It is reported that the air is bent."

"What?"

"The air is bent where the disappearances have occurred. There are some who have seen it without disappearing, or being taken, or whatever is happening. They describe a bend, a curve, as if the air itself were a malleable thing. They say you feel it more than see it."

"And have you witnessed this yourself? Has the Protector?"

"I have not seen this for myself. And the Protector is responsible for the entire town. She dare not risk her own disappearance."

"I see. These witnesses are reliable?"

"I believe so. But we need more information."

Ah. "And that is why you offer me my life."

"Yes. I want you to accompany me to where the air bends. We will then report back to the Protector what we...experience."

"Why you?"

"I am the Protector's most trusted counselor."

"Why me?"

"As I said, you are known to be sensible. Intelligent. There are some of us who can't understand why you chose the life you did."

Malander could feel his freedom waiting on the other side of the cell door, so instead of saying, "What makes you think I chose it?" he said, "Sensible men can still be unreliable."

"You have no reason to be so. Besides, what kind of life the Protector returns to you will depend on the quality of the information you bring back."

What kind of life? He pushed it aside. Life was life. Still, he could not resist: "And what if I simply run away?"

"I will take precautions that you do not."

He looked over at the new guard, who seemed to have grown larger in the time he had been standing there. "And what if I, too, 'disappear'?"

Linander almost smiled. Not quite, but almost. "Then the town will have saved itself the expense of a hangman. Now, are we agreed?"

Malander looked past the Protector's most trusted counselor. Outside the window there was a sky with a whole world under it. For the second time, he bowed. "Counselor Linander, I am the Protector's servant. Take me to where the air bends."

* * *

The journey began inauspiciously, with the Protector granting them generous provisions, but no horses. "She expects us to walk to her phenomenon?" he demanded of Linander as they prepared to leave town.

"The town has none to spare. Besides, the Protector wishes to keep this simple. The district authorities remain fools, but still, there's no need to alert them with a parade of riders leaving town."

"And how would they know?"

"You'd be surprised."

Malander doubted that, but he was not ready to let this go just yet. "I thought this was an emergency. I would presume time to be of the essence."

"If you quit talking and start walking, you will be where you need to be by this time tomorrow."

"And how many people might disappear in that time? How many cattle?"

"We have more cattle than horses."

"You're content to walk when you could ride?"

"I serve our Protector," the counselor replied.

And so Malander found himself walking through the town with Linander and the Protector's man, whose name was Pandal and who, no longer within a jail cell, seemed a more normal size. It was the middle of the week and the streets were neither full nor empty. The Protector had granted an ample meal before their departure, but the months Malander had languished in his cell had left him with a continual want unconnected with actual hunger or thirst. As they passed the baker's, he wanted bread; when they reached the tavern, he wanted beer. He slowed ever so slightly as they passed the latter, but Pandal prodded him, none too gently, with his walking staff, while Linander never broke stride. Instinctively, Malander's hands went to his belt before he remembered that his knife and cudgel were for the moment in Pandal's care. He decided that, if he made it back from this unusual errand, he would let the fool Dill go but might have to pay Pandal an unannounced visit.

They reached the limits of the town without further delay. Pandal halted them, removed the pack he carried on his back, and gave it to Malander. "This should get you through till your return. If you return," he added with a smile.

"You're not along for the rest of our grand adventure?"

Pandal tapped his staff on the ground, raised it, and pointed down the road that led away from Caspel. "A day's walk, give or take, and then another half day beyond that. Linander will keep you on the path well enough."

Malander looked over at his new guardian, who nodded almost imperceptibly. So be it.

As Pandal turned to leave, Malander said, "Pardon, sir." The Protector's man turned back with an annoyed look. As Malander held out both his hands, the annoyance remained, but Pandal duly returned Malander's knife and cudgel. The Protector's man looked intently at Linander, said, "Watch yourself," and then he was gone.

The guard need not have concerned himself. Malander had already decided that he would stick to the plan he had been given, at least until they reached their destination. The goal was to put as much distance between himself and the hangman as possible, so why not take advantage of doing so not in escape, but in sanctioned travel? Linander was safe with him. For now.

Malander shifted the pack on his back. He was out of practice carrying such weight and silently cursed the Protector for her almighty cheap ways. Linander, whose pack was the same size as his own, stood comfortably, waiting. "Well, let's be off, then," Malander grunted. Linander gestured ahead of them—after you—and Malander began walking.

The road to the north was well-kept and they made good time. As the town fell away behind, the land around them thickened; scattered trees turned to forest and the fields disappeared. Now that there were no bakeries or taverns to distract him, Malander looked up at the sky. A few clouds here and there, but still a cheering blue. A barely-discernable dot in the blue grew larger, and Malander strained to see what it was. It was a bird—the same kind he had seen through the window of his cell. Black like a crow, but larger wings, and a beak that seemed almost too big. It descended to a few yards above their heads, circled once, then again, and then flew away, also heading north.

"What kind of bird is that?" Malander asked, not expecting an answer. Linander had not said a word since they left town.

"I don't know the exact name," Linander replied, "but you see them in the district from time to time."

Malander looked at his—companion? guard?—and laughed. "So, you remember how to talk."

"When there's something to say."

"Oh, there's always something to say. That's how the world works. People talk, decide, act."

The Protector's most trusted counselor returned to silence.

"Come, now that you've started, let's keep it going. Tell me of yourself, Linander. If we're on this task together, we should know something about each other."

"Why?"

Rather than reply truthfully, "So I can find an advantage for when I will inevitably need it," Malander paused as if in thought. "Perhaps we don't need each other's life stories. But there ought to be something." Another pause. "Let me ask you a question, and if I think you've answered truthfully, you can ask me one."

"So we become familiar on your terms."

Smarter than he thought. "So we can feel enough familiarity to engender trust. We have no real idea what awaits, do we? We will rely on each other to survive." He started to reach over and clap Linander on the shoulder but thought better of it. "Well?"

"All right."

And easier than he had expected. "Splendid! Tell me this, then: why does the Protector have such a low opinion of the district authorities?"

Silence, then more of the same. Finally: "To be an administrator at any level is to be convinced that those in the levels above you are at best inadequate, most likely incompetent, and at worst malevolent. The Protector is an administrator." A pause, briefer this time. "A very good one. We are fortunate to have her. And she is not mistaken in her evaluation of her superiors."

"How do you know she's not?"

"That's two questions."

Malander laughed, but before he could formulate a clever reply, Linander continued. "I've served other Protectors, and I've seen the same game played out. Sometimes the Protector is on a level with the district authorities, and they—understand each other. But when you have a Protector who actually brings a mind to her duties, as ours does, things can get complicated. You may find yourself dealing with things you should not have to deal with, because if you don't, nobody will."

"You mean this—bent air we've been charged with investigating? Why are her superiors so unconcerned?"

"And that's three questions. My turn."

"Very well."

"Why did you make such an issue of the horses?"

"What?"

"This is a reasonable journey on foot. The Protector's decision not to give us horses was understandable, and even if it weren't, she owes you neither convenience nor comfort. Surely you must realize that. So why complain about the actions of the person who holds your life in her hands?"

First smarter, then easier, and now cannier. Malander was beginning to wish he had just kept looking at the sky. "Do you know how it feels to be sated? To conclude a good meal, or finish off the last tankard, or complete a job and know you did it right?"

"That's four questions, but the answer is yes."

"Well, I don't. Not really. It is my lot in life to be unsatisfied. I continually look for the convenience, the advantage, the extra bit that will leave me feeling as if I have gotten what I want. The horses were the extra bit. Why should we walk if we can ride?"

"And that extra bit was more important than your life?"

"That's two questions, most trusted counselor."

"I believe that particular horse left the stable a few minutes ago."

This time he did clap Linander on the shoulder, as he roared with laughter. "Excellent! Indeed it did. So I'll answer: you aren't the only one who is impressed with our Protector. That she would mount this expedition at all convinces me she would not let my annoying ways distract from a larger problem."

Linander sank back into silence. Malander, beginning to sense the rhythms of his assigned companion, let the silence persist until the counselor said, "I already know you're right. It's good you understand what's at stake."

Malander was not sure that, in fact, he did, and started to ask another question, but stopped himself. He had already gotten more information than he expected. Let it lie for now.

He looked up at the increasingly cloudy sky. "Best get as many miles under our feet as we can before dark. Then we can see if there's a spot where these trees will step back and let us make camp."

They did, and there was, and they did. Malander, expecting no more than bread and cheese and water, was delighted to find that part of his pack's weight was also meat and ale. They ate well, and when they lay down for the night he almost felt satisfied. But his head still buzzed with questions, and he wondered if he would sleep at all. Then the food and the ale and the day's walk after months of sitting all seized him at once, and he relaxed within their grip and slept.

* * *

In Malander's dream, he was on his back and someone with no face rode him, squeezed him between thighs like stone. The sensation took his breath away.

Then he woke and the dream was gone, but there was still weight on top of him, and he still couldn't breathe.

He opened his eyes to a dawn sky the color of parchment and the bloated face of Dill above his own. The jailer's hands encircled his throat. Dill smiled as if in greeting. "Good morning, convict," Dill muttered. "Here—let me hug *your* neck."

Malander tried to grasp for his belt and its weapons that he had laid carefully within reach before he slept, but the jailer's legs pinned his arms to his sides. He tried to shift beneath the jailer's weight, tried to throw him off, and failed. The pressure increased.

Then, just as the world started to go away, there was a barely-discernible blur of motion behind Dill. The jailer's smile disappeared as he fell away from Malander and thumped to the ground. Malander gasped and jerked into a sitting position. The world came back, and its most prominent feature was Linander standing in front of him, holding Malander's cudgel, recently applied to the back of Dill's head.

"Are you all right?" Linander asked.

Another gasp followed by a hacking cough. "I will be," Malander said as he rose, swaying, to his feet. "Just give me a moment." He turned to where Dill lay moaning in the dirt, kicked him once, twice, then dropped to his knees, wrapped his right arm beneath the jailer's chin, pressed his left against the back of Dill's head. "I feel better already," Malander said, and began to twist and squeeze.

"Malander, stop! We need to know who sent him. Let him go!"

Malander paused. The jailer's eyes began to bulge. "Oh, very well," he said. Dill fell gasping back into the dirt.

Linander squatted in front of Dill and grabbed him by his hair. "Who sent you?"

"No one," the jailer gasped. "I came on my own."

"Horseshit! He hasn't got it in him to do this without orders, and pay."

"I tend to agree," Linander said. "So, jailer, once again: who sent you?"

Tears ran down Dill's face. "No one!"

Linander released him. "If you insist. Malander, pray continue."

"No!" The jailer began to weep in earnest. "No, it was—it wasn't my fault! They offered me so much more than she ever did—"

"The Protector?" Linander asked.

"Yes! That bitch! They promised me if I did this, I would prosper, and she would suffer! Treating me like the straw on the cell floor. Treating us all—"

"'They,' who?" Linander pressed.

"They never gave their names." Dill now sat staring at the ground. "After they gave me a first payment, when they left I heard one of them say the name Colbine."

For the first time since they had met, Malander thought he saw on Linander's face something that could pass for anger. "Who is Colbine?" Malander asked.

"The Secretary to the district authority." Yes, definitely anger. "That's his official title. More accurate would be Enforcer, Enabler, Hirer of Assassins and Obscurer of Plots. His masters decide what should be done, and he sees that it is."

Malander rubbed his still-aching throat. "Why me?"

"Me as well, I'm sure. So we don't reach our destination."

"And what do they know that we don't?"

"Perhaps everything. They may have sent their own people already. Or perhaps nothing. The simple fact that the Protector wants us to go there may be enough for them to want the opposite." He moved towards his bedding, began to gather his things. "We must hurry. They may have sent others."

Malander cleared his throat, an act he instantly regretted. "If I may—"

"What?"

Malander gestured towards Dill, who sat staring gloomily at the dirt.

Linander stared at them both, turned away, and resumed packing.

By the time Linander hoisted his bag onto his back, Dill lay face down and motionless.

"Was that absolutely necessary?" Linander asked.

"I believe so."

"There's no time to bury him."

"No concern of mine," Malander said. "I've done enough work before breakfast."

As they headed out, Malander looked up and saw a bird, the same kind as before, circling above the trees. He wondered if it would swoop down to sample the dead man lying in the dirt. But it just circled once more and headed north. They followed.

* * *

Malander had assumed that when they reached their destination the forest would thin. He had not realized it would give way altogether. As the trees grew fewer and fewer the air around them changed, grew thick; the hair on his hands floated as if underwater. Finally, they were greeted by a flat plain the likes of which he had not seen since he was a young man and had journeyed to the west because there was no reason for him not to.

In point of fact, Malander was not sure if he had ever seen such land at all. The soil was unnaturally smooth and did not give beneath his feet. Flat and bare as if no one had ever thought of trees.

"She said there were houses here," Malander said. "I see no houses."

"Gone with their dwellers," Linander said. He paused and pulled the straps on his pack tighter. "I suspect we are almost there."

"How will we know when we are?"

"If what we were told is true, we'll know."

Linander resumed the pace, and Malander walked behind in silence. For the first time since being freed from his cell, he wondered if he had made a mistake in following through this far. He should have taken his cudgel to Linander after he finished off Dill and then headed east, where there were still trees and an ocean to boot. Talk his way onto the first ship out and put all his wretched miscalculations behind him.

Perhaps there was still time. There was a half-day's light; he could get back to the forest and find the road to the sea. He had known it once and was sure he could find it again. He rested his hands on both weapons that hung from his belt and edged his way closer to Linander.

"We're here," Linander announced.

Malander halted and looked past his intended victim. "How do you know? There's nothing here."

"Look deeper."

Malander continued to stare at the emptiness in front of them. Then he realized, with as profound a sense of shock as he had ever felt, that although there was nothing there, there was—something—there. There was a shimmering, as on an excessively hot day, but not generalized within a line of sight. This was clearly outlined, with the borders extending only a few yards to either side of them. Whatever he had expected, he didn't think it would be this small. Beyond that, and the shock that he still felt, were two contradictory impulses. The first was to turn and run all the way back to Caspel, and when he got there to keep running.

The other was to walk up to this thing that did and did not exist and touch it. He took a step towards it then stopped and cursed himself for a fool. Then he took another step, and another.

Malander looked over to his right where Linander had been standing and saw that the most trusted counselor was not there. Fascination and fear were promptly overtaken by panic. For the first time in his life, he simply did not have any idea what to do next. Such a state of affairs frightened him even more than the nothing-thing that shimmered in front of him.

Then he looked to his left and saw Linander walking towards

him, writing in a leather-bound book. "Well? Where did you go?"

"Around this phenomenon and back again."

"And?"

"It appears to extend behind about as far as it does to either side."

"Is it—doing the same all over as it's doing here in front of us?"

"Yes."

Malander looked carefully at Linander. Outwardly his travelling companion was as calm and unflappable as usual. But when Malander looked into Linander's eyes, he saw something different. He saw that, in addition to anger, Linander was capable of feeling fear.

"Well," Malander said. "Now what?"

"The Protector wants information, so information she shall have."

"Such as what you're writing down in that book?" A useless observation, but as long as he was talking with Linander, the attraction and repulsion of this—whatever it was—seemed to have not quite as strong a hold on him.

"In part." Linander reached around into his travel sack—still on his back—and took out a horseshoe.

"You traveled all this way with that in your sack? And us with no horses? For what?"

"For this," Linander said, and tossed the horseshoe at the shimmering bend in the air...

...where it disappeared.

Linander blinked twice, wrote something in the book, and sat down on the ground. In the silence that followed, Malander felt the pull of the nothing-thing once more. He resumed his progress towards it.

Linander sprang up, ran over, and grabbed Malander's arm. "What are you doing?"

"Gathering information for the Protector. Isn't that what we're supposed to do?"

"Yes, and that's what we've done. We've fulfilled our mission."

"Don't you want to find out what happened to the horseshoe?"

"Not at the cost of our lives, no."

"I was supposed to die today anyway, remember?"

"Let's head back to Caspel. That way neither of us has to die."

Malander stopped walking. Linander was right. He had signed on to this lunatic mission, he had killed Dill, he had come closer to killing Linander than the counselor would ever realize—and for what? For freedom. For life. And now all he had to do was turn around and walk away.

But he was not going to. He did not understand why, and in yet another emotion that was new to him, he was content not to know.

When he paused, Linander's grip loosened. Malander moved quickly towards the shimmer. "No!" Linander cried as Malander put his hand out and touched it, then thrust his hand inside it, and then followed with the rest of him.

As he was absorbed by the shimmering something-nothingness—an experience curiously lacking in sensation—he sensed someone beside him.

Then the someone was gone, and Malander experienced nothing.

Literally nothing. His awareness of his own thoughts was all there was. No sight, no sound, no touch. No time. Nothing.

Malander's thoughts raced, and he realized he had no sense of how long he had been like this. He tried counting his breaths, only to realize he was not breathing. And yet he felt no pain. He felt nothing.

Was this forever? He tried to think of how he might end it by ending himself, but his mind was becoming as still as his lungs.

After five minutes or perhaps a hundred years, there was a touch—a touch!—on his arm. Someone gripped him and pulled.

And then he and Linander stood outside the thing that was and was not there. It had returned to its seamless form. Above it, the bird that had come with them from Caspel circled and dived, then circled some more as it orbited the shimmering not-thing.

Malander shuddered as the air passed in and out of his lungs. Linander watched him carefully. "Are you all right?"

"No. How could either of us be?"

"I cannot report any injury," Linander said.

"No injury? No marks, perhaps," Malander said as he quickly inspected himself. "But how can either of us be well after that... nothingness." He shuddered again.

"Nothingness? What do you mean?"

"The void! The nothing! How can you be so calm?"

Linander paused. "When we crossed over, you had disappeared. I went in search of you. It took a while, and I had almost given up, but when I returned to where we entered, you were there, standing silent and motionless. When I touched your arm, we were here again."

Malander stared at him in disbelief. "Where did you go? What did you see?"

Linander told him, at some length. When the counselor was through, Malander shook his head and stared at his hands, which were still trembling. "That is not what happened to me."

"You can tell me on the way back to Caspel. The Protector will be eager to hear our reports."

At the mention of the Protector, Malander's hands steadied and he realized what he had to do. "I'll tell you. But I won't tell her."

"What? Why not?"

"Because," Malander began. Eventually, but long before they got back to Caspel, Linander agreed.

* * *

Malander had never been in the Protector's official rooms. Ordinarily he would have been surprised at how spare the space was, how empty, not that far removed from his cell, except there were no bars on the windows and the floor was reasonably clean. But Malander was past the point of being surprised by anything.

If there was any source of surprise, it was the Protector's relative youth. She was no longer young, but no older than Malander himself. In keeping with her rank, the Protector of the Town of Caspel was dressed plainly and covered fully. Her hair was drawn up efficiently beneath the golden cap that signified her office. Her amber eyes seemed to catch what little light was in the room. Malander was immediately convinced those eyes missed nothing. He wished he had asked for a cup of water.

The Protector closed the leather-bound notebook that Linander had been scribbling in, put it on the small table beside her, and leaned back into the sumptuous chair—almost more throne than chair—that was the only indulgent thing in the room. "My most trusted counselor took copious notes, made useful diagrams, measured well."

"Linander is a person of great wit and skill, Madame Protector."

"And yet," she said, gesturing at the book, "all this tells me little. I need to know what you experienced after you went through—into?—this thing."

"Surely Linander gave you a full report?"

"Yes. But I want to hear from you."

Malander paused, looked at his old friend Pandal, who stood smiling beside the Protector's chair. There was nothing to it but to trust Linander and hope for the best. "We found ourselves in a location much the same as that we had just left, but with grass and trees and flowers. It seemed undisturbed by the phenomenon that had drawn us in. We walked for a while and came upon a village where the people were..."

"Go on."

"They were like us, but they were dressed differently. Their clothes were brightly colored and had a sheen to them that seemed something other than cloth or leather or fur. Nobody seemed to notice us until the cart almost ran us down."

"The cart?"

"A metal cart that moved by itself. It had no horse in front of it."

The Protector leaned forward. "A horseless cart. Wonderful. Continue."

"The man driving the cart cursed us for careless fools and sped away. This drew the attention of some young people walking by. One of them laughed and asked us if we were late to the Ren Faire."

"And what is that?"

"Madame, I have no idea. We retreated into an alleyway..." There followed an account of the various marvels of the magic village, carefully coordinated with what Linander had told him. He hoped he had kept it all straight. "And when we found our way back to where the air was bent on that side, we walked through and returned."

"I see."

"The gods' own truth, Madame, I swear."

"No need for swearing, Malander. I believe you."

Malander hoped the Protector did not notice how his body sagged with relief.

"However, there is one very important thing I have yet to hear."

Not done yet. So be it. "And that is?"

"If the two of you could just walk back through to our side, why not the others? Why have my other citizens who disappeared not come home?"

A point he and Linander had in fact discussed. "Perhaps they don't care to return, Madame Protector. Or perhaps they simply haven't returned yet. Time seems to pass differently in that other place." When they had emerged, the sun was still in the same part of the sky it had been in when they entered.

"Perhaps, indeed. A sensible reply, Malander. Like everything else you have said. Had I heard all this only from you, I might have my doubts. But Linander described the same thing.

Exactly," she said, giving him a look that Malander hoped he never saw again. "And I believe Linander in all things."

"You are quite right, Madame, to trust your counselor."

"Quite right, indeed. And quite struck by the fact that you have become such fast companions, given that you were two steps away from killing him before you crossed through the bend in the air."

Malander stared at the Protector. "I beg your pardon? You are misinformed. I did no such—"

"You approached Linander from behind. You were reaching for your cudgel. If you start lying to me now, I shall have to rethink our agreement."

"But how—"

The Protector rose and walked past Malander to the other side of the room. She returned carrying a large object covered in a richly-designed cloth. She set the object on the table next to the book and removed the cloth.

It was the bird that had followed them on their journey. It sat silent and motionless on its perch.

Malander gaped at the bird. "Your pet, Madame Protector?"

"Not quite. Observe." She took the bird's upper and lower beaks in each hand and pulled them open. And kept pulling. But rather than the creature's skull cracking, its beak simply continued to open, wider and wider, until the Protector could reach into the bird's maw and withdraw a silver orb. The bird's beak snapped back to its normal size. The Protector tossed the orb into the air between her and Malander, where it hovered. She clapped her hands once, and it grew transparent. Malander could see a small image of himself and Linander walking. His hands were on his weapons as he came closer.

"Enough! Please, Madame. Enough."

She clapped her hands twice again, and the orb was opaque once more. She plucked it from the air like an apple from a tree and set it on the table. "I'll replace it in the bird later. You seem to have reached your limit of wonders."

Malander carefully clasped his hands in his lap. "I am more grateful than ever for your investing your time in me. Clearly you had no need of my services at all."

"Oh, I did, absolutely. I was not going to risk myself on this expedition." She frowned. "I did not really want to risk Linander, at least not to the extent of my counselor turning explorer of other worlds. I made that clear before he left."

Malander supposed he should offer at least one truthful response. "In fairness, Madame, it might not have been Linander's idea. I believe your counselor may have been pulled through simply by proximity to the phenomenon."

"And that, too, was careless. But never mind." She sat back down in her chair, whose elegance Malander now realized was not indulgence, but an expression of power.

"Madame, what sorcery, if I may ask—"

"You may not." She paused. "I will say that those of us who worry about the wisdom of the district authorities occasionally must take extraordinary steps to live up to our title of Protector. A few of us have—connections—beyond our towns." She smiled. "It is a large world, Malander, full of many things. But surely you understand that now."

Malander bowed his head toward the Protector. "I do indeed. So much so that I most humbly request that I be allowed to take my leave so I can resume a life that I do understand."

"Of course. You did what I asked. You may go." As Malander rose, she added, "I would strongly suggest that you leave this town, and that rather than resuming your life, you begin a new one."

Malander bowed again. "I will carry your wisdom with me always, Madame Protector."

"I doubt it. But consider what I have said. And, of course, say nothing of what you have seen. The world is large, but it is finite. If I want to find you, I can." She gestured toward the orb, and then towards Pandal.

Malander gave a final bow and exited the room. The bird remained on its perch.

Outside, Linander waited. "All is well?"

"Oh, certainly. She tried to get me to remain and take your job, but I politely refused."

"Is that why your hands are trembling?" The counselor paused, then said, "She showed you the bird, didn't she."

Malander shuddered. "You knew nothing of that, trusted counselor?"

"I did not."

"And it doesn't terrify you?"

"Not as long as it is in her hands and not someone else's."

Malander laughed without mirth. "Of course. What could go wrong?"

Linander led him to the stables, informing Malander that the Protector had authorized his being given a horse for his journey. Malander laughed again. "She must really want me gone."

"I believe she does."

As Malander mounted the horse, Linander said, "A moment before you leave."

"Yes?"

"I still need to understand why you insisted on claiming that what happened to me happened to you. Why not just tell her the truth of your own experience?"

"Why are you still speaking to me after you learned I was ready to kill you?"

"Because you are leaving and not coming back, and because I knew what you were before we left."

"There's your answer, counselor. Our Protector knows what I am as well. I did not want her getting any ideas about sending me back. Or sending anyone back. If it were not for this latter point, I might not have returned to Caspel at all."

"She certainly will send more people if she deems it necessary."

"By then I hope to be shipboard and far away from here."

Linander looked up at him. "You really did all that you were accused of, didn't you?"

"Everything. Yes."

"Then I hope your journey is a safe one."

"And I hope you do not have to go on such a journey as ours ever again." He paused, then added, "Grant me two last questions."

"Very well."

"Now that the Protector has her information, what is she going to do with it?"

"Consult with the other Protectors who share her concerns about the district authorities, I suppose. Develop a coordinated strategy. Find a way to relocate anyone within the vicinity of that location without letting anyone know what it is. And since she now knows one of her own was working for Colbine, do this all as quickly as possible."

"That seems wise." Linander had insisted they tell the Protector about Dill. The fact that it was not a topic in her conversation with Malander told him she was as capable of ruthlessness as he. He wasn't sure if that was good or bad, and he had no desire to find out.

"And your second question?"

Malander paused. "Are you a man or a woman?"

Linander stared silently at him, and Malander thought he had finally done something to cause the counselor genuine offense. Then Linander smiled and said, "I am myself."

Malander returned the smile, turned the horse, and rode out of town. As he made his way toward the turn that would take him to the coast, he tried, and failed, not to think of what he had experienced on the other side of the bend in the air.

Malander had no memory of Linander's taking his arm and pulling him back home. His gratitude would be eternal, but his gratitude paled beside his terror.

Was that what lay ahead when all was said and done? Was that his fate for his crimes? Was this how it all played out—the Linanders getting a new world of puzzles to be solved, the Malanders being removed from any world at all?

He pushed such thoughts away as best he could. Then he reached the turn that led to the sea, and took it.

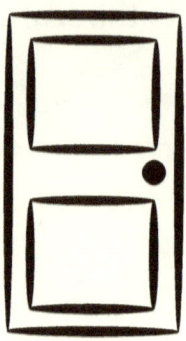

All the Lost Places

Jaime Lee Moyer

Static was all I could get on the radio after I stopped for gas in Calliope Valley and the reception got worse as I climbed up Smuggler's Mountain. I turned the sound up, letting white noise wash over me. Right now, I had a lot to think about.

This was my first trip home since Aunt Lilly died. The first time she wouldn't be waiting with a hug and a mug of chai. Bittersweet didn't come close to how this trip felt. The house and all the land belonged to me now, a gift I hadn't expected. I hadn't expected Lilly to slip away before I could say goodbye either, but her death wasn't the only kick in the teeth I'd gotten this year.

A decade of work had vanished in a flash of grenades and rocket fire. Archaeologists in the wrong place are in as much danger as anyone and claiming I was Dr. Emma Jordan hadn't protected me. I owed my life to a fast-talking assistant who convinced the government soldiers I wasn't a spy. An embassy helicopter evacuated me three days later and got me on a plane.

Through aspen trees shining gold and white in the afternoon light, I spotted the turnoff. Bare blackberry canes lined the road. Rounding the last curve of the driveway and seeing the house brought tears to my eyes. This was home.

I'd come here for the first time just after I turned six. That summer I'd named Lilly's mountaintop cottage The Palace and the name had stuck. I'd spent more of my childhood here than any of the far-flung places my parents had lived and worked. My mother had sounded relieved when I told her I wanted to stay with my aunt full time. I was only nine, but Lilly never questioned my decision and years later admitted to me that she'd known it was inevitable. Dragging a child around the world was a burden Mom and Dad once thought they'd wanted. Discovering they were wrong was painful for all of us. I became Lilly's daughter in everything but name.

The house looked the same, expectant and waiting for us to come home, but everything else had changed. I thought about Aunt Lilly's last letter and pulled the pale blue envelope out of my backpack. I'd memorized the message weeks ago.

Dearest Emma,

There is so much I wanted to tell you, to explain and teach you. If you're reading this, my lawyer passed on my letter and I never got the chance.

Running out of time was never part of the plan. In a perfect world I'd have eased you into the responsibility, not left you in the dark about what was coming. That's not at all fair to you, and I know asking you to trust me is even less fair, but this is where we are.

I'm leaving you The Palace. You love the house as much as I do and you've proven you can handle the isolation. The deed is already signed over and I've ordered a new, bigger generator and arranged for installation. You should probably look into solar panels soon (in case the power grid fails), but all the other major repairs were done last spring. The money I left to you should be more than enough to keep you going a long time, and to restock immediately. You'll find a list of what I consider critical supplies in my desk.

Someone who can help you understand what's at stake will find you soon. I don't want you to be surprised by who shows up, and I wish I had a name to give you, or could tell you who to watch for—but I can't. You'll recognize the right person when the time comes. Promise.

Be strong, Em. I already know you're brave.

All my love, Lilly

When the two of us were together Lilly rarely held anything back, but nothing she'd ever written was straightforward. My aunt's letters always hinted at secrets she wouldn't commit to writing. This letter was more cryptic than most.

The little girl inside who'd never backed down from any challenge my aunt offered was intrigued. The grown woman who'd almost died just months ago was nervous. Discovering I was mortal had made me more cautious. I still wasn't sure if that was good or bad.

Getting all the food, clothing, and my laptop inside took longer than I thought. I sank into a porch chair and watched the sun slide toward the top of the trees, unable to avoid thinking about the mysterious responsibility I was supposed to shoulder. Winter was supposed to be weeks away, but the air already smelled like snow. Snow and ice would make everything more difficult.

I eyed the meadow that stretched all the way to the aspen grove, and past the trees to the rock columns that thrust toward the sky. As a kid I'd wondered why the rocks only glittered at sunset and not noon, but that was last on the list of weird things about those rocks. Aunt Lilly never laughed when I told her about hearing voices or seeing things I couldn't understand. Her joking explanations varied over the years, ranging from fairy rings, to rips in space and time, and finally settled on the meadow being haunted. I couldn't disprove any of it—and I'd really tried.

Now I stared at colored sparks glittering in the frost-burned meadow grass closer to the house, each one identical to the glimmer atop the columns. A double row of cloudy white rock used to circle The Palace, front to back, but the glimmer was the only sign the border was still there.

Night replaced day between one breath and another. Stars winked into existence, filling the sky until it was covered with glowing silver mist, and studded with diamond-bright shards. The constellations I'd watched while growing up would wheel past in the next few hours, old friends I'd missed living on the other side of the world. I'd missed Lilly's stories about them even more.

A cold wind snaked its way under the porch eaves, making me shiver, and thoughts of stargazing vanished. Another gust tore through the trees and raced toward the house, shaking branches and rattling dying leaves. The mournful note riding the wind was too close to the sounds Lilly called *mountain ghosts* and brought back memories of all the times my aunt woke me in the middle of the night and hurried me into the shelter in the basement.

I'd only been really afraid once. All sixteen-year-olds have dramatic imaginations, but I hadn't imagined the keening wind, the shouts and angry voices in the meadow, or the truck engine roaring toward the house. My aunt had hustled me down the steps and hid me in the safe room. I'd never forgotten the rifle in her hand, nor the look in Lilly's eyes when she shut the door. My aunt let me out sometime after dawn, red-eyed and sleepless. By dinnertime I'd worked up the courage to ask what had happened and why I'd slept in the basement. She'd given me a lame excuse about an overturned prison van and a man hunt. I knew it was a lie, but let it go.

Now I regretted not pushing her. I'd lost track of all the times Lilly met strangers in the meadow or shut the front door before I could see who'd knocked. As a kid, I hadn't thought much about it. I couldn't stop thinking about it now.

I leaned against the front doorjamb, breathing in the scent of woodsmoke, and listening. Sound echoed off rock faces and down canyons in the mountains, distorting distance. Mountain winds worked the same way, almost never blowing in a straight line. The fire I smelled was likely miles away, and there was no telling if the smoke came from a campsite upslope or a cabin further down. How quickly the odor faded reassured me the fire wasn't on my land.

Convincing myself the baby I heard crying was miles away was more difficult. I'd heard too many babies cry in small towns and smaller villages not to recognize the sound. Almost all of those little ones wailed with hunger or the need to be held. The lucky ones had a mother close by and stopped crying quickly.

This baby kept crying. I was having a really hard time talking myself into believing this was just another ghost.

The odds that someone had left an infant on the far side of the aspen trees were almost nonexistent. I'd talked myself out of grabbing a flashlight and searching the meadow when a somewhat older child began to sob and call for her mother.

Mami, Mami...no me dejes...Mami...

My heart sank.

"Oh God, Lilly," I whispered. "Is this what you want me to do? How do I find them?"

I forgot all about the flashlight and hurried down the porch steps, but I'd only gone a few feet before the cries faded away. A big part of me was relieved, even as I strained to hear every sound riding the night winds. Guilt made my stomach churn, but I turned back toward the house. My fingers tingled with cold by the time I got up onto the porch and got the front door open. Tomorrow, while the sun was high and the air warmer, I'd explore as much as possible.

Lilly converted my bedroom into an office when I went to college, but left my bed in place for visits home. The chest at the end of the small bed held clean sheets, blankets, and a stack of romance novels tied together with a blue ribbon. A sticky note in Lilly's handwriting clung to the top book. All the note said was *Welcome home*, but that was enough to make me cry.

Fifty pages into *The Pauper Prince and the Shop Girl*, I fell asleep. My dreams were full of pirate ships and sword fights and not being able to hear what Lilly shouted from the crow's nest.

* * *

I jerked awake a few hours later, my heart pounding and disoriented. A glance at the alarm clock told me the power was off and explained the near total darkness. Snow covered the ground when I pulled the curtain aside and looked out.

Nothing explained the man shouting and pounding on the front door.

"Lilly! Wake up and let me in!" *Bang bang bang!* "Lilly, where are you? Open the door!"

Groping in the desk drawer finally yielded a flashlight. I grabbed my heavy walking stick, more for its weapon potential then because I needed the support on the wooden floors. The stranger kept hammering on the front door and yelling for Lilly, panic rising in his voice, until I yanked the door open wide.

He put a hand up to shield his eyes from the bright flashlight. The next second, he shoved through the door and shouldered it closed. "Turn the damn light off unless the door's shut. You're making both of us a target. Is Lilly upstairs?"

Reflex gained from years of living in unsettled areas made me point the light at the floor, but I didn't turn it off. This guy was a stranger and using Lilly's name didn't mean I should trust him. Not even close.

"Who are you? And what do you want with Lilly?"

The look he gave me wasn't friendly. "Adam. Who the hell are you?"

Twisted lines were tattooed down one side of Adam's neck and disappeared into his collar. Another tattoo covered the back of his right hand, but in the uncertain light I couldn't see the design clearly. He was tall, with brown eyes and scruffy dark hair, and needed a shave. His build would fit either a runner or a swimmer, but I couldn't imagine him as either one. He was wound too tight and the way he paced showed the violence coiled under his skin. My newfound sense of self-preservation said I didn't want him as an enemy.

The small child sleeping on his shoulder didn't do much to change my opinion. A striped wool blanket covered the little one head to feet, and about all I could see was long dark hair and a small fist holding tight to his coat. Long hair wasn't much to go on, but odds were the child was a girl. She began to fuss until Adam murmured nonsense in her ear and pulled the blanket up to keep the light out of her eyes. She sighed and went back to sleep.

Dragging a little kid up the mountain in a snowstorm didn't make any sense—not unless he really needed my aunt's help. And if he'd come seeking Lilly's help, the little girl in his arms was along for the whole ride, good or bad. Kicking him out wouldn't bother me, but I couldn't do that to her.

"I'm Emma...Lilly's niece." Adam turned to stare at me. "She's not here, Adam. I'm sorry, but Lilly—Lilly died months ago."

"Ah, shit...Lilly Belle." He flinched and shut his eyes. "She said she was fine the last time I talked to her, and gave me crap for worrying. What happened?"

His reaction settled some of my doubts. My aunt was Lillian to everyone but a few longtime friends and family. Only a select group was allowed to call her Lilly Belle, a pet name from childhood. A stranger wouldn't know that.

"She caught pneumonia, but she was too stubborn to see a doctor," I said. "The infection overwhelmed her system. She... she was gone overnight. I missed saying goodbye."

"Yeah," Adam said. He cleared his throat. "So did I."

The outside lights flickered a few times and came back on for good, bathing the entryway in a bright halogen glow that let me turn off the flashlight. Adam shifted the child on his shoulder and appeared to come to a decision. "How much did Lilly tell you about this place or what we do?"

"I grew up in The Palace, but so many deeply weird things happened here, I can't claim to know anything about any of it." Tears filled my eyes, unexpected and embarrassing. "Lilly wrote me a strange last letter, too, apologizing for not being able to explain what I was supposed to do or what I'm responsible for. She promised someone would show up to teach me the ropes. You're a part of that, aren't you?"

Adam grimaced. "What makes you think so?"

"Men don't usually arrive in the middle of the night, pound on the door, and shout for Lilly to open up. I wouldn't forget something like that happening before," I said. "And I'd have to be an idiot not to pick up on the fact something's wrong. Clue me in, Adam. Maybe I can help."

"Maybe covers a lot of territory. Most of it's swampland," he said. "Let me think. I'd counted on Lilly being here."

A bright light flashed through the front windows, lighting up the entryway and the front hall, followed by a loud bang that made my ears ring. The power was out again when the light faded. Transformers on the mountain blew up two or three times a winter, but the explosions were rarely this loud. I stood there for a few seconds, heart pounding, before flicking on the flashlight.

Adam shoved the end of the flashlight down to point at the floor. "You don't learn, do you? Here, take Ileana for a second and give me the flashlight."

He shoved the light into a coat pocket and put Ileana on my shoulder. She held on tight and was lighter than I'd thought.

Adam came at the closest window by the front door from the side and brushed back the curtain to peer out. Watching the tattoos on his neck and right-hand start to pulse and glow made the hair on my neck stand up. I found myself stepping back toward the shadows, finally taking to heart his warning about not making myself a target.

"Ah...shit, someone followed us. The nexus is cycling open." Adam ducked low and rushed towards me. "Into the safe room, Emma, right now. Go, go, go!"

He took Ileana and ran for the basement steps. I followed as fast as I could. Aunt Lilly had conditioned me to move when I heard those words, and ask questions later. And I had lots of questions for Adam. Lots.

The wind grew louder, full of remembered voices howling around corners and echoing under the eaves, trapping me in memories. Women cried, children begged and pleaded, and men screamed in rage, each of them trapped and knowing they couldn't escape. One of the voices was the government troop commander, arguing with my assistant Nikki about whether I was worth saving; another was Nikki's voice pushing back. My heart pounded, much the way it had each time one of the soldiers pointed a gun at me and Nikki got between us. I knew they weren't really there, but I couldn't stop hearing them.

I made it to the top of the basement steps before I tripped and went down hard. My breathing was already ragged, coming too fast and burning my throat. Knocking the wind out of myself sent things cascading from bad to worse. Now I couldn't breathe at all. Even so, I grabbed the handrail, hauled myself to my feet, and rushed down the stairs.

Adam held the safe room door open, waiting for me. The pulse of his glowing tattoos—blue and green and gold—was hypnotic, and the voices faded back into the wind. As soon as I made it inside and dropped to the floor, he slammed the door shut. The pain in my back hit me then, hard and fast, and scared the hell out of me. I curled into a ball and bit back a scream as wrenched muscles spasmed, mindful of Ileana and Adam.

Ileana tiptoed around me to go to Adam. She clung to his arm and whispered in his ear, and he pulled her into his lap. More whispers between the two of them went right over my head. I thought they were speaking Spanish, but I wasn't sure.

"Emma?" Adam touched my shoulder. "Ileana wants to know if you're okay, or if you need her to make it better. She's worried about you."

"I'm worried about me, too." Gritting my teeth and rolling on my back didn't help, but it didn't make things worse, so I stayed there. "But it's not the kind of thing she can make better."

"She wants to try," Adam said. "I say you let her."

Ileana watched me from the safety of Adam's lap, eyes wide and her expression too solemn for anyone that young. I'd no idea what she thought she could do, but I'd hurt her by saying no and would likely hurt her more when she failed. Either way, I was screwed.

"Fine...tell her to have at it. Just don't make me move."

More whispers flew between them and Ileana climbed off his lap. She stood at my feet, staring at me with those big brown eyes, and put her hand on my leg. My pain levels instantly spiked up to fourteen and I screamed. Spasms rippled down my spine and it took all I had not to let my leg kick out.

All bets were off once I blacked out.

* * *

When I opened my eyes again, the wall clock showed I'd been out for hours. Afraid to move, I rolled over carefully. Nothing hurt.

Ileana was sound asleep on the other side of the room, sprawled across the bed in the boneless way only tired children can sleep. Adam still sat next to me, knees up and back to the door, watching me. He smiled, but that didn't erase the tired droop to his shoulders. My hunch was he'd stood watch and hadn't slept at all.

"Welcome back," he said. "How are you feeling?"

"Confused." I braced myself and sat up, hoping that wasn't a mistake. My back felt fine. "How the hell did Ileana do...that?"

"She was born with the ability to take away pain. Don't ask me how it works." Adam rubbed his eyes and yawned. "Lilly gave me the scientific explanation the last time we rescued a kid like Ileana. Most of it went right over my head, but it has something to do with disrupting electrical signals between damaged nerves and the central nervous system."

I wanted to tell him to cut the tabloid crap—but I couldn't. Living with Lilly had conditioned me to take the weird and bizarre at face value and to believe what was right in front of me. I believed too easily at times, but I couldn't deny what had happened.

"How did she—"

"Get this way? The short answer is selective breeding and gene manipulation, and no guarantees on the result. Ileana's worth a lot of money on sixty different worlds, including this one."

"Wait—sixty worlds? You're joking, right?"

He shook his head. "Not even close. They closed the bidding early because I was getting too close, or it would have been more. For every kid who turns out like Ileana, there are hundreds, maybe thousands of failures."

I stared, struggling to wrap my head around all this. "How many worlds are there?"

"With nexus technology? No one knows for sure." Adam scowled. "The long answer to your question involves profiteers on both ends of the nexus, smugglers, and human trafficking. Breeding cartels are big business. The scum in charge keep what they're doing hidden in war zones and refugee camps, or anyplace people are stuck with no way out. Lilly called those the lost places."

"Because people trapped there lost all hope," I said. "First time I heard her say that was to a store clerk in town. They were arguing about something in the newspaper."

A thump over our heads jerked Adam's head up. He stared at the ceiling, head cocked to one side and listening. My heart raced until I saw him relax.

"Something changed four or five years ago." He pointed at Ileana. "Right about the time she was born, the number of rescues Lilly and I did quadrupled. Almost like these lowlifes suddenly got permission to operate openly. That's when Lilly started talking about bringing in someone to help us."

"Meaning me."

"Unless she has another niece I don't know about." His smile was more than a little brittle. "Now we're down to two again, and only one of us knows what he's doing. I won't hold a lack of enthusiasm against you."

Memories of crying babies at the dig site being fed, and children calling for their mothers at night, came back to haunt me. Thinking about how many times Ileana and kids like her had called, never getting an answer, was deeply sad and made me angry. "I might be deeply pissed at Lilly for keeping secrets my entire life, but she wanted me here. Count me in."

"Lilly had solid reasons for not telling you when you were young," Adam said. "She also warned me that you'd commit without knowing what was involved. You just proved her right."

I sighed. "Did you want me to say no? I didn't ask for this, Adam, I was volunteered. If there's something I need to know, *tell me*. Maybe start with what Lilly expected me to do."

"Lilly wanted you to take over where she left off. In the simplest terms, she kept objects traveling through the nexus from leaking into this world. Not all worlds have a failsafe in place, or anyone to watch out for what gets sucked into an open nexus." He crossed his arms and I saw him struggling to overcome his annoyance. "If she was still around, whoever or whatever is banging around upstairs wouldn't be there. She'd have shut them out before they cycled through."

"Even if this is where they meant to end up?" I asked.

"Yeah, even then." He glanced at Ileana and lowered his voice. "Run of the mill smugglers deal almost exclusively with inorganic cargo. A lot of them are opportunists, like the group upstairs. See an open nexus, follow where it leads. They don't have very sophisticated nexus systems, but they don't need them. Human traffickers are constantly upgrading. No one will deal with you if your goods keep arriving dead or brain wiped. Lilly managed to keep a step ahead."

"Aunt Lilly had advanced engineering degrees. I'm an archeologist." More thumps sounded overhead and my panic levels went off the charts. "And how did she do all this? I've never found any sign of equipment or computer systems to control anything that sophisticated. And I know crap all about what Lilly was doing. What if you or one of the kids you rescue dies because I screw up? You have to find someone else."

"There is no one else, Emma. Try to calm down and think for a second," he said. "You and I both know Lilly never tossed people into the deep end unless they could swim. She gave me a crash course in the basics, but I was supposed to be emergency backup. Lilly made notes on all critical operations and said you'd ace the system hacks in less than a month. I believed her. You should too."

"You seem to have all the answers. Why don't you run the nexus systems?"

"I've got a job already." Adam held up his right hand, showing me the softly pulsing tattoos. "Hunters track the monsters to the cesspool they came from and take back the people they stole from this world. Most of the time they take kids, but not always. I've pulled adults out, too, and their transition back to normal life is a crapshoot. Women make it back with their minds in one piece more often than the men."

A long series of thumps and sharp bangs shook the ceiling, making me jump, and frayed my nerves even more. Adam's only response was to glare at the ceiling.

"How long will they keep that up?" I asked.

He leaned back against the door and shut his eyes. "Until they get bored or the nexus starts to cycle closed. Try to ignore the noise. The door won't open until they leave or I'd go upstairs and chase them off."

"Alone?"

Adam opened one eye to peer at me and closed it again. "Yes. Alone."

I became painfully aware I should probably be terrified of Adam and wasn't. He called himself a hunter, but the calm he projected said there was more to it than that. I stood, realized I had nowhere to retreat, and climbed into one of the squeaky top bunks. Facing the wall and shutting my eyes let me pretend to sleep. I wasn't in the least bit sleepy, but I needed to sort the chaos whirling through my head and edge toward a choice.

Ileana scrambled up the ladder a few seconds later and snuggled in between me and the wall. The room was warm, but she trembled from head to toe. I put an arm around her and hummed pop songs in her ear until she fell asleep again. I didn't know any lullabies.

Adam cleared his throat to let me know he stood next to the bed. "I'll take her if you want. She doesn't like to sleep alone."

"She's fine. Leave her here." I brushed the hair back from her face. "What happened to her mother?"

"I don't know. If smugglers can make grabbing a child look like a political kidnapping, they leave the mother behind. Otherwise—mothers are in the way." The lower bunk squeaked as he stretched out. "I'd been looking for Ileana for months. By the time I found her, they were ready to make the handoff to an off-world buyer. He never arrived."

"Did the buyer back out?"

Adam rolled onto his side before answering. "Not by choice. I blew up the nexus with him inside."

"Oh," I said, my heart hammering. "All right."

"It's okay to be shocked, you're new to this," he said. "But this is the world I live in. I don't have room for second thoughts or regrets."

I pulled Ileana closer and remembered the rifle in Aunt Lilly's hand as she'd locked me in the safe room. Lilly wouldn't have hesitated to shoot someone to keep me safe; I knew that in my bones. Memories of life with my aunt, of all the unexplained incidents and strangers that came and went, took on a new, darker meaning. She'd lived in Adam's world and never let me see.

She'd never had to. I could only pray I'd be that lucky.

"No second thoughts or regrets is the best way to handle life in general. Lilly must have told me that a million times, but I'm a slow learner." My decision clicked into place. "And she wouldn't have wanted me to take over here if she didn't have faith I could handle it all. Lilly would want me to have a little faith in myself, too. When the crew upstairs leaves, I'd like you to show me where she hid the nexus controls. And I should get started on her notes too."

The bed creaked and I pictured him sitting up. "Emma...are you sure?"

"Positive. I can't promise not to freak out at first, but I'll try not to melt down when you're around."

"I'll forgive you if you do," he said. "I was only sixteen when a hunter yanked me off a street corner. Ike's six foot five and he wasn't having any of my attitude. I'd never been that scared of anyone."

"Is that when you got the tattoos?"

"The tattoos happened over the next two years. Once we knew the ink wouldn't kill me, Ike made me earn each design."

Adam kept talking once he'd started, telling stories and answering questions. He was the last person I'd have expected to show up, but I already knew he'd do his best for me. Lilly had trusted him. I should too.

* * *

A month went past in a blur. I got the hang of the computer codes, and knowing the difference between false alarms, and when something—or someone—was traveling through the nexus. Telling friend from foe was the hardest part; at least until Adam clued me into the big secret.

"Hunters have all the codes to nexus points on this world. It's built into the tattoo patterns and updates automatically," he said. "You don't have to worry about shutting out a hunter and anyone they're transporting by accident."

I tossed a dishtowel at his head, but missed by a mile. "Telling me from the start would have been nice. Do you know how much I've stressed over that?"

Adam whispered to Ileana, making her giggle, and my annoyance dropped away. He always sat with her at mealtime, coaxing her to eat more. She followed me from morning to night, but Adam was the one she clung to when she got scared or felt unsure. He was also the one who made her laugh. I needed to learn more Spanish if I wanted to be in on the joke.

"Sorry. I've never taught a newbie before and I forgot." He held out a sliver of apple and Ileana opened her mouth wide, doing her best baby bird impression. Adam glanced at me. "But I got a message from Ike this morning and that reminded me. I've got to go away and don't know when I'll be back. Tell me now if I should call in the cavalry to help out."

"When do you have to leave?" I asked.

"Today. I need to be gone by sunset." He looked me in the eye. "Yes or no on backup, Emma."

I shook my head. "I can handle things alone. Ileana is the one I'm worried about."

I'm a really bad liar, but other than a raised eyebrow Adam didn't call me on it. He fed Ileana another piece of apple and smiled when she ate two more on her own. "Yeah. I'll explain it all. She'll be okay."

"Ask her to teach me Spanish while you're gone," I said. "That will give her something to do other than miss you."

"Good plan." He grinned and began whispering in Ileana's ear.

I went back to drying the dishes he'd washed. Ileana wasn't the only one who'd miss him.

After lunch, Adam took me out to the meadow for shooting practice as always. Lilly taught me to shoot, but he'd made target practice a part of the daily routine. Guns were a last line of defense, but he wanted me ready.

He'd spent the last hour reviewing all the safety protocols about strangers. His critique of how I reloaded the rifle, however, was the last straw. I put the safety on and stomped back toward the house without a word.

"Emma!" Adam hurried to catch up. "Where are you going?"

"Inside." I glared at him. "I'm not stupid, and if this was a normal trip you wouldn't be treating me like...like...I'm too dim to tie my shoes without instructions. Either tell me what's wrong or leave me alone."

"You're not stupid." Adam took the rifle in one hand and held my arm with the other. "Not so sure about me. I should have trusted you, but Ike—well, he doesn't know you. Let's go inside before Ileana gets bored with watching through the window."

We leaned against the counter drinking coffee, while Ileana drew pictures of bright colored birds, huge spotted cats, and broad-leafed jungle trees. I guessed it was the little she remembered of home.

"Hunters have been chasing rumors that a cartel of traffickers were planning a new transfer point on this side of the border." Adam smiled as Ileana showed him the latest drawing. "The people who sold our budding artist are in the thick of making this happen. Wars and kidnappings further south are providing a lot of cover for their operation. Long story short, Ike found the new nexus after it powered up for a test run. We're going to shut them down for good."

I set my coffee aside, trying to make peace with how dangerous this trip was, and that he might not come back.

"Where?"

"A camp in the desert," he said. "The biggest lost place on this side of the border."

Ileana came to me, wrapped her arms around my legs, and I picked her up. "What happens to the kids in that camp?"

"Most of them have parents somewhere and we'll find all we can," he said. "We have safe places for all the other kids, too. Don't panic if I'm not back for a few days. I will come back."

I was too choked up to say anything, but Ileana wasn't so restrained. She grabbed the front of Adam's shirt and pulled him close enough to whisper in his ear.

"Ileana thinks you need a hug and says I need one, too. She says grownups always forget to hug the people they care about." Adam wrapped his arms around both of us and held tight. "Smart kid. Much smarter than me."

I wasn't going to argue. I wasn't any smarter.

Sunset had come and gone before Adam dressed to leave. The hunter's clothing he'd pulled from a trunk in the basement drank the light, making him difficult to see even in Lilly's brightly lit office. A small arsenal hid inside his jacket, deep pants pockets, and the pack on his back. I'd watched him tuck all the weapons away, but the bulges smoothed into shadows.

He held his hands out and spun in a circle. "Remember this trick and where I hid things, Emma. Hunters count on people not knowing where their weapons are."

"And I might need to know where yours are." My heart sped up. "Or where to start aiming to hit another hunter's cache."

Adam flipped off the lights, plunging us into darkness. All the other house lights were off, and he took my arm for the walk to the front door, keeping me from losing him in the dark.

"Exactly," he said. "I'm suspicious under the best circumstances, but Ike's last message really bugs me. Something's got him shook, but he brushes questions off and tells me not to worry. Promise me you'll crank being careful up to an eleven. Double that if another hunter shows up looking for me, or claims to be carrying messages. React first, think later."

Anything that bugged Adam made me outright paranoid. "I won't take any risks. Promise."

"Thank you." He hugged me tight before opening the door. "I call dibs on a welcome back hug. Stay safe so I can collect."

"Deal," I whispered. "You stay safe, too."

He disappeared into the night.

I locked the door and waited for the flash of light signaling the nexus had opened, and the soft sigh of a hunter entering and being recognized. Silence told me Adam was on his way.

Paranoia started with grabbing a rifle and a box of bullets and carrying them down to the safe room. My back started to complain before I got down the steps, but not enough to change my mind about sleeping in the basement. The rack Adam had mounted on the wall kept the rifle well out of Ileana's reach. I'd leave it there. Other rifles waited upstairs.

Ileana was awake when I got into bed. I still didn't know any lullabies, but '80s pop always put her to sleep. One of us needed to get some rest.

The way my head replayed my conversation with Adam, I knew that wouldn't be me.

* * *

Two days later, Adam returned. He pounded on the door as he had the night I met him, only this time he yelled for me and Lilly both.

"Emma, Lillian, open up! Where are you? Lillian!"

A warning, likely the only one he could give me. I rushed into the kitchen and scooped up the half-empty juice box and the sandwich I wanted Ileana to finish. "Ileana, go, go, go! Hurry!"

We'd worked on that phrase for weeks before Adam left and she took off running for the basement. When I reached the safe room, she was already perched on the edge of the bunk, wide-eyed and frightened. I dumped her lunch on the table. Grabbed a rifle and flipped off the safety.

"*Comer, niña.*" I kissed Ileana's forehead. "*Silencio.*"

She nodded as I locked her inside.

Back in the front hall, I swung the door open and leveled the rifle at the men on the doorstep. Approval that I'd understood his message flared in Adam's eyes.

A stranger stood much too close behind him, using Adam as a shield. He was much older, and the dull hunter's tattoos on his neck were in stark contrast to Adam's bright designs. Either his tattoos were faded with age and disuse—or fakes. This man wasn't tall enough to be Ike, and the nexus hadn't greeted him as a hunter. Whoever he was, he wasn't a friend.

I said the first thing to pop into my head. "What are you doing here? I told you not to come back."

Adam reached for me. "Don't be that way, babe."

The stranger yanked him back. "Knock that crap off, I'm not falling for it. Call your aunt out here, darling. Tell her Sargent Jesse wants to barter."

I aimed for a spot over his head and pulled the trigger, chambering a new round as he ducked behind Adam. "My name isn't darling. Now get off my porch before my aim improves."

Jesse called my bluff. The long knife he'd kept hidden flashed into view and slashed Adam's earlobe. Adam hissed with pain, but didn't move. Something other than the knife kept him from going after Jesse. Something I couldn't see.

"This isn't a wager you can win, sweetheart." He pressed the blade tight against Adam's neck. "You can either give me the little girl Lillian is hiding, or I can keep cutting on your boy here. You decide."

He thought I was too scared to pull the trigger. But Aunt Lilly wouldn't have backed down and I couldn't either.

"All right. I've decided." I shifted my aim to a spot between his right ear and jaw, the biggest piece of Jesse I could see, and squeezed the trigger.

Adam screwed his eyes up tight as the shot whizzed past his head, but he didn't flinch until Jesse's hand jerked and the knife sliced his tattoos. He staggered away from Jesse's body to the porch steps, tore a silver disc off the back of his coat, and threw the disc as hard and far as he could. It exploded in midair.

Half the old smuggler's head was gone, sprayed across the porch and melting snow in the yard. More splatter coated Adam's jacket. He kept a shaking hand pressed to his neck and I locked the door once Adam was inside. The body on the porch could wait.

All I wanted to do was puke. I held it together enough to get Adam into the kitchen and clean his wound. Blood seeped from a thin line across his tattoos, but the bleeding wasn't heavy, and the cut was already closing. He claimed his tattoos weren't magic, but I had my doubts.

He stood to peel off his gore encrusted jacket and the stench undid me. Heaving into the sink wasn't any fun, especially when I couldn't stop. The way my arms and legs shook and threatened to collapse was less fun.

Adam looped an arm around my middle and petted my hair. "He didn't leave you another choice. I've had to make those snap decisions, Emma. I know how hard pulling that trigger was, and how shitty you feel. The whole trip was a trap, a setup to find Ileana. Try to remember you kept her safe and you saved my ass in the bargain."

He held me tighter when I started to cry. I couldn't stop wondering how many times Lilly kept me safe and I hadn't known.

Safe for now didn't mean safe forever. Adam fought a war the well fed and well-off knew nothing about. All the lost places were nothing more than fleeting images on a screen, easy to flip past, or stories in the paper that never touched their lives. Never became their fight.

Ileana made this my fight. I couldn't walk away or pretend not to see.

Aunt Lilly expected better of me.

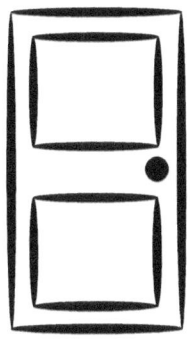

Onward to Glory!

Jason Palmatier

"Don't touch it!" Willoughby yelled.

Jimmy Johnson looked away from the shimmering circle of blue-edged scenery on the basement wall to glare at Willoughby. "Why not, Will? It's a portal, plain as day. If we aren't supposed to touch it then why'd it suddenly appear?"

"Because we tapped into the arcane powers of evil by drawing the sacred circle just like the module said!" Terrence yelled from the far side of the room. He'd been there ever since the portal had sprung to life within the confines of the dry-erase circle they had drawn on the unfinished sheetrock of his parents' basement. Between him and the thing that had caused him to wet his finest pair of plaid gamer shorts lay the full spread of Willtasia, the fantasy world Willoughby had created in sixth grade and in which they all still adventured today, six years later. Amidst the D20s, yellowed, eraser-holed character sheets, and nacho chip crumbs sat the Warlock's Revenge adventure module open to the Hideous Inner Chamber page. On that page, in exquisite detail with numerous callout boxes clarifying minor points, lay an Arcane Portal sketch with the obviously bullshit "Do Not Draw In Real Life!" caption scrawled over it. Always up for an artistic challenge, Willoughby had taken it as his honor-bound duty to draw the circle, exactly as pictured, to the exact scale mentioned in the side notes, on Terrence's basement wall.

And everything had been fine until that absolute turd, Jimmy "I can't leave stuff well enough alone" Johnson decided to recite the gibberish verses printed on the bloody scroll inset on the opposite page.

"Jimmy, why'd you have to read those stinkin' words!" Terrence yelled, pulling at his damp drawers.

Jimmy's glare deepened. "What are you two talking about? There's a portal to another dimension on your basement wall. Look at it!" Jimmy stabbed his finger at it for emphasis as he spoke. "A portal. To another. *Dimension.* Right there!"

Willoughby swallowed.

Terrence shook.

"You guys are missing the entire point of this unbelievable situation," Jimmy said. "How many times have we sat around this very table and said how cool it would be if we could somehow step into Willtasia and actually be there? Be our characters rather than just pretending that we were them? Swinging swords, bashing orcs, hurling fireballs—I'm talking the whole saucy enchilada here, people. And now it's right there, in front of us and all you can do is complain about its existence?"

"Wait, wait, wait. We don't know that that's Willtasia. It was conjured from a third-party module set in a generic realm. It could be anywhere!" Willoughby countered.

Jimmy shook his head in disappointment. "Willy, Willy, Will-Will. Have you lost your artistic eye? Have the thousands of hours of scenery creation and miniature painting burned your rods and cones to crumbling cinders? Look, right there…" Jimmy pointed to a stone ruin poking from the underbrush near the back of the scene, finger coming perilously close to touching the surface of the portal.

Willoughby frowned, but leaned in despite himself, peering at the unnervingly realistic image as it rippled under the touch of his breath. "The Aqueduct of the Ancients! The remnants of the once great civilization of Gwenthani that fell into ruin after the Tabtherian Schism!"

Jimmy nodded his head. "Exactly."

"It's even got the Sigil of Binding on it from the First Age..." Willoughby gasped.

"Yep. The crest you made when Gwen said she'd go out with you, then joined the group. Plus, if you look real close, it's also got everything you added to it after you broke up with her over that 'Tab was never a real soft drink' debacle."

"I can't believe you broke up with her over a soda," Terrence said from his spot of safety.

"It's a conspiracy! Tab never existed! No one has a can to prove it, and even if they did it could have just been 3D printed or hand painted on a generic can! It's 2018 people, you can make anything with a little money!" Willoughby retorted vehemently.

Terrence rolled his eyes and shook his head. Jimmy just pressed his lips together and let the storm pass. After a bit Jimmy said, "Okay, so we all agree that that's Willtasia in there?"

Willoughby smirked but gave a grudging nod.

Terrence just stared like a squirrel facing a Rottweiler.

"Good. So I say the only logical course of action is to jump through this thing right now," Jimmy said.

"What?!" Willoughby shouted.

"Are you crazy?!" Terrence cried.

"Not at all, Terrence. Not at all," Jimmy retorted.

"We should report it to the authorities! Get some scientists in here to study it!" Terrence yelled.

"Terrence, you and I both know that if we try to bring some sort of authority figure in here that portal is going to implode back into drywall faster than a 'no' to your prom date request."

"I've never asked a girl to prom!"

"Exactly, because you knew what would happen. So, to keep this thing humming we're going to keep it a secret and dive right into it."

"Uh, uh. No way," Terrence crossed his arms and shook his head.

Jimmy regarded him for a second.

"Tell me, what do you have to look forward to tomorrow, Terrence?" Jimmy finally said. "A math test? A hard shove into a locker followed by some uncaring laughter? Another two hours of anonymous online gaming while your never-ending-crush Stacey makes out with your arch-nemesis Vance a mere twenty-five feet from your bedroom window? Is that what keeps you all the way over there on the other side of the table instead of right here, ready to jump through a portal and live out your wildest fantasy fantasies?"

"Whoa there, Jimmy," Willoughby said.

Terrence glared at Jimmy. But then his jaw stopped shaking. It closed, real slow, and clenched. "You know what, Jimmy? You are an ass. A complete, hairy, pimple-laden ass that smells like dirty ass! And sometimes I hate you so bad I just want to shove a pencil up your nose and watch the lead dance inside your pierced eyeball as you scream."

"Hey now..."

"But then I realize that, though you may be a dick for making me feel like a pants-pissing loser who rolls natural ones in real life, you are still one-hundred percent correct. And I can't really call myself a logical human being if I don't own up to that fact and say, yes, I am afraid of losing all that. Because *I don't want to die!*"

Jimmy nodded his head. "Fair enough. But who says we're going to die? You've all seen the movies, read the books. You know that as soon as we jump through that portal we're going to *become* our characters. We'll splash through that thing and land on our feet fully armored, or robed, and ready to kick serious Willtasia ass! I'll be the oddly clever barbarian warlord, you'll be the sneaky, secretly good thief, and Willoughby will be the taciturn dwarf healer who saves all of us from near-death while not revealing any game-master-only knowledge!"

Willoughby raised his eyebrows and nodded his head. "Terrance, you have to admit that does sound pretty cool. I just wish we had a few more players to even up any odds."

Jimmy scoffed. "Pshaw! All the losers who've ever been a part of this group but dropped out because of 'other life commitments' can suck my sticky-fingered, low-rolling D20! This is *our* time! The *real* players are finally going to get their due! So, are you with me?! Are you ready to jump into the adventure and live out your dreams?!"

Willoughby nodded his head, feeling Jimmy's amped-up speech energize him, buying into the glorious vision of it all. But Terrence shook his head, eyes flicking from Jimmy's euphoric face to the shimmering scenery behind him and back in rising panic.

Then he saw it.

"Holy cow! Is that my backpack?" Terrence suddenly shouted, pointing at a well-worn leather shoulder bag lying almost completely hidden in the bushes near one edge of the portal view. Willoughby and Jimmy turned and looked. "It is! It is my lucky backpack! The one I dropped when we were running from the bugbear war party and ran into that pack of vinebears!" Terrence cut his distance to the portal by half to get a better look. "And it still has my potions in it!"

Sure enough, the swirling blue and red contents of multiple small vials could be seen glowing through the half-open top flap of the bag. Jimmy's eyes narrowed. A small smile tugged at one corner of his mouth. He turned to Terrence.

"You want to touch it, don't you, Terrence?" Jimmy asked.

Terrence's eyes flicked to Jimmy's face then back to the backpack and vials.

He licked his lips. His eye twitched. After years of gaming together Willoughby could almost read his friend's thoughts: just a few steps, a jump, a heroic landing on ninja-quiet feet and then a deft snag. All of the die injustices of the past two years would be snuffed out, relegated to the tawdry lore of yester-game, and a new age would dawn, an age filled with 15s, 16s, 17s, 18s, 19s and yes, glorious, foe-piercing 20s! And all of it was Terrence's for the taking if he just plunged through a portal that shouldn't exist into a land built solely from the questionable imagination of his sorta-friend Willoughby Parnel Winereb and grabbed it—just grabbed it—and ran back out.

"What do you say, Terrence?" Jimmy said, stepping closer to his friend. "You ready to get back your mojo? Reclaim your claim to fame? Buy a ticket on the Adventurer Express to Awesome Town?!"

Terrence stared at the bag, body shaking. The images in Willoughby's fertile mind morphed, unbidden, conjured the conflict that must be raging in his friend at that critical moment: a nugget of desire burned within Terrence—a desire to be somebody, do something, to break out of the cage of normalcy that held him tightly and run free, like a gazelle bounding on the open savannah, dodging lions and cheetahs, hoping it didn't break a leg in a meerkat hole and fall thrashing about on the ground while some hyenas or maybe even an oddly carnivorous giraffe began feasting on its entrails—

"Nope! Not going to do it!" Terrence declared.

"Oh, for crying out loud!"

Jimmy seized Terrence's "You Got Game?" t-shirt right on the D20s and dragged him through the portal.

"Wait!" Willoughby cried as he dove after them.

* * *

Thud.

Willoughby stood up. Jimmy stood up. Terrence lay on the ground, whimpering. "Oh, yeah! We did it!" Jimmy yelled. "Bring it on, Willtasia!"

Willoughby frowned, swallowed hard. "Uh, Jimmy?"

"There's no time for losers, Willy! We are the champions now. I'm going to smash and bash my way to glory and there isn't a single thing—*wah aaaa uh uh aaaa uh uh aaaaaaa!*" Jimmy's boasting suddenly cut off as a filthy spear-point emerged from his chest and lifted him two feet into the air.

"You're not your character, Jimmy!" Willoughby shouted in horror. "You're just you!"

Jimmy looked down at the triangle blade that protruded from his chest. His hands closed around the filthy shaft that followed after it with painful, slurpy slowness.

"*Glaaahhb glubaaahhhb*," Jimmy said.

His body suddenly swung to the side, legs dangling limply, revealing a seven-foot-tall bugbear with dreadlocks and a REO Speedwagon tattoo on its flattened, fanged face. The muscles that bulged under its short, matted fur bespoke bonus damage and the bones that dangled from its boiled leather armor were not entirely clean.

"Bugbearious Maximus!" Willoughby cried.

The bugbear's lips curled upwards in a cliched, GM-has-been-awake-too-long grin. He tilted his head back and roared, drooly spittle and leftover bits of gnome flying from his reeking jaws.

"I told you we should have quit that night before you made up anymore lame bad guys!" Terrence yelled. "An REO Speedwagon tattoo? I mean, come on!"

But Willoughby wasn't listening. Instead of worrying about his past GM faux-pas he was staring in disbelieving shock and half-remembrance at the quaking saplings and exploding bushes that were rapidly approaching the bugbear from behind. Terrence followed his fixated gaze and uttered a horrified "What is that!" seconds before a herd of vinebears burst into the clearing, bowling over Bugbearious Maximus and thundering past Willoughby and Terrence. Bulky and green-brown, with three thorny, vine-like appendages sprouting from each shoulder, the vinebears snorted through their sap-dripping snouts at the band of bugbears that crouched at the ready behind their fallen leader.

"Vinebears are supposed to be solitary, Will!" Terrence yelled angrily as he scrambled to the edge of the battlefield.

"It was late!" Willoughby shouted in his defense.

"*Ugh buh guh blaaahhhh...*" Jimmy said, red, frothy drool oozing from the corner of his mouth onto the ground where he now lay.

"Jimmy!" Willoughby scrambled over and grabbed his friend's arm as the vinebears bellowed in rage and charged. The bugbears set spears to insteps to blunt the onslaught and roared back. Willoughby tugged, Terrence whimpered, and Bugbearious Maximus stood, drew his wickedly curved sword and leaped onto the back of the closest vinebear. Vine sap flew and dreadlocks whipped wildly around as the battle was joined.

"Terrence, help me!" Willoughby yelled between grunts.

Terrence scrambled over, probably because getting closer to Willoughby meant getting farther away from the battle, but maybe, just maybe, because Jimmy's shirt was completely awash in blood and he had gone very, very pale.

"Oh, no, no, no. That's a lot of blood, Will," Terrence said. "I don't think he's going to—*blech*!" Terrence hurled orange fiesta-chip-barf all over Jimmy's oozing wound.

"Jesus, Terrence! You're going to give him an infection!" Willoughby said.

"Uhg. I... I don't... I can't..." Terrence started.

"*Uhhhhgggggg...*" Jimmy's eyes rolled back and his head slumped to the ground.

"He's dying! We've got to do something!" Willoughby shouted.

Terrence looked up at Willoughby with saucer-sized eyes that slowly lost focus in dismay, looking through him, behind him—

"My backpack! It's full of healing potions!" Terrence shouted, leaping up and grabbing the strap, pulling against snags until it popped free. He rummaged through the inside until he found the biggest potion of healing he remembered having. He uncorked it, very heroically, with his teeth, and poured it down Jimmy's throat.

"Careful! Don't choke him!" Willoughby cried as Jimmy sputtered and gagged.

Their friend pulled in a ragged breath once, twice. Then his eyes blew wide open and he screamed, thrashing on the ground and ripping at his clothes. After a long minute he stopped and gasped, "Oh, man, did that hurt. It was like someone was shoving my flesh into a George Foreman grill and just holding it there. It was terrible." He blinked his eyes and rolled his neck. "But it really works, I'm telling you. I mean, I feel great! I'm ready to get right back at it, just like in the game. If I had some armor and a sword I'd be—" Jimmy stopped, noticing the looks on his friend's faces. "What? What is it?" He looked down. "Oh, my God, the spear is still in me!"

Ripping at his blood-soaked, barf-encrusted shirt, he found the skin of his chest perfectly healed right up to and around the shaft. "What am I supposed to do now?!" he wailed.

A vinebear gave him his answer. It stumbled into him, green blood streaming from its slashed face, and impaled itself on the pointy end of the spear. The vinebear bellowed in renewed pain, thrashing about, bucking wildly, snapping the front half of the spear with a two-vine grab and pull. Jimmy fell to the ground. A charging bugbear rammed its spear home in the vinebear's side but lost its grip as the beast reared back onto its hind legs. Weaponless, the bugbear spied the shaft sticking out of Jimmy's back and seized it. It placed a foot between Jimmy's shoulders and tugged, like it was pulling a fork out of a tough piece of meat. Once. Twice. The shaft popped free with sick, flesh-ripping sounds on the third attempt. The bugbear spun the shaft above its head like a bo staff, winging off chunks of Jimmy-organs as it did so.

"Ah, dude, that is just too sick!" Willoughby yelled, grimacing.

Terrence dry heaved next to him.

The vinebear leapt, the bugbear parried and they both disappeared back into the maelstrom of blades and jaws. Jimmy lay face down in the dirt of the road, his back a mess of freshly torn flesh.

"Quick, we gotta help him make a save versus death!" Willoughby yelled as he scrambled for Terrence's backpack. He flipped Jimmy over, ignored the gore, and poured a full flask into his friend's unresponsive mouth. Then he waited.

"Uh, oh. I think we're too late," Terrence said. "That bugbear must have pulled out too many of his organs!"

"*Bleh-heh-heh!*" Jimmy sputtered for a second time, grabbing at all parts of his body at once.

"Quick, grab him and we'll get out of here!" Terrence said.

"For once, I agree with your cowardly instincts, Terrence!" Willoughby grabbed Jimmy's left arm, Terrence grabbed the right and they yanked with every ounce of gamer strength they had, groaning and cursing as their friend thrashed.

Only then did they think to check if the portal was still there...

It was.

With a final great heave they plunged through it, leaving the magic and madness of Willtasia behind.

* * *

"*Waaaaa!*" Jimmy screamed.

"Shut him up! My parents might be home!" Terrence yell-whispered.

Willoughby clamped a hand over Jimmy's mouth and pressed *hard*. After a moment Jimmy stopped fighting and looked around.

"Are we back? Did we make it?" he asked after ripping Willoughby's hand away.

Willtasia sat atop the gaming table, corn-chip odors wafted on the central air induced breeze, and high-backed chairs sat ready for gamers.

"Yeah, we made it back. We're home!" Terrence yelled with building excitement. Then he paused. "Wait, did any of that really happen?"

"Uh, yeah," Jimmy said, pulling on his torn and bloodied shirt. "Ah, dude, is there Dorito barf all over me?!"

Terrence avoided his gaze, then swore. "The portal is still here!"

Willoughby and Jimmy turned and found the portal still open, shimmering and showing the vinebear versus bugbear battle in all-to-real detail. Luckily the melee seemed to be moving away from the portal towards the ancient ruins of the Gwenthani.

"We got to close that thing down before something comes through to this side!" Terrence said.

"How do we close it?" Willoughby asked.

"I don't know!" Terrence yelled. They furiously paged through the adventure module. "There's nothing here about closing it! It just has the incantation to open it!"

"Ah, great, what are we going to do now?" Willoughby wailed.

But Jimmy began nodding his head, eyes narrowing as he looked at the partially complete southern end of Willtasia. "I have an idea."

Ten minutes later they slumped into their gaming chairs, sweat running off their foreheads and blisters forming on their tender, dice-rolling hands. The portal now sat behind a double layer of plywood nailed to the studs in the drywall around it and reinforced with diagonal running two-by-fours.

"Well, there goes my expansion tables for Willtasia," Willoughby said.

"You can buy more wood later. I'm just glad Terrance's parents gave us free rein down here, otherwise there'd be a lot of questions coming," Jimmy said.

"Yeah, but now what? If something big comes along it could blast right through that," Terrence pointed out.

"True, and we need that to hold until we're ready to go back in there," Jimmy mused.

"Go back in there?!" Terrence yelled with parent-alerting volume. "You almost died—twice!"

"Almost, Terrence. Almost. But I survived and we all made it back and now we know that if we go through that portal we're going to be ourselves. No mondo growth spurts, no avatar assumption, just us, in there, battling it out with the beasts and burdens of medieval fantasy. So we're going to have to get buff."

"Wha—what are you talking about, Jimmy?" Willoughby asked, thoroughly confused.

"I'm talking about seizing the day, Will. I'm talking about becoming who we are truly supposed to be, I'm talking about—"

"Exercise! You are talking about exercising until we get ripped like some yahoo jock football player!" Terrence wailed in betrayal.

"Exactly! Football players...I should have thought of that before. What time is it?" Jimmy suddenly asked.

"Uh," Willoughby looked at his phone. "Like four-thirty?"

"Perfect! That means Vance should still be over at Stacey's making out," Jimmy said.

Terrence's face lost all color. "No. No, no, no, no. We are not going to talk to Vance about this, or Stacey. And they are not making out! They're doing homework together!"

"Riiiggghhhhhttt. Okay, Terrence, you just keep thinking that and Willoughby and I will go over and have a little chat with them. Come on, Will."

"Uh, do you think that's a good idea, Jimmy? I mean, look at you..." Willoughby said

Jimmy looked down at his tattered, soiled clothes. "That will just make it more believable. Now get moving!"

Jimmy shoved Willoughby towards the stairs, cutting off his confused reply. Terrence stood nervously for a second then glanced over at the light leaking through the seams in the plywood and stumbled after them.

"Wait up!"

* * *

Stacey's door swung open.

"Oh, uh, hi, Jimmy," Stacey glanced down at Jimmy's torn, befouled shirt and tried valiantly to hide her discomfort. She failed. "What, uh...what's up?"

"Hi Stacey, is Vance here?" Jimmy asked.

"Uh...yeah...we're just working on some homework..."

"Great, so is he dressed?"

"What?"

"Stacey, what's the square root of ten?" Vance yelled from somewhere near the kitchen.

"Vance! It's Jimmy Johnson! We need to talk!" Jimmy yelled past Stacey into the house.

A chair scraped linoleum. Vance poked a scowling head around the dining room wall. His scowl deepened upon seeing Jimmy.

"Jimmy who?" Vance asked.

"Jimmy Johnson. We've shared at least one class every year since the second grade."

Vance looked nonplussed.

"Anyway, me and my friends here are in need of some help and you have what we need."

Vance took this in for a bit. "I don't need any band booster popcorn." Vance's head disappeared back around the dining room wall.

"We aren't selling popcorn! We need the best football player on the team to show us how to get into shape so we can dominate in Willtas—*mpppfffhhhh*!"

Willoughby had clamped a hand over Jimmy's mouth and flared his eyes. "Are you crazy?! Don't tell him about the portal! Just tell him we need to get in shape!"

"Portal?" Stacey said as she stood in the middle of everything, completely ignored except by a fawning, hiding-in-the-background Terrence.

Vance stomped up to the door. "Did you just call me the best football player on the team?"

"I did," Jimmy stated flatly.

"Do you even watch football games?" Vance asked with narrowed eyes.

"Well...no, but—"

Vance scoffed and started stomping back towards the dining room.

"Wait! I haven't actually seen you play but I've heard that you are the best. I mean, everyone knows that you're the best."

Stomp, stomp, stomp, stomp.

"Everyone says I'm the best football player on the team?" Vance asked.

"Of course! They've been saying it for years!" Jimmy said with an almost-genuine smile.

"Hold on a second," Stacey said, holding up a hand for emphasis on the holding. "What is this about a portal?"

Willoughby cringed. Vance looked down at Stacey sharply, something indescribable flickering behind his eyes. Jimmy pointed a finger in the air in an attempt to take command of the situation and said, "We just need to get into shape for a... ah...for a..."

"We opened a portal to a fantasy world of Willoughby's creation in my basement and now we need to get buff so we can adventure in it!" Terrence suddenly blurted.

"Is that why you are all bloody?" Stacey asked, pointing at Jimmy's shirt.

Jimmy attempted to smooth his t-shirt while looking her straight in the eye. "Yes. I got stabbed by a bugbear and then thrown about by a vinebear—hey I just realized there's an overabundance of bears in this adventure—"

"It was late! I was tired!" Willoughby shouted, exasperated.

"—fair enough, fair enough," Jimmy conceded. "But then we were able to heal me with some of Terrence's dropped potions and get back through the portal and now we're here, looking to get buff."

Stacey nodded as if Jimmy had just described how they'd gotten home late after an all-night party. "Okay, show it to me."

"Uh..." Willoughby started. "We kind of boarded it up."

Stacey turned to him and said with frightening finality, "Show it to me."

* * *

"Wow. That looks like a portal to another dimension all right." Stacey pulled her eye back from the seam between two plywood sheets. "So when you go through it you are just the same as you are here?"

"Yep. That's the problem. We got over there and then the bugbears started kicking our asses immediately. I don't even know if Vance here could handle them," Jimmy said.

"Yeah, that would be a problem for you guys," Stacey said, nodding her head thoughtfully.

"Hey! What do you mean by that?" Willoughby said indignantly.

"My dad's made me take Tae Kwon Do since I was four and I throw javelin for the track team, so I should be golden," Stacey said.

"Whoa, whoa, whoa!" Willoughby suddenly said. "You sound like you're thinking of actually going in there. Plus, you are taking all of this in way to easily. You should at least be skeptical that any of this is real and confused about the particulars, like bugbears and potions and stuff."

"Confused? I've logged over a thousand hours of screen time in Fantasy War 7," Stacey said, frowning.

"You play Fantasy War 7?!" Terrence blurted, his wrist aching at the memory of his past marathon gaming sessions on the exact same title.

"Really?" Jimmy said, expressing genuine interested in another human being for the first time since any of them had ever known him. "What's your screen name?"

"Alduth Bloodraker," Stacey said.

"You're Alduth Bloodraker?!" Terrence blurted yet again, mind officially blown and splatter-graphed on the far wall. "But, but...I've played with Alduth Bloodraker every night for the past three years and completed every single quest with him."

"You mean, her," Jimmy pointed out helpfully.

"Really?" Stacey said. "What's your screen name?"

"Kingpunch Kittyhammer," Terrence said.

"You're Kingpunch?" Stacey said.

Terrence just nodded vaguely. "But...that's not possible. I play when Vance is over at your house and you're making out with him."

"Excuse me?" Stacey said, with an offended glare.

"I mean, helping him with his homework!" Terrence yelled, completely failing to cover his tracks.

Stacey nodded knowingly, not forgetting his earlier comment, but forging ahead. "Yeah, I always play while he's here and only help him out when he really needs it. He's pretty smart, actually. I'm not even sure why he keeps coming over."

Everyone turned to look at Vance—who had unexpectedly followed them to Terrence's house—with fresh eyes, but they stopped when they saw his face.

Vance stood stock still, licking his lips and sweating. His hands shook almost imperceptibly. His eyes, deep blue and for some reason fear-soaked, kept darting to the model of Willtasia and back again, as if he both didn't want to see it and longed to see it more than anything.

"Uh...Vance? You okay?" Jimmy asked.

Vance didn't respond. He just swallowed hard and tried to back out of the room. He failed.

"Hey, get him some water, Will," Jimmy said, gesturing to the unused steins with glued together dice for handles that hung on one end of the table. Willoughby grabbed one, filled it from their all-night game cooler and held it up to Vance.

Vance's wild, trapped eyes darted down to look at it. They locked onto the D12 midway down the handle.

Waaaaaa!" Vance flailed, knocking the stein away and stumbling backwards. He tripped on a chair and landed in the chair behind it. His arm hit a blank character sheet and a bag of dice, knocking both into his lap. He stared down at the paper and spilled dice in horror. "G-g-g-g-get it off...get it off!" he screamed.

Everyone stood frozen.

"Um...what is going on?" Jimmy finally asked.

"I can't have this stuff on me or around me! You've got to get it off!" Vance yelled.

Willoughby moved forward, uncertain, and removed the dice and papers. He retreated slowly, afraid to make any sudden moves. Vance calmed somewhat, but his chest still heaved. He leaned his forehead onto his hand for support but saw that his elbow was within twelve inches of the Eastern edge of Willtasia.

"Aaaaa!" Vance leaped up, wiping furiously at his varsity shirtsleeve. "Oh, this is bad! This is bad!" he said. He paced about the room shaking his head and swiping at his body like he had the heebie-jeebies.

"Ok. Alright. This is a little too weird so I'm just going to ask this: what the hell is going on, Vance?" Jimmy said.

"I can't be around this nerd stuff! Don't you understand?! I've spent my entire middle grade and high school years building up my coolness, doing all of the cool things, excelling at everything that cool people think is cool so that they'd think that I was cool, and all of this is threatening that! What would my teammates think if they walked in here and saw me standing next to an over-the-top, awesomely-detailed map of a fantasy world that doesn't exist but should and that I want to be a part of so bad I can hardly keep my hands off of that gleaming pile of dice and that sweet, sweet blank character sheet! After all these years it's got me!" Vance clutched at his head and stumbled about, finally tripping and catching himself on the edge of the table with one hand. He stared down at black dice with blazing orange numbers on them, eyes and mouth and lips fighting with themselves until he finally reached out a shaking hand that paused, then drew back, then shot forward and seized them and rolled—ROLLED!—all of them in a bouncing, clacking mass that rebounded off the back edge of the square and flopped, face up, their probabilities cemented in absolute reality.

A strange, delicate relief spread across Vance's face. His lips quivered, his eyes danced in their sockets. "That felt really good," he said. Then he turned his head away in shame.

"Your homework!" Stacey suddenly yelled. "I wondered why you kept coming over for help when you seemed to be smart enough to get it on your own. You were coming over to watch me play Fantasy War 7!"

"Yes. I tried to stop myself, but the images of epic battles and heroic deeds invaded my dreams, messing with my head. I started dropping balls and missing plays at practice. My grades started to slip. But when I came over that first time and you started playing Fantasy War 7 while I worked I realized I'd found the perfect cover: dumb jock needs help with his homework. I got to experience the joy of high adventure without anyone knowing I was doing it."

"Hmpf. And here I thought you were making out the entire time," Jimmy said, shaking his head at the novelty of the entire thing. "But in reality, Terrence and Stacey were making out, at least in a platonic, digital, hack-and-slash way, while you secretly indulged your true love: fantasy gaming. That's totally epic. You seemed to have the perfect life and we were the losers, but in reality we were being our true selves and enjoying it and you were denying yourself what you really wanted and were completely miserable trying to be whatever you thought other people wanted you to be. I mean, Terrence's life looks like a model of perfection compared to your effed up existence."

"But now, with these dice in my hands...it's all over," Vance shook his head sadly. "I can feel the coolness seeping out of me into them. And right when I hit prime chick-scoring age!"

"Uh, you were, like, hanging out with Stacey every day for months while she played the one thing that your soul really desired. Why didn't you ever hit on her?" Jimmy asked.

"She's kind of a barbarian, smash-with-an-ax girl and I'm more into the flame-handed sorcerer chicks," Vance said with dead seriousness.

"Umm...and you think you are going to find that kind of girl on the cheerleading squad?"

"Don't judge me!" Vance yelled.

"Uh, I'm on the cheerleading squad," Stacey said.

Everyone turned to look at her.

"Is there anything you can't do?!" Willoughby shouted.

"Give me a minute—let me think." Stacey rubbed her finger on her lower lip as she considered the question.

"But none of that matters now," Vance said, eyes becoming despondent. "It's all over. It's...all over." The dice rolled onto the table from his limp, defeated hand. He didn't even look at them.

Jimmy's eyes took on that special gleam that meant he sensed opportunity/blood in the water. He began shaking his head. "Oh, no, no, no, Vance. It isn't all over. It's just beginning. Think of it! You, us, diving through that portal and cleaning up villainy like it was going out of style. It'd be like you running to the net and head-butting a screaming ball in for a game saving goal!"

"That's a soccer analogy," Stacey said. "Vance plays football."

"Doesn't matter!" Jimmy retorted, "The point is Vance can live out his long-held dream in real, actual life. And in a bonus twist of fate his concentration on athletic coolness actually qualifies him even more than us to realize that dream right now. But to survive over there you are going to need our years of gaming and Willtasia knowledge. So what do you say? Will you train us to be ultra-buff and ready to rumble? Will you help us help you realize your lifelong dream of fantasy-adventuring awesomeness?" Jimmy paused dramatically, eyebrows raised.

Vance hesitated, toying with the edge of a character sheet. Then he looked up at Jimmy's maniacal eyes. He looked down at Jimmy's torn, bloodied shirt. He slowly looked around the room at each undecided, thoughtful, terrified face. He took a deep breath.

"Yeah, alright. I want to do it."

"Woohoo!" Jimmy shouted, pumping his fist in the air.

Willoughby swallowed heavily, Terrence almost fainted, and Stacey held up a finger and said, "Okay, got it. Macrame. I totally suck at doing macrame."

"But if we're going to do this," Vance continued, "we're going to need a team. The best players you've ever had. Who else should we get?"

Jimmy looked to Terrence. Terrence looked to Jimmy. They both looked to Willoughby.

Willoughby pressed his lips together and glared. Vance noted the tension.

"Who else should we get?" Vance asked again, looking right at Willoughby.

* * *

Ding dong

Click-clack. Squeeeeeekkkk.

"Hello, Will."

"Hi, Gwen. I just wanted to know if—wait, what's that?"

"A can of Tab."

"What do you mean?"

"It's a can of Tab soda, Will. I bought it online. They still make it. They've made it since 1963. Drink it."

"Uh..."

"Drink it, Will."

"You've kept a can of Tab by the door ever since we broke up?"

"Drink it!"

"Okay! Okay!"

Pop-fizzzzz.

Glug. Glug.

Buuurrrrrppp!

"Wow, that is actually kind of good."

"Now do you believe that Tab is real, Will?"

"Well, yeah. I mean, here's a can of it, I just opened it and drank some and it doesn't taste like anything I've ever had before, so...yeah. I think Tab is real."

Slam!

"Gwen, wait! We need your help in Willltasia!"

* * *

"Aahhggg!" Terrence fell to his stomach on the ground, sweating profusely, quaking arms useless.

"That was three pushups, Terrence!" Vance yelled. "Three freaking pushups!"

Willoughby walked through Terrence's back gate, alone.

"How'd it go with Gwen?" Jimmy asked.

Willoughby kept his eyes on the ground. "She isn't coming."

"Then why is she behind you?" Jimmy asked.

Willoughby spun around, eyes blowing wide open to find Gwen, glorious, evil-elf-slaying Gwen, standing with one hand on the half-open gate. Her stocky frame and no-nonsense glare were set off by her full head of curly brown hair. Willoughby's heart melted.

Gwen let the gate close behind her.

"Gwen? I thought you still hated me. Why'd you come?" Willoughby asked.

"Because you were an awesome game master and Willtasia was an awesome place. If you, and it, need help, I'm in," Gwen said.

"Yeah, but this is diff—"

"Bah!" Gwen held up a hand. "I'm in. What do we need to do?"

"Move! Right now!" Vance yelled. "Twenty laps around this yard people and I want them done yesterday!"

Inspirational thumpa-thumpa music played. The plywood sheets with orcish axes buried in one side were removed and a fancy, scrap-metal gate affixed in their place, barred with authority. Nerds sweated and roared and pumped iron while wearing pilled, cotton headbands. Online articles were studied and medieval armor boiled, sewn, riveted, and donned. Bo staves and Renaissance Fair swords were twirled and swung under the tutelage of Stacey. Vance was schooled in hack-and-slash, cryptic rune puzzles, and scattered component reassembly plots. Three long summer months later, the party assembled.

"Wow, we look like positive bad asses," Willoughby said, admiring the shining armor he had purchased with credit on the Internet.

"Yes. Yes we do," Jimmy said, nodding his head. He swallowed. "Are we sure we want to go through with this?" he asked.

"What are you talking about?! You were the one who pushed us to do this in the first place!" Willoughby shouted.

"I know. But standing here, getting ready to open that door and jump through, made me remember how much those healing potions burned."

"Get a spine, Jimmy!" Terrence yelled in a deep, steroid-infused voice. He rolled his thick neck and flexed his muscles, his definitely-not-a-thief-anymore leather armor creaking against the swelling of them.

"It's kind of scary how your body took to weight lifting, Terrence," Vance observed.

"Shut up and open the door!" Terrence yelled, veins bulging on his forehead in 'roid rage.

"You know what? I just realized something," Willoughby began, hands resting on the head of his great mallet, fingers partially covering the "Tab is REAL" runes inscribed upon it. "This portal is more than just a portal into Willtasia. It's really a portal that led us into the hidden lives of those around us. It pulled us out of our comfort zones and into a greater world, where we discovered who we really were, what we could really be, and that we were not alone. There were people right next to us who were just like us, who wanted the same things as us, had the same dreams that we did, and we didn't even know it."

Terrence took Stacey's armored hand in his, jaw unclenching for a fraction of a second as he looked lovingly into the eye slits of her Greek-inspired, full-coverage helm. They shared a brief finger squeeze and bent for an awkward hug, her backpack of sharpened track javelins clinking into the hilt of his massive, two-handed sword.

Gwen nodded in agreement with Willoughby, the head of her highly sharpened Ace Hardware battle ax resting on the concrete floor; dual, braided ponytails rubbing on the Tab-can shoulder pauldrons of her studded leather armor. "Hear, hear, Will," she said, clapping him on the back with her single, heavy metal gauntlet.

"It was an escape," Willoughby continued after smiling back at her, "just like gaming, but this time into the future, *our* future, the one that we shaped for ourselves, just like we shaped Willtasia. This portal is a portal to adulthood."

"What the hell, Will?" Vance said. "This isn't about some namby-pamby life lesson, this is about hacking and slashing our way to victory. So can that literary crap and start swinging!"

"Amen to that!" Terrence yelled as he threw the crossbar up and yanked open the door.

"Now, all to me!" Vance bellowed, pointing his school-colors shield with authority at the shimmering light of Willtasia. "Onward to glory!"

And together, as one, they leapt into the portal.

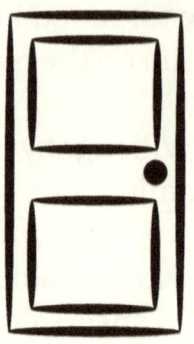

Hard Times in the Vancouver Continuum

Andrija Popovic

"Officer Malcolm Hayes. Please report to Continuum Police Department headquarters right away."

Relentless and polite, the message would not stop until I answered. I slotted my phone into the charger and pulled my gauntlet from its holster. When the gauntlet paired with my phone, I answered the call.

"Hayes. What's the situation?" I popped open my dresser and pulled the plastic off a fresh set of clothes.

"Hey, Malcolm. It's Delia. Captain wants you in right away. Said skip his office and go straight to tracking." Delia ran dispatch; had for over forty years. Should have retired when we became the new model for "public/private cooperative law enforcement" but the department would literally burn to the ground without her.

"Gonna take me an hour, at least." Even on Sunday nights DC gridlock would swallow you whole.

"You're cleared to run your lights. Traffic control will be routing you." I winced as the gauntlet fused with my arm. The opalescent blue casing softened, adhering to my dark brown skin. Ultrafine wires tapped my nerves and merged us together. The gauntlet and I were one. My phone became just another eReader. Delia now whispered in my ear.

"And Malcom...it's Isabella."

Bella.

I looked over at my tiny writing desk. Dollar store notebooks, all sporting a faux leather cover graphic and filled with my scratchy first-draft poems, scattered across the battered plastic desktop like dead leaves. They surrounded a tiny framed painting of a Mediterranean town rendered in colored pencil. I'd given her the best set I could afford. She gave me the art in return.

Next time, she'd said, *I'll give you a real leather notebook. You can write poems when we're in the Med together.*

"I'm on my way." I pulled on my flak vest and armored shirt. I ran my fingers across the little drawing's cheap frame before grabbing my jacket. Setting the door locks, I flipped the condo to "away" mode. I wouldn't be back for a while.

* * *

"Romania?!? Seriously? Mal, who schedules trips to the Romanian continuum? Do they want vampires? Because that's how you get vampires..."

* * *

The tracking room at CPD felt more like the control tower at Reagan-National than a police station. Screens surrounded the dispatch pit, showing updates on the authorized portal openings to various fictional continua: tour groups visiting the 70's Studio Comedy continuum; sci-fi conventions running the Gernsback continuum; vacationers traveling to various Universal Television continua (70's for folks who wanted an old school *Buck Rodgers* thrill, 80's for anyone who wanted to play *A-Team* or *Knight Rider*). Every discovered, tagged, and authorized continuum was listed in glowing blue-white letters.

In the center of it all was the CSW, the "Current Standard World."

The board I focused on was hidden in the back, near the conference room. It was an old dry-erase board with a grid painted on the surface labeled "Active Breaches." Despite heroic erasure attempts, the ghosts of the names "Serrano & Hayes" still appeared under the "Assigned" column. Now, only my name showed, written in red over the others. Bella's name appeared under the case description, where we kept the perps and breach locations.

Serrano (Vancouver Continuum)

Oh, Bella. Never wanted to see your name up here. Why did you run?

"Mal. Get in here."

Captain Johnson waited by the door to Conference Room One with Byron, our squad's senior mission controller. The two were a study in contrasts. The tall, lean Johnson towered over Byron's muscular, fire-hydrant-shaped figure. I jogged into the small, white-board covered room. The Captain closed the door behind us and flipped the tiny windows to reflective "privacy" mode.

"Byron's going to update you. I've got to access your clearance levels." The captain touched his gauntlet to mine. The blue crystal "eye" on the back of my palm snapped open. His crystal flashed red. Tiny filaments stretched from his gauntlet to mine and connected our biomechanical companions.

"An hour ago, one of our routine sweeps pulled up an unauthorized portal connection from a known coyote ring. We thought it'd be one of those rough 'tear and toss' jobs. But the signal was clear and fixed. When patrol took down the door, the coyotes were dead. Body cams confirmed Isabella Serrano, with an active gauntlet, transitioning out of our continuum. When the portal closed, everything was trashed by an improvised EMP device. We were only able to recover bits of the destination based on the transport media, drug cocktail, and reports of unusual flares in other sections."

I swallowed. Bella went on the run after oversight supposedly found her trafficking in illegal transport media. When her gauntlet went dark, we assumed the safeties had kicked in. But Bella knew her way around the tech. She'd jailbroken her gauntlet. Brilliant, beautiful Bella.

The Captain's gauntlet retracted its tendrils. I flexed, not feeling any different. When I visualized the transfer media, the lodestones allowing me to connect to the fiction of each continuum, I found every file was unlocked. I now had access to continua that only our private sector partners—portal survey teams, oversight, and ESWAT—could use. "So, where did she go? Somewhere locked down? Did she take anyone with her?"

"No and no on the last two." Byron pulled up an after-incident report on his touch-screen computer and flung it to my gauntlet. "All we could track down is she went into the Vancouver continuum."

"Which one? Any of our usual stops?" The Vancouver Continuum covered thousands of fictional realities. Most coyote "tear & toss" missions were to one of the Vancouvers—it had stood in for home in so many TV shows. Everyone wanted to go to a clean, beautiful version of their home with no traffic, pollution, or run-down neighborhoods.

People didn't realize those Vancouvers were also settings for criminal thrillers, too. They were filled with sex offenders, serial killers, aliens, and other weirdness. Undocumented travelers often ended up as bizarre sculptures made by overly-artistic murderers obsessed with classical mythology, or worse. Bella and I had spent most of our shifts there, rescuing illegals from their hopes of a better life.

"She jumped into the Washington, D.C., iteration." The D.C. on TV that no D.C. native ever recognized. We knew it very well.

"I think I know why she's there. We busted—"

The Captain fired me a quick look, then motioned to Bryce. A few sharp gestures, and Bryce gave us a thumbs-up sign. Confused, I looked to the captain.

"Sorry. Our 'partners' have taken an unhealthy interest in this case. Bryce has looped this room. Don't want oversight getting more than necessary." The Captain put his hand on my shoulder. "Bella was one of us. She was family. Your heart wasn't the only one broken when she bolted. All the old timers? We wanted to be talking about engagement parties and wedding gifts for her in this room. Not hunting her down."

"Then why am I here?" My stomach tightened. "If corporate oversight knew about us, why do I still have a badge?"

"Because fuck oversight and ESWAT, that's why." I almost jumped. The Captain only swore when he meant it. "Bella's one of us. She's family. You know her better than anyone else. You can find her, see why she ran, and try to keep her safe. That's why I unlocked your gauntlet. That's why we're stonewalling our 'partners' as much as we can."

"Amen," said Bryce. He put down his touchscreen. "Go. Find her. Keep our girl safe. We'll back you up."

I took a breath, wiped around my eyes, and said, "Thank you."

The Captain slapped my back. "Outstanding. Let's get you racked and ready to go.

* * *

Byron and the Captain hustled me to the transition chamber. They strapped me to the transit frame and confirmed my gauntlet's drug factories were fueled for the trip. I took a breath, relaxing my muscles as the cross-shaped frame rotated me onto my back. Icy cold transit drugs leached into my veins. Static—salt-and-pepper glitches in reality—ate at the edge of my vision. I focused upward, at the blue pinpoint glowing above me.

The static merged into rainbow-hued waveforms. Sound twisted in my ear, pitch and tone distorting like a lost radio signal. Overhead, the blue pinprick opened into a roaring portal. Thin lines of blood dripped between my teeth and down my throat as my gums bled. I gurgled and screamed. Static overtook my body, erasing it bit by bit. Great chunks of my existence floated up into the light. I saw my feet, hands, and legs drift away on gobbets of tortured reality.

And then, I was in Vancouver (Washington, D.C., version).

* * *

"Yeah, I know. I should talk to a counselor. But, does all this never get you down? There are company dudebros out there using daddy's money to get into the 80's ski school continuum, and we're busting working folk jumping to Vancouver."

"It bugs me. But that's how it is. This isn't a TV show."

"If it was, I'd hang the producer, Mal."

* * *

The Vancouver version of the D.C. medical examiner's office gleamed. Janitors kept the marble floors spotless. Every inch of the wooden security desk glowed, polished to a perfect shine. Even the metal detectors looked fresh off the factory floor. Men and women in well pressed suits and uniforms, badges shining bright as sunlight, poured into the atrium-like lobby. Down in the morgue itself, the tile walls glowed, shiny and spot free.

It was an amazing lie. The D.C. government did their best, but once you got past the front door, everything felt thirty years old. It was noisy, ugly, and smelled *off* because of the orange scented enzyme cleaners they used on everything. I'd been there too many times to believe the gleaming, ultramodern Vancouver version.

Not many folks visited this continuum. D.C. city council had a ban on portal trips to other versions of the District. Tourism money kept the city alive. The travel ban kept out travelers but made it a perfect spot for shady deals. The morgue had a perfect set-up for keeping transit media at just the right temperature. It also appealed to our CI's weird sense of humor.

Cady spit up his dinner when he saw me walk into the slab room. Pad Thai noodles marred the gleaming floors. I had my gauntlet up before he could run. "Calm down, man. I'm here for information, not you."

"Mal. Dammit! You should have called!" Cady started wiping up the spill. He looked like "Asian morgue technician number one" from central casting, an extra designed to give the impression of diversity. This made him an effective coyote and in-continuum info broker. He seemed to belong, and the world went with the idea. "What's this about?"

"Isabella."

"Fuck me." Cady opened a body drawer and pulled out a slab containing a fully stocked bar, complete with mini-fridge. He selected a Jim Beam bottle, tumbler, and an ice sphere from the set up. "You want one?"

"No, thanks."

"Your loss." Cady fixed, poured, and drank in one fluid motion. "Just to save time so I can get back to escaping: she was here. She knows she's being hunted—didn't even bother with the old 'I'm going to use my stolen police gauntlet to de-rez you back to reality so slowly your teeth will fall out' threats."

Cady smiled, wistful. I tried not to laugh. CI relationships were built on an odd sort of trust. Bella knew we could work with Cady when he reacted to her hard-boiled patter with his own. It felt like my job was to remind them we were working, not recreating scenes from the *Miami Vice* continuum.

"She was worried about me, Mal." Cady put down his drink. "Told me ESWAT was on her tail—not you, but ESWAT in specific. Surprised they're not here already. You guys always treated me well. Those executive action mercenary fuckers—"

"Are exactly who we're trying to protect her from." I leaned close. "Please. What did she want from you?"

Cady reached into the freezer section of the mini-fridge. Behind the ice sphere molds sat stacks of blue crystals, ready for gauntlet absorption. Delicately, he handed one to me. Etched on the surface were the words "VC FicActu."

"She wanted access to Vancouver. Not the real Vancouver, or any of the other continua, but Vancouver playing its fictional self. It's high level access only, so she needed updated transit media." He leaned back against the body drawers. The ice sphere clinked in his tumbler, melting against the heat of his palm. "I also hooked her up with some in-continuum items.

She was specific—wanted photo ID along with cash and credit. Like she was traveling somewhere in and around fictional Vancouver."

Cady handed me the crystal. I dropped it onto the palm of my gauntlet. It melted into an azure puddle. Lines of deep blue data poured through the gauntlet's system. I leaned against the wall, taking shallow breaths as the new media drizzled into my nervous system.

"Thank you," I nodded to Cady. "You'd better get going."

"Already have transit plans." He reached into another corpse freezer and pulled out a handful of roadside magnesium flares. Striking them alight, he threw one into the freezer with the transit media and closed the door. He let the others burn down his bar before picking up his drink and closing the body drawer. "Tell Bella I said hi."

"I will." I started to leave, then paused, and put on my best old-timey gangster voice. "Oh, and not a word of this to the heat. Otherwise, your face is going to play paddy-cake with a phone book, got it?"

"Not bad!" Cady took a swig from his drink. "Now get going, ya mug."

I pulled out my in-world cell phone and started dialing. It was a convenient fiction, letting me communicate with Byron. As I walked down the hall, reporting to the Captain and asking for transit to Vancouver actual, I thought I heard Bella's laugh echoing down the hallway.

I stopped and closed my eyes, trying to imagine what she looked like after a year on the run. And then, the morgue hallway ripped apart. A new Vancouver continuum called me.

* * *

"You know, I can't blame someone for wanting to run. To see if they can live in one of the continua. Doesn't matter how bad things look in the serial killer version of LA 'cause, if you're a background character, you get to just live there. Camera doesn't focus on you. You're just the guy pushing the lawn mower, or talking with someone on the stoop."

"But, who the hell tries to get into a Soviet NeoRealist continuum? Film students? Guys who get off on Brutalist architecture?"

"Yeah. Something about that still bugs me, Mal."

"Uh-oh. You got that look. So much for sleeping tonight."

"Shut up. You can sleep anywhere, lug. But I'll try and keep the phone pointed away from you, 'kay?"

"Promises, promises, Bella."

* * *

"Malcolm Hayes, INTERPOL. We're in pursuit of a known fugitive." I showed my ID to the lady behind the counter at airport security and immediately asked her to track down a passenger for me: Isabella.

In the real world, getting an identification on a passenger took time, interactions with airport security bureaucrats, and phone calls to my superiors. But in fictional Vancouver International Airport, everything was a few keystrokes away.

"Agent Hayes? Aiden Duchamp, head of security." Aiden was a big, beefy man with a crew cut, tight shirt, and worn-out tie. Everything about him said "two weeks to retirement" or "character actor." I shook his hand.

"Thanks for your cooperation. Have you found anything?"

"Yes. Let me show you." He walked me to central security—a stereotypical office filled with flat-screen monitors. On the biggest monitor, the one designed for audiences to see clearly, was Isabella. Her passport photo sat on the left side of the screen. On the right, a driver's license photo. She'd cut her hair, tinting it auburn instead of just leaving it coal black.

"At first, we thought she'd be trying to hide her destination. But she bought tickets and followed all the usual steps. Acting just like everyone else." Aiden laughed. "Guess that's the key? Blend in?"

"Blending in is what she does. Where's she heading?"

"Toronto. She took a direct flight from there about twelve hours back." Toronto. Another big hub city. Bella could have jumped there using her gauntlet. She had her pick of Toronto continua. Why take an in-continuum flight? Was she leaving a trail? Was this a trap for the ESWAT team?

I muttered something about copies and getting them sent to a superior. Digital files were emailed to me. Byron was already skimming the information from my gauntlet when I called back in. "I need to take an in-continuum flight."

There was yelling in the background. The Captain was unloading on someone—likely corporate oversight. Time was tight. "OK, I'm seeing what we can do here. Think she's trying to jump out of the continuum while pursuit is in the air?"

"I don't think so." I looked around the busy airport. "If she hops a flight from Vancouver here, like one of the residents, she lands in the fictional version of her destination. I think that's the point. She needed to make sure she went to Toronto, but Toronto *playing* itself."

"Gotcha. FYI, Toronto playing itself is another high-level clearance continuum. In-continuum flights would get around any alarms."

I heard Byron cover his mic and talk with another background voice. "That was the Captain. We're setting up a fictional INTERPOL chartered flight. It'll get you to Toronto as fast as possible."

"Thanks."

"One other thing." Byron took a breath. "Delia did some digging, off books. Remember that ring of relic smugglers? Looks like Isabella spoke with them. She may have in-continuum items."

"Do you know what?"

"Delia doesn't know yet. We'll update you when we can." Another mystery. Objects translated from the different continua just became props. Airwolf became a helicopter with some special effects rigs attached. But to the right folks, having their own personal (as close to reality as possible) Airwolf was enough.

"Can you get me the eyes on the ground I asked for?"

"Yeah. They'll be waiting for you. You sure it'll work? Resonance tracking through the gauntlets is much more efficient."

"You think our Bella would fall for that? She's got decoys up. I know it." My phone chimed. The charter flight was ready for boarding. The paperwork came just about the same time, handed to me by the head of airport security himself.

"Good luck." Aiden smacked my arm with a big, meaty palm. "And try to get some sleep on the plane. You look like five miles of rough road."

"Will do. Thanks."

I let Byron know my flight was inbound. Before I could blink, I was walking into the charter jet. Everything was brown leather, padded, and very fancy. There was even an old school stewardess with a short skirt offering me a drink when I sat down.

I said no, thank you, and buckled myself in. I tried not to fall asleep. I went through the files, focusing on the mission, on Bella. I downed cups of rich coffee, filled with cane sugar. The flight was moving at the speed of plot. The last thing I needed was sleep.

Which is why sleep hit me, right as I closed my eyes for the briefest of moments.

* * *

"Wasn't this how it started? Fucking after a bad run?" Cool blue light poured in through the Venetian blinds. It made our skin three steps darker compared to the hotel's bedsheets.

"Bella, it started when you said, 'Can I sketch you naked?'"

"Oh, no, Officer Hayes. You started it with that poem. Tell me, were you trying to out-sexy the Song of Solomon?*"*

Bella stretched out. She pulled me close, toying with the curls along the nape of my neck. I rested against her shoulder and watched sweat bead on her naked skin. AC barely worked, but we didn't care. It was out of District and unmonitored. It worked just fine for us.

"Why did they do it? Hell, Mal, why?"

"I don't know." I rubbed my eyes. "ESWAT didn't have to breach like that. We were close. You almost had the stolen transfer logs processed. We could have tracked it up the line—"

"'Follow drugs, you get druggies and dealers. Follow the money, and you don't know where it goes.'"

"Did you just quote The Wire at me? Really?" I fought the urge to poke her in the belly button.

"This time, it fits. I've been thinking about the whole raid." She touched the small scar where her gauntlet dug into the back of her hand. "They didn't fully purge the transfer logs from my gauntlet."

"What?"

"Yeah. I kept a hidden copy. Just in case. I'm gonna take a look at it. Quietly. Maybe our so-called 'private sector security partners' didn't want us digging into the transfer destinations."

"You're seeing things. There are no big conspiracies, Bella."

"No conspiracies, just folks trying to get away with shit. Besides, I just want to be sure we didn't end up wrecking someone else's investigation, that's all." She leaned down and kissed me. We lingered, tasting each other. When I opened my eyes, she just kept looking at me.

"Ever think there's a continuum for us?" She rested her hand on my chest. "The retired cop continuum, where we can live on a beach somewhere. You can write poems for fancy magazines. I can afford real paint for my paintings. We could make arepas for tourists when times get tight."

"That would be nice." I ran my hand along her flat belly, over her breasts. She purred like a cat when I kissed her. "But I'll take the here and now. This is real. And this is all I want."

And then I leaned down and made farting noises on her belly. She burst out laughing and hit me with the pillow.

* * *

"You sure this is it?" The two ravens standing on my car gave me the clearest of stink eyes. I wasn't in the best mood. Dreams in continuum were never just dreams. I smelled her on my skin. It meant I was close. When I left the airport, the ravens were waiting for me. Byron had translated them from another Toronto continuum. If they were good enough for a wayward Norse god, they would work for me.

Didn't mean they weren't a pain to work with. They led me on a roundabout chase to the outer edges of Toronto. It was nearly night, and the lights soaked everything in sodium orange and fluorescent green. When they circled a parking lot, I stopped my car, got out, and looked at the building.

Exotica. The club sported a neon sign flashing pink and red, with a lady's silhouette surrounded by strings of lights. All the windows had similar strings, but otherwise the building was almost aggressively nondescript. The ravens landed on the sign, cawing and casting odd shadows over the street.

The door had a sign, handwritten, which said "Closed for inventory." I popped the lock with a credit card and walked into a completely different building. The outside promised cold brick and blue paint. The inside was tropical. Faux palm trees surrounded the tables, the stage, and cast shadows over their painted counterparts on the walls. The dancer's stage was jet black, with silver clamshell lights illuminating the stripper's runway.

Along the wall were rock-like caves, leading to the kitchens and the dressing rooms. Despite it being an inventory night, music still played through the sound system. Leonard Cohen's "Everybody Knows" shook the miniature jungle of fake palm trees and plastic leaves. I raised my gauntlet, keeping close to the fake forest, and got ready to de-rez anyone who came too close.

"Dude, we're closed!" Through the trees, up in the DJ loft, a tall man, his long curly hair caught in a blue bandanna, pointed to me. He angled two lights into my face. World washed out for a moment. Spots crossed my eyes. As he talked about calling the police, and yelled about security, I held onto a tree as my vision adjusted.

On the stage was a lone dancer in a schoolgirl uniform. She swayed to the music, back and forth, but kept her back to me. Long, black hair fell in ringlets along her crisp white shirt. She had her hands crossed in front of her, as if hugging herself while Leonard Cohen sang. I raised my gauntlet and said, "Turn around! Hands up!"

She did. It wasn't her. Just a face too beautiful for a club like this, singing along to the song as she danced. *"Everybody knows... Everybody knows."*

I heard the whir before I saw the shadow behind me. Isabella raised her hand. She wore an elaborate jeweled glove, with a crystal in her palm and chains trailing to a bracelet made of blue scarabs. Light, more intense than the ones from the stage, drowned me.

* * *

"Mal. Lie still. We've got minutes until ESWAT hits this place." At first, I thought it was another flashback from the dream. But when I opened my eyes, I saw palm trees, blue lights, a comfortable chair, and the woman I loved training a stolen fictional weapon on me. Bella must have brought it from another Toronto continuum, this one where the *Stargate* series was filmed. That explained the in-continuum cash she needed.

Bella was dressed to fit in. She wore the same schoolgirl outfit as the dancer, but it clashed with the Egyptian-style jewels around her neck and wrists. Her jailbroken gauntlet glowed on her right hand. Tendrils moved from her arm to mine, connecting us, transferring drugs and data.

"ESWAT? No, look, the Captain—"

"Cap sent you?" Bella looked up and around. We were on the second floor, in one of the private booth spaces reserved for lap dances. The hushed tones of Leonard Cohen continued. Did they never play anything but this one song? "That's sweet of him, but it only buys us a little more time. ESWAT is going to come in, heavy. They'll shoot us, righteous kills, and oversight will say we were colluding to sell restricted transfer media to coyotes."

"What? No, look, I don't like the corporate guys, but they wouldn't kill cops."

"Yes, they would. After what I found, they'll catch us long enough to drain our gauntlets for data and then set up a fake shootout." She glanced around, eyes tracking the entrances.

"Bella, what did you find? What's worth all this?" I sat up, trying to get some feeling back in my legs.

"I found what they've been hiding." Bella looked at her gauntlet, focused and cold. "The Europorn continuum."

"The what?"

"You heard me."

"There's no such thing." I flexed my hand. There was nothing but silence on the comm channels. Bryce and the Captain were gone. Either Bella had blocked all contact attempts or ESWAT were incoming. "If there was, there would be tours going there all the time. Same with the Van Nuys continuum. They just don't exist."

"*They do, Mal.*" Frustrated, she took a breath. "High value continua aren't just locked down. They're hidden. Kept off books." She pulled up a continuum map from her gauntlet. The holographic spiderweb drifted between us. "See. The coyote we busted had an uncensored map."

"Uncensored?"

"They hide them in plain sight sometimes. Remember the Romania and Soviet Cinema continua? Or the Philippines continua that's always locked down because of malaria risks?" Bella wiggled her fingers, manipulating the map. "I couldn't get enough data for a transfer just by the map. So, I took a risk that whoever they had coming after me, their gauntlet would be unlocked. Thought I'd be hitting an ESWAT officer. I got lucky. Cap sent you."

"Don't think it was luck, Bella. He was talking about wedding gifts..."

She laughed. "Cap was always sentimental. The data in your gauntlet is the best present we could get. And this place— similar theme and aesthetics for the Europorn continuum—

easiest for a connecting breach. There are no active patrols here. Monitoring is slight. Who comes to Toronto playing itself?"

"Why? Why keep it away when they could be selling tours?" I looked around. No windows, so no entry there. Front and rear entries only. Maybe through the offices. If ESWAT was breaking in, they'd be arranging to cover the exits.

"They are selling tours. And properties. And new lives. We're just not fucking rich enough to afford them." Anger tinged her eyes. "What do they call our world on the board?"

"Current Standard World."

"Wrong." Bella zoomed into the center of her continuum map. She tapped on it and expanded the name.

CSW. CrapSack World.

"Everyone knows things are falling apart. But the folks with means, the company folks, they've found a way out." She ran her hand along my chin. "But now, so have we! We can get in. Can you imagine what it'd be like to become a background character in the Europorn continuum?"

"I'd write poetry on the beach. It'd get published in French literary magazines. Printed ones, not on-line like I do now." Needles danced along my legs. "You'd paint every day and sell artwork to tourists until a gallery owner catches on to your work. And every night, we'd make love until we fell asleep under the moon." It was a good dream. I wrote about in my dollar-store notebooks. Bella sketched it with her colored pencils. It was our dream.

On the dance floor, I could see figures in black tactical gear moving out of the exits like wraiths. Mercenary dream killers. "It's too late, Bella. ESWAT's here. People like us don't get to have our dreams come true."

"It's never too late."

She started adjusting the continuum map. Drugs churned through the gauntlet. She unsnapped the weapon from her hand and threw it over the railing, onto the floor. There was no warning. Automatic fire ripped the air. A bright blue flash, followed by a Wilhelm scream, and the ESWAT team flew backwards as the weapon's power pack detonated.

Bella kissed me. "Please. Come to the beach with me."

"Oh, Bella." I buried my face in her hair, inhaling her. Stray locks stuck to my tears. "I wish I could go. But what about everyone else? Your family? The Captain? Bryce and Delia?"

Another series of flashes. More screams. Bella must have gotten a lot of toys from the Stargate continuum. She cupped my cheeks and looked me right in the eyes.

"We can help them. We can get them out. But we can't do it dead." She touched her forehead to mine. "You trust me, partner?"

Strippers screamed below us. Leonard Cohen's voice died in harsh electronic gurgle. "Always."

"Good." She smiled. And then, her eyes widened. "DOWN!"

The rest came in strobing, overexposed images. Gunfire ripping from an ESWAT weapon. Three shots which should have hit me center mass vanishing in a cowl of blue light. The Egyptian necklace around Bella's throat glowing like a protective eye. My hand holding hers close. Bella activating the transfer.

Everything slowed. Everything froze. Static tore at the edges of my vision. The barrier generated by Bella's necklace slowly cracked as the ESWAT team raised their gauntlets, ready to de-rez the barrier and everyone inside it. Above me, the world cracked. A ray of sunlight hit me on the face. It was so warm, so inviting. I wanted to swim in it.

But then static caught me. It mingled with the howl of the de-rez functions of the gauntlets. Blood poured from my nose and gums. My eyes blurred in pain. A great electronic snarl overtook me as the de-rez guns in ESWAT's gauntlet fired.

The barrier crashed. Bella threw herself over my body. The world caved.

* * *

"You're right. The porn does sound classier in French."

"Shut up." Bella reached out and pinched my nipples. "You've

got to admit, this is more fun than American porn. Look, they're in an amazing house in Ibiza, discussing Anais Nin, and then the repressed Spanish Catholic girl gives it up to the really hot dude."

"You just envy her."

"I envy her life." She curled against me, playing with the dark thicket of hair on my chest. "Someone said movies are dreams. And dreams are wishes the heart makes."

"Dreams are wishes, huh? So what's this, then? A wish for an easy life with lots of love, culture, and sunshine?"

"Yeah! Why not? That' not a bad wish..."

"If wishes were fishes..."

* * *

The sun dripping through the wooden slats of our house woke me up. It rolled onto my eyes, warm and sweet as honey. I rose from the bed, pulled on some shorts, slipped my feet into two leather sandals, and looked around. The breeze caught the mosquito netting around the four-poster bed. We didn't need it—no one got malaria here—but the netting glowed blue under the moonlight when we made love.

After gathering my leather-bound notebook, a pen, and a fresh glass of iced tea, I stepped out onto the porch. The deck hung over a rocky coastline, somewhere Mediterranean. The white stucco walls and orange-tiled roof looked just like all the other homes. Narrow alleys gave us access to the cobbled city streets. If we needed a sand beach, it was an easy walk, as was everything else. Further up the mountain were the manor villas. We avoided those—occasionally they housed rich jumpers looking for a weekend of debauchery. Our little home could exist in the background, out of focus, as a part of the fiction no one really noticed.

"About time you woke up. The publisher called. Good news about the new collection of poems." Bella lay on the deck. She wore a white sarong, the Egyptian jewelry slash personal shield, tanning oil, and nothing else. An old radio chattered away beside her. "They were well received. You'll be a posthumous bestseller."

At first, I thought she was talking about my actual poems. But I remembered she'd been in contact with one the runners from the Van Nuys continuum. Cady and his contacts confirmed what we suspected after our second month here: the authorities wrote us off as dead—with the Captain, Bryce, and Delia backing this conclusion. They'd sent a "Congratulations on your Engagement" card along with the news.

Our gauntlets were bricked, stripped of all communications and tracking functions. They were fancy eReaders now, filled with transfer media. Selling the data, bit by bit, kept us in out-of-continuum gear. We would be prepared if ESWAT or a different "private executive action" company turned this continuum into a location for a spy film action sequence.

I sat down beside her. "And your art?"

"Selling well. There will be another gallery showing in one of the Atlanta continua. We may have guests." Guests meant Bella's parents. Mine had passed, rest their souls, but her folks lived in perpetual gridlock down in the Atlanta metroplex. The money we'd gotten in CSW through our data sales would pay for a "vacation" through a fake tour company. They'd make their way to an Atlanta continuum and then slowly fall off the grid. We couldn't get everyone out, but it was a start.

"Having your folks around will be...interesting."

"They love you. Quit being so negative."

"Wish I could." I reached over and took her hand, kissing it. She smelled of sweat, coconut, and sea salt. She tasted like paradise. Adjusting the pillow behind my head, I opened the journal. It felt so good, writing in a book, scratching ink onto pages with real texture. "How long do you think we have? Before it all crashes in?"

"I wish I could say." Bella sat up and stretched. She looked at me, licking her lips, and took my glass of tea from the table. She took a long sip. Condensation dripped onto her sun-dark skin. "Might be today. Might be two years from now."

"So live while we can?"

"Exactly." Bella leaned in, over my poems, and kissed my nose. She ran her hand up my leg. "But who knows? This is Europorn continuum. It's full of happy endings."

I groaned and bopped her in the face with my pillow.

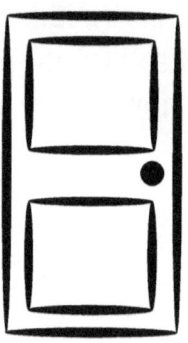

The Cracks in the Road

Patrick Hurley

"Rain's coming down hard again," Caleb said.

"That don't mean squat," said Rafe, spitting off to one side. Reddish gray hair sprang out from beneath his faded ball cap, curling around his prominent ears. He pulled a card from the deck in the center of the black folding table, examined it, and smiled. "It's summer. You get summer storms. All's we got to worry about is if some jerk with bald tires takes the curve on 15th too tight and gets hisself killed."

From around the table came a chorus of grunts. All the crewmen (which included one woman) seemed cast from the same mold as Rafe. Their faces were lined, their wiry forearms had farmers' tans turning pale just past the elbow. They all wore thick denim overalls over tar-stained t-shirts. Steel-toed boots covered their feet and thick leather gloves poked out from their overalls' side pockets.

The road crew sat in a breakroom comprised of mismatched chairs, half-empty vending machines, and a bulletin board covered in tacked-on forms no one ever read. Through the breakroom's dusty window, one could see a fleet of dirty yellow plow trucks parked in a large garage. On the sides of each door read "COUNTY" followed by a serial number.

Only Caleb, who'd mentioned the rain, looked different. His denim overalls still possessed some of their original blue; his work boots maintained some semblance of a shine. Though Caleb was nineteen, his thin neck and large Adam's apple de-aged him in the eyes of his colleagues by several years. He had yet to learn the important workplace skill of knowing when to keep one's mouth shut.

"It's the third day in a row it's been like this," said Caleb, picking up a card when his turn finally came. "And I swear it only rains around the garage. Soon as I leave the parking lot, it's sunny."

Stares were traded around the table. Caleb saw them and ground his teeth. Rafe called and everyone showed their cards. Groans and mutters of "shee-yit" issued forth as the red-headed foreman collected his winnings.

"I'm taking Jeannie out tonight," Rafe crowed. When he saw Caleb still staring at him, his grin vanished with a sharp growl. "Kid, I been working the county for twenty-five years, before you was even a gleam in yer daddy's eye. Abe's been here for twenty-eight. Marcia twenty-three. Darryl twenty-one. Randy and Doug are both at twenty."

"Twenty-one," Randy muttered, while putting a dollar in the pot for the next hand.

"You was on disability for eight months," Rafe said, "so I say twenty. Point is, we been doing this awhile, and we know the weather 'round here. Trust me when I say this shit's normal."

"How come we never take D Avenue north?" Caleb blurted out, before any more grunts and nods could end the discussion. The crew looked at him in surprise. "We drive it south, but always jog over to E when we head back. How come that road needs patching so much anyways? We're repairing it five times as much as any other, but I've never seen a single car drive it. It's not even on most maps!"

"Just an old road," said Marcia quietly.

"It's not just that," Caleb said, unable to stop himself. "Everyone goes quiet when some guy named Rusty is brought up. And what's up with that horseshoe over the door? Why do you all tap it when we head out?"

They were all staring at him now, and Caleb realized he hadn't put a dollar in the pot. He did so, and mumbled, "I just wondered. You act like there's more to this job, but besides shoveling roadkill, holding a stop sign, and spreading patch, what do you all do?"

He didn't mention Marcia's frequent stops for naps at a deserted cul de sac, or Abe's habit of stopping in the bar for two hours at lunch, or Darryl's perpetual smell of cannabis. Nor did Caleb mention that, at least twice now, he'd sworn he'd heard singing and laughter during the strange localized rainfall.

Caleb had gotten this summer job with the county road commission through his mother, who hated the thought of her son not working while he was home from school. She'd talked to a friend at church, who talked to her husband, who talked to his boss, and then Caleb was buying steel-capped boots and getting fitted for an orange hardhat.

He mostly didn't mind it. The roads outside town were surprisingly beautiful, full of twists and turns through lush green forests whose floors were coated with vivid wildflowers, leading to lookout points over indigo lakes or past serene golden fields of farmed wheat. His colleagues were a bit rough around the edges, but they told good jokes and hadn't hazed him much. They even let him join in the dollar poker game, played during the final fifteen minutes of every workday, just before clocking out.

Yet something had been bothering Caleb for the last few weeks. Not just the rain or the voices, nor the secrets and shared looks, but something out of the corner of his eye, a flicker he couldn't quite see. Like a burr in the foot, the discomfort had grown until Caleb let it all out, even though he knew Rafe had a short fuse and little tolerance for him.

The crew stared at Caleb in shocked silence. Rafe's face underwent an interesting series of changes. Instead of reaming him out, the foreman turned to Abe and asked, "What you think?'

Abe's half-lidded eyes raised ever so slightly. "Might be worth looking into."

Rafe nodded. He jabbed a calloused finger at Caleb. "Tell you what, Joe College," his boss said. "How 'bout you ride with me tomorrow, see if we can get you some answers to all these pressing questions?" He examined his cards and threw them down. "Shit. I'm out. Shift's over anyway. Let's get the hell out of here."

They all stood to leave, making sure to slide their timecards into the punching slot before heading toward the door. As always, each reached up to the old horseshoe nailed over the exit and tapped it once before stepping out. Even Caleb had taken to doing this, not wanting to break the tradition. He found Rafe waiting for him in the parking lot, smoking a cigarette.

"You got any crosses, rosaries, shit like that on you?" Rafe asked.

Caleb stopped, confused for a moment. "Nossir. I'm not religious. I tell my friends I'm agnostic with Catholic tendencies."

Rafe grimaced. "Don't know what the hell that means, but if you do have any religious stuff, leave it at home. Don't wear it when you come in tomorrow."

"What?"

Rafe sighed. "Just don't, kid. See you tomorrow."

Caleb watched Rafe climb into his pickup and peel out. The rain had begun to die down, and by the time Caleb exited the parking lot, it had stopped.

* * *

The cab in Rafe's rig was the cleanest Caleb had ever ridden in. The others all featured wrinkled magazines on the shotgun seat, cans rolling around on the floor, and empty fast food bags on the dashboard which blew around if the windows were left open. Rafe's cab was the opposite; there weren't even crumbs in the seat creases. The only personal touch Caleb noticed was a photo of a middle-aged woman he figured must be Jeannie.

"Buckle up, Joe College," Rafe said as he turned the ignition. "We're rolling out."

Caleb had enough sense to keep his face blank, but thought, *Does this jerk actually think we're cops or something?*

They rode in silence for the first fifteen minutes. Caleb's stomach still churned from last night's tacos and this morning's gas station coffee. He knew the roads they took, but soon Rafe turned down one he'd never seen before, a single-lane dirt path splitting a row of tall trees, so narrow Caleb would have missed it if they'd been driving at full speed.

The new road looked pretty, lined with dark pines and high grass, but Caleb realized he had no idea where they were. After a while, the silence began to grate on him.

"So why no crosses?" Caleb asked. "Like, are you an atheist or something?"

"Don't want to piss anyone off if I don't have to," Rafe said, staring straight ahead as he drove the county truck up to an intersection. They'd arrived smack dab in the middle of E Avenue, a two-lane asphalt road that went by one gas station, two farms, then nothing but fields and trees. When Rafe turned south on E and then west on 9th, Caleb realized that, for the first time ever, they were about to head *north* on D Avenue.

"Piss who off?" Caleb asked as they turned down D.

Rafe was silent for so long Caleb thought he might not have heard the question.

"Here's the thing, kid," his boss said. "We been doing this a long time and get used to their juju. That's why we need a fresh set of eyes on the road."

Caleb stared at Rafe. Was he in the car with a crazy person? "Um. Don't get mad, but I have no idea what you're talking about."

Rafe barked laughter like a gunshot. "Don't worry, Joe College. You will."

They continued to drive down D Avenue. Coming from this direction, it looked different. The fields seemed hazier, more indistinct, as if they were driving through a morning mist. The wind picked up the further they went on, enough so the plow truck swayed gently from side to side.

"What I want you to do, Caleb," Rafe said, "is look for any cracks or potholes. Got it?"

"Um, okay," said Caleb, startled at being referred to by his first name. They drove on, a bit slower than before, and Caleb tried to concentrate on the road in front of them. It began to rain, but Rafe turned on the windshield wipers, switched on his lights, and slowed even further. The sky had darkened quite a bit, but Caleb did as he was told, searching the deserted road for—

"There!" Caleb shouted. Indeed, before them was a large, jagged crack across both lanes, ending in what almost looked like a small sinkhole on the road's western side. Lightning flashed, and for a brief second, Caleb though he saw the crack glow, showing something else underneath, but then it grew dark again.

Rafe hit the brakes. "Hot damn, there she is!" he cried. "Should have been another few years before one this big came through. Someone must be getting restless."

He shifted the rig into park and clapped Caleb on the shoulder. "Grab your gear, kid, we got some patching to do."

As Caleb hopped down and put his vest and hardhat on, Rafe flipped on the rig's flashers, and set up orange cones on either side of the road. Then he proceeded to unhitch two heavy shovels from the latches on the trailer side.

"Should we use cold or hot patch?" Caleb asked as he went around to the back trailer.

"With this rain, probably better to use the cold stuff."

Caleb nodded, picked up two heavy plastic buckets, and jumped down from the bed. There was another flash, and for a second, Caleb thought he saw an indistinct silhouette just off the road.

"Did you just see—"

Rafe placed the shovel in his hand. "C'mon, kid. Let's get patching."

They popped off the sealed top to each bucket and dug into the shiny, speckled tar with their shovels. Caleb's nostrils filled with the oily chemical scent of newly opened cold patch. As a team they began to shovel the tar over the crack in the road, then patted it down with the flat of the shovel so it sealed smooth.

The rain came down harder. Caleb thought he heard laughter once or twice, but Rafe worked so fiercely, he didn't bring it up, just continued to shovel. When they got to the large hole at the side of the road, Caleb looked at Rafe, his eyebrows raised. "Shouldn't we call in a truck to regrade that?" he asked.

Rafe grunted. "No time. We just got to fill 'er up. Trust me, ain't no one going to report us to the EPA on *this* road."

Filling the hole with patch was long, arduous work. The rain annoyed Caleb, but at least it kept him cool while he shoveled. Just as the cold patch level drew even with the rest of the road, thunder boomed across the sky. Caleb glanced around. Rafe had vanished. Caleb thought he saw someone by the truck and went over to check what his boss wanted him to do next.

It wasn't Rafe.

Though it was pouring rain and the haze made it difficult to see very far, Caleb could tell whatever stood just off the road couldn't be human. The face was too long and narrow, the cheekbones pointy enough to cut glass. Its gleaming eyes were slit like a cat's and that hair... Hair shouldn't glow.

The creature gave Caleb the most beautiful smile he'd ever seen. Caleb started to ask him—or was it a her?—a question, but then the creature began to sing.

The voice promised Caleb everything he ever wanted. It showed him glorious visions, promised all would be well if he'd just drop the iron from his hands. Caleb's shovel hit the ground with a discordant clang, but the song drowned that out, too.

The small part of Caleb that wasn't entranced noticed the thing's smile grew as it beckoned him to the crack which had somehow widened, despite its recent patching.

As Caleb drew within arm's length of the creature, it raised a hand over its shining hair. An obsidian dagger gleamed in its clawed grip like a black star, but Caleb barely noticed. Before it could bring the dagger down, another dark shape rushed at them both from the mist. Caleb almost cried out a warning, but instead let himself be lost in the song.

There was a loud thud as Rafe's shovel connected with the back of the creature's head. The song ended in a painful wail, and Caleb came back to himself to find his boss standing over a collapsed body, his shovel dripping with blood—blood that looked greenish-blue. The body at his feet no longer looked quite as beautiful with the back of its skull caved in. The creature's cat eyes had widened in shock, but they moved no longer.

"I—you—what did you do?" Caleb finally managed. Rafe ignored him, walked over to the rig, jumped in and picked up his two-way radio. "Car One to Base, Car One to Base."

Abe's voice came crackling back over the two-way. "This is Base, what's your sitch, Car One?"

Rafe spat. "Calling in a Code Blue, Abe. We got a partial breach, and we need to get all trucks out here quick. Bring everything. Honey. Salt. Patch. The works. Make sure the front office knows about it. You better believe we're getting some overtime for this."

"Roger that. We'll see you in a few."

Rafe nodded and set his radio back on the receiver.

"What the fuck did you do?" cried Caleb, pointing at the body.

"Saved your life."

"Fucking killed him." Caleb babbled. "Killed him. Killed him. Killed—"

Rafe slapped him. He was wearing his gloves, so it didn't hurt as much as it could have, but it still sent Caleb spinning.

"Killed *it*," Rafe said in a tone that, for him, qualified as gentle. "Understand?"

"You just smashed his head in, and all he was doing was singing!" said Caleb. He missed the song and hated himself for this.

Rafe rolled his eyes. He crouched down by the body and turned it over so Caleb could see the jagged, obsidian dagger still clutched in the creature's hand.

"I've seen what happens to folks who get stabbed with this," Rafe said. "Believe me, you don't want it to happen to you."

Caleb gaped at the wicked looking blade.

"Nothing like poppin' yer cherry, right, Joe College?" Rafe gave Caleb his first genuine smile ever. "That right there is a fucking elf."

* * *

It started a couple hundred years ago, Rafe said. The roads appeared not long after the area had been settled by a motley crew of Dutch, German, and Irish. No one knew where they led; no one knew who made them. The settlers took to calling them fairy roads, like their legends from the old country. Why fairy roads would appear in the New World was a mystery, but some said the land had been sacred to the Potawatomi before they'd been driven off. In any event, no one laughed when the disappearances started.

"Used to be," Rafe claimed, "if you stepped out at night and heard music in the air, you'd turn yourself right back 'round if you knew what was good for you."

After the town incorporated, the county decided to take action. They paved over the roads, using asphalt laced with iron shavings blessed by a local minister. The disappearances stopped right after that, so the county took it upon themselves to always maintain the roads no matter the cost. The job was passed along from father to son (or daughter, in Marcia's case) and here they were today.

"I don't know where the roads came from," Rafe said. "Nobody does."

Caleb couldn't think of anything to say. He still wasn't sure he hadn't gone crazy.

"What I *think*," Rafe continued, "is when folk moved out here, they brought their own legends with them and the land woke them. They been real quiet the last few years, and I was hoping they'd stay that way. It's why I didn't want you to bring any religious crap. They don't like it and I didn't want to attract their attention."

Most years were fine. The roads stayed silent and didn't cause any trouble. But every once in a while, it began to rain in localized spots. Laughter could be heard over the wind. The paved roads began to crack and pothole. It was hard for the regular road crew to see it because they'd been exposed to so much fairy magic over the years. That's why they hired kids like Caleb, Rafe explained. "Fresh eyes see better than old ones. Guess you're the lucky one who gets to see the shit in action."

Caleb glanced down once more at the obsidian dagger. "That knife. Was that what happened to your friend Rusty?"

Rafe tensed and then let out a breath. In a tired voice, he said, "Something like that."

Caleb nodded. "So what are they really? Aliens?"

Rafe looked at Caleb as if he'd just asked his most stupid question yet. "Ain't you ever read Spenser? *Midsummer's Night Dream*? Yeats?" Rafe cussed at Caleb's blank face. "The state of education these days. I checked all that shit out from the library after I started this job. Kid, they're fairies. Elves."

"Like in *Lord of the Rings*?"

Rafe considered this, stroking his jaw. "Naw, them fellas are supposed to be good, right? Angelic and shit. That ain't these guys. These are more like Celtic Gentry. Fuckers who poison cows, kidnap folk, and leave changelings."

Caleb hadn't been much for science fiction, but he recalled folk stories from his youth. He examined the fallen creature's cat-slit eyes, the clawed, tapered fingers, the glowing hair matted with blue blood, and the angular face. It looked beautiful and terrifying, but it certainly didn't look human.

The rain had died down to a drizzle, but Caleb still felt cold. "So what do we do about the body?" he heard himself ask.

Rafe took off his hat and pointed. "Just watch."

Caleb followed his boss's finger to where the elf's body lay. A sunbeam broke through the clouds, and as it fell on the body, the elf faded away into wisps of golden pollen. A bright cluster of posies sprang up in the shape of the fallen body. Moments later, its obsidian dagger melted into black dust.

Caleb almost collapsed to his knees and had to steady himself against the plow truck.

"Takes some getting used to," said Rafe, "but you *do* get used to it."

There were tears in Caleb's eyes, but he couldn't say why. Years later, whenever a beam of sunlight broke through rain clouds, he'd once again feel a strange sadness.

"What do we do now?" asked Caleb, his voice hoarse.

Rafe took out a packet of honey from his vest pocket. "First, you wanna take this here and dab it 'round your ears."

Caleb took it. "What does it do?"

Rafe began coating his own eyes and ears with another packet. "Protects against their magic. Once you finish warding yerself, we're gonna wait for the others to get here. And while we do that, you're gonna pick up a shovel and we're gonna keep watch."

* * *

They didn't have to wait long before hearing the loud rumble of the county fleet. Five yellow plow trucks converged on their position in the middle of D Ave. As one, the side doors opened and the road crew got to work.

Marcia drove her salt truck along the western side of the road, spreading a thick layer of salt along the edge and the widening crack.

"I thought salt was for icy roads," said Caleb.

"Most salt is," Rafe said, nodding. "This load's different. Got it blessed special by Father McCready from my parish."

Caleb shook his head in disbelief. "And the patch?"

"The patch is a special mix. Has bits of tar and iron fillings. Tar's good for the road and the pointy-eared bastards don't like the iron, which is why they're always bringing wind and rain when they can. Wears down the roads and rusts our equipment."

As if his words had summoned it, the clouds darkened, and rain began to fall.

"Goddammit," Rafe muttered. "All right folks, we better make this quick. Soon as Mar finishes spreading the salt, Doug and Randy can leave the offerings. After that, Abe draws the symbols just like always. Darryl, I want you on your fiddle if any get through." He turned to Caleb. "You and me are on shovel duty."

Caleb shook. "You mean we patch the road?"

"Hell no!" There was a wild look in Rafe's eyes, almost as if he was enjoying himself. "If any get through, I want you to whack the shit out of them with your shovel, hear?"

"Our shovels," Caleb pointed out, "they're not iron."

Rafe nodded. "Steel's even better than iron when it comes to elves, kid. It's an iron alloy—like super iron."

A thunderclap drowned out Caleb's reply. Seconds later, Marcia pulled away the salt truck and Randy ran up with a thermos in his hand. He knelt at the side of the road, where the crack crossed the border and seemed to fade out into a distant field. With great reverence, he placed the thermos on the ground before the crack. "This here is milk from my farm's best cow," Randy said. "I, um, leave it as an offering, oh lords of earth and fire."

Soon as he was done, Doug ran up and took his place. He knelt, opened his lunch pail, and pulled out a large loaf of bread. "My wife Loni's fresh-baked bread. I leave it as an offering to you, oh ladies of air and darkness." He placed it next to the thermos of milk.

"Why are we giving them bread and milk?" Caleb whispered to Rafe.

"Not all the elves are evil, kid. Some just want a little offering, a little remembrance and they're on their way. So we leave that for 'em and hope they're satisfied with it. The good ones usually are."

"What about the bad ones?" Caleb asked.

Rafe ignored the question and instead hollered, "Abe, you're up."

Despite the rain, Abe knelt down and pulled a willow branch from his overalls. Caleb watched in fascination as the old man drew strange symbols in the thick layer of salt with the skill of a classical calligrapher. Celtic knots, pentagrams, and whirling circles that made Caleb's head feel dizzy. As Abe continued, the wind picked up, and Marcia and Doug ran over and held up a tarp to keep Abe's work from getting blown away.

In the midst of the road, the crack widened and jagged out into the western field and up into the air, which somehow split open with a loud boom of thunder.

Beyond it waited the fairy host.

Their armor glittered beneath the strange stars of their world, their eyes glowed blue. With the sounding of a war horn, they began to march forward. A dozen stopped at the border to consider the offerings of bread and milk. These fair folk wore gold in their hair and more ornate armor. They looked older and kinder than the elf Rafe had killed. They each took a piece of bread or a sip of milk, bowed gravely to Rafe and the crew, and then disappeared back through the crack in the world.

Other elves, younger and fiercer, mocked their retreating elders. These wore leather and furs, had painted their faces in red streaks. They charged forward, but cried out as soon as their feet touched the salt runes, falling to the ground in pain. Once they could get to their feet, they limped back through the breach.

Several, larger and stronger than the rest, managed to force their way across the salted runes, and pulled black daggers from their belts.

Standing beneath Randy's umbrella, Darryl drew his bow across his fiddle. Caleb gaped as the old pothead began to play a wild reel almost as compelling as elfsong. The elves who'd made it past the salt dropped their daggers and began to sway with the music, began to dance and caper and sing. Led by Darryl's fiddle, they danced their way back through the crack between worlds.

Now just one stood on the road. He was the largest of the invaders, the most beautiful. He wore a glittering mail shirt, leather breeches, and had a sword strapped across one broad shoulder. He'd painted his face in whorls of blue and red. Caleb thought he resembled the elf Rafe had killed.

The elf drew a sabre of blue crystal and said something in a language Caleb couldn't understand.

Rafe called back, "We don't speak that here, slick."

The elf smirked. "Shall I speak to you in your tongue then, ape?"

"Don't have much to say," answered Rafe. "Might be best for you to get back to where you come from."

"I have a better idea," said the elf. "Face me in single combat. With entry to your world as the prize."

Rafe laughed. "Don't see why I should."

"Because you have killed one of mine." The elf pointed with his sword to Rafe's shovel, still coated in blue-green blood. "And some time ago, I killed one of yours."

For a few seconds, the only sound to be heard was the pattering of rain on the road.

"You killed Rusty?" said Rafe, his voice almost a whisper.

Abe looked at Rafe and shouted, "Boss, no!" but Rafe held up a hand.

"Yer gonna pay for that, you pointy-eared fuck."

Both elf and man shrugged off their shirts and Caleb's heart sank. Rafe's back and arms looked like iron cords. He had what Caleb's friends liked to call "old man strength"—the kind of wiry muscle that helped get a job done. Yet compared to the elf, Rafe looked like a decrepit geezer way past the prime of his life.

They bowed to one another. The elf charged, blue crystal sabre raised over his head. Rafe waited patiently, hands on the shovel held in front of him. Just before the sword hit, he brought up the shovel and deflected the blade with an explosion of blue sparks. The elf looked surprised. Rafe returned to his previous stance, face calm, shovel held in front of him. Again, the elf sliced at him, again Rafe deflected the blow.

For a brief moment, Caleb thought it might be an even match, but then he noticed, off to the side of the road beyond the crew, another elf still crouched in the grass, drawing a black arrow back against a curved bow. Caleb charged, shovel raised over his head, a loud scream bursting from his mouth. The elf had time to gape as Caleb brought his shovel down, smashing the bow from his hands. Caleb raised his shovel again, but the elf backed away, hands raised, and ran back through the cracks between the worlds.

Rafe only glanced Caleb's way for a moment, but it was all his opponent needed. The elf lashed out, disarming Rafe with a sudden, deft flick of his blade. As the foreman's shovel clattered to the ground, the grinning elf drew back his sword for a finishing blow.

Instead of backing up, Rafe kicked the elf in the crotch with his steel-toed boot.

The elf screamed and fell to the ground, clutching his groin. Rafe kicked away his sabre. The rest of the crew circled around the shuddering creature, their faces grim.

"This is for Rusty," Rafe said, and it began. They kicked the elf with their steel boots, hitting it in the shoulders, in the ribs, in the ass. It screamed and tried to crawl away, but a rage had come over them, and Caleb knew they wouldn't stop until they'd kicked this creature to death.

"Guys, he's had enough," Caleb shouted, but his crew couldn't hear him. Caleb remembered the first elf's song, he remembered the grave look of respect on the faces of the elder elves who'd taken the bread and milk and left. *They're not all bad.* Without giving himself time to think, he tackled Rafe, just as the foreman was about to put his boot through the unconscious elf's face.

"What the fuck are you DOING!?" Rafe roared.

"It's over, man," said Caleb. "It's done. You won."

Rafe threw Caleb off him and screamed, "You don't know what that bastard did! You don't know nothing, little shit!"

"It's not worth it, man," Caleb gasped. "Please. We're better than this. We're better than them, right?"

By then the crew had stepped back, their anger blown out like a candle. Just as Rafe was about to shout something else, Abe put a hand on his arm. "Maybe the kid's right."

The foreman shuddered. He closed his eyes. Caleb thought he saw tears.

"Shit. I know he is. Shit. You're right. Shit."

Rafe opened his eyes and looked at his crew. "Take that asshole and toss him through the breach. Maybe they'll see what he looks like and be less apt to cross. Hell, maybe they'll even appreciate we showed mercy. Not that he deserves it."

Doug and Randy carried the battered elf to the hole in the world and tossed him through. The rest proceeded to shovel and patch up the crack in the road.

"And don't come back, you sumbitch," said Abe, spitting on the last bit of the patch as they smoothed it over. The wind died, the skies cleared, and the tear through the world sealed itself with a final boom of thunder.

The crew didn't say anything after that, just got back into their rigs and drove back to base. Caleb followed Rafe into his cab, but the look on the man's face made him scared to say anything. When they got back to the garage, Rafe stopped Caleb just before he reached the breakroom door.

"You wanna come back next year, you'd be welcome."

The foreman held out his hand. Caleb blinked and shook it. Rafe's grip was like a vise, and though Caleb couldn't feel his fingers for the next few minutes, he did feel proud.

The crew played cards without mentioning what had happened. Caleb knew now why they kept silent about what happened on the road. Some things didn't need to be talked about. For the first time since joining the crew, he even won a hand at poker.

* * *

Only Abe and Rafe stayed behind after everyone else had punched out, sitting at the folding table, putting away the cards. The garage fell silent. The tools and yellow trucks seemed to glow in the fading summer light. Abe took a swig from his flask and cuffed Rafe in the shoulder. "Guess he weren't as soft as you thought."

"Hmph," Rafe said. "Guess not."

"Why'd you offer him a job?" Abe said. "You know he'll forget everything when he goes back to college at the end of the summer, just like all the others."

"Saved my life," Rafe said. "Plus he made the right call at the end. Sometimes it's best to show mercy. Might be more to him than we thought. We'll see what he remembers, won't we?"

He spat on the ground. Outside the garage, the sunlight glinted off the windows of the parked plow trucks. Far off in the distance, a storm cloud gathered, but to Rafe, it looked just like any other summer storm. He didn't think it'd hit for a while.

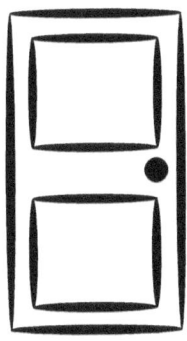

About the Authors

JACEY BEDFORD is a British writer, published by DAW in the USA. She writes science fiction and fantasy. Her *Psi-Tech* space opera trilogy consists of *Empire of Dust, Crossways,* and *Nimbus.* Her historical fantasy trilogy comprises *Winterwood, Silverwolf,* and *Rowankind.* Her short stories have appeared in anthologies and magazines on both sides of the Atlantic, and have been translated into Estonian, Galician, and Polish. She's the secretary of Milford SF Writers Conference for published SF authors. (www.milford.co.uk) She's been a folk singer with vocal trio, Artisan, and has sung live on BBC Radio4 accompanied by the Doctor (Who?) playing spoons. www.jaceybedford.co.uk

F. BRETT COX's debut collection, *The End of All Our Exploring: Stories,* was published by Fairwood Press in 2018. In addition to the stories in this collection, his poetry, plays, essays, and reviews have appeared in numerous magazines and anthologies. With Andy Duncan, he co-edited the anthology *Crossroads: Tales of the Southern Literary Fantastic* (Tor,

2004). He is a co-founder of the Shirley Jackson Awards and serves on the award's Board of Directors. He is also a longtime member of the Cambridge Science Fiction Writers Workshop. A native of North Carolina, Brett is Dana Professor of English at Norwich University and lives in Vermont with his wife, playwright Jeanne Beckwith.

JAMES ENGE lives in northwest Ohio with his wife and two crime-fighting, emotionally fragile dogs. He teaches Latin, Greek and mythology at a medium-sized public university. His stories have appeared in *Black Gate*, in the ZNB anthology *Guilds and Glaives*, in *Tales from the Magician's Skull*, and elsewhere. His first novel, *Blood of Ambrose* (Pyr, 2009) was nominated for the World Fantasy Award in 2010; and the French translation was nominated for the Prix Imaginales in 2011. You can reach him through Facebook (as james.enge) or on Twitter (@jamesenge) or, if all else fails, via his website, jamesenge.com.

ANITA ENSAL has always been intrigued by possibilities inherent in myths and legends. She likes to find both the fantastical element in the mundane and the ordinary component within the incredible. She writes in all areas of speculative fiction and has stories in several fine anthologies including Love and Rockets and Boondocks Fantasy from DAW Books, Guilds & Glaives from Zombies Need Brains, The Book of Exodi from Eposic, and the novella, A Cup of Joe. She will be re-releasing The Neighborhood series in 2019. You can reach Anita (aka Gini Koch) at her website, Fantastical Fiction (http://www.ginikoch.com/aebookstore.htm).

Nebula Award winner **ESTHER FRIESNER** is the author of over 40 novels and more than 200 short stories. She is also the creator/editor of the Chicks in Chainmail series (Baen Books). The sixth, Chicks and Balances, appeared in July 2015. Deception's Pawn, latest in her popular Princesses of Myth YA series (Random House), was published in April 2015. Esther is married, a mother of two, grandmother of two, harbors cats, and lives in Connecticut. There is no truth to the rumor that her family motto is "Oooooh, SHINY!"

JOHN LINWOOD GRANT is a professional writer/editor from Yorkshire, UK. Widely published in anthologies and magazines, he writes contemporary weird fiction, and also stories of murder, madness and the supernatural – such as his 'Tales of the Last Edwardian' series, including the 1920s hoodoo-woman Mamma Lucy. His latest novel is The Assassin's Coin, from IFD, featuring Mr Edwin Dry, the Deptford Assassin, who also features in his new collection A Persistence of Geraniums. He is editor of Occult Detective Quarterly, plus anthologies such as ODQ Presents and Hell's Empire. He can be found on Facebook, and at his popular website greydogtales.com.

KATE HALL is a speculative fiction writer currently residing in Lubbock, Texas. When she isn't writing, she is a bookseller, an amateur tea connoisseur, and a semi-pro cat and baby wrangler. You can follow her on Twitter at @katherine_hall1 or on Instagram at @akatehall.

NANCY HOLZNER is the author of the *Deadtown* urban fantasy series. She's worked as a medievalist, corporate trainer, technical writer, and editor. Nancy lives in Ithaca, New York, where she teaches writing at Ithaca College.

PATRICK HURLEY lives in Seattle where he enjoys taking long, hilly walks and eating far too much sushi. He's had fiction published in dozens of markets, including Galaxy's Edge, Cosmic Roots & Eldritch Shores, Flame Tree Publishing, Abyss & Apex, and The Drabblecast. In 2017, he attended the Taos Toolbox Writers Workshop where he wrote "The Cracks in the Road." He was one of the finalists for the Baen Fantasy Award in 2018. Patrick is a member of SFWA, STEW, Codex, and the Dreamcrashers.

JULIET KEMP lives in London with their partners, child, and dog. Their fantasy novel *The Deep And Shining Dark* (Elsewhen Press) and their YA SF novella *A Glimmer Of Silver* (Book Smugglers) both came out in 2018, and their short fiction has appeared in various places. In their free time, they go bouldering, tend their towering to-be-read pile, and get over-enthusiastic about fountain pens. They can be found online at http://julietkemp.com, or as @julietk on Twitter.

VIOLETTE MALAN is the author of the Dhulyn and Parno sword-and-sorcery series (now available in omnibus editions) and *The Mirror Lands* series of primary world fantasies. As VM Escalada, she's the author of the Faraman Prophecy series, *Halls of Law,* and *Gift of Griffins.* She's on Facebook, she's on Twitter, and website-wise check either www.violettemalan. com or www.vmescalada.com. She strongly urges you to remember that no one expects the Spanish Inquisition.

JAIME LEE MOYER lives in a dry land of cactus and cowboys, while dreaming of tall trees and the ocean. She writes novels about murder and betrayal, friendship, ghosts and magic, and she feels it's only fair to warn you that all her books are kissing books. Jaime is the author of *Delia's Shadow, A Barricade In Hell,* and *Against A Brightening Sky,* published by Tor Books, and *Brightfall,* coming from from Jo Fletcher Books on 9/5/19.

JASON PALMATIER is co-creator/co-writer of the fantasy graphic novel *Plague* published by AAM-Markosia and a contributor to the indie comic series *Lords of the Cosmos* by Ugli Studios. His short stories have appeared in the Zombies Need Brains anthologies *Clockwork Universe: Steampunk vs Aliens, All Hail Our Robot Conquerors* and *Guilds and Glaives.* He has completed two novels, *War Mind,* a near future military thriller about a dystopia controlled by music, and *Xenoslammer*, a parody/rage piece that is best described as "Cards Against Humanity meets Aliens".

STEVEN HARPER PIZIKS was born with a last name no one can reliably spell or pronounce, so he usually writes under the name Steven Harper. He grew up on a farm in Michigan but has also lived in Wisconsin and Germany, and spent extensive time in Ukraine. So far, he's written more than two dozen novels and over fifty short stories and essays. When not writing, he plays the folk harp, lifts weights, and spends more time on-line than is probably good for him. He teaches high school English in southeast Michigan, where he lives with his husband and youngest son. Visit his web page at http://www.stevenpiziks.com or http://www.stevenharperwriter.com

ANDRIJA POPOVIC is a native of the Washington DC metropolitan area who indulges in photography, spends entirely too much on books, and occasionally adds to the #NoirAlley chats on Twitter as @andrian6. His stories have previously been published in Daily Science Fiction and the anthologies ALIEN ARTIFACTS, THE DEATH OF ALL THINGS, and the forthcoming WAR ON CHRISTMAS. For more, check Biomechanoid Blues (biomechanoidblues.wordpress.com)

IAN TREGILLIS, the son of a bearded mountebank and a discredited tarot card reader, is a physicist and writer. His published novels include the Milkweed Triptych (BITTER SEEDS, THE COLDEST WAR, and NECESSARY EVIL), SOMETHING MORE THAN NIGHT, and the Alchemy Wars trilogy (THE MECHANICAL, THE RISING, and THE LIBERATION). His short fiction has appeared in numerous venues including Tor.com, Fantasy and Science Fiction, The Best Science Fiction and Fantasy of the Year, and Best New Horror. He and his wife live in New Mexico with a pampered cat. www.iantregillis.com @ ITregillis

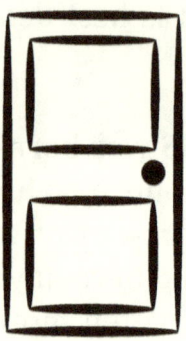

About the Editors

PATRICIA BRAY is the author of a dozen novels, including *Devlin's Luck*, which won the Compton Crook Award for the best first novel in the field of science fiction or fantasy. A multi-genre author whose career spans both epic fantasy and Regency romance, her books have been translated into Russian, German, Portuguese and Hebrew. She's also crossed over to the dark side as the co-editor of *After Hours: Tales from the Ur-Bar* (DAW, March 2011) and *The Modern Fae's Guide to Surviving Humanity* (DAW, March 2012), *Clockwork Universe: Steampunk vs. Aliens* (ZNB, June 2014), *Temporally Out of Order* (ZNB, August 2015), *Alien Artifacts* (ZNB, August 2016), *Were-* (ZNB, August 2016), *All Hail Our Robot Conquerors!* (ZNB, August 2017), and *Second Round: A Return to the Ur-Bar* (ZNB, July 2018).

Patricia lives in a New England college town, where she combines her writing with a full-time career as a systems analyst. To offset the hours spent at a keyboard, she bikes, hikes, cross-country skis, snowshoes, and has recently taken up the noble sport of curling. To find out more, visit her website at www.patriciabray.com.

* * *

S.C. BUTLER is a writer living in New Hampshire with his wife and son. He is the author of the Stoneways trilogy: *Reiffen's Choice, Queen Ferris*, and *The Magicians' Daughter*, published by Tor Books; and a contributor of short stories to several anthologies and magazines. He made his editorial debut with the anthology *Submerged.*

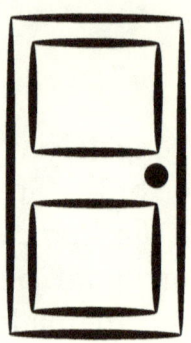

Acknowledgments

This anthology would not have been possible without the tremendous support of those who pledged during the Kickstarter. Everyone who contributed not only helped create this anthology, they also helped solidify the foundation of the small press Zombies Need Brains LLC, which I hope will be bringing SF&F themed anthologies to the reading public for years to come . . . as well as perhaps some select novels by leading authors, eventually. I want to thank each and every one of them for helping to bring this small dream into reality. Thank you, my zombie horde.

The Zombie Horde: Colleen Champagne, Robert Coleman, Elena Beghetto, Mark Simon Phillips, Corey T, Sarah Cornell, Jenny Barber, Larisa LaBrant, Emma L, Jim Gotaas, Arturo, Lavinia Ceccarelli, Karen Thomas, Carol J. Guess, Meg Leader, Ian Harvey, Joseph Hoopman, John Green, Cyn Armistead, Jason S. Clary, John T. Sapienza, Jr., Carolyn C, Jen1701D, A.A. Jankiewicz, Santiago Akira Kitashima, windypenguin, Dr. Kai Herbertz, Michael Kohne, Pat Hayes, Joanne Burrows, Alan

Smale, Sheryl R. Hayes, Michael A. Burstein, Todd V. Ehrenfels, Kaiqua, Anonymous Reader, David Holden, Neil Clarke, Jaq Greenspon, Michael D'Auben, Eagle Archambeault, Kristi Chadwick, H Lynnea Johnson, John Winkelman, Studio 9 Games, Joe Hauser, Misty and Todd Lambert, Michele Fry, Shaun Kilgore, Regis M. Donovan, Steven Halter, Roger Simmons, Penny, Gabe Krabbe, Simon Dick, Chris Gerrib, Justin P. Miller, James Williams, Sachin Suchak, Mark Carter, Kelly Melnyk, Tory Shade, Harvey Brinda, Howard J. Bampton, Ivan Donati, Cheryl Preyer, Michael Halverson, Sean Collins, Kiya Nicoll, GMarkC, Michael Fedrowitz, Sharon Wood, David Zurek, Stephanie Lucas, Glori Medina, Jakub Narębski, Jörg Tremmel, Andrew Hatchell, Stephanie Cranford, Susan Oke, Sidney Whitaker, Engel Dreizehn, Andrea Terdik, John Markley, Amber Bryant, Meagan Pledger, Ian Chung, Pam Blome, Sebastian Müller, Cody Black, James Moriarty, Judith Mortimore, Karina Kolb, Ronda Sanders, Chrysta Stuckless, Mark Kiraly, Michelle Palmer, Craig Hackl, Beth Kampa, David Perkins, Brendan Burke, Carl Wiseman, Andrija Popovic, Anna Rudholm, Beth Lobdell, Cat Wyatt, Chad Bowden, Kevin Kibelstis, Patricia Gates, Scarlett Eisenhauer, Molly J., Robert Gilson, Grant Canterbury, Tina and Byron Connell, Rob Fowler, Michelle T., Darrell Z. Grizzle, L.C., Gabriel Cruz, Vicki Greer, Russell Martens, Samantha T., Ron Oakes, Ben Nash, Miranda Floyd, Wolf SilverOak, Tommy Acuff, John Senn, Kevin Winter, Cat Girczyc, Pat Knuth, Betsy, Claire Sims, Jeremy Audet, Whitney Gutierrez, Christine Hale, James Conason, Andy Pfrimmer, Wendy Cornwall, Barde Press, Mark Slauter, Jo Good, Tina Nichols, Myca Arcangel, Chloe Nagle, Tasha Turner, Sheelagh Semper, B. Keith Dunn, Jude, Jennifer Berk, Hoose Family, Nirven, Terry Williams, Leah Webber, Katherine Matthews, ChillieBrick, Jennifer Robinson, Jaymie Larkey Maham, Ian M. Fowler, Martina W., Brenda Rezk, Céline Malgen, Jennifer Priester, Cory Williams, Brendan Lonehawk, Tina Noe Good, Katherine Malloy, Margaret Bumby, Cheryl Losinger, andrew ahn and sin soracco, Pierre Gauthier, Susan

Simko, Kate Barela, Colette Reap, Danan Bradley, Steve Lord, Götz Weinreich, Scott Raun, William Leisner, Scott Drummond, Julie Kovac, Kristine Smith, Michael Stearns, Veronica Kavanagh, Tim Jordan, Debbie Matsuura, Rick McKnight, Nick W, Josie Ryan, Cathy Green, A.Chatain, Toni Lichtenstein Bogolub, Brad Roberts, Stephen Ballentine, Melanie McCoy, Jamieson Cobleigh, Anne Burner, Lutz F. Krebs, Francesca, Jillian and Doug Zeigler, Peggy J, eric priehs, Christine Ethier, Patti Short, Colbey, R.J.H, Mary Alice Wuerz, Helen, Robert Claney, Gina Freed, K. Hodghead, Clariben Huntington, Ginger Field, Katrina Coll, Leila Qışın, Amanda Nixon, Tom Powers, Charles Budworth, RKBookman, Jenni P., Leonie Duane, Brian D Lambert, Dagmar Baumann, Gavran, Michele Hall, Graeme, C. L. Werner, Andrew J Clark IV, jjmcgaffey, Anne M. Rindfliesch, Gary Phillips, Stacey Kaye Manuel, Andrea Watson, Abby Kieser, Aysha Rehm, Angie Hogencamp, Elizabeth Klandrud, Annalise M., Taryn, Peter Thew, Mark Newman, Tim Jones, Donna Gaudet, Michael Kahan, Craig "Stevo" Stephenson, T.D. England, Mark Hirschman, Niall Gordon, Jerrie the filkferengi, Sheryl Ehrlich, Edward Ellis, A. Eddy, Elektra Hammond, Uncle Batman, Sean and Catherine Kane, Gail Morse, Sarah Klapper-Lehman, Erik T Johnson, Bonnie Stewart, Eleanor Russell, Amanda Hudson, Kerry aka Trouble, Stephanie Slavin, Kristin Coley, Rebecca M, Koen Andrews, Matthew Aronoff, Rachel Shell Vance, Evergreen Lee, Margaret St. John, Jonathan S. Chance, Mark Lukens, Jenn Whitworth, Yankton Robins, Carl Dershem, Erin Himrod, L. E. Doggett, Andrew Foxx, Ruth Duggan, Jonathan, Greg Vose, Danny Dyer, Beckey and Steve Sanchez, Shirley, Jesse N. Klein, Meg Fielding, Guy W. Thomas, Chantelle Wilson, Linda Pierce, Alexander Smith, Jason Tongier, Brenda Moon, Nathan Turner, Anthony R. Cardno, Catherine Gross-Colten, SusanB, compiledwrong, SwordFire, Amelia Smith, Chris Brant, David Rowe, Michael Bernardi, Kayla Sinclair, Joe Stech, Ronald H. Miller, James Lucas, Barbara Matzner-Volfing, Natascha McGilvray, Louise Lowenspets, Mark Featherston,

Deanna Harrison, Phillip Spencer, Susan Carlson, Liz Tuckwell, rissatoo, Brent Johnson, Duncan's Books and More, Chris Matosky, Matt Hope, Mervi Mustonen, Kerry Ebanks, Michelle Brenner, Karen the Griffmom, Sarina McKown-Goh, K. R. Smith, Gretchen Persbacker, Camille Lofters, Andrew and Kate Barton, Q Fortier, Sally Qwill Janin, Paul Alex Gray, Kitty Likes, Chris, Carol Mammano, Lisa Howard, Rolf Laun, H. Rasmussen, Sharan Volin, Lace, Elisabeth Bender, Frank Nissen, Steven Mentzel, William Hall, R. Hunter, Deirdre Murphy, Simba, Lisa Rich, Kathryn Haines, Mary Hargrove, Charissa Weaks, Marty Poling Tool, Dan R. Herrick, Chris McLaren, Curtis Frye, Nancy M. Tice, Elizabeth, Carla Hollar, Olivia Montoya, Paul McErlean, Sarah Eyermann, Amy Rogers, Deborah Torrance, Mark Manning, Barbara Silcox, C. Joshua Villines, NewGuyDave, Kevin Niemczyk, Max Kaehn, OgreM, Kixie K. Nowell, Ichino, Chloe Turner, Robby Thrasher, Yosen Lin, Tanya K., Daniel O., Caitlin Mininger, A.J. Abrao, Louisa Swann, Fred and Mimi Bailey, John H. Bookwalter Jr., Kevin Looney, Alex Shvartsman, Mom, Alyssa Hillary, Isaac 'Will It Work' Dansicker, Steven Howell Wilson, James McIntosh, Axisor, Olav Rokne, Michael M. Jones, Jason Palmatier, Belkis Marcillo, Elaine Costa, Jennifer Dunne, Mud Mymudes, Jules Jones, Melissa Shumake, laura robbins, Julie Holderman, Lizard L., Cliff Winnig, Rhiannon Raphael, Cherie Livingston, Amanda S., Tom B., D-Rock, Y. H. Lee, Kristin Evenson Hirst, Tibs, Linda, Keith E. Hartman, R Kirkpatrick, Yaron Davidson, H. Kriesel, Mike M, Elaine Tindill-Rohr, Kathryn Allen, Cat Rambo, Walter Prawak, Kayliealien, Crystal Sarakas, Elizabeth Gray, Lynn Kramer, Michelle Botwinick, Sharon Sayegh, Becky Allyn Johnson, Tom Berrisford, Erin Penn, Taylor Alcantar, Shawn Blackhawk, Missy Katano

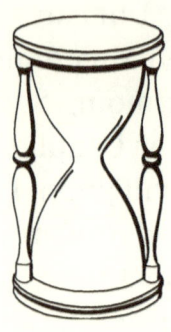

Also Available from ZNB!

Temporally Out of Order

It's frustrating when a gadget stops working. But what if the gadget is working fine, it's just "temporally" out of order? What would you do if you discovered your cell phone linked you to a different time? Or that your camera took pictures of the past?
In this collection, seventeen leading science fiction authors share their take on what happens when gadgets run temporally amok. From past to future, humor to horror, there's something for everyone.

Join Seanan McGuire, Elektra Hammond, David B. Coe, Chuck Rothman, Faith Hunter, Edmund R. Schubert, Steve Ruskin, Sofie Bird, Laura Resnick, Amy Griswold, Laura Anne Gilman, Susan Jett, Gini Koch, Christopher Barili, Stephen Leigh, Juliet E. McKenna, and Jeremy Sim as they investigate how ordinary objects behaving temporally out of order can change our everyday lives.

Also Available from ZNB!

Alien Artifacts

What might we run into as we expand beyond Earth and into the stars? As we explore our own solar system and beyond, it seems inevitable that we'll run into aliens ... and what they've left behind. Alien artifacts: what might they reveal about us as we try to unlock their secrets? What might they reveal about the universe?

In this anthology, nineteen of today's leading science fiction and fantasy authors explore how discovering long lost relics of alien civilizations might change humanity. Join Walter H. Hunt, Julie Novakova, David Farland, Angela Penrose, S.C. Butler, Gail Z. Martin & Larry N. Martin, Juliet E. McKenna, Sharon Lee & Steve Miller, Andrija Popovic, Jacey Bedford, Sofie Bird, James Van Pelt, Gini Koch, Anthony Lowe, Jennifer Dunne, Coral Moore, Daniel J. Davis, C.S. Friedman, and Seanan McGuire as they discover the stars and the secrets they may hold—both dark and deadly and awe-inspiring.

Also Available from ZNB!

Were-

Werewolves rule the night in urban fantasy, but everyone knows there are other were-creatures out there just as dangerous and deadly, if not as common, each with their own issues as they struggle to fit into—or prey upon—society. What about the were-goats?
The were-crows and were-wasps?

Here are seventeen stories of urban fantasy by today's leading science fiction and fantasy authors that introduce you to some of those other were-creatures, the ones hiding in the dark background shadows, waiting to bite. Join Seanan McGuire, Ashley McConnell, Susan Jett, Eliora Smith, David B. Coe, April Steenburgh, Gini Koch, Mike Barretta, Elizabeth Kite, Danielle Ackley-McPhail, Jean Marie Ward, Katharine Kerr, Sarah Brand, Anneliese Belmond, Faith Hunter, Patricia Bray, and Phyllis Ames as they take you into the hidden corners of our world to see some lesser known were-creatures. You may want to bring along some silver ... just in case.

Also Available from ZNB!

All Hail Our Robot Conquerors!

RRRAWRRR!!! ZZZZZZTTTTT!!! ZZZZAAAAPPPPP!!!

The robots of the 50s and 60s science fiction movies and novels captured our hearts and our imaginations. Their clunky, bulbous bodies with their clear domed heads, whirling antennae, and randomly flashing lights staggered ponderously across the screen and page and into our souls—whether as a constant companion or as the invading army threatening to exterminate our world. We can never return to that innocent time, where the robot overlords could be identified by their burning red eyes or our trusty robot sidekick would warn us instantly of danger—

Or can we?

With a touch of nostalgia and a little tongue-in-cheek humor, here are fifteen stories from today's leading science fiction and fantasy authors that take us back to the time of evil robot overlords, invading armies, and not-quite-trustworthy mechanical companions. Join Julie E. Czerneda, Brandon Daubs, Tanya Huff, Brian Trent, L.E. Modesitt, Jr., Jason Palmatier, Jez Patterson, Gini Koch, Lauren Fox, Sharon Lee & Steve Miller, Philip Brian Hall, Rosemary Edghill, R. Overwater, Helen French, and Seanan McGuire as we step into the future with a nod to the past. Hold on to those stun guns. You may need them!

Also Available from ZNB!

The Death of All Things

Lie.
Cheat.
Bargain.
Fight.
Accept.
Bribe.
Conquer.
Evade.

No matter what humanity tries, Death always wins. Or does it?

Discover the answer in The Death of All Things, where twenty-two writers take their shot at the Grim Reaper with explorations of the mythical, fantastical, and futuristic bonds between life and death. Learn the cost of mortality, the perils—and joys—of the afterlife, and the potential pitfalls of immortality ...

Featuring stories from: K. M. Laney, Andrea Mullen, Faith Hunter, Kendra Leigh Speedling, Jason M. Hough, Julie Pitzel, Shaun Avery, Christie Golden, Leah Cutter, Aliette de Bodard, Andrew Dunlop, Juliet E. McKenna, A. Merc Rustad, Ville Meriläinen, Amanda Kespohl, Mack Moyer, Fran Wilde, Kathryn McBride, Andrija Popovic, Jim C. Hines, Stephen Blackmoore, and Kiya Nicoll.

Also Available from ZNB!

Submerged

Everyone has their eyes set on the black depths of space … but what about the deep abysses of the ocean? What dark monsters swim unseen beneath the waves? What ancient wonders lie hidden, waiting to be discovered? What sirens call, either here on Earth or in the icy waters of a far off planet … or even at the bottom of a wine glass? So much remains to be explored below the surface, where light fades and the pressure kills.

Here are seventeen stories from today's leading science fiction and fantasy authors that take us into those depths, whether we want to or not. Join Seanan McGuire, Michael Robertson, Esther Friesner, F. Brett Cox, Wendy Nikel, Marsheila Rockwell & Jeffrey J. Mariotte, Jody Lynn Nye, Bill Kte'pi, Jenna Rhodes, Susan Jett, James Van Pelt, J.C. Koch, Misty Massey, A. Merc Rustad, David Farland, Sara M. Harvey, and Nicky Drayden as they explore unfathomable trenches, underwater volcanoes, and abyssal plains. Take the plunge … into the Deep End!

Also Available from ZNB!

The Razor's Edge

One man's insurgent is another man's freedom fighter...

From The Moon is a Harsh Mistress to The Hunger Games, everyone enjoys a good rebellion. There is something compelling about a group (or individual) who throws caution to the wind and rises up in armed defiance against oppression, tyranny, religion, the government—you name it. No matter the cause, or how small the chance, it's the courage to fight against overwhelming odds that grabs our hearts and has us pumping our fists in the air.

Win or lose, it's the righteous struggle we cherish, and those who take up arms for a cause must walk The Razor's Edge between liberator and extremist. With stories by Blake Jessop, William C. Dietz, D.B. Jackson, Gerald Brandt, Sharon P. Goza, Walter H. Hunt, Sharon Lee & Steve Miller, Kay Kenyon, Steve Perry, Seanan McGuire, Christopher Allenby, Chris Kennedy, L.E. Modesitt, Jr., Alex Gideon, Brian Hugenbruch, and Y.M. Pang.